THE VILLAGE VICAR

ALSO BY JULIE HOUSTON

Goodness, Grace and Me
The One Saving Grace
An Off-Piste Christmas
Looking for Lucy
Coming Home to Holly Close Farm
A Village Affair
Sing Me a Secret
A Village Vacancy
A Family Affair
A Village Secret

THE VILLAGE VICAR

Julie Houston

An Aria Book

This edition first published in the UK in 2023 by Head of Zeus Ltd,
part of Bloomsbury publishing Plc

A CIP catalogue record for this book is available from the British Library.

ISBN (PB): 9781803280028
ISBN (E): 9781803280004

Cover design: Robyn Neild (illustration); HoZ / Jessie Price (design)

Typeset by Siliconchips Services Ltd UK

Head of Zeus
First Floor East
5–8 Hardwick Street
London EC1R 4RG

WWW.HEADOFZEUS.COM

For all my wonderful women friends.
You know who you are!

THE CHURCH TIMES

June 5th 2021
We are so sad that Ben Carey, our vicar for the past five
years, is leaving the village
But we are just as excited at finding someone to step into
his shoes at
All Hallows Church
Westenbury
Our church, here in the beautiful village of Westenbury, is a
rural parish situated between the industrial towns of West
Yorkshire with a rapidly growing population.
AND WE NEED YOU!
Can you
bring vision, passion and a hunger to see God's kingdom
flourish?
Have you
sensitivity, empathy and compassion for those who might
be experiencing difficult times?
Will you
be a figurehead and ground yourself in our rural parish
and community?
It will also help if you
have a good sense of humour
like custard creams
keep sermons short but interesting
wouldn't mind mowing the vicarage lawns every now
and again

For an informal conversation about the post, please contact
the (new) Bishop of Pontefract (our very own Ben Carey)
Interviews will be held at the church on 3rd August 2021

PART ONE

I

May 1984

Westenbury Vicarage

'Well, look who it is.' Glenys Parkes glanced up from the sausage meat she was expertly encasing in flaky pastry, wiped her hands on the front of her faded pinny and moved to kiss her younger daughter. 'You never said you were coming home?' Glenys took in Alice's lack of suitcase, her grubby looking bare feet in their leather sandals and her skimpy flowing dress, quite unsuitable for this overcast, chilly May morning in Yorkshire. 'You look frozen. Here.' Glenys threw her mauve M&S cardigan in Alice's direction but, although Alice caught it, she placed it on the battered armchair in front of her and went, instead, over to the sink to fill the kettle.

'I need coffee,' Alice said. 'Don't suppose you've any decent stuff?'

'Sorry, love, this is Westenbury, not Paris. The coffee's the Co-op's instant. I'll have a mug if you're making one. So, have you just landed at Manchester? Was that a taxi that dropped you off?' Glenys peered out of the kitchen window at the car slowly making its way back down the vicarage driveway.

Alice laughed. 'Actually, bagged a lift from some bloke on the flight. Lives five miles or so away. Got talking to him and guess who it was? It was that Bill bloke...'

3

'Bill bloke?' Glenys frowned as she moved Alice to one side and finished the job of making the coffee herself.

'You know, the earl or the count or the lord or whatever he reckons to be.'

'Oh, Bill Astley?'

'He's a lord or something?'

'Bit more than a lord.' Glenys glanced in Alice's direction. 'He's the Marquess of Heatherly, lives at Heatherly Hall on the way over to Midhope. Place is a wreck from what I gather. He never got over his first wife dying years ago; she was trapped in a fire at some big house party in Scotland and he went in, tried to save her. But he couldn't. His son, Henry, has gone off the rails a bit too, I heard. Lives in Wales in a commune. Anyway, Bill's a total eccentric. Has wives and mistresses galore. Very arty. He's a sculptor or something.'

'Artist of some sort,' Alice nodded. 'Oils I think.' She paused. 'He invited me to a party.'

'I assumed you were here because of *our* party.' Glenys looked up sharply and, when Alice didn't answer but yawned and rubbed at her mascaraed eyes, went on, 'You do know it's your father's birthday today?'

'Yes, absolutely,' Alice lied. 'That's why I'm here. You know, a surprise and all that? Where is the Very Reverend Cecil? Not still in bed, is he?'

'Have you ever known your father stay in bed in the morning? He thinks 7 a.m. is a lie-in. No,' Glenys went on, attacking the uncooked sausage rolls with a brush and beaten egg, 'he's got a wedding this morning, but he'll be back for the party.'

'Right.' Alice yawned and rubbed at her eyes once more. 'Look, do you mind if I crash out for a couple of hours? I was at the airport just after midnight last night hoping for a last-minute flight. And then I got talking to the Bill bloke and... you know...' Alice yawned again.

'You look like you could do with a shower.' Glenys looked

pointedly at Alice's chipped nail varnish on the end of what were decidedly dirty feet.

'More than likely,' Alice agreed. 'But I need a bit of a kip first. What time does this extravaganza kick off?'

'People are coming about six.'

'Early do then? So how many have you got coming? I don't think I've ever known Dad to have a party before.'

'Well, he *is* sixty.' Glenys sighed volubly. 'I had to persuade him to do this. You know what he's like. Not the most sociable of men.'

'Mum, he hates everyone.'

'Oh, don't exaggerate.' Glenys flapped a hand in Alice's direction. 'He likes Margaret Gillespie.'

'Only because the simpering fool does anything he asks. And it wouldn't surprise me if it *was* anything.'

Glenys tutted. 'Oy, stop that right now. She's in charge of the choir and flower rota.'

'And the scouts and WI. You know, Dad would have been a lot better off married to her. You'd have had time to get on with your painting then.' Alice glanced across at her mother. 'Have you done any recently?'

'Some. I'll show you later.' Glenys didn't look up but, instead, pointed to the door leading to the long, tiled corridor and flight of stairs leading to the large chilly bedrooms on the first floor. 'Go on, get some sleep. I'll wake you for a shower and a bacon sandwich in an hour or so. You look as if you could do with a good meal. As well as a good wash,' she added taking in the paint-encrusted fingernails. 'You've lost weight too. Are you eating properly?'

Ignoring this, Alice asked, 'So, who've you got coming?'

'You know – the usual.'

'The usual?' Alice reached for a banana from the glass fruit bowl that had sat on the kitchen table as long as she remembered, unceremoniously peeling and demolishing the fruit in three greedy bites. It was obvious there was some sort of do going on – the regular Coxes, and flyblown pears from the vicarage orchard had been joined by tangerines, mangoes and even kumquats.

'The Hastings, the Browns, the new verger and his wife. And, of course, Susan and Richard with Virginia.'

'How *is* the sprog?'

'The *sprog*? For heaven's sake, Alice. Six years living in Paris hasn't changed you.'

'OK, OK. *Ma nièce. La petite enfant.*'

Glenys's face softened. 'Oh, she's really lovely. Very bright. You know, for a four-year-old. Way ahead of any of her little friends at nursery. Your father adores her. Quite taken with her, he is. She sits at the front of church with Susan, and knows the words to the Lord's Prayer and "O God, Our Help in Ages Past" already.'

'Bloody hell. God help *us*,' Alice grinned and, catching her mother's eye, they both started to giggle.

'I thought Susan would have popped out another couple by now. She's so much into all that mothering thing.' Alice shuddered slightly. 'I tell you now, any kids I have in the future – and don't get your hopes up, Mum, I do *not* want kids – would have to be born by caesarean. I can't be doing with all that huffing and puffing and ending up like a road accident down below.'

'Alice!' Glenys glared in her daughter's direction. 'For heaven's sake, don't talk like that when your father gets back. You know he can't be doing with anything gynaecological. Anyway,' she went on when Alice just grinned, 'it just doesn't seem to have happened again for the pair of them. I don't ask; it's Susan and Richard's business.'

'Maybe they don't have sex. Mind you, Richard's rather fanciable; it's that lovely Scouse accent. Quite a turn-on...'

'Get to bed, you baggage,' Glenys said almost nervously, glancing at the outer door. 'Dad'll be home any minute and I can't have any friction. Not on his birthday.'

'Friction? *Moi?* I'll be the dutiful daughter – have you got a spare card and a box of Thorntons hanging about anywhere – and I'll toast him with a sausage roll and then leave you all to it once again.'

'Stay a few days, love.' Glenys went to hug her daughter.

'You're always welcome home, you know you are.' Glenys relinquished her hold and bent to put the sausage rolls in the oven. 'Bloody oven's not hot,' she swore. 'Damned thing.'

'Mum, you've complained about that oven ever since I was a kid. Get Dad to cough up for a new one. Or persuade the church coffers to buy you one.' Alice gave the rusting stove a kick and a temperature light came on.

'Thanks, love. You always knew how to control the bugger. Go on, go and have a few hours' sleep and then you can tell us everything you've been up to. I don't suppose you're back for good?'

''Fraid not. Just a familial visit to remind you I'm still alive. A couple of days and I'll be off again.' Alice took another banana and, this time, chewing the overripe flesh thoughtfully and almost lasciviously, headed in the direction of the stairs to the old childhood bedroom she'd shared with her older sister, Susan. Despite there being four large bedrooms in the vicarage, once her father had claimed two for himself – one to sleep in, claiming Glenys was restless and wanted the light on to read, as well as the small box room for the safe keeping of his vestments, robes and chasubles – Alice and Susan had been left to share the prettiest room overlooking the grounds of the Victorian house.

The girls hadn't minded; convinced ghosts of Vicars Past roamed the draughty corridors, they were more than happy to bunk down together. They'd always got on, although, once they'd hit their teens, Susan – very much her mother's daughter – had gone along with her father's wishes, heading off to teacher training college in Liverpool before returning to take up a post at the village primary school both she and Alice had themselves attended as little girls.

Alice had had none of it. Once she'd hit sixteen and discovered the joys of sex, drink and illicit substances, as well as the fun of baiting her father, she knew there was a whole wide world of culture, art and enjoyment out there, totally alien to the Rev Cecil Parkes. And one in which she intended to immerse herself fully.

Alice didn't think her mum – but especially her dad – would want to know the real reason she'd run off into the night and made the decision to come home. Being caught *in flagrante* or, in Yorkshire parlance, *at it*, with Yves, by his mad wife, Martine, as she brandished a carving knife in both their directions had been a bit exciting, if not downright frightening. Were the French still not arrested and tried for *crime passionel*? If not, Martine could have cut off Yves' todger as well as slit her own throat and been acquitted by a jury.

Yes, it had definitely been time to get out of there until things cooled down. How the hell Martine had known Alice was having a bit of a fling with fellow artist Yves – and that's all it was, *a bit of a thing*, nothing heavy, just very enjoyable sex – and, furthermore, had obviously followed them and eventually managed to take her chance with the communal buzzer on the door (just like something out of a damned spy film) before creeping up the stairs to Alice's loft bedsitter, knife to hand, was beyond her. Alice grinned as she snuggled down into the tiny single bed she'd slept in as a child, remembering Yves' quite magnificent erection shrivelling to nothing more than the size of those snails they'd scooped out of their garlicky shells just a few hours earlier as Martine's knife glinted evilly at her husband's penis. She could still taste and smell both the garlic and Yves on her breath, and she gave an involuntary little shiver as she remembered her limbs wrapped round his, his mouth on every conceivable – and inconceivable – part of her body.

What was it about French men? God, they were good lovers. They could come and come again – a bit like Glenys's *cut and come again* fruit cakes, which always tasted better when given time to mature. Alice grinned to herself. Shame Yves was now *pas plus*, having been carted off by Martine, like the little boy he was, back to where he belonged.

Alice had thought on her feet, weighing up a couple of

options: turn up at Luc's, with whom she shared the small studio in a backstreet behind the Jardin Sauvage Saint Vincent, or get away completely and find refuge – just for a couple of days – back home at the vicarage in Westenbury, Yorkshire, where she'd grown up. She'd gone for the second option, taking the chance while Martine was hysterically crying and begging Yves' forgiveness (*his* forgiveness for heaven's sake?) to grab her bag and passport and the clothes she'd been divested of just half an hour earlier. As well as the bundle of francs she'd earned from actually selling a couple of oil paintings, and which was intended for the rent she owed the landlord, before taking *Le Taxi* she couldn't really afford to the airport at Orly.

But, Alice admitted to herself now, as the soothing chatter of sparrows in the vicarage garden below her open window began to lull her to sleep, she was tired. Tired of painting stuff no one seemed to want. She was existing hand to mouth, selling a painting here and there, getting her kit off and life-modelling for other artists in the eclectic neighbourhood of Belleville when the rent was due and there was nothing in her bank account or her pocket. She'd already had several run-ins with the landlord who, fed up with arty types who didn't cough up their francs on time, was constantly threatening her with eviction.

She knew she was good – bloody good, in fact – but the trouble was, despite being the shining star of her intake on the fine arts degree course at UCL, the one who was predicted to go far, no one, it seemed – now that she was living and working in Paris – appeared to agree with that sentiment. She'd been so excited when she'd been given a place at the École Nationale Supérieure des Beaux-Arts school of fine arts across from the Louvre in the sixth arrondissement (financed by her art-loving grandfather who had disliked his objectionable – and objecting – son-in-law as much as the Rev Cecil's village flock appeared to) and she had adored her two years there. It seemed her father's objections to Alice continuing her studies in Paris (an expensive and unnecessary waste of time and money when she was only going to end up teaching the subject or, more than likely, an out-of-work arty layabout sponging off the state on her return) were being realised. Not that she was about to return. The very idea of abandoning her beloved Paris with its vibrancy and energy emanating from the culmination of hundreds of years of cultural and artistic encouragement, its special light, its architecture, that first sight of Monet's *Water Lilies* at the Musée de l'Orangerie...

No way was she leaving Paris for a job teaching art in cold, miserable West Yorkshire as her father constantly suggested, on the few occasions she now saw him. Teaching art to a bunch of spotty adolescents at Westenbury Comp, where she'd herself been a pupil, filled her with horror. Kids who thought art was a great get-out from doing the more onerous academic subjects: pimply boys without the soul to appreciate texture or colour; spoilt princesses whose daddies showered them with expensive folders and art materials while affecting a duplicitous pride at their offspring's creativity when it had become more than obvious the academic A-levels they would need for medicine, dentistry or law were out of their grasp. And Cecil would be proved right – were she to slink back home – when he'd told her she'd come to nothing with her ridiculous artwork, and that she'd end up with a bastard in the gutters of Paris along with the other down-and-outs and retrogrades who made their way there.

Alice had laughed at that. Actually laughed out loud, not sure whether Cecil was meaning some bastard man – he'd been quite correct, several times over, on that score – or the true, literal meaning of the word. As well as left debating whether her father had been reading *Down and Out in Paris and London, Les Misérables* or, much more likely, *The News of the World*, which he professed to despise but which was, nevertheless, delivered and devoured every Sunday after church service.

Alice slept.

2

'Jesus!' Alice woke with a start several hours later being eyeballed by a fair-haired tot who continued to stare, even while Alice gave back as good as she got. This was becoming a game of who would lose their nerve and look away first and, while Alice conceded that, as the adult round here, she should be doing just that, there was something in the little girl's determined eye that made Alice refuse to admit defeat and give in.

'What on earth are you doing?' Susan Quinn's head had appeared round the bedroom door and was taking in the strange, almost frozen tableau of aunt and niece.

'She started it,' Alice sniffed, sitting up in bed and pulling down her dress that had somehow rucked up into her knickers.

'She hasn't seen you for nearly a year, Alice. She's trying to work you out. You know, who you are. *And* you're in her bed. That's the one she sleeps in when she stays here with Mum and Dad.'

'Well, tell her I haven't eaten her porridge as well.' Alice yawned loudly.

'You tell her,' Susan laughed. 'She does understand English, you know.'

'Do they talk at this age?' Alice frowned and, turning, contemplated Virginia once more. 'How're you doing, Suze?' she continued as Susan reached down to hug her younger sister. 'How's life in the village? Richard?'

'All well. All good. Nothing much changes.' Susan lowered her voice. 'You smell of garlic and red wine and... and...' Susan pulled a face.

'Sex?'

'I was going to say *Gauloises*, but now you've mentioned it, yes, you know...' Susan glanced down at her daughter who still appeared fascinated by the aunt she didn't know; who had filched, and was in, her usual bed. In the middle of the day.

'Is she poorly? Has she got tummy ache?' Virginia turned large, disdainful blue eyes – Cecil's eyes, Alice thought with a slight shiver – to her mother. No wonder the Rev Cecil was so taken with this first granddaughter of his when she looked so uncannily like him. Always self-satisfied and opinionated to the point of egotism, if not downright smugness, Cecil would love this little shadow, this little reflection of himself, following him everywhere he went.

'It was mine first, kiddo,' Alice said, patting the girl on the head. 'The bed, I mean. I get first dibs in it.' She yawned again, stretching. 'God, I'm starving. You and Richard should come over to Paris for the weekend,' Alice said suddenly, turning to her older sister. 'You know, come and see where I am.'

'I know, I know, we must. We've been talking about it for ages and then, well, something crops up: life happens, kids get ill, Dad needs help with his flock...' Susan trailed off, pulling a face.

'I'd tell him to flock off,' Alice sniffed, yawning some more while stretching out her arms to the ceiling.

'I've really missed you, Alice, and I've not been to Paris since that school exchange when I was sixteen.' She laughed. 'You know, when Dad just knew I was going to come back pregnant and stinking of garlic – not sure which he thought was the worst crime. It was the year after the Paris riots and he was convinced my head was going to be turned by insurrection.'

'You *were* brave,' Alice laughed, remembering. 'You came back with your long hair gone and that fabulous gamine haircut Dad was almost apoplectic about. His little daughter was suddenly no more, and you stood in the kitchen, all French and breathless, with hair that gave you cheekbones, your blue eyes huge in your face and your skirt up to your backside.' Alice laughed again.

'And you kept playing Jane Birkin's "Je t'aime... moi non plus". All that heavy breathing with Serge Gainsbourg. God, I was jealous. And, you said, from then on you were to be called Suzy, not Susan. *And* you refused to do any piano practice after that trip to Paris. I was only fourteen or so, but I remember being totally impressed with you and determined that one day I was going to live there, if just for two weeks, with that French family who had made you grow a pair.'

'Grow a pair? A pair of *what*?' Susan frowned, not understanding. 'Well, you certainly succeeded,' she went on. 'You got away.'

'But you're OK, aren't you?' Alice scrutinised her sister's face. 'You never really wanted to leave Westenbury?'

'No, I'm fine. Really. I'm back doing three days at school – Mum has Virginia one day and she goes to nursery the other two – and we're actually thinking of moving house.'

'Moving?'

'Oh, not away. Not from this area. I know Richard sometimes thinks he'd like to be back in Liverpool, but he's been made head of faculty at the poly now. We'll be here for ever...' Susan trailed off.

'You don't sound too happy about it?'

'Oh, I am, I am, honestly. It's just...'

'Just?'

'We'd really like another baby.'

'And it's not happening?'

Susan shook her head. 'Richard is so lovely.'

'He is,' Alice nodded in agreement. 'I could even fancy him myself.'

'And I know he'd love a son. You know, to take to cricket, to football, to watch Everton...' Susan stopped. 'Come on, Dad's just got back. Don't let him catch you in bed, smelling of booze, sex and fags. You'd be playing right into his self-righteous hands.'

'Blimey, not like you that, Suze?'

'No, well, you've managed to escape him. I don't seem able to.'

'Come to Paris. Just you and Richard – leave Virginia with Mum and Dad. Give yourself some time off.'

'I will, I promise. Something to really look forward to,' Susan laughed. 'Come on, get showered, put your dutiful daughter face on and, for God's sake, don't wind him up any more than you have to. It is his birthday, after all.'

By 9 p.m. Alice had had enough. She'd accepted, without recourse to retaliation, her father's snide criticisms of her hair ('a couple of *oiseaux* nesting in there, Alice?'), her dress ('from a Frog flea market, Alice?'), her paint-ingrained fingers ('still biting your nails, Alice?'), smiling, instead, with a serenity she certainly didn't feel, but which she knew irritated Cecil more than any caustic response. In desperation, after she'd explained for the third time her work and life in Paris to the verger, the chaplain attached to the local hospital who suffered not only horrific halitosis but a quite pungent body odour and then again to the local Conservative councillor and his anorexic wife (who, for some reason her father had attached himself to recently) she'd downed as much of the cheap, acidic Liebfraumilch as she could stomach, resigned to getting through the seemingly interminable evening through a haze of alcohol.

There'd been an hour or so's relief, once she'd escaped the antagonism of her father and the clutches of his worthy, but stultifying disciples, when she'd been able to talk to Richard about her life in Paris, able to admit to him – and to Susan once she'd put Virginia into the bed Alice had only recently relinquished – that her life across the channel wasn't totally panning out as she'd intended. Tall, smiley and with that wonderful, unaffected Scouse accent that had Cecil pulling pained expressions at his son-in-law's lack of the Queen's English, Richard Quinn was one of the nicest men Alice had ever met. He was funny, at times irreverent and, best of all, he adored Susan.

But, once the guests began to make leaving noises – buttoning cardigans and fastening coats against the chilly spring night air, shaking hands and saying *God Bless*, and *Happy Birthday, once again, Vicar* and a childfree Richard and Susan were off for an early night (sex at the optimal time, she wondered idly?), Alice weighed up the idea of slipping away herself. Restless after snoozing the day away under the blue candlewick bedspread, as well as now pretty drunk from the Co-op's cheapest bottles of wine (Rev Cecil Parkes was notoriously mean, not averse to watering down the communal wine if he thought the congregation were taking advantage of his generosity), Alice considered her options: staying to help Glenys clear away the debris of the little soirée while catching up with life in Westenbury these past ten months, or actually turning up at Lord Bill's place in the next village. She'd have to get a taxi over there and cash was short. She was on the verge of telling herself she really couldn't be bothered with the latter option, when her father returned from the front door where he'd been seeing off the last of his guests.

Cecil deigned to pick up a couple of lipstick-rimmed glasses (they must have both belonged to the Tory MP's wife, as Alice couldn't recall any of the other women wearing a scrap of even foundation or face powder, let alone lipstick in the garish pink that now smeared the best lead crystal glasses that only came out at Christmas and birthdays) before leaning against the stove and folding his arms in Alice's direction.

'So, you've still not given Toulouse-Lautrec a run for his money then, Alice? Mind you, with his legs – or lack of them – I wouldn't have thought that was too difficult a task.' Cecil grinned, but there was an undercurrent of sneery disdain she recognised from old. When she didn't answer, refusing to be drawn into the argument on which, she knew, he was intent, Cecil carried on, his bullying tone filling the kitchen, reverberating across the

Formica-topped worksurfaces, lifting and swooping around the lacy cloth-covered table and black plastic padded chairs. There appeared little chance of escape: Glenys had gone to check on the sleeping Virginia and Cecil was determined to push home his advantage.

'Not made your name yet, then? Not been discovered as the next best thing? Didn't I tell you it would all come to nothing, you gallivanting off to Paris to bed down with those Frog arty types and work-shy shirkers? And all those Algerians who shouldn't be there in the first place? Are they still hanging around doing nothing? You need to be careful with that lot, Alice.'

'What? What *are* you on about, Dad?' Alice felt the palms of her hands grow sweaty and she moved them down and across the flimsy material of her cotton dress as she fought to keep her temper. She could argue back, tell him that her two very best friends, Nazim and Walid, with whom she spent much of her time in the Barbès neighbourhood near Montmartre, were from Algeria, but what was the point?

'I never liked the French.' Cecil was obviously off on one, speaking so heatedly that spittle gathered in tiny pools at each corner of his thin-lipped mouth. 'Soon lay down and gave in once the Jerries moved in on them.'

'I don't think they had much choice, Dad,' Alice muttered, looking for escape, relieved when Glenys came back into the kitchen.

'Weren't averse to collaborating...' Cecil continued, unaware, or simply not caring, that no one was listening. He'd had plenty of practice at that, every Sunday when he preached, long and hard, loving the sound of his own rhetoric, to a rapidly dwindling congregation.

'Look, Mum,' Alice said, taking hold of Glenys's arm and moving her back into the long oak-clad hallway, 'I think I'm going to head over to Bill Astley's place for an hour or two.'

'Come on, I'll give you a lift up there, then. I've barely had anything to drink. If I leave the two of you together here, you'll only end up arguing...'

Although not generally given to crises of confidence when faced with new situations, even Alice felt something akin to a slight misgiving as Glenys dropped her off at the huge metal gates before driving off in the direction she'd just come. Alice was left hovering, unsure how to access the grounds, feeling foolish, as well as unconvinced there was anything akin to her idea of a party going on in the house itself.

House? That was a misnomer for a start. This truly was some sort of stately home, a castle even, and, while she'd always known about the place, of course, had even visited on a trip from junior school when the class topic for the term was Tudors and Stuarts, the notion she'd one day be invited back for a party here had never entered her head. And to be honest, how much of an invitation was it?

Alice had found herself sitting next to the middle-aged, ponytailed and bearded man on the flight from Paris and, had he not leaned over, asking if she'd like a drink from the trolley just as, exhausted from the trauma of being held at knifepoint by Mad Martine, she was dropping off to sleep, she doubted she'd have exchanged a word with him.

Flights, Alice had always maintained, were for catching up on sleep, books and movies while downing as much alcohol as was humanly possible. Especially on hurriedly obtained early morning flights such as the one she then found herself on. As this flight from Paris to Manchester Airport was no more than an hour long, and she'd no reading material with her, the majority of the above inducements were necessarily discounted and, instead, she'd just closed her eyes when her neighbour had laid a hand on her arm. Despite it being only 6 a.m, he'd bought them both a large gin and tonic and spent the whole flight asking her about herself, laughing uproariously as she'd admitted to her close shave with death a few hours earlier.

It was only as they landed that she realised, somewhat guiltily, she'd not asked anything about him but accepted gratefully – once they worked out they lived only several miles apart – the lift in his car waiting at the airport car park. As he'd pulled up on the drive at the rectory, he'd proffered a business card, told her there was a party going on at his house that evening and why didn't she come along? There would be a couple of artists she might enjoy meeting, and he'd like to see her again. Just, you know, he'd laughed, if only to confirm she was over the shock of her boyfriend's penis being on the point of amputation.

Alice had returned his laughter, deciding she liked this man a lot, but it was only as she walked slowly up the drive to the huge rectory door, glancing at the card he'd handed her, did she realise that the guy with whom she'd shared her escapade of the evening, as well as his gin, was actually William Astley – call me Bill – twelfth Marquess of Heatherly.

And now Alice was regretting leaving the rectory and a catch-up with Glenys in order to spend the evening with some much older man she really didn't know, who'd possibly conjured up some mythical party in order to get her out here. She looked at her watch. It wasn't quite 9 p.m., but the early May evening was rapidly drawing in and the hall loomed hugely solid, and ridiculously imposing, in its acreage of grounds. Apart from a couple of lights in a bank of upstairs windows, the rest of the place appeared dark and uninviting. Alice took hold of the central gates, a couple of yards down from where she'd first alighted from Glenys's old Morris Minor, and shook them ineffectually.

She was just about to set off to the nearest pub or telephone box – whichever would manifest itself first – in order to spend money she didn't have on a taxi back to Westenbury, when the gates shuddered and groaned before inching open slightly. At the same time a variety of lights were activated, illuminating the house in front of her. Two men, each with some sort of guard dog – Dobermans, Alice thought – appeared at the gates as they continued to slowly move back on themselves.

'What's your name, love? Have you got an invite?' The man, Alice gleaned from his accent, was obviously local. 'Are you invited?'

'Well yes, sort of. I think so.' Alice felt silly, standing there, waiting to be let in. 'I met Bill this morning. On the flight from Paris,' she added, as if that were justification enough for hanging around outside this great pile of a house. 'Bill invited me...' Alice fumbled in her pocket for the card Bill had handed over.

'Right, love. It's OK. You the artist? Whose boyfriend nearly parted company with his todger?' Both men grinned, eyeing her up somewhat lasciviously and Alice pulled at her jacket in order to cover bare flesh at her neck and breasts. Even the dogs, seated now but panting slightly, kept their unblinking eyes on her face. 'Right, come on then. The do is in Bill's private apartment at the other side of the house. You've come round to the back here, love. Lucky we spotted you on the camera.'

3

'Alice?' Bill Astley walked from the middle of the room where he appeared to be entertaining a crowd of party-goers with some tale or other, and came towards her, one hand held out in welcome, the other clutching a large glass of something presumably alcoholic. 'Great that you were able to make it. You managed to get away from your own party? Was your father OK with that?' Bill's vowels were clipped, aristocratic – a sharp contrast to the guests at her father's party. 'Come in, come in, come and have a drink. You look frozen, darling.'

Alice *was* cold. It had been much warmer in France and, when she'd run off from her studio apartment and into that dark but mild Parisian night, she'd grabbed just one other dress apart from the one with which she'd hastily covered her nakedness. Cotton, ridiculously flimsy, and totally unsuitable for the chilly Yorkshire evening, which was always several degrees below the optimistic weather that had been forecast. She realised she was now underdressed, not sartorially but because most of the other thirty or so people either standing or seated in the huge, fabulously plush room were dressed warmly in jackets or hadn't yet discarded overcoats. One very beautiful and elegant woman was swathed from head to toe in scarves. Alice had been sure guests at a lord's do would all be in some sort of evening dress. Black tie at least. Obviously not.

'Here,' Bill grinned, handing Alice an exotic, vibrantly

coloured shawl. 'It's always bloody freezing in here. Costs the very devil to heat and I've already had the estate manager on at me today to not put any heating on now that we're – apparently – into summer. Goodness, you are cold, darling. Hang on...' Bill moved back towards a drinks' cabinet, returning with a large heavy glass tumbler of amber liquid. 'This'll warm you up.'

'Or knock me out,' Alice gasped, coughing slightly as the alcohol made its way down her throat. 'Jesus, what *is* that?'

'My father's legacy.' Bill laughed at Alice's contorted face. 'The old bastard might have left this great pile for me to do something with...' Bill waved an arm almost crossly in the direction of the walls opposite where a plethora of former Astleys gazed down disdainfully at the present company below them '...but he did have the good sense to lay down a cellar full of Scottish single malt as well. If left unopened, they improve with age and go up in value.' He laughed once more. 'Allegedly. I prefer to drink it. Right, has that warmed you up a bit? Would you prefer a glass of wine now?'

The whisky had, Alice conceded after knocking it back too quickly, certainly done its intended job of warming her up, but back home in Paris she'd trained herself to drink the cheap Bordeaux, which suited her purse as well as her palate, and she accepted the proffered glass of red wine gratefully. Sipping at the beautifully smooth liquid, she realised she'd said hardly a word since being escorted up to this part of the house by the two Doberman-toting lackeys ten minutes earlier.

'Have you always lived here?' she now asked, realising it was probably a somewhat banal question. 'Sorry, that was very much along the lines of "do you come here often?"' she added, embarrassed.

Bill laughed at that. 'My family's been here for centuries. Since William – you know, the Conqueror – sent up his barons to knock the marauding peasants into some sort of shape.

The first actual Marquess of Heatherly – William, like me – presumably pulled in a few royal favours in order to be granted more land, as well as obtaining permission from the king to build a much bigger place here. I reckon it was still a pretty wild place to build a hall, seven hundred years ago.' Bill shrugged, and downed his own whisky. 'That's how it was in those days. The peasants had tried to revolt in the 1300s but hadn't got very far against the ruling aristocracy. And, to answer your question, no, I've had many years away from the family seat. I was sent away to school at an early age and then drafted into the army, at the very end of compulsory National Service. I could probably have got out of it – you know, got my father to pull a few strings – but ended up in the Guards. I tell you, Alice, being forced into Eton and then the army has had me fighting against all authority ever since.'

'Right,' Alice grinned. 'I always reckon my sister and I having to put up with my dad's authoritarian way of bringing up kids was bad enough, but I suppose it was nothing compared to what you had to go through.'

'Oh, it wasn't all bad. I then went up to Oxford and drank a lot and was a member of the Bullingdon Club which, when I look back now, I can't believe I was involved in.'

'Oh, what's that?'

'A totally elitist establishment for rich kids who'd been at Eton and Harrow...'

'And this place *isn't* elitist?'

'I didn't say it wasn't.' Bill frowned. 'Inheriting this lot isn't easy, you know.'

Alice laughed out loud. 'Oh, come on. For heaven's sake. You tell that to Arthur Scargill and the miners out on strike just down the road, that living *here* –' Alice raised her glass of wine, which appeared to have been filled to the top once more, in the direction of the trappings of wealth around her '– isn't *easy*.' The glass's contents spilled over onto her hand as she did so.

'You tell *them* it isn't *easy* –' Alice laughed in disbelief once more '– and you'd soon be carted off to the guillotine. Where you and all your lot deserve to be.' Alice swayed slightly and she realised she was very drunk. The whisky and wine, on top of the wine she'd drunk at the vicarage, on nothing but a couple of bananas and a sausage roll, were taking their toll.

Bill put out a steadying arm and smiled. 'You know, the last thing I expected, as the third son, was to have anything to do with the ancestral line. I'd always been aware that Heatherly Hall, together with the title, would pass ultimately to Gerald or Simeon, my two elder brothers, but unfortunately – both for them and for me – neither of them returned from sorties across the Channel during the war. Both dead before they were twenty, and within two months of each other. Suddenly, with no other siblings, I was – at the age of five – in line to be the next Marquess of Heatherly. I was only six or seven by the end of the war. My parents had divorced and I was living in London with my mother, when I wasn't at school.'

'Blimey.' Alice stared. 'How did all that make you feel?'

'Pretty good to be honest. I hadn't really had much to do with Gerald and Simeon; they were just another pair of grown ups. Knowing you're going to inherit the hall and title does give you a certain superiority, a distinct feeling of one-upmanship when you're sharing a dorm with the other boys.'

'But?'

'There's always a but, isn't there? I soon realised what I would be facing and by the time I was in my early twenties and living and working in London – the swinging Sixties were just waiting to happen – the last thing I wanted was to be living in and in charge of a draughty, run-down pile in West Yorkshire. Castle Howard, up in North Yorkshire, realised that the only way forward was to diversify, mainly by opening to the public. My father should have followed their example and gone down the same route.'

JULIE HOUSTON

'But you did eventually? Open to the public, I mean. I came here on a school visit when I was at junior school.'

'Yes, we used to allow local schools to come and have a wander, and I hired someone to be a bit of a guide, give a talk, but we didn't really get going officially until the mid-Seventies. We eventually followed suit, but very probably should have done it much earlier.'

'And is it working out?' Alice asked. 'You know, charging and letting the proletariat in to see what you're all up to? Must be a bit like being at the zoo? With you as the attraction? You know, pay your money and watch the posh folk at work and play.'

Bill laughed. 'No, it's not like that. To some extent, throwing open the doors has worked, although the costs still mount up. We're nowhere in the same league as Castle Howard, which has its connection with Anne Boleyn and the delights of North Yorkshire to bring in the crowds. We do have a farm shop now where we sell our own honey from the apiaries we have up in the meadow; and a tea room trying hard to compete with Bettys over at Harrogate and Ilkley.' Bill paused and smiled and Alice thought, not for the first time, what a lovely smiley face this Marquess of Heatherly had. He really was quite fanciable. Or was that the alcohol talking? She thought it very probably was.

'And,' he went on, while Alice continued to take in every aspect of his untidily long, now greying hair and his rather merry, very dark eyes, 'while we've not quite got the lions that the Marquess of Bath decided to bring in at Longleat, we do have a petting farm as well as the working farm that's always been here. We have some rare-breed sheep, as well as the usual daft Yorkshire flock that wander out into the road and get run over if we're not careful.'

Alice laughed at that, remembering how the Reverend Cecil had once careered into the hedge when trying to avoid one such

24

specimen and, forgetting his two daughters were in the back seat, had come out with the quite foul invective one wouldn't expect from a man of the cloth.

'What we're really hoping is that the law will change at some point soon so that we'll actually be able to hold civil ceremonies here, but I think that's many years off. We already host wedding receptions in the ballroom, and that's working well so far, but we really want to invest in making the hall the complete go-to wedding venue of Yorkshire.'

'Goodness.' Alice shook her head. 'It never occurred to me that so much was necessary, you know, just to make a few quid to keep the place up and running.'

'To actually keep it standing.' Bill shook his head in turn. 'Anyway, enough of my troubles. I invited you here to hear more about your painting in Paris. Come on, I'll show you some of my stuff.'

'I always feel I'm just on the verge of making it, you know?' Alice sighed heavily as she followed Bill Astley along a couple of stone-flagged corridors and climbed what seemed a huge number of stairs. The higher they climbed, the chillier and bleaker the air appeared. 'I sell a couple of pieces,' Alice was saying to Bill's back as she fell into line behind him, 'or, out of the blue, there's a flurry of interest from the major art galleries. I was so near to having an exhibition at the *Galerie Marion Meyer*; worked for months, day and night towards it, and then it all fell through at the last minute.'

'I'm sorry, that's hard. I was in Paris myself for two years, probably working on the same streets, going through the same merry-go-round of hope and anti-climax as yourself.'

'Really? When did you fit that in? I thought you lived in London?'

'After Oxford, in the Sixties, I did the whole London thing, working in the City, enjoying the clubs and the permissive society, as it was dubbed then.' Bill turned as they climbed yet another flight of stairs and he grinned down at her. 'Long before your time, of course.' He sighed and went on, 'But eventually, it began to pall. I wanted to paint, wanted to study art. Where else but Paris, as you've found out for yourself? Being a part of the English aristocracy helped of course, as well as having the means to finance the life of a down-at-heel artist. I'm embarrassed to admit I didn't starve in a garret like the majority of trying-to-make-it artists there. I had a couple of exhibitions at two not very well-known galleries. Lived the life. Loved every minute. And then my father died and I had to come back here, playing at being the lord of the manor, pretending I knew what to do...' Bill Astley broke off as he opened the door at the very top of the stairs and switched on several lights.

'Oh. Oh...' That was all Alice appeared to be able to utter as she stared, transfixed at what was in front of her. Every wall, from floor to ceiling, as well as the actual ceiling itself in what was a long gallery, stretching seemingly forever, was covered in enormous canvases. Huge, vibrant oil paintings alive with exotic flowers; flying and swooping tropical birds; trees whose limbs became entangled with those of naked men and sultry wanton women, their heads thrown back in abandonment. The paintings were at once harmonious and extravagant, created with, from what Alice could decipher, complete artistic control. It was, she thought, like being in Paradise crossed with Sodom and Gomorrah, a benign deity crossing swords with the devil. Or was it a peace treaty?

'Blimey.' Alice continued to stare, but found herself reaching out a hand to Bill Astley waiting silently at her side. 'You are *so* talented,' she finally breathed. 'Why on earth aren't you still painting? Famous? Known for all this?' She set off, slowly, still holding Bill's hand, along the length of the gallery, stopping occasionally to absorb a particular nuance of the artwork, but needing to continue, to take in every aspect of what was to come. She came to a sudden halt and stood, spellbound, at the beautifully created image of one man and one woman now in front of her. The semi-naked man, his legs muscled and rippling like some Ancient Greek warrior, were wrapped lovingly around a woman dressed only in a thin, transparent shift, his mouth on her secret places, her shift rucked up as she abandoned herself up to what was obviously a quite explosive climax.

It took a man who knew women, who had experienced the wanton sexuality portrayed in this gallery, to create art such as this and Alice felt shivers of lust go through every part of her body.

'You're cold,' Bill said. 'I'm sorry, I'll take you back.' He put a hand to her shoulder, in order to steer her back the way they'd come.

Alice turned and just stared at this man who'd had the ability to create the tumult of feelings she was now experiencing. Jealousy, yes – she was jealous of his skill, she knew, but this man who could handle paint and brush with such expertise, skill and knowledge, who appeared to know a woman's mind as well as her body's desire, was filling her with such lust, she felt her nipples harden involuntarily. 'I'm not cold,' Alice said finally, 'I'm just totally blown away with it all. With the... you know, the passion you've put into all this.'

Bill Astley appeared to hesitate, was about to manoeuvre Alice once more back to the closed door of the gallery, but his hand moved instead from her shoulder, down her bare arm and to her breast, unhindered in any undergarment. His thumb moved slowly and gently across the thin cotton of her summer dress and, as she leaned forward, wanting more, he slipped a cool hand to her throat, stroking gently downwards before opening the top button of the bodice. Bill stepped back, seeking permission to continue and, when Alice took his hand once more, returning it to the buttons, he undid each one in turn before bending towards her, taking an erect nipple in his mouth.

With a gasp of lust that took them both by surprise, Alice opened her eyes, taking in the beautiful, erotic tableaux on the ceilings above her and on the walls surrounding her, and smiled before holding out her arms to Bill Astley, twelfth Marquess of Heatherly.

4

November 1984

'Right, OK, let's go over to Paris and see this thing of Alice's for ourselves.' Richard Quinn wafted the flyer advertising: *Alice Parkes – An Exhibition of Watercolour* towards Susan as she sat at the kitchen table marking a pile of exercise books.

'It's November,' Susan frowned. 'How will we get there?'

'What's November got to do with it?'

'Well, you hate flying. You know –' she started to laugh '– ever since we took off from Manchester for Majorca and landed at Liverpool ten minutes later.' Susan laughed again as she remembered Richard clutching onto her hand, intoning and directing a constant liturgy of Hail Marys to a Catholic god he'd duly resurrected, after years of professing disbelief. 'It's going to be cloudy and rainy and bumpy up there in November.'

'Yes, alright, alright,' Richard agreed somewhat huffily. 'I'm sure I can take a couple of something to make me sleep. It's only an hour or so... Or –' his face brightened '– how about we take the car and go by ferry? I like boats.'

'Virginia is sick in the car. She'll probably throw up on a boat too.'

'No, we're not taking Virginia. I want this to be a bit of a holiday for you. Let her stay here with your mum. Or, we could always take her over to *my* mum and then we could sail from Liverpool.'

'Isn't that the wrong direction? Don't you get to America if you sail from Liverpool?' Susan laughed again. Richard might be Dean of Faculty in charge of Sociology at the local poly, but he was bloody hopeless at directions. 'And if we drive, are you sure you know which way to go?'

'Down the M1 to Dover, the ferry across to Calais and then down to Paris. No sweat. Probably take six or seven hours at the most.'

'It's November, Richard. There'll be fog and big waves and people's vomit blown back at us as we all stand on deck throwing up together.' Susan paused and considered. 'And have you ever driven on the other side of the road?'

'Hitched through Europe as a student. You know that. Got as far as Greece,' he added proudly.

'Yes, but a) you weren't driving and b) you were lucky not to be thrown into a Cretan jail for smoking dope. I still don't know how you got away with that one. If they'd done as they should have, you'd probably be just getting out...' Susan glanced at the calendar on the wall '...about now.'

'Good job the desk sergeant fancied me then. Right, that's a plan. A long weekend. We can tie it in with your days off from school and my upcoming reading week at the poly.' Richard rubbed his hands, before draining his glass of wine. 'And don't tell Alice we're coming. Let's surprise her.' He wafted the flyer once again and then pulled a face as he read out the words in Scouse-flavoured French:

Musée de Monmartre du 11 novembre au 3 décembre
Une exposition d'aquarelle
Aquarelles de Nouveaux Artistes
Jean-Pierre Laurent   Jules Garnier   Maurice Bouchard
Alice Parkes

'She's last on the list,' Richard frowned. 'Do you think it means anything, Suze?'

'Yes, it means she's last on the list. She's not French; she's not a man.' Susan looked up from her marking once again. '*I* don't know, Richard; I'm sure it means nothing. She's brilliant, you know she is, and this is a real breakthrough for her. Just go and book all the tickets we need and start planning the route. And then practise driving round roundabouts the wrong way. Just let me get on with this.' Susan was beginning to feel irritable: Richard, at times, was as annoyingly persistent as some of the kids in her class. And she'd been totally convinced she was pregnant again. Her period was two weeks late and her breasts were full and heavy, just as they had been when she was first pregnant with Virginia, but as she marked – her red pen stabbing evermore furiously at ticks and crosses – the faint cramping she'd felt earlier that afternoon became intense and, as she stood to fill the kettle, she immediately recognised a tell-tale leakage at the top of her legs. Susan dashed the water into the kettle with such anger the liquid spurted out over her hand and onto the kitchen floor.

'Richard, that's the same damned church we passed ten minutes ago, I'm sure it is.' Susan hunted in the well of the VW GTI for the map. 'Just slow down a minute will you. I can't read in the car – I'll be sick.'

'There's loads of *églises* in France; the French are all good, God-fearing Catholics like me. I don't know how you can tell one church from another. We're right, I'm sure we are. We're on the A26 now.'

'No, we're *not*. That *is* the same church, and we're still on the N216. Look, look, there's a Paris sign.'

'Where?'

'Richard, for God's sake, don't overtake on the right side of the road.'

'I am on the right side.'

'No, you're on the left... God's sake... Get over on to the right...'

'Jesus, you're confusing me now. There! Paris sign again. Shit, it's the other way.'

'Next roundabout, Richard. Turn round...' Susan clamped a hand over her eyes as a tantivy of angry French horns blasted in their direction. 'Let me drive. For God's sake, let *me* drive.'

Three hours and fifty-nine minutes later, Richard drew up on the *Bois de Vincennes*, squeezing the car inexpertly between two others once a much smaller Citroën had pulled out and sped off in the opposite direction. 'We're nowhere near the hotel,' Susan complained, scanning the map.

'Look, we're here now. Let's just leave the car and walk. Find the exhibition and find Alice.'

'She's not bound to be there, you know. I mean, I can't imagine all the artists just sit there, ready to chat about their work, waiting to accept cheques if they sell their stuff.'

'*I* don't know,' Richard said irritably. 'I don't know how it works. We should have told your sister we were coming.'

'It was you who didn't want to. You who wanted to surprise her...' Susan broke off and stood stock-still, staring across the road towards a pavement café.

'Well, you agreed it would be great to surprise her. What's the matter?' Richard turned in the same direction, frowning as he tried to decipher what it was Susan was looking at. 'Is it Alice? Is she over there?'

Susan shook her head. 'No, it's nothing. OK, come on, leave the stuff in the car and let's ask where this place is. We can at least see Alice's paintings, even if she herself isn't there.'

'Nice one.' Richard folded his arms and stared at one particular watercolour of Alice's. 'Don't think I realised just how good your sister is, Suze.'

'How do you know these are hers?'

'The name on them's a bit of a giveaway. As are the red dots. She's sold most of them. Look.' Richard was impressed. 'Good price as well. She can buy us a bevvy or two when we actually find her.' He looked round the large airy room, its smooth white walls broken haphazardly with artwork, to where just a handful of people were gathered around one particular painting by Alice Parkes. 'Can't see her anywhere here though.'

'*Excusez-moi?*' Susan was already trying out her rusty schoolgirl French on whom she assumed to be the proprietor. '*Nous sommes regarder Alice? Alice Parkes, le artist?*' Susan waved a hand in the general direction of Alice's canvases. '*Où-est-elle, s'il-vous plait?*'

'She was here two minutes ago.' The man spoke perfect English and Susan felt a frisson of irritation. What was it about anyone trying out the bit of foreign language they knew, whether it be in Spain or Germany or, particularly, in France? The natives just wouldn't let you have a go. They had to come back at you in English, determined to show just how rubbish the English were at speaking the local lingo. And how proficient they were at yours. 'I'm sorry, you've just missed her. Ah, here is her friend now, looking for her too, I think.'

Susan and Richard turned simultaneously, assuming it to be one or other of the French or Algerian artists Alice shared much of her life with. Susan's face remained impassive as the man walked towards them, smiling at her while obviously trying to work out where he knew her from. 'Hello,' he greeted them. 'Are you here to see Alice's work? Do you know her?'

Richard laughed. 'Susan is Alice's sister.' He reached out a hand. 'Richard Quinn, Alice's brother-in-law. You don't happen to know where she is, do you?'

'Bill Astley. Friend of Alice's from home.' He turned back to Susan. 'Well, fancy that... Small world. I didn't know you and Alice were related?'

'Why would you?'

'Do you two know each other?' Richard asked, smiling.

'We met years ago at school,' Susan said. 'Bill came in to give my kids a talk on knights and castles.'

'Oh *right*,' Bill smiled, obviously relieved. 'I knew I recognised you from somewhere.'

'You're a historian? You know all about knights and castles?' Richard smiled in turn.

'Bill *is* a knight,' Susan said, somewhat shortly. 'And lives *in* a castle. Well sort of...'

For a second, Richard appeared nonplussed and then grinned. 'Ah, you're the Marquess of Heatherly? Got you. Nice to meet you, lad. Should I bow and scrape a bit?'

'Please don't. I'd arranged to meet Alice here this afternoon. I'm a bit early. Had a coffee and cognac over the road – it always seems OK to drink during the day here in Paris, don't you think? Are you here to persuade her to come back to the UK?'

'Back to England?' Richard and Susan spoke as one. 'Why would we do that?' Susan went on. 'She loves it here. I can't see her ever coming back. Especially now as her painting appears to have finally taken off.'

'Right.' Bill appeared at a loss. 'Alice does know you're here? She knew you were coming?'

'No, all a big surprise,' Richard smiled. 'We've been threatening to fly over for years, but you know, work and family – as well as a bit of a fear of flying I appear to have taken on board – have got in the way. I gather you're a bit of an artist yourself, Bill? Is that how you know Alice? I mean, do you actually *know* her, or are you just visiting a fellow Yorkshire artist...?' Richard broke off as the gallery's outer door opened and the three of them turned towards it.

'Oh my God, Alice.' Susan could do nothing but stare as her little sister stood, apparently unsure what to do next.

'Shit.' Richard stared open-mouthed.

'You've a couple of visitors, Alice.' Bill Astley walked towards her and, taking her arm, brought her over to where the other two seemed frozen to the spot.

'You appear to have put on a bit of weight, Alice,' Susan finally managed to get out as, scowling, Alice stood in front of her, defiantly meeting her sister's eye, like one of Susan's ten-year-olds being told off for using a black biro instead of the regulation fountain pen and Quink blue cartridge.

'As you see,' Alice snapped crossly.

'I'm assuming that's not from scoffing too many croissants, éclairs or crème brûlée?' Richard attempted levity as Susan and Alice squared up to each other.

'Shut up, Richard,' Susan snapped back. 'Alice, you're *enormous*. When are you due?'

'A couple of months.' Alice was petulant now. 'It's fine, it *will* be fine… it'll all be sorted.'

'A couple of months? But, Alice, you're huge for seven months pregnant…'

'Six actually.'

'But… twins? You must be having twins?'

'Try again.'

'What do you mean?' Susan stared.

'What Alice is trying to say… I'm sorry, Susan, is it…?' Bill was apologetic. 'What Alice is trying to tell you is that there are three of them.'

'Jesus, Mary and Joseph.' Richard blew out a long breath.

'No, not those three,' Alice said tartly. 'Look, can you just forget about all this? If you hadn't just turned up, all of you, out of the blue without an invitation, none of you would have been any the wiser.'

'You're going to have three babies, Alice, three children, and your own sister would be none the wiser? What the hell is the matter with you?' Susan's face was grim.

'I didn't ask for there to be three of them.' Alice was cross now. 'I didn't know there was even *one* of them until it was too late. Do you think I'd have, you know, gone ahead with all this, let it get to this stage, if I'd realised?'

'What are you talking about? You're an intelligent grown woman, Alice, although, standing there in front of me now, I can't see much sign of any intelligence whatsoever.' Susan, who so longed for the chance to have just one more baby in her arms, the chance to be pregnant again after so many years of disappointment, looked with something akin to distaste at her little sister. 'You always were such a *baggage*, Alice.'

'Susan!' Richard turned on her. 'Stop it. You're not being helpful here.'

'Exactly,' Alice said, her arms reaching round to the small of her back. 'Hang on, I need to sit down.'

Bill Astley immediately reached for a nearby chair and Alice sat with a grateful *whoomp*. 'If you'd just stayed at home, instead of jumping out at me like bloody Cilla Black, none of you would have been any the wiser. I'd have given birth and had them adopted and that would have been it. Job done.'

'Cilla Black? What's Cilla Black got to do with it?' The other three stared.

'*Surprise, Surprise*. It's one of the English programmes we get over here. I've become quite obsessed with it.'

'Adopted?' Susan started. 'No way, Alice. You are not having my nieces or nephews adopted.'

'I'm sorry, Susan, I don't think you have any say in the matter. There is no way I want *one* baby, never mind three. How the hell do you think I'm able to look after three babies? Here? By myself?' Alice paused, one eyebrow raised. 'This exhibition is going to New York next year. And I'm going with it.'

'You selfish cow. You self-indulgent, spoilt, lazy bitch...' Susan found that she was crying, tears and snot and mascara coming away on the back of her hand as she attempted to stop the flow of tears. 'What will Mum and Dad say?'

'Mum and Dad won't *know*, unless you tell them. And, Susan, don't you *dare* tell them about this. Mum would be distraught and Dad... well, we know what the Very Reverend Cecil would say.'

'Do you know,' Susan said through her tears, 'next time Dad has a party, and you happen to just turn up, as you did last time, we can call it a Tarts and Vicars' party.'

'Stop it, Suze.' Richard was angry now. 'That's not worthy of you, calling Alice names. She's made a mistake. Everyone makes a mistake sometime in their life.'

'Some mistake. And what does the father think of all this? Do you even know who the father *is*?'

'Thanks, Susan, for that.' Alice eyed her big sister who was standing, fists clenched, glaring down at her. She paused. 'He's standing right beside you.'

'What?' Susan screeched, almost apoplectic with rage. 'You've had sex with *Richard*? With my *husband*? He's given you *three* babies, when I don't appear to be able to have just one more? One *little one* more. I knew you always fancied him. You've always wanted anything *I've* got...'

'What?' Alice shouted in turn. 'Oh, for fuck's sake, Susan, don't talk so bloody daft.' She actually started to laugh, somewhat hysterically. 'Standing at the other side of you, you moron.'

All three turned to Bill Astley who was standing calmly, taking it all in. 'Guilty as charged,' he said, holding up his hands. 'I'm not sure if multiple births run in families, but my mother was a twin.'

'Pity you didn't think to point that out at the time,' Alice grunted. 'Look, I'm dying for a pee. Can we perhaps go somewhere for a drink?'

'I've told Alice I'm more than happy to be of financial assistance where I can be.' Bill ordered coffee, cognac and water in fluent French. 'I like children. I've told her she's welcome to have one of the cottages in the grounds of Heatherly Hall.'

'But you have a wife?' Susan stated. 'Don't you? Aren't you married?'

'I have an *ex-wife* and several children of my own and, if I'm being honest, several friends...'

'Friends?' Susan glared at Bill. 'Do you mean mistresses? Live-in lovers?'

'Susan, you're beginning to sound like Dad. You've got the same hectoring, self-righteous tone as him.'

'My first wife, Elizabeth, died a long time ago.' Bill paused for breath, the words obviously painful for him to speak. 'And my ex-wife, Diana, lives in California, no doubt sharing her bed with one of her many lovers.'

Susan tutted crossly at that, but Bill just smiled, taking no further notice of her disapproval. 'My arrangements are all fairly amicable. It does all become somewhat complicated, as well as expensive, I grant you, but as I say I've offered Alice one of the cottages and am happy to put my name on the babies' birth certificates.'

'And if there's a boy in there, lad?' Richard leaned forward, his Scouse accent becoming more pronounced. 'Is he in line to the throne, as it were? You know, will he get his hands on Heatherly Hall? Just asking for a friend,' he protested, as both Susan and Alice kicked out at him and Bill frowned.

'I'm afraid that ship sailed a long time ago,' Bill smiled. 'My son, Henry, at the moment living in Tregaron in Wales, will inherit.'

'Look, Bill's family is his own affair,' Alice said determinedly. 'I've already started to make arrangements with the people who will be involved. These babies are going to live in France. They will *be* French...'

'But...'

Alice held up a hand as Susan started to interrupt. 'You're not changing my mind, Susan. I am *not* keeping them. 'There are two successive steps in the adoption process in France: an administrative procedure and a judicial one. The administrative step enables the applicant to obtain an "*agrément*". This assent is required in order for the prospective adopters to be put in contact with a child likely to be adopted.'

'And are they going to be adopted singly?' Susan interrupted. 'Are they to grow up not knowing they have brothers and sisters? That they are triplets?'

Alice had the grace to look slightly ashamed, but only for a split second. 'I don't *know*, Susan. I mean, to be honest, I can't see someone wanting to adopt three of them all at once. You know, buy one, get two free...'

'These are *babies*,' Susan howled, 'not effing boxes of soap powder.'

'You never could bring yourself to say "fuck", could you, Suze?' Alice said, almost sadly. 'Look, if you hadn't decided to pay me this surprise visit, you'd have been none the wiser about all this. Just go back to Westenbury, tell Mum and Dad you've seen me, the exhibition has been really successful and at some point I'm moving over to New York with it. I might settle there. Who knows? Live for today, I say.'

'Alice, your babies – *my* babies as well – will be split up from each other.' Bill Astley spoke quietly, emphasising the word 'my'.

'I'll ask if they can stay together.'

'Like starting at high school?' Richard murmured. 'You know, can the best friends from junior school be put in the same class?'

'I'm sorry.' Alice was resolute. 'I can't just demand they be kept together. Who would want to take on three brand-new babies?'

'Me,' Susan shouted. There were pinpricks of red in her otherwise white face. 'Me. *I'll* take them. *I'll* adopt them. *I'll* have them. *Richard and I* will have them.'

'Hang on a minute, Susan...' Richard's head had shot up and he was shaking it in confusion. 'How are we going to cope with four children all of a sudden? You'd have to give up work. We've only got three bedrooms.'

'I'm *happy* to give up work,' Susan shouted. 'I *want* these babies. They're my *family*. And, Richard, we're thinking of moving. You know we are.'

'Only if you were carrying on working. A bigger mortgage and three extra kids to bring up? Jesus, think of the nappy bill, the shoe bill, the university bill...'

'I'd be happy to contribute,' Bill interjected somewhat stiffly.

'No, I didn't mean *you* to think of the bill, Bill.' Richard rubbed a hand over his eyes before reaching for the other man's pack of Gauloises, shaking a cigarette from its pack and lighting it, drawing smoke long and hard into his lungs.

'I didn't know you smoked, Richard.' Alice eyed her brother-in-law through the plume of smoke ascending towards the nicotine-painted low ceiling where it joined the by-product of a thousand other cigarettes smoked at the table.

'I don't,' Richard said, glaring at Alice, before reaching for Susan's cold hand and squeezing it tightly.

PART TWO

5

October 2021

Westenbury

ALL HALLOWS PARISH CHURCH NEWSLETTER

We are delighted to announce that the Reverend Rosa Quinn is joining us as our new vicar this week. She will be licensed by the Bishop of Pontefract, our very own Ben Carey, who as you know left us to be that bit nearer to God several months ago. Reverend Quinn graduated from Durham University with a first-class degree in Business Management, and spent ten years working in London before relinquishing her high-flying career in finance in order to carry out God's work. She has just completed three years as curate in the parish of Worksbrough in Nottingham and is very excited, not only at the prospect of her ministry with us, but also at returning to the village where she was brought up and went to school. You might be aware that our new vicar is the granddaughter of the Rev Cecil Parkes, who was incumbent at our church for thirty very long years, and who is planning to move back into the vicarage...

'Left us to be nearer to God?' Eva Malik frowned, wafting the parish newsletter towards Rosa. 'Is Ben Carey dead then?'

'I hope not,' Rosa said shortly, grinning at her sister who was now fiddling with the rusting vicarage gate. 'He's coming over from his hallowed office in Pontefract next week to *bless me and all who sail in her* sort of thing. You know, swear me in, as it were?'

'You're going to have to get some WD40 on this gate,' Eva said. 'Bugger, that's one nail down. And,' she went on, 'who the hell is responsible for writing this newsletter?' She wafted the paper in Rosa's direction once more. 'The wording sounds like Grandpa Cecil is moving back in here, rather than you. Blimey, if the parishioners are thinking that the Rev Cecil is back, they'll be heading for the hills, and you'll end up preaching to an empty house every Sunday.'

'Hilary Caldwell,' Rosa said, leading the way up the broken concrete path to the vicarage door before searching in her bag for the key.

'What about Hilary Caldwell?' Eva asked, catching up with Rosa, who now had everything from her bag out on the windowsill in an effort to find the recalcitrant key. 'Haven't seen *her* for years.'

'Oh, this is a good start, isn't it? A bit of breaking and entering on my first official day here, because I can't find the damned key?' Rosa fumbled in the back of her jeans before pulling out a huge key and, with a victory salute skywards, and a '*Thank you, God*,' fitted the key with some difficulty into the lock and pushed open the front door to the vicarage. 'Hilary Caldwell? *She's* written this stuff about me.'

'Hilary Caldwell is on the parish council?' Eva stared. 'Last time I saw her she was snogging the life out of Duncan Makepeace behind the bus shelter down by the rec. Just after we'd all finished A-levels.'

'Well, Duncan must have reckoned her snogging passed muster,' Rosa grinned. 'She's Hilary Makepeace now and, apparently, one of the churchwardens. She was on the interviewing panel with Ben Carey and a couple of the lay preachers when I came for the job. I couldn't believe it when I saw it was her – she's gone all rarefied. Asked if I'd like a *scon* rather than a *scooone*, once the interview was over and the tea trolley came out.'

'Hilary Caldwell rarefied?' Eva pulled a face. 'She was as rough as a box of frogs at school. She once told me she'd nicked, and knocked back, a six-pack of Babycham – it was her granny's favourite drink apparently – and then fellated three of the upper-six in turn...' Eva pointed out of the kitchen window '...down there in the graveyard. Just remember that when she's offering you a *scon* in future. And, she needs to improve her English if she's going to continue writing newsletters like this... Oh look, Rosa, this is priceless.' Eva started laughing.

'What?' Rosa turned back to Eva.

'In the classified ads, at the bottom.' Eva pointed a gloved finger.

'What? Ah right.' Rosa started giggling herself as she read out loud:

'GIRLIE WANTED FOR CHURCH FOOTBALL TEAM – must be fit and have some idea about scoring. See Colin Wicks on the field behind the church on Tuesday evening.'

'Great stuff. Right, we're in. Gosh, Rosa, it doesn't look any different from when Grandpa Cecil was in charge, does it? Didn't Ben and Sarah Carey do *anything* to the place in the few years they were here? Look, the kitchen cupboards are still the same disgusting snot green that Granny Glenys used to complain about when we were kids.'

'Granny was far too busy keeping out of Cecil's way as much as she could to really care about the state of the kitchen...' Rosa broke off as Hannah, the third of the Quinn triplets, came through the kitchen door bringing in a blast of chilly autumn air along with her.

Hannah took in the old-fashioned units as well the upright, three-ringed Tricity cooker that had eventually replaced the worn-out stove that had been the bane of Glenys Parkes' life in her reign at the vicarage, before glancing upwards at the badly painted wooden creel suspended at a strange angle above their heads, not unlike some mediaeval rack of torture.

'Well, you'll certainly have to fight the good fight with that, Rosa,' Eva said, following Hannah's gaze to the ceiling.

'It'll be fine. *I'll* be fine. It'll all be good,' Rosa said with a conviction she wasn't really feeling. 'I'm going to paint it all myself. They warned me the vicarage needed a complete makeover when they tried to persuade me to take up the offer of that tiny little flat at the other side of the village instead. Apparently, according to Hilary Makepeace anyway – who appears to have become my new best friend – the area's property department administrator had written advising the parish county council and diocese of their responsibilities regarding the vicarage, and that now was perhaps as good a time as any to follow the housing committee's advice to sell the place on. I would imagine flattening the vicarage and selling the land to a developer was what they were advising.

'Anyway, when I turned down the offer of the flat and said I'd only take the post if I could also take on the vicarage, it was almost a case of washing their hands of me. You know, here was a bit of a troublemaker: not only a woman – when I can guarantee not only Hilary Makepeace, but the rest of the female brethren were wanting a young, single male to have fantasies about and to invite over for lunch after the Sunday service – but a bolshie one at that. When I laid my cards on the table, and said I'd love the post but only if I could live in the vicarage, they weren't happy about it.'

'I'm surprised they offered you the job then.' Eva pulled a face. 'Especially knowing you could turn out to be a chip off the old Rev Cecil block. I'm amazed they even let you through the door when they realised that.'

'There wasn't a great deal of competition,' Rosa admitted. 'Vicars appear to be a bit thin on the ground at the moment, especially now we're expected to take on at least one other parish as well as our main one. A girl I was at college with has ended up with three churches to administer to. Can you imagine? Anyway, according to Hilary Makepeace, who took me to one side before the final decision was made, it was a toss-up between me and the bloke I'd seen wandering nervously through the graveyard earlier, talking to himself. Or possibly God – I wasn't quite sure which...'

'A toss-up between you, the nervy nerd or *God*?' Eva stared. 'You actually pipped The Almighty to the post?'

'No! Let me finish!' Rosa started to laugh. 'You *always* jump in before I've finished! The vicar in the graveyard was talking to *himself* or God. When I finally caught up with him, he was then having a one-sided conversation with one Cyril Fletcher, who apparently met his demise drowning in the village duck pond after too much ale at The Jolly Sailor while celebrating his brother's wedding back in 1910. When my fellow interviewee turned to talk to a real-life human being – and I know this isn't a kind thing to say – his halitosis nearly knocked me into the grave alongside Cyril Fletcher.' Rosa laughed again. 'I know, I know, not a very Christian thing to say.'

'They *were* hoping to sell this place, you know,' Hannah said. 'Or at least do it up a bit and rent it out at great expense. Mum told me. Anyway,' she went on, walking over to the fridge, which was humming loudly and insistently, 'at least you won't starve. Mum said she'd been out shopping for you. God, you're going to have to do something about this bloody humming – it'll drive you mad.' Hannah opened the fridge door and all three peered in. 'Look at this lot: cheese, eggs, chicken, sausages, Mum's usual corned-beef sandwiches. There's enough to feed an army.'

'She's making sure you eat properly so you don't get sick again,' Eva said matter-of-factly. 'We're *not* going through all that again.'

'*We?*' Rosa pulled a face. 'I think you'll find it was *me* who went through it all.'

'And we were with you every step of the way,' Hannah protested. 'Me and Eva. And Mum and Dad.'

'I know, I know,' Rosa smiled. 'I know you were.'

'You *are* OK now, aren't you?' Hannah frowned. 'I mean, you would tell us if you weren't? You don't think you've taken on too much? This is a big parish to handle. And living in this great mausoleum? All by yourself?'

Rosa laughed. '*You* live all by yourself, Hannah.'

'Yes, and I love that. But I've not been through what you've been through, Rosa, and my little house is tiny. And modern. And I can lock it up and leave it and go off for a couple of weeks whenever I want without having to worry about the grass needing cutting.'

'That's because you've no lawn,' Eva protested. 'That's why you never have to worry about the grass needing cutting – you haven't *got* any grass.'

'Exactly,' Hannah beamed, reaching for a bottle of wine cooling in the fridge. 'Right, shall we wet the baby's head as it were? Celebrate your being the new village vicar, Rosa?' She opened cupboards looking for glasses. 'God, stingy things, they've left you just four glasses – cheap things, free with petrol as well, by the look of them. Whereas, you, Rosa,' she went on, warming to her theme, 'will have to be out with the Flymo every minute of the day you're not praying: mowing the lawns, tidying up the churchyard, clipping and manicuring the grass around the graves. And that's after a day administering to the sick and elderly with chicken soup and dumplings…'

'Isn't that a Jewish thing?' Eva asked doubtfully. 'You know, the chicken soup?'

'I'm sure Rosa's Christian brethren will appreciate it just as much as the Jews.'

'I don't have to mow the lawns and tend to the churchyard, do I?' Rosa looked worried. 'The parishioners took it in turn to do that in Nottingham. Maybe I should have taken up the offer of that flat instead of this place?'

'Just bat those big chocolate brown eyes of yours at some gorgeous young lackey in your congregation and…'

'Gorgeous and young are not adjectives that describe the Westenbury congregation,' Hannah interrupted Eva. 'If they were, do you not think I'd be here every Sunday morning on the dot of 10.30 a.m. instead of taking my chances swiping left and right on Tinder? Gone are the days –' she sighed '– when a young girl could take her pick from the packed pews of rampantly lusty farmers' sons.'

'Young girl?' Eva snorted. 'You're thirty-six, Hannah. Time's running out for the pair of you.' She turned to her sisters and raised an eyebrow.

'Well, if it's running out for us, it must be for you too, you daft thing. We're only, what, two-fifths through our allotted time on this earthly journey towards the grave? Rosa and I have got all our lives ahead of us; can do what we want, go where we want while you, on the other hand, Eva, have taken the conventional path of marriage and motherhood and, because you're a bit bored with it all, a bit frustrated with the day-to-day sameness of it all, are jealous of our freedom and are determined to tie us up... or tie us down...' Hannah trailed off, a superior look on her face. 'Or something like that.'

'I'm not frustrated with my life,' Eva returned crossly. 'I have a fulfilling and meaningful career as a dentist.'

'Looking in people's mouths all day long?' Hannah smirked. 'While you try to have some sort of conversation with the person sitting in the chair with a gob full of metal? Or with one or other of the posse of dental nurses you've taken on, who're equally bored stiff standing there administering that spit-sucker thing while wishing they'd done beauty and hairdressing instead.'

Rosa laughed at that, and at Eva's face. 'Come on,' she soothed, 'where's that wine? Mum and Dad said they were going to come down again as well.' She looked at her wristwatch and then out of the kitchen window. 'Oh, hang on, they're here – get out another couple of glasses, Hans. Or cups or something.' This was followed by a banging of the outer door, the clattering of nails along the tiled corridor and then a mad flurry of whining and barking as a crazed ball of hair and fur flung itself into the kitchen.

'Jeez, you damned dog. Get down, Brian.' Eva examined the expanse of tights above the black suede boots she was wearing but, nevertheless, bent down to join in with the general patting and welcoming of the blonde-coloured Cockerpoo.

'He doesn't get any more grown-up, does he?' Rosa smiled, caressing the creature's silky ears until he was a squirming mass of ecstasy. 'What is he now? Eighty-four in dog years?'

'You wouldn't know he was twelve, would you?' Richard Quinn said proudly, kissing each of his three daughters in turn. 'How lovely to have all three of you together again,' he smiled. 'We should have asked Virginia to join us and then we'd have had a full set. You could do with a dog here yourself, Rosa,' he added, gazing round at the kitchen. 'God, it must be twenty years since I've been in this place. Twenty years since Cecil finally took off to that great vicarage in the sky.' He laughed. 'I bet he's still arguing the toss at the pearly gates, telling St Peter it's his God-given right to enter. If Peter has any sense, he'll have pointed him in the other direction.'

'Oy, do you mind? That's my dad you're having a go at.' Susan Quinn took her turn at hugging each of her daughters, but holding on to Rosa for seconds longer than was necessary. They'd so nearly lost her and, with her here, now, not only in her arms but back in the village, Susan sent up her own silent prayer of thanks.

'I was merely pointing out facts re the Rev Cecil,' Richard replied, squeezing his wife's arm. 'So don't go all holier-than-thou on me now. You've done your share of criticism of the old sod.'

'And don't swear in the Lord's house,' Susan added primly, still not happy with the dissing of her father.

'It's not the Lord's; it's Rosa's now. God forbid,' Richard added, turning to where Rosa was flicking through the post that had been collected by Susan earlier and left on the kitchen table.

'Are you sure about this, sweetheart? Living here in this great pile all by yourself? Come and stay with Mum and me. At least until the rest of your furniture comes up from Nottingham?' Richard gazed round the soulless kitchen once again and shivered slightly and, when Rosa smiled, shaking her head at his proposal, he went on, 'Hell, I remember standing in this very spot the first time your mum brought me home to meet Cecil and Glenys. Your Granny Glenys was lovely, so welcoming, but Cecil had taken himself off to what he called his inner sanctum – that room along the corridor, Rosa – and was waiting for me like something out of a bloody Dickens novel. Given that I was Catholic and a Scouser, as well as the prospect of someone in his family who not only liked to spout the Labour Manifesto but was also a sociology lecturer, there wasn't a huge welcome for me at the vicarage. I tell you, if I hadn't loved your mum to the moon and back, I'd have been off. Out of there before you could say 'Is the Pope Catholic?'

'But he allowed you to marry?' Rosa asked.

'Couldn't stop us,' Susan jumped in. 'My father was already on pretty bad terms with Alice; he didn't want to lose me as well. He knew he had to try and be fairly pleasant or we'd have gone to live in Liverpool.'

'I was certainly up for that,' Richard went on, 'but your mum wanted to be around for Glenys. If your grandmother had had any sense, she'd have washed her hands of the old devil once Mum and Alice had left home.'

'He wasn't very pleasant to us three when we were kids,' Eva remembered. 'Totally different with Virginia, of course. She was the one he really loved – if he ever loved *anyone* other than himself,' she added.

'Cecil could never come to terms with you three being a result of *Alice's sinfulness*, as he used to call it. And even though your real father…'

'You're our *real* father,' Rosa, Eva and Hannah chorused as one, as they so often had done over the years.

'And even though your *birth father*' – Richard amended – 'was a marquess – *is* a marquess – and Cecil Parkes was one hell of a snob – he couldn't forgive Alice for deserting you three and bringing what he saw as total disgrace to the family name as well as making him question his Christian values on forgiveness.'

'How is Alice?' Rosa asked. 'Have you heard from her recently?'

'She's not been well,' Susan replied, unwrapping dishcloths and tea towels, washing-up liquid and Brillo pads before placing them in kitchen drawers and under the sink. 'She worked so hard on that last exhibition and, while it received the usual accolades and fabulous reviews, I think it tired her out. She *is* nearly seventy now, and riddled with arthritis, but she still keeps on working, still insists on pushing herself.'

'How do you know?' Rosa asked. 'You've not seen her for years. Not since we all went over to New York to see her and her exhibition in the Metropolitan Museum of Art. That must be over twenty years or so ago.'

'We speak on the phone,' Susan said. 'Regularly. She always asks after you girls. There was a big spread on her and her work in the Saturday *Guardian* review a couple of months ago. I did send it to you, Rosa, didn't I?'

Rosa nodded and then made to tidy away the empty glasses. 'Right, if you don't mind, you lot, I'm going to get on, unpacking a bit more stuff…'

'We'll help you.' Susan was adamant.

'…before I have a governors' meeting across at Little Acorns.'

'Not on your first night here, Rosa. Come home and eat with us,' Susan pleaded. 'Or I'll stay with you here and cook for you? What about your bed? Is it made up? Is it aired?'

'Mum, stop fussing, I'm fine. I promised Cassie Beresford, the head teacher at Little Acorns, I'd go over there to have a welcome drink and meet the other governors at seven.'

'Don't overdo it, love,' Richard said. 'Give yourself time.

You don't want to make yourself ill...' He didn't actually say the word *again* but it hung in the air like a bad smell.

'I'm going to sort myself out a bit, have a long soak in the bath.'

'Is the hot water on? Is it up and running? It was always so temperamental.' Susan felt the radiators in the kitchen, which were just gurgling into life.

'And then devour a big plate of beans on toast. And if it means I fart my way through my very first governors' meeting at the school, then so be it. Go on, all of you, get off to where you need to be.'

'Your dad and I don't need to be anywhere...' Susan started to say, but Richard picked up his coat, whistled for Brian who was now stretched out on the rug in front of the open fire in the sitting room, despite it not being lit, and attempted to manoeuvre Susan towards the door. 'Come on, girls, leave the village vicar to sort herself out. Give her a bit of peace and quiet.' He gave Rosa a hug, whispered, 'We're always here if you need us,' and ferried the others out in front of him.

'Will it ever get any easier?' Rosa wondered out loud as she lowered herself into the hot water and closed her eyes. Had it been a mistake coming back to Westenbury, with all its reminders of him?

She knew her calling to the church, albeit quite late on and certainly coming as a shock to her family and all who knew and loved her, was most certainly not a mistake. Sometimes she was quite amazed that it had taken thirty years before she was able to acknowledge, even to herself, that this call to follow God and do his work was what she'd probably really wanted all of her life.

Rosa sniffed a couple of times, determined she wouldn't cry, but found herself catching a warm tear on her fingers before it dripped unceremoniously onto her breast and into the bath water. She brought two fingers up to her mouth, enjoying the saltiness on them and then, unable to stop the dam bursting, lay back and gave in to her emotions.

'No,' she sobbed out loud to the steam that was now rising and condensing on the glazed, curtainless bathroom window. 'Oh God, I can't see that it... ever... will.'

6

Eva drove the five miles or so back to the house she shared in the village of Heath Green with Rayan and their two girls, Laila and Nora. She didn't put the car above the 30 m.p.h. speed limit, didn't overtake a couple of slow-moving elderly drivers or the tractor that pulled out from one of the fields in front of her, even when the farmer beckoned her forward, indicating, with an impatient wave of his hand, that it was safe for her to do so. She was in no hurry to get home.

Rayan was covering the late evening shift at the dental practice they owned at the very end of the main street through Westenbury village. The business was thriving and, according to both their accountant and their growing list of patients, seemed to be going from strength to strength. So much so, they'd recently taken on two new junior dentists, one a female graduate from Sheffield University and the other a more experienced dentist Rayan had interviewed for the job a month earlier and who was still to start at the practice. With three receptionists, two dental hygienists and a plethora of dental nurses on board, Rayan had, the year previously, bid and been successful both in acquiring and obtaining planning permission for two of the neighbouring shops in order to knock through to make a couple of additional surgeries. While Eva was certainly not averse to growing and expanding the practice, she did feel a sense of guilt at their taking over what had originally been small family-run businesses in the village.

As little girls, once Virginia had been taken and dropped off at the village school where, at one point, Susan herself had been a teacher, the just-four-year-old triplets would be ordered to hold hands ready to walk along the paths by the school and the church, in preparation for crossing the busy road to the many wonders of the village shops. Whichever two of them managed to get there first would hang possessively on to Susan's own, while the third – dependent on who she was wanting to exclude that morning – would somewhat sulkily take another sister's hand and, on the barked order of *now* from Susan, the four of them would run across the road and into the magic kingdom of the streets of shops. Thirty years on, the village was all very different. And, while the village school the triplets had attended was still there, it too had changed and grown dramatically. Once a small C of E village school, under the auspices of All Hallows where, it was very strange to think, Rosa was about to be ordained, the primary school was now Little Acorns and was, apparently, with head teacher Cassie Beresford at the helm, held up as the very model of good practice, particularly in its approach to early years education.

Eva wondered, idly, if Rosa would spill the beans on any insider knowledge gained from her now being a member of the school's governing body. She doubted it. Rosa, of the three sisters, was the one with integrity. Bloody hell, she must have it in spades, and a whole lot more, giving up her high-flying career in the city, the beautiful London apartment in Wandsworth she'd lived in while climbing that greasy pole in order to reach and go through the glass ceiling. Hmm, too many metaphors there, Eva mused as the three-way traffic lights finally allowed her to move on.

And now it appeared Rayan would actually be examining patients' mouths in what had formerly been the shoe shop. The plans incorporated a brand-new surgery for herself, as well as for Rayan who, after much further training, had expanded into the lucrative world of orthodontics. As well, Rayan now offered Botox injections two evenings a week. Eva had, after some hesitation, lain back in her husband's surgery chair and allowed him to practise pumping rat poison into her forehead. She'd been a bit concerned she'd end up with a mask-like face or, worse, one eye lower than the other, and suggested, instead, they reverse positions and she'd try it out on Rayan first. Just in case. But she had to admit, he'd had a cool, steady hand and done a pretty good job, although, apart from Susan asking if she'd done something to her fringe – or was it her eyebrows? – she herself couldn't see a great deal of difference. Maybe if she'd been twenty years older which, she supposed, was the mean age of the women happy to give themselves up to Rayan's administrations along with a filling to a back molar or root canal, she might have seen some improvement. Eva had not fessed up to either Hannah or Rosa she'd had Botox. She had a feeling neither would approve.

It was almost half past five by the time Eva pulled up in the drive of their large, neo-classical box in Heath Green on the outskirts of Westenbury village, and the rain that had been threatening for most of the afternoon was now here, falling heavily. The black-painted front door with its huge brass knob and knocker – Eva always wanted to laugh at those words, childish as that might seem – opened slightly and Nora, presumably having heard her mother's car pull up, was already behind it, waiting impatiently for Jodie, their Australian part-time nanny, to open it fully.

'Hello, my darling girl.' Eva walked up the slippery, leaf-strewn garden path and reached for her daughter just before Nora set her bare feet on the wet concrete.

'Where Daddy? Want my daddy?'

'Oh,' Eva crooned. 'Won't I do, sweetie-pie? I've missed you. I need to give you one great big hug.'

'No, I's sorry,' Nora said politely, 'I's want just Daddy.' Nora struggled in Eva's arms and, digging her elbow into her mother's right breast, Eva let her down on the wooden-blocked floor of the entrance hall. 'No, sweetheart, you can't go out there in the wet,' Eva went on, pulling her none too gently back in. 'It's cold and wet out there. Brrr! Brrr! Brrr!'

Nora gave Eva the full extent of the *get a life, Mother* look she'd been practising and polishing for the past couple of weeks. 'Upsidaisy,' she added, for no particular reason that Eva could make out, before patting Eva's knee sympathetically and turning back into the house.

'Has she been hard work, Jodie?' Eva asked, following the pair of them down the hallway to the kitchen.

'Is a frog's ass watertight?'

'Sorry?'

'You've got a visitor,' Jodie replied, ignoring Eva's response and instead catching up with Nora who was running along the length of the hall, her pyjama bottoms spiralling down her sturdy little legs as she went. Jodie picked her up, expertly throwing her over her shoulder and tickling her until she giggled hysterically. 'Jeeze, Nora, you'll sleep flat out tonight.' She bent down, blowing raspberries on Nora's bare tummy.

'A visitor?' Hell, Eva thought, she was in no mood for visitors.

'Yep,' Jodie answered over her shoulder. 'She arrived in a taxi this arvo. She's already cleaned out your fridge and kitchen cupboards and is now in the process of turning the kitchen into the best little Curry House in the North.'

Eva's heart sank. Surely Rayan's mother hadn't taken a taxi all the way from Bradford? Despite Rayan telling Azra that she really *must* let them know when she was coming to stay, rather than just turning up, unannounced, this was the second time in two months she'd put in an appearance without advising them of her imminent arrival first.

'Ah,' Azra greeted Eva through a cloud of steam. '*As-salamualaykum*. Hello, lovely girl. How are you?' She smiled, adjusting the *dupatta* which had fallen from her head to around her shoulder before turning back to the stove and stirring furiously at the pan there. 'Now, I know you weren't expecting me, but

I also know how hard you both work at that tooth place. And what a naughty little girl that Nora is.' Azra smiled indulgently, chucking Nora – who had escaped Jodie's arms – affectionately under her chin. 'She has grown now. She looks just like Rayan now, don't you think?'

Seeing Rayan was six foot tall with a beard, Eva couldn't quite see it. 'How've you got here, Azra? Why didn't you tell us you were coming?'

'Ah now –' Azra grinned, showing perfectly white, straight teeth '– if I'd told you, you'd have stopped me coming on bus. I know Rayan. He'd have said it was too much like hard work coming over here to this cold, back-of-beyond place on National Express. He'd have sent me a ticket for train or he'd have driven over in big fast car of his to pick me up and I don't want that. I know how busy he is.'

'Right,' Eva said, desperate for gin but, instead, reaching for the kettle. 'Really, you know, Azra—'

'It all alright,' Azra beamed, bending down to pat first Nora on her dark curls and then Eva's arm. 'Don't you worry about me. I get Hadhira to take me to Leeds Bradford Airport.'

'The airport?' Eva frowned. 'Why? Where were you wanting to fly off to?'

'No, not to *fly off to*.' Azra started to laugh and then, remembering her administrations at the stove, turned back to whatever it was she was stirring. 'Best place to get National Express Coach. It take just over hour to get to Midhope. Full of people coming back from Lanzagrotty and Tenerifey. And then,' she added proudly, 'I get taxi here from bus station. Hadhira tell me to take taxi when I get to town bus station. Cost a bloody fortune, but Hadhira give me money.'

I bet she did, Eva thought. Rayan's younger sister, also a dentist but in their native Bradford, would have been more than happy to have a break from her mother who had moved in with Hadhira and her GP husband, Sabir, and their two boys when Rayan's father had died three years previously.

'Now,' Azra said, 'I making *Shab daig* for tomorrow's tea.'

'What's that, Mrs Malik?' Jodie, pulling on boots and a thick woollen jacket against the rain waiting outside for her, wound a voluminous scarlet scarf around her neck and peered into Eva's best blue Le Creuset casserole pot in which something meaty and slightly noxious- smelling was boiling and rolling.

'OK, Jodie.' Azra smiled indulgently. 'You want I teach you to make it tomorrow? It night boiler.'

'Night boiler?' Jodie gave the pot a stir. 'Go on then, spill the beans. What's in there, Mrs M?'

'No, Jodie, no beans at all. Meat. You girls need meat. Good for the blood. Good for periods. Give you healthy babies.' Azra's eyes widened and she winked at Eva. 'So, always mutton, beef, and turnip. But I make it even better and put in big chicken as well. No beans. Will boil all night long and tomorrow, tomorrow we have *big feast.*'

'I love chook,' Jodie said, grinning at Eva, who was pulling a face of despair. 'Did you stop off at Sainsbury's on the way here then, Azra, to buy all this food?'

'No, I brought it all with me, packed in my clothes.' Azra indicated the huge battered, wheeled suitcase still standing by the kitchen door where she'd obviously deposited it earlier, and Eva's heart sank. It looked as though Azra was here for the duration.

'Good on ya, Mrs M,' Jodie grinned before returning a sympathetic face in Eva's direction as Azra searched in Eva's cupboards for salt. 'Rightio, I'm off, both of yous. Here in the morning. Bye, my darling.' She blew a kiss and jangled her car keys in Nora's direction. 'Off on the lash, tonight,' she added for Eva's benefit. 'Girls' night out.'

'Oh, you are all naughty girls,' Azra laughed, shaking enough salt into the Le Creuset to send the blood pressure of the whole of Westenbury soaring. She elbowed Jodie affectionately. 'If I took a drink, I'd be joining you on lash myself.'

'Actually, Azra, got a bit of a hot date later on.'

'Well good for you, love,' Azra beamed again. 'One date is better than two raisins.'

'Is that right?' Jodie started to laugh and, elbowing Azra back, she teased, 'You should get out there and have a bit of fun yourself, Azra.'

'Oh, go on with you,' Azra chortled, flapping her *dupatta* in Jodie's direction before bringing it up to wipe at her eyes. 'Now, you be careful, Jodie, looking for husband. You are sure to marry man either beautiful or ugly – if ugly, that will be punishment enough; if he very sexy...' Azra's head waggled in mirth... 'you will have to share him with all the others.'

'As long as he knows what he's doing in the sack, and got a bob or two as well, he'll do for me.'

'Oh you.' Azra chortled some more. 'You girls. You have such *fun*...' She turned back to the stove. 'Now, we have *Aloo Gosht*, with *Gulab Jamun* for afters for tea tonight. We need to fatten this one up a bit,' she went on, patting Eva's behind through her black tailored work skirt. 'A man likes a bit of padding when he comes home from hard day's work pulling out teeth.' She fingered her own ample backside. '*Gulab Jamun* – fried dough and syrup – that'll do the trick.'

Much as Eva wanted to keep Nora awake in order to spend some precious time with her, to read to her, to chat with her in order to try and ingratiate herself in her daughter's affections when it appeared only Rayan would do, she felt a guilty sense of relief when Nora drooped on her shoulder and was fast asleep before her head touched the cot mattress. She glanced at her watch – an hour or so before Rayan would be home after picking up six-year-old Laila from her classmate Matilda's house, on his way back from the surgery. She'd had to remind him to do just that or, with his head full of the new plans for the surgery, of his plans for world domination – or village domination at least – and of all things dental – he'd be home, tired yet buzzing, sans one daughter.

Eva stripped off to the buff and made her way to the shower but, catching sight of herself in the full-length mirror, stopped to appraise her body. While she, Hannah and Rosa all looked very much alike, being trizygotic triplets they were no more identical than if they'd been ordinary sisters born to the same parents at different times. They were all dark-haired and brown-eyed as were both Alice and Bill, but now, Eva acknowledged, after two pregnancies she was the only one of the three whose bosom – without help from the sturdy M&S bra – was heading south, while the silvery lines and tracks of stretch marks on her abdomen and thighs bore witness to carrying those babies in her body for nine months. Eva lifted up both breasts, sucked in her stomach and did a couple of pelvic floor lifts but she knew, compared to her sisters' unravaged bodies, she now came in a poor third in comparison.

Of course, *absolutely*, she wouldn't swap her two gorgeous girls for her old unmarked, lithe body back again, but if there was something like Boob Botox to give her droopy pair a bit of a helping hand, she had a feeling she'd be in the front of the queue. Eva shook back her thick shoulder-length dark hair and then, piling it on top of her head, pouted the classic model pose in the mirror. No, nothing helped. What on earth was the matter with her? Was it the post-summer blues? October, with the thought of a long miserable winter ahead of her? No, she quite liked winter with its wardrobe of suede and leather boots, cashmere sweaters and big scarves and coats. Was she peri-menopausal? Surely not at thirty-six? Although, to be fair, only last week one of her mates from uni had rung her, crying down the phone that, now she'd made the decision to try for a baby before she hit the watershed of being forty, she'd apparently left it too late – she was already well into the change.

Did she, Eva, want another baby? No, absolutely not. Was

she as excited as Rayan about the expansion of the practice? Not very, no. Was it the fact that, after fifteen years of being with Rayan – eight of those being his wife – she wanted more? Eva raised an eyebrow at her reflection in answer to that one and when, still trying to work out exactly what it *was* she was wanting, she finally, if silently, asked that other woman in the mirror: *Do you want another man? A lover?* the other woman stared right back at her, but didn't demur.

'You silly bitch,' Eva eventually sniffed, reaching for one of the soft pink towels on the heated radiator and heading for the shower.

7

Hannah breathed a silent *fuck it* as the long chain of brake lights ahead of her turned red and the traffic heading east on the early morning stretch of motorway came, yet again, to its customary standstill. She pulled on the brake of the Fiesta before turning up the volume of both the car radio and the heater. If she had to sit here, on this long stretch of motorway, with stonking great immobile European lorries and trucks snorting on every side of her like white prehistoric beasts, she might as well have some decent music. With an impatient *pillock*, she obliterated some stuttering cabinet minister who was losing the battle with Radio 4's Justin Webb, allowing *Clean Bandit* instead to flood the car's interior. She didn't normally go for electronic, electropop bands such as this, but one of the kids she regularly dealt with at court was big into Jess Glynne and had persuaded her to listen along with her, sharing her earphones in an invitation Hannah thought it inadvisable to turn down. It was one way, Hannah supposed, to get a fourteen-year-old looked-after child – who not only had a history of attacking the staff at the homes she was sent to, but also of self-harming – onto her side.

Rain. Again. Hannah swore once more as water lashed at her windscreen. She wasn't a nervous driver; was more than happy to shoot along in the fast lane, overtaking the heavy traffic in the other two lanes, but the rain was adding to the build-up of traffic and, glancing at the car's console while attempting to nudge into the third lane, she knew she was going to be late for work yet again. At least the sudden downpour gave her an excuse for her tardiness but, pulling a face at herself in her rear-view mirror, she was furious with herself for the real reason she'd still been in bed less than an hour earlier.

After too many late arrivals that week at the youth court where she was an officer in the Youth Offending Team, once she'd left Rosa and the others at the vicarage, Hannah had promised herself an early night in order to catch up on some much-needed sleep. Instead, she'd spent her evening binge-watching some unmissable TV drama – which, at its conclusion, she'd declared totally *missable*, throwing a cushion at the screen, cross with herself for wasting time watching it. Unable to catch up on the sleep she knew her body craved, she'd taken her laptop into bed with her and written lengthy WhatsApp messages to ex-uni friends who were now living in Canada, Australia and, for some reason Hannah couldn't quite fathom, on Tresco in the Scilly Isles.

Anything to stop her picking up her phone in order to message him and tell him it was all a mistake; she couldn't go through with it after all.

As soon as she'd walked into the vicarage kitchen the previous afternoon, she'd assured Eva – with a simple nod of a head to Eva's raised questioning raised eyebrow – that yes, she'd finally done it. She'd told him, the evening before, she just couldn't do this any longer; he was never going to leave his wife and, after nine months, the relationship was going absolutely nowhere except with Ben going back, every evening, to his wife and two children.

Here *she* was, her job that of protector of children, the majority coming from some sort of broken or abusive home, and yet for the last six or seven months she'd been carrying on with a daddy to two small children. There *he* was, with the two children in Croatia; in the garden hanging on to the rear end of the boy's bike as he finally managed to ride it without stabilisers; on Easter Sunday six months ago, in the midst of his little boy and girl excitedly sitting amidst a veritable mound of Easter eggs. And without any words on the Facebook page needing to tell her how Ben had then been called into the hospital to use his clever hands and expertise to save the life of an elderly man. Knocked down and left with head injuries as he crossed the road after spending his own Easter Day with his daughter's family, by some high-on-drugs kids who, more than likely, would end up in the court she was now battling her way along the motorway to get to. And how, after making her way back from her own parents' Easter Sunday lunch with Rosa and Eva, Rayan, Laila and Nora, as well as Granny Glenys, plucked out of her care home for the occasion, she'd left early, pleading a headache, but knowing that Ben was waiting for her back at her house.

Eva had given her the look, the one that said: *For heaven's sake, this is Easter; has he no conscience? Have you no shame?* And, ignoring the look, she'd driven back, desperate to have him for herself, and taken him upstairs to her bedroom, given him her very own special Easter present before relinquishing, as she knew she must, this man that she loved, once more to his own waiting family.

Shame shot through Hannah as the cloudburst abruptly ceased and the traffic began to move forwards, slowly at first and then with momentum. Shame that, like an alcoholic lies about never touching a drop ever again, it had taken less than twelve hours after reassuring Eva yesterday that yes, she had finally finished the affair with Ben, had blocked his number from her phone and asked him for her key back, for her to answer the door to him at six this morning – just over three hours ago. He'd stood on her doorstep, eyes almost drooping with fatigue after yet another night of call-outs to cover more junior staff who'd rung in sick and said, simply, 'I can't do this, Hans. I can't be without you.'

And so it went on. As did the deceit and the shame; the not getting on with her own life instead of hankering for the one she couldn't have. Hannah indicated left off the motorway and, clenching her teeth with the tension of it all, joined the queue of traffic making its way towards the city centre, the courts and her office.

'Busy morning for you,' Shirina, the youth court usher, called after Hannah as she opened her office door, dumped her coat and laptop and took a grateful mouthful of the strong Costa coffee she'd ordered at the bar next to the court building.

'I know, I know, sorry. Rain as well as the usual gridlock on the motorway.'

'They're all waiting for you,' Shirina frowned. 'That sarcastic big bald bloke – you know, the one who seems to hate kids? – is chairing the bench and already getting the hump at having the magistrates retire because we've nothing ready for them yet. Oh, and Kath's the legal adviser.'

Thank heavens for small mercies, Hannah thought, draining her coffee before opening the lid to hook out the chocolate-powdered foam left on the rim and sides. Kathleen Donnelly, who'd been doing the job for years, knew what she was about and would keep the court moving seamlessly through the different cases as professionally as she could. She'd argue the toss with some of the more bolshie advocates doing their utmost to persuade both the magistrates and the YOT that their fourteen- and fifteen-year-old clients were at best little angels, at worst mere scamps who were utterly remorseful and who wouldn't *ever* be back in front of the magistrates. *Ever again.* Until the next time, Hannah wanted to add. These advocates very conveniently forgot that for a child to actually appear in the youth court (and sometimes Hannah wanted to remind the court professionals that these *were* still children despite the downy hair on their upper lips, the tattoos and air of world-weary ennui), they'd quite probably – and rightly, in her view – had numerous out-of-court disposals and police cautions before actually appearing in front of a bench of youth magistrates for the first time. 'Right, Shirina, OK, just give me two minutes to get my laptop up and running and then I'll come into court.'

Hannah scrolled through her morning's list, frowning at the

names of a couple of kids who were only two months into their respective six- and nine-month referral orders, but who'd been arrested jointly for having bladed articles in a public place, as well as riding off on another twelve-year-old's brand-new bike after apparently following him into the local park.

When she was up to date with the coming morning's work, reminding herself of who was who and of their past history, as well as quickly scanning through the numerous reports written by members of her team, she studied the list for any children new to the court system. It always surprised laypeople, with little or no experience of youth justice, that there were only two outcomes for a child pleading guilty in court for a first offence. A detention and training order – basically the nick – or a referral order. As the whole aim of the Youth Offending Team was to keep any child out of custody, 99 per cent of newbies, as Hannah liked to think of them, would be given six- to twelve-month referral orders, which would then be supervised by Hannah and others in the team.

After tossing the coffee cup expertly into the bin beside her desk, Hannah walked into court, taking her seat at the side until she was asked to comment, depending on what stage they were at, on how a child was actually progressing on a particular order, or to advise the best way forward for a 'newbie'. Her heart sank at the hectoring tone of the magistrate who was already speaking to the fourteen-year-old standing in front of the bench of three.

'So, young man, can you explain to us why you thought it was a good idea to take and drive your mother's car? And take your hands out of your pockets first.'

Oh, for heaven's sake. Hannah glanced across at the magistrate who was getting into his stride.

'Dunno really.' The boy looked at his feet, chewed on his fingers and then gazed round the room.

'Could you look at me when I'm talking to you?'

Oh Jesus... Hannah closed her eyes briefly.

'Well, what *were* you thinking?'

The boy shrugged. 'Nowt really. Just thought it'd be a good idea.'

'At three in the morning? When you're fourteen and you don't know how to drive? Have no licence or insurance?' The magistrate harumphed loudly before blowing his nose into a pristine white handkerchief. 'You just wait until you're appearing in the adult court in a few years' time. They'll throw the book at you.'

Oh, great stuff, nothing like the assumption that the kid was going to end up as a hardened criminal in the future... Hannah adopted a look of mild benevolence, imagining a hard-backed copy of *War and Peace* to hand and the utter joy of throwing it at the sanctimonious old bastard's bald head, without her getting the sack for doing just that.

'So why do it, Kyle? When you know you shouldn't?'

'I were bored.'

'Bored? At three in the morning?' Big Baldy Bloke looked genuinely mystified. 'Why weren't you asleep like everybody else at that time of night?'

'Dunno.'

The magistrate conferred with each of his colleagues in turn and then looked directly at Hannah. 'So, can we hear from the Youth Offending Team now? Miss Quinn?'

'Sir.' Hannah rose from her seat and, for the next minute or two, outlined the best possible way forward for the fourteen-year-old youth. 'A nine-month referral order with supervision, where Kyle will meet to negotiate a contract of reparation to his mother and to the community, as well as a programme of work to address his offending behaviour...' Hannah heard herself smoothly spouting the correct words, followed by Kyle's mother at the back assuring the court that she wouldn't be letting him out of her sight for one minute. There'd be no sloping off to see his mates.

Good luck with that one, Mum. Hannah bowed her head, the benevolent smile pasted once more on her face.

'And he'll be having to wash up and make his own bed to pay off the court costs I've been landed with,' his mother continued from the back of court.

'Right, OK, thank you, Mrs Bradshaw,' Kath Donnelly ventured.

But Mrs Bradshaw was in full swing and she was going to have her day in court, now she'd got going. 'He's learned his lesson, 'as our Kyle, and, as his girlfriend is pregnant with his first child…'

His *first child*? Ye Gods and all his little angels. Even Hannah, hardened as she was to the goings-on of preteens, teens and adolescent youths, blanched a little and felt some sympathy for the look old Baldy now offered up to young Kyle.

'…he'll have some responsibility to keep him on the straight and narrow. You know, becoming a family man, like.'

'Right, thank you, Mrs Bradshaw.' The magistrate smiled an on/off smile and shuffled his papers like a BBC newsreader at the end of his shift. 'You're free to go, young man, but don't go without seeing Miss Quinn first.'

Half an hour for lunch when, despite Hannah telling herself she would absolutely *not* pick up her phone to see if Ben had left a message, repeatedly did just that. She was feeling depressed and impatient with herself that, for heaven's sake, she was pathetic; she hadn't even been able to manage a day without him. She was an addict. She needed Al Anon. Or to leave the area altogether. The country even. She'd always fancied working in the States. Did they need youth workers over there? She'd email Alice once she got home and ask her opinion.

Funny, she mused, and not for the first time, that Alice might be her and her sisters' birth mother, but none of them had ever contemplated anyone but Susan as their mum, and Alice as anything but Susan's sister – their aunt. It was as though Alice had lent her womb for the sole purpose of growing the triplets for Susan and Richard. A bit like tomatoes in a growbag. This wasn't a new idea, but one that Eva had mooted years ago, and it still made Hannah want to laugh every time she thought it. Alice the Growbag, for heaven's sake. How would the three of them have fared had Alice decided to keep her babies and raise them herself? Or given them up for adoption, as apparently had been Alice's intention? Scary thought that the three of them could have been scattered across France – one in Paris, one in Nice and one in Normandy maybe? Eva had always bagged Paris for herself, being kind enough – she said – to allow the other two to choose any other destination *en France* for themselves.

Eva, Rosa and herself had, of course, discussed the whole strange situation of their birth many times over the years but particularly when the three of them were going through a somewhat bolshie adolescence and Eva had said she was off. Off to France where she belonged. Leaving bloody cold Yorkshire, with its lack of artistic talent, to be French and find her true destination. Or off to live with Alice in New York and become a famous artist – like her talented *real* mother. All three of them had shown off a bit – well, quite a lot actually – particularly when doing GCSE Art and whenever Miss Woodrow, the ageing art mistress who promoted gentle watercolours rather than the vivid oils the three of them favoured, had the gall to criticise their portfolios, making suggestions they all ignored.

Hannah spent the last five minutes of her lunchbreak on her laptop googling career opportunities both in Australia and New York. Maybe if she told Ben she was leaving the UK, it would spur him on to come with her. She spent the last two minutes googling opportunities for brain surgeons in those two far-off places as well. Oh, for heaven's sake. Hannah knew she couldn't live with the guilt of Ben leaving his two beautiful children. And yet she appeared to be able to live with the guilt of encouraging Ben to spend time in her bed.

Hannah slammed down the lid of her laptop. Three minutes to drink yet more coffee and shove the three gingernuts she'd filched from the basket of individual packs in the magistrates' retiring room while reading:

POLITE NOTICE – REFRESHMENTS FOR SOLE USE
OF MAGISTRATES

Hell, she was going from bad to worse – adulterer to thief. But wasn't she already a thief – taking Ben from his wife and children?

Hannah sighed, picked up her laptop and files and headed across to the youth court once more for the afternoon session.

'Eyes down, look in, we're off again,' Kath Donnelly said, catching up with Hannah along the corridor from her office. 'We've a kid from somewhere down south in this afternoon. Serious stuff. I've spent all lunchtime trying to get in touch with the Youth Offending Team in his home town, but not had much luck. I think they've all gone to the pub.'

'I could murder a gin myself,' Hannah grinned. 'Rhys Johnson? He the one you mean? He's moved over to my neck of the woods, apparently, but I don't have the full low-down on him, or his family or why they've moved to Westenbury. Is he here? I need to see him before he comes into court.'

'Not yet, as far as I can see. He might be talking to his solicitor. There's a couple of other cases we can be dealing with until he arrives.'

Hannah spent the next hour speaking on behalf of one case of criminal damage, one possession of Class B drugs and one assault by beating before turning to the magistrate who'd replaced the morning's chair of the bench.

'Now, has this other child turned up? Rhys Johnson?' The magistrate looked over her glasses at Shirina, the usher.

'Just arrived, ma'am. Just having a last-minute word with his brief.'

'Apologies, ma'am...' Mr Nasir, whose law firm was well known for taking on the most difficult of youth cases, ambled into court, running a hand through his sparse hair. He pulled out papers, waving them for a few seconds before addressing the bench. 'Ma'am, I represent Rhys, but we're having a bit of a problem actually getting him into court.'

'Who is he with?' the motherly magistrate asked. 'Is it a parent or some other appropriate adult?'

'His father, ma'am. He'll be pleading not guilty to a number of *going equipped* as well as an actual *domestic burglary*.'

Hannah rose from her seat in the well of the court. If his father was having problems actually getting his son into court, it was her job to persuade him in, to reassure him, explain what was going to happen, answer any questions he or his father might have. It always reminded her of persuading a mulish horse into its box. 'I need to see him for two minutes, now he's actually appeared.' She nodded the usual courtesy to the court and made her way to the door just as it opened and a tall, fair-haired man entered the room, followed by a scowling, pale-faced fourteen-year-old. The man halted, seemingly unsure where to go, but when he saw Hannah, he actually stopped in his tracks.

Oh My God. Hannah closed her eyes briefly before locking them onto Joe Rosavina's own, unable to look away.

Which one out of her and Eva was going to be the one to tell Rosa? Tell her that, like in some third-rate cowboy or gangster film, Joe Rosavina was back in town?

8

The rain had returned on Hannah's journey home, the spray-filled motorway loaded with impatient truck drivers travelling westbound at speed, either desperate to get home for their tea or to reach Liverpool, the docks and the continent for their allotted time on the ferries, and who had scant regard for Hannah in her little red Fiesta.

Fed up of constantly battling the spray that her wipers were manfully trying to overcome, she pulled into the slow lane, reduced her speed and then made the decision to leave the motorway at the junction before her customary exit back to the village. She'd spent ten minutes after leaving work ringing and leaving messages for Eva both at home and at the dental practice. Eva's mother-in-law had answered her landline and, while Hannah normally enjoyed a bit of banter with Azra, this time she'd cut her short, despite Azra laughing down the phone, wanting to tell her what *that naughty Nora* had been up to with Eva's brand-new full (now empty) bottle of Miller Harris's Scherzo eau de parfum and a bag of chapatti flour. The receptionist at the practice said it was one of Eva's half-days for not working and, Hannah wasn't to hold her to this – or quote her on this, she'd added – she thought her boss had plans to take the girls somewhere after picking Laila up from school.

Not being able to track Eva down, Hannah took the earlier exit and instead of heading for her own address, or for either of her sisters' places, made the decision to call in instead at Heatherly Hall to see Bill.

The three girls had grown up used to calling their birth father

Bill instead of *Father* or *Dad*. They had only ever recognised one *Dad* and that was Richard, who had accepted and brought up the triplets with as much love and devotion for them as for his firstborn, his natural daughter, Virginia. Richard had never favoured Virginia above herself, Eva and Rosa which, considering Virginia was not only the eldest and probably, with Susan's blonde hair and big blue eyes, the prettiest of the four girls, as well as being his birth daughter, was somewhat surprising.

Virginia had always been the apple of the Rev Cecil's eye – his adored and favoured granddaughter – sobbing quite uncontrollably at the old man's funeral when she was twenty and in her second year of teacher training, while the Trips were just fifteen, bolshie and unable to shed even one tear over a grandfather who'd never had a particularly kind word to say about any one of the three of *them*. Boys, alcohol and cigarettes – as well as an unswerving devotion to the Backstreet Boys – filled every waking moment for the fifteen-year-old girls that wasn't already taken by an all-consuming desire to paint and to be as famous as their Turner-Prize-winning birth mother, Alice Parkes.

Funny, Hannah reminisced as she put the Fiesta into second gear and wound her way up the wet roads to Heatherly Hall, by the time the girls were doing A-levels and planning their future careers, while art was still a love of all three of them – but particularly Eva, who'd persuaded sixth-form college to let her do A-level Art along with the sciences needed for entry to dentistry – none of them were considered talented enough, even by themselves, to go on to a career in the art world.

While she, Hannah, had gone to Manchester to do a degree in social sciences and Eva had spent five years at dental school in Sheffield, it was Rosa who had gone from strength to strength in the City, becoming the first woman to be awarded both the UK National Forum Award and the *Sunday Clarion*'s Future Management Award. It was all beyond Hannah, who had never been particularly driven or ambitious in her chosen career, but she, Eva and Rayan had all travelled to London with Richard and Susan to see Rosa receive her accolade.

And now look at Rosa: the village vicar, following in the footsteps of the dreadful, sanctimonious Reverend Cecil Parkes and living in that ghost-filled, scruffy mausoleum of a vicarage.

Totally unaware, Hannah could almost guarantee that Joe Rosavina had returned to Westenbury as well.

Hannah drove past the main entrance of Heatherly Hall, which allowed access when the farm shop and the petting farm were open to the public, as well as entry to the flourishing wedding venue that had been incorporated into, and now taken over, the west wing of the hall. Instead, she motored to the next T-junction, turning right before stopping at the huge black iron gates which, almost forty years earlier, had led Alice not only to Bill's party, but also to Hannah's own conception.

The girls knew the whole story of the circumstances of their birth, but more so after their first visit to New York to see both the sights and Alice when they were just sixteen. Alice had scrutinised each of the girls in turn, turning their faces to the light while seemingly searching for any of her features in their own. She'd not seen the girls, not returned for a visit to the village, since they were six or so, and had appeared more interested in their physical characteristics – *definitely Bill's eyes*, she'd concurred while holding Rosa's face in dry paint-stained hands – as well as any blossoming potential artistic talent, rather than how well they might be doing at school, their friendships, favourite foods or how the three of them all got on together.

The girls had spent an exciting – if exhausting – five days with Richard, Susan and Virginia (home from studying education at Leicester for the Easter break) walking for miles, stopping on every street corner for yet another Starbucks, taking in the whole heady ambiance of the Big Apple and all it offered, vowing that, one day, they would come and live here, share an apartment overlooking Central Park and be like the fabulous girls in *Sex and the City*. The series had first been aired on TV a couple of years earlier, but Eva had managed to get hold of the DVD doing the rounds at school and, while Susan – as well as Virginia, apparently – had not thought it suitable for young girls of sixteen, Richard had laughed and said of course it was. Where else were they going to learn more about their birthmother's adopted city?

After long and tiring days taking in the delights of New York, Ellis Island and the American Museum of Natural History, their early evenings were full of art exhibitions at the New Museum – the seven-storey building dedicated to all things modern in every medium – where Alice was currently showing her latest work – as well as at the MoMA PS1 out in Queens, where the girls took in every aspect of the cutting-edge contemporary art on show there. Each of them, privately, vowed this was where they were meant to be; ten or twenty years into the future, their own work would be feted and applauded, gazed upon and written about, in this very art gallery in which they now stood, mouths open in awe and admiration.

So, every evening, with aching feet, but buzzing from all they'd taken in during the day, the six of them would be taken, by Alice, to various watering holes around the city. Sometimes she was alone, at others accompanied by one of the many men – and women – with whom she was either having, or with whom she had been in, a relationship, and they would all hoover up pastrami, clam chowder and huge lumps of authentic New York cheesecake.

And while, at the end of the five days, Virginia and Susan proclaimed themselves utterly exhausted and ready for a bit of normality and a good cup of Yorkshire tea, the triplets were loath to return to their looming GCSEs, the acne-faced boys with whom they'd once considered themselves in love back at Westenbury Comp, as well as the mundane ennui of village life. All three of them had fallen in love with Alice, copying her mannerisms, her Yorkshire-tinged-with-New-York accent, her disregard for any social rules and niceties, as well as her penchant for chain-smoking Nat Sherman cigarillos.

Back in the UK, the girls bought Cohiba Mini Classic – the least expensive they could find – puffing and choking, eyes streaming over their GCSE art projects as all three dreamed of stardom in the art world like Alice, their much-celebrated artist mother. Eva even asserted she was changing her name to Eva Parkes, writing her new handle on all her exercise books as well as refusing to answer to her former name when the register was called at school. It was only when Hannah pointed out that she now had the same surname as that curmudgeonly old malcontent, the recently deceased Rev Cecil, and that people at school might think she was mourning his passing, that she grudgingly reverted to Quinn.

All this went through Hannah's head as she passed the cottage on the estate she'd been allowed to live in when, unsure where to go after returning from university, but not wanting to live back at home with Susan and Richard, Bill had offered it to her for as long as she required it. She'd gone on to do a fair bit of travelling, working in Australia and New Zealand, Thailand and South America but, eventually she'd returned to the UK, training as a YOT officer, and gratefully accepting Bill's offer for her to return to the estate cottage. After three years living there, Richard began to moot the idea of mortgages and pensions and a financially secure future for herself and, with some help from both Richard and Susan as well as from Bill himself, she'd bought the two-bedroomed townhouse up towards Norman's Meadow, which she adored. And which she considered her safe haven after long days working with the area's disaffected youth.

'Hans!' A little dark-haired, brown-eyed bundle of energy toddled towards Hannah as she let herself into Bill's private apartment in the east wing of the hall. It was, she noted, looking somewhat cleaner and more in keeping with the rest of the house than on her previous visit. Bill's estate manager must have finally found another band of cleaners after the last pair were dismissed when security had hauled them out with a couple of solid silver ancestral candlesticks in their bags. What on earth had they been planning to do with them? Hannah mused. How do you dispose of fifteenth-century solid silver without drawing attention to yourself? Gumtree? The church newsletter's *For Sale* ads?

'Hello, my darling Nora.' Hannah swept up her niece, kissing and tickling her until she was giggling and hiccupping in delight.

'You'll have her throwing up all over you.' Eva came out into the hallway to greet Hannah. 'Bill's just fed them both huge knickerbocker glories.' Without waiting for a response, Eva held Hannah's eye. 'Are you OK? Are you alright? You know, after finally finishing it all with Ben?'

'Absolutely,' Hannah lied, not returning Eva's look.

'Oh, for fu—' Eva altered her words, knowing Nora was taking it all in and would be repeating it verbatim once back at home, '...flipping heck's sake. You've *not* done it, have you?'

'Yes, I did,' Hannah snapped back crossly. 'I did.'

'But a few hours later he was back in your bed, *unable* to be without you?'

'I 'able...' Nora stumbled over the word, '...'able to be without you, Hans. I *love* you.' She snuggled herself into Hannah, planting sugary-smelling wet kisses onto her aunt's neck.

'I don't want to talk about it,' Hannah said, exchanging sloppy kisses with her niece and reluctantly replacing Nora on the carpet before making her way into the huge, baronial sitting room that had once been, apparently, Heatherly Hall's ballroom. It was the same room Alice had been escorted into almost forty years earlier and, while the central heating had been upgraded, ensuring the room was now a good deal warmer than when Alice had walked into it, the same grotesquely in-your-face chandelier hung from the ceiling and the artwork – that had survived being sold to pay yet more tax bills – hung in their same positions on the walls.

Large murals and frescoes filled the main expanse of the ceiling, with small related adornings surrounding its lower layers. Apotheosis scenes, cherubs and those depicting popular biblical stories looked down benignly, while a surfeit of gilding was the principal element used to outline tiers, highlight important medallions as well as offering additional sparkle around chandeliers. Or probably, Hannah had eventually realised, just as a means of expressing wealth.

'Darling, how are you doing?' Bill rose slowly from his chair, good manners superseding the obvious pain in his arthritic knees and hips. 'You look shattered. Have those evil little toerags been giving you the runaround again?'

Hannah tutted. Despite Bill's almost lifelong support of what might be considered left-wing issues, he wasn't averse, when the mood took him – usually when he was in pain with his joints – to spouting right-wing dogma. 'You know as well as I do, Bill, kids are not evil. No one is born bad…'

'Phhuff,' Eva interrupted. 'You haven't had to get down and dirty with Sylvia Faraday-Brown. She constantly comes into the surgery complaining about her bridge or – excuse the non-PC handle – that a bunch of Irish navvies could have done a better job on the root canal I carried out at her last appointment. I tell you, that woman is a nightmare. Now, she *must* have been born bad.'

'Sylvia Faraday-Brown?' Bill grinned. 'Once had a bit of a thing with her, girls. She was a bit of a goer if I recall.'

'OK, OK, we don't want to know.' Hannah put her hands over Laila's ears as Eva's elder daughter sat on the carpet at Bill's feet, ostensibly doing her reading homework, but really earwigging and taking in everything of the grown-up conversation.

'Ooh, your hands are cold, Aunty Hans.' Laila released herself and turned to Bill. 'What's a goer, Bill?'

'Goer,' Nora said solemnly. 'I's a goer.'

'So, what's up, Hannah? Still embroiled with your doctor?' Bill patted the space on the sofa next to him, and Hannah gratefully sat. She could have done with a stiff gin and tonic but she was driving and, having seen the damage fifteen-year-olds could create when in charge of alcohol and a taken-without-consent vehicle, she never, ever, combined the two.

'Are you poorly, Aunty Hannah?'

'Poorly?' Hannah glanced down at Laila.

'I hear that you're seeing the doctor a lot.' Laila said it without guile, but Hannah knew her six-year-old niece was a bright, tough little cookie who wasn't averse to sticking her pretty little nose into grown-up affairs.

'Just a touch of Dr Strangelove Syndrome,' Hannah said, straight-faced.

'Which, just when you've convinced everyone you're over it, appears to come back and you're forced to submit to it once again, ending up in bed for several hours,' Eva added, sniffing sanctimoniously. 'Until it leaves you once more, feeling sicker and more let down than when it arrived.'

'Right.' Laila obviously knew she was being talked over but couldn't quite work out what it was. She came out fighting. 'Chloe Evans in Year 6 has got puberty. Her sister, Belle, sits next to me and she told me that Chloe has to carry an ST... no, I think it's a TS... round with her in her lunch box. You know, just in case.'

'In case of what, darling?' Bill was trying not to laugh.

'In case she gets hungry, I suppose. I think it must be a Tomato Sandwich. Or possibly a tuna one.'

'I think you're going to have to do the birds and bees talk, Eva.' Bill was roaring with laughter.

'Oh, I know all about *that*,' Laila said scornfully. 'It's when a daddy puts his penis in a mummy's wagina. But before you can have a baby, you have to eat tomato sandwiches every month.'

'Definitely, the talk, Eva,' Bill grinned. 'Right, Laila, how about you take Nora and go and hunt for the Twix biscuits I've hidden in the butler's pantry?'

Greed at finding Biscuit Treasure was obviously fighting suspicion that this was just a ruse on the grown-ups' part to talk grown-up secrets, and Laila waivered. Greed overcame scepticism and, taking Nora's hand, Laila ran off.

'Something's happened,' Bill said, lowering his voice. 'I know you, Hannah. Has the doctor chap finally left his wife?'

'No, nothing like that,' Hannah sighed. 'Would that he had. Although,' she added, 'I'm not sure how I'd managed the guilt at his leaving his children, if he ever did.'

'I'm sure you'd find a way,' Eva said primly.

'Will you stop getting at me, Eva? It's bad enough that Rosa will be preaching from the pulpit every Sunday morning without *you* joining her at every opportunity.'

'Eva is jealous, Hannah,' Bill stated calmly as Eva flushed unbecomingly. 'She yearns for the excitement of an adulterous affair, for the heart-stopping moment when a love-object notices you for the first time; holds your eye for longer than you both know is necessary; that first forbidden kiss...'

'I most certainly am *not* jealous,' Eva said furiously. 'What a ridiculous thing to say, Bill. I'm totally offended.'

'You are my daughter, Eva. And Alice's daughter as well,' he said in the same matter-of-fact voice. As if that explained everything. 'So,' he went on, ignoring Eva's mouth that was working itself up to form contradictions and, turning from her and back to Hannah, asked, 'What is it, Hannah?'

Hannah hesitated, turning from Bill to Eva. 'It's Rosa.'

'What's Rosa? Oh, please don't say it's come back again?' Eva's hand flew to her mouth, genuinely distressed.

'No, she's fine. As far as I know.' Hannah hesitated. 'It's Joe. It's Joe Rosavina,' she said, shaking her head. 'It's Joe who is *back*. Back in Westenbury.'

There was silence for a few seconds as the other two digested this nugget of information.

'I thought he was still in London?' Bill said finally. 'Are you sure, Hannah? This will demolish Rosa. Make her ill again.'

'Absolutely certain. I spoke to him. He was in court today.'

'Bit old for the youth courts, isn't he?'

'He was acting as responsible adult.'

'Responsible? Joe?' Eva spat the three words. 'You can't put those together in the same sentence.'

'*Appropriate* adult, I mean,' Hannah said, tutting. 'I always get the two words mixed up.'

'Appropriate: ditto re Joe Rosavina,' Eva broke in crossly. 'So, has he left his high-powered job in London to crawl back to Yorkshire to train as a youth worker or something?'

'No, no,' Hannah tutted again. 'I didn't get the full story. He was acting as appropriate adult for his stepson.'

'His stepson? The *baggage's* son? Was she not there as well then?'

'No. I really didn't get the whole low-down of why on earth Joe was in court. And with his fourteen-year-old stepson. By the time I'd gathered up all my papers and run after Mohammed, my colleague who was dealing with their case, they'd disappeared onto the concourse and I had other clients to see. What I can tell you is that the pair of them – Joe and his stepson – are back in Westenbury. They're all living with Joe's parents at his old address.'

'Oh Lordy,' Eva closed her eyes. 'Who's going to tell Rosa?'

'Oh Lordy,' Nora beamed, coming back into the room, her mouth and hands sticky with melted chocolate. 'Lordy, Lordy, Lordy...'

9

It was probably Eva's fault the three of them had all fallen in love with Joe Rosavina.

Returning from their five-day visit to New York where they'd unearthed the delights of the city, as well as the enigmatic, talented woman who was their birth mother – actually their *mother*, for heaven's sake – the three of them had become querulous, depressed even, with their situation of being Year 11 sixteen-year-olds with two months of revision for eleven GCSEs. All three agreed there was absolutely nothing to look forward to in their dull, insular little lives. Even the potential excitement of the much-anticipated move from Westenbury Comp to the nearby sixth-form college at the start of Year 12 (where the students wore their own clothes instead of any regulation uniform, called the teachers by their first names and were generally groomed to become *real* students two years hence) had faded to a mere triviality compared to the high-pressured pizzaz and the élan of those heady days in New York.

Virginia returned gratefully to Leicester to complete her second year of education studies, stating that it had all been a bit much, really, don't you think? And remaining quite unimpressed with her Aunt Alice's lifestyle in the States. She'd spent the eight-hour journey home eschewing the in-flight entertainment and complimentary alcohol, involving herself, instead, in the intricate planning – which appeared to Eva, sitting next to her, to be nothing more than glorified spiders' webs – for her Early Years teaching practice in the coming weeks ahead. She broke off only to eat and digest the stringy chicken in its glutinous grey sauce, declaring it the best meal she'd eaten since leaving Westenbury almost a week earlier.

For the triplets it was heads down, noses to the grindstone, seemingly for ever (her life, Eva declaring despairingly loudly from her room, over before it had even started) as they tussled with quadratic equations, comparisons of Lady Macbeth with Desdemona and, especially for Eva, who needed high science grades in order to study the difficult chemistry, physics and maths at A-level, revising the periodic table and trying to get into her head the differences between atoms, molecules, elements and compounds. Susan was constantly on hand, up and down the stairs every two minutes with delicious things on trays 'to keep you going' and joined by Richard – on long-term sick leave after his involvement in a car accident – available to advise on the relevance of the Duke of Bridgewater to the building of the northern industries canal system or the Amazon Basin to the Peruvian economy.

When the exams were finally over, the Year 11s had drifted away from school in an anti-climax of dribs and drabs, rather than leaving with the bang they'd envisaged, apart from Hilary Caldwell, who'd celebrated her final exam by losing her virginity to one Spike Overton in the Jolly Sailor car park. She'd declared, quite volubly to anyone listening, the whole business to be utterly *climaxic*, and suggested, nay urged, any virgins still left in Year 11 to unfetter themselves from the chains of innocence and go for it.

'Go for it?' Eva had scoffed. 'With the likes of *Spike Overton* and his mates? *I* intend saving myself for a tall, fit, broad-chested New Yorker in his twenties, preferably a talented artist, rather than handing it on a plate to a pale, weedy village nerd. How do you think he came by the nickname *Spike?*' she added, grinning and bending her little finger in derision.

With the GCSE exams finally over and the whole of the summer ahead of them until sixth-form college started in September, the three of them went to work for Bill. Or, to put it more accurately, for the Heatherly Hall Management Team. Dressed in their navy-blue polo shirts with the white embroidered badge depicting the hall and, below, its logo, *Heatherly Hall Staff*, Susan would either give them a lift to work, or they'd hop on the Number 45 double-decker which dropped them right outside the front gates.

Bill had warned them they were not to expect any favouritism, no nepotism because of who they were and, indeed, wasn't averse to calling out either one or all three of the girls if they were caught idling or late turning up for work. Jobs were many and varied, and while some were more popular and sought after, others most certainly were not.

After six weeks working most days on the estate, all three were getting cheesed off with the work and more than ready to relinquish it, the following week, for the start of their new venture at sixth-form college. 'If I'm in with those sodding hens and peacocks again,' Hannah said crossly as the three of them walked across the manicured lawns, dodging the many sprinklers keeping the grass green and watered, 'I'm going to complain to Bill.'

'He wouldn't listen. He'd just tell you to get on with it and suck it up,' Rosa said, her mouth full of the toast and Marmite she'd brought with her on the bus. 'God, do you realise we've fifty years of work ahead of us before we can claim our pensions? Fifty years of having to get up before 7 a.m. Fifty years of not having the time for a nice breakfast.' Rosa adored both her bed and her breakfast, but often found it difficult to relinquish the former for the latter.

'Well, *I* don't want to do these bloody jobs,' Eva sniffed, 'but I'm not giving in now – much as I hate being in that damned petting zoo.' She lifted up the hem of her polo shirt, sniffing at it. 'I still smell of those bloody pigs,' she added, before blurting out, because she couldn't contain her idea any longer, 'I've saved every single penny Bill has given us in wages.'

Hannah and Rosa both turned towards Eva as they drew up outside the site manager's office. 'You've never saved a penny in your life. You bought that new jumper from River Island a couple of weeks ago,' Hannah pointed out.

'I know, I know, I hadn't thought about it then.'

'About what?'

'Going back to New York in October. You know, at half-term.'

'Mum and Dad won't let us go back by ourselves.'

'I didn't say I was going with *you two*.' Eva was adamant. 'I'm going to stay with Alice. In her apartment. By myself.'

'What about us?' Rosa frowned. 'We want to come.'

'There comes a time, in every triplet's life, when she has to make her bid for freedom,' Eva started loftily.

'Sounds like you've been arrested,' Hannah smirked.

'It will happen to both of you in time,' Eva said with some degree of condescension. 'As the oldest of the three of us—'

'By twenty minutes, you pillock.'

'And being the first to become a woman—'

'What, because you started your periods two months before me?' Hannah tutted. 'And four months before Rosa?'

'No,' Rosa said impatiently. 'It's because she handled Spike Overton's, you know, *spike*.'

'I most certainly did *not*.' Eva raised an eyebrow, but didn't quite meet the other two's eyes.

'Yes, you did, you know you did. *We* know you did.' Hannah was adamant. 'And, if you think you're legging it back to New York without us, you can jolly well think again.'

'Oi, will you three stop gassing and get in here so we can sort you out with your jobs?' Jim Mitchell, Deputy Estates Manager, rapped on the open office window. 'You're late as it is. Everyone else has been at it ten minutes. Right.' Jim glanced down at his clipboard. 'Hannah, you're cleaning the holiday cottages with the chambermaids.'

'Oh, I hate cleaning toilets.' Hannah pulled a face.

'Eva, in with Pinky and Perky.'

'Bloody hell. The pigs again? Don't you know, young sir, I'm related to a marquess? I'm practically a princess.' Hannah and

Rosa started giggling as Eva gazed straight-faced, and defiantly royal, at the deputy manager. 'And you don't place princesses with pigs.'

'Aye, well, you find the bloody pea under twenty mattresses and you can have the day off, love. Otherwise, pigs it is. And you, Rosa, Maureen needs some help over in the café. Karen's gone home. *Women's problems* apparently. Again.' He paused, scratching his head. 'I'm sure she only had 'em two weeks ago.'

'Keeping tabs on our menstrual cycles now, Mr Mitchell? And, it's not fair, Rosa putting on her pinny to help serve cream teas while I'm in the pigs again.'

'And I've got to have my hands down some disgusting, skiddy toilet.' Hannah gave a dramatic distasteful shudder.

'Hey, listen, you three, you're late as it is. Don't start calling the shots, complaining about pigs and periods just because of who your dad is, or I'll have Mrs Howard after you.'

That sobered them up. Bill in a bad mood was bad enough, but Mrs Howard, who'd organised the smooth running of the Heatherly Hall estate for years, was in another league.

'And,' Hannah shouted after Eva as she made her way over to the petting zoo where, already, a queue of overeager kids with harassed mothers was waiting for access, 'don't even think about going to bloody New York at half-term without me and Rosa. Got that?'

'Rosa!'

Rosa looked up from dolloping mayonnaise into a bowl of mashed boiled eggs, but couldn't see where the voice was coming from.

'Behind you,' Eva whispered. 'I'm down here.'

Rosa turned, a mayonnaise-coated spoon still in her hand, before walking over to the open floor-level window at the rear of the Tea and Cake café. 'What are you doing down there?'

'I've escaped the pigs for five minutes. I've just got to tell you—'

'What, that you're off to New York without us? Well so be it,' Rosa said coolly. 'You're right; we need to have a little independence from each other. I might just take myself off to the Scilly Isles... or somewhere...'

'The Scilly Isles?' Rosa could just see the top of Eva's dark head as she lay on her stomach at the open window. 'Bloody *silly* idea. Scotland will be freezing in October.' Geography had never been the girls' strong point.

'And New York won't be?'

'Shut up about New York for two minutes. This is much more momentous.' Eva paused. 'Listen, you're not going to believe this. Guess who's here?'

'Margaret Thatcher? Mahatma Gandhi? The Backstreet Boys?'

'Yes!'

'Mahatma Gandhi? He's dead, isn't he?'

'The Backstreet Boys! Well one of them anyway.'

'Oh, don't be so daft... Coming, Maureen, won't be a minute...' Rosa turned back to the open window.

'I can smell... pigs.' Maureen Hardcastle, coming into the kitchen from the café, lifted her nose and sniffed. 'Have you got that egg mayonnaise yet, love? There's a couple of people wanting an egg sandwich already.' She sniffed the air once again. 'I'm sure I can smell pigs.'

'It's the eggs, Maureen. You know, the sulphur dioxide in them.'

'Hmm, they can sometimes smell a bit as though our Ron's dropped one. Come on, lovey, get a move on with it.' Maureen picked up the tray of Fat Rascals and, without another word, returned to the front of the café with them.

Rosa bobbed back down to floor level. 'So, the Backstreet Boys are here, are they? Duh?'

'Just Nick Carter.'

'Right.' If there was one boy – just one – to whom Rosa was prepared to offer her virginity, in fact prepared to beg him to *take it* from her, it would be Nickolas Gene Carter, singer with the Backstreet Boys. Most nights, Rosa fell asleep to fantasies of Nick Carter doing unmentionable things to unmentionable parts of her body. Her bedroom wall was covered with photographs of the blue-eyed, blond-haired demigod and while, to some degree, both Eva and Hannah shared her obsession with the singer, they weren't averse to cheating on him with Ricky Martin, Montell Jordan and even, for heaven's sake, Hannah, with Michael Jackson. But *she* was constant. She, Rosa, was Nick Carter's constant tin soldier; her whole body would burn into a little tin heart for him. She would—

'Rosa! Come back? Why are you staring into space with a dripping mayonnaise spoon in your hand like some sort of loon?'

'Where is he?'

'In the alpacas.'

'Nick Carter, best singer with the greatest band in the world, is mucking out the alpacas?'

'Tell Maureen you need the loo and go and see for yourself.'

'There's a loo here.' Rosa lifted the spoon, indicating a door on her right.

'Well tell her you've got to take a message to Mrs Howard.'

'What sort of message?'

'*I* don't know. You're good at making up stories – you won that prize for creative writing last term.' Eva was getting impatient. 'I can't crouch down here much longer. My legs are getting stiff. I need to tell Hans over at the cottages about Nick and then get back. I'm in the shit if I'm caught going AWOL.' She stood up. 'But I'm going to have another look at him before I go back to the pigs.'

'Rosa! Egg mayo!' The generally unflustered Maureen was getting irate. 'And I need them teacakes splitting into two and buttering. Butter's in t'fridge. You'll have to soften it in the microwave or t'bread'll be all over t'shop...'

Rosa, who, since she was a little girl, had always hated being told off, hurried to do Maureen's bidding, spending the next three hours in the kitchen behind the café cutting and buttering teacakes, washing lettuce, crying over a pile of chopped onions and, when it was nearing lunchtime, helping Maureen and Marion serve sandwiches, quiche, millionaire's shortbread and myriad coffee and Cokes. There was a veritable army of waiting mums with prams, out-of-control toddlers accompanied by irritable grannies as well as the old bloke in charge of grounds and maintenance who, always on the dot of one, downed tools and made his way to Tea and Cake for his usual cup of 'strong Yorkshire tea and ham sandwich on white, love'.

'You've done a grand job, there, lovey,' Maureen eventually said, wiping at her brow. 'Go and sit yourself down with a Coke and a sandwich. The quiche is good today – broccoli and Stilton, no less; bit posh, that, for round here. Mind you, you are a marquess's daughter...' She trailed off, taking in all of Rosa's features: the thick brunette hair tied back in its neat ponytail, huge dark eyes and full mouth.

Everyone round these parts, and especially those who worked here at the hall, knew the story of the Marquess of Heatherly, the artist Alice Parkes and the adopted triplets. It was old news, today's fish and chip wrapper, but just occasionally people – teachers at school, the boys who the triplets had just snogged and, particularly, the staff here at the hall – would stop and stare at the girls, looking for a noble brow, a royal wave, a superior, blue-blooded nod of the head and want to know more. Why had Alice Parkes abandoned them? What was their relationship with Bill Astley now? What did the marquess's 'real' children think of the three of them?

The novelty of being a triplet was hugely accentuated by the circumstances of their birth; the famous, Turner-Prize-winning birth mother who, along with David Hockney and Damien

Hirst, was indisputably one of Britain's most famous artists, an internationally revered icon who had well and truly become a household name. Throw in a bit of English aristocracy to the mix and to describe all this as a big deal would be an understatement.

'Just going to get some fresh air, Maureen, if that's OK?' Rosa took a cheese and beetroot teacake from under its glass case. 'I'll eat this as I walk.'

Maureen glanced up at the café clock. 'Be back in half an hour, love. The afternoon tea lot will be in soon wanting their cream teas; it's become really popular with young mums since we've added a glass of fizz to the deal. Oh, and put that teacake into a paper bag.' Maureen handed one over. 'Don't let Mrs Howard see you eating it in the grounds. You know what she's like – not the "*done thing*" apparently…' Maureen air-quoted the words with her fingers '…you know, staff having a picnic with food from the café.' She raised an eyebrow and sniffed. There was no love lost between the café manager and the estate manager.

Rosa made her way over to the alpacas, taking surreptitious bites of the loaded sandwich before popping it back into the paper bag. She had a bit of a thing about beetroot at the moment. She'd always had these food idols, which tended to last just a couple of weeks at the most, but were pretty intense in their following and application at the time: there'd been Hellmann's mayo, Branston pickle, horseradish and a particularly tart bottled mint sauce from Tesco – which she'd lavishly added to everything for a good few weeks before losing interest. Now it was beetroot, and she'd loaded extra onto the sandwich admiring, from an artistic stance, the red stains on her fingers and the now-pink white bread; loving the acidic, vinegary taste as it hit her lips and tongue.

By the time she'd skirted the pigs and baby lambs – which were now bouncing adolescents, she supposed – and stopped to laugh at the antics of a family of ducklings being persuaded into the water by their impatiently bossy mother, she'd downed the last glorious morsel of cheese and double helping of beetroot and was ready to stake out this Nick Carter lookalike over in the alpaca shed.

Rosa stopped in her tracks – Nick Carter *was* here. He was actually here in front of her. A tall, blond-haired boy was letting himself out of the gate while pulling a navy sweater over his head. He raised an arm and, in doing so, his navy sweatshirt parted company from his low-slung belted Wranglers, a glorious line of dark hair spreading upwards from his groin to his naval. Rosa stared. Of course, it wasn't Nick Carter himself. That would have been totally and utterly ridiculous. This boy standing in front of her, totally unaware of her presence as he searched in his jeans' pocket for something, was, if possible, even better than the singer. He fished out a roll-up – flattened from the pressure of the denim – and a lighter from the back pocket, before bending slightly away from the breeze to light the flimsy paper. It flared large and yellow for a second, the flame eating the paper hungrily before reaching the few strands of tobacco, and the boy inhaled deeply and stood. He started in some confusion as his eyes met Rosa's own, before turning to look behind her at the two other girls gazing down at him from the wall of the alpaca pen.

'Can I help you?' he asked politely as the three of them continued to stand and stare in silent reverence.

Eva, always the most forward of the triplets (Alice to a T, Granny Glenys had always affirmed), broke the burgeoning silence. 'We're just wondering why Nick Carter has left the States to muck out alpacas for the Marquess of Heatherly? Are you on tour in the UK and setting up a video shoot? Or are you in some sort of rehab? You shouldn't be smoking those –' Eva nodded towards the roll-up in the boy's fingers '– if that's the case. Or is it the drugs and booze that you're trying to get over? I read recently that you admitted your parents had an alcohol problem and that you had your first drink when you were just two?'

'Sorry? My parents are *alcoholics*? How do *you* know my parents?' The boy frowned. 'My mother never touches anything except a sherry before lunch on Sunday, and dessert wine with Christmas pudding.'

'So not rehab then?'

Hannah pushed Eva out of the way while Rosa continued to drink in every detail of this demigod standing in front of her. He was tall, over six foot as far as she could see, and with the physique of a rugby player. She did hope he wasn't a rugby jock – they always ended up with cauliflower ears and bent noses. 'We've not seen you here before,' Hannah smiled, putting a warning hand on Eva's arm who was about to launch once more. 'We're the marquess's daughters. Who are you?'

'The marquess's daughters? Oh yeah? And I'm Rumpelstiltskin.' He shook his head, ground the tab beneath his feet and closed the gate behind him. 'And *you*,' he added, as he walked past Rosa, 'are obviously some sort of female vampire.' He strode off in the direction of the staff kitchen.

'Female vampire?' Rosa turned to Eva and Hannah.

'You look like a lion who's had his head in a zebra kill,' Eva crowed. 'Well, *you're* out of the running, Rosie Posie. Just down to you and me, now, Hans.' She whipped out a Rimmel blusher compact, opening it up and handing it to Rosa as she laughed evilly.

Mortified, Rosa took in the beetroot-stained mouth and lips, the smudge of red on her left cheek. She'd fallen in love with a boy who'd never look twice at her now.

'Where the hell's Jodie?' Eva glanced irritably at the clock on the microwave. 'And that clock's wrong. Can you fix it, Rayan? It's driving me mad.' Eva handed the box of chocolate coated cereal to Laila who looked up in surprise but grabbed at it almost lasciviously while she had the chance, and before her mother changed her mind. Sugary cereals, along with concentrated fruit juice, were usually a no-no at the Malik breakfast table but Azra – similarly banned from eating them at Rayan's sister's house – had obviously smuggled the packet in along with the other booty she'd ferried here on the National Express coach from Leeds Bradford Airport.

'Jodie *told* you she was going to be late,' Laila said prissily. 'Don't you remember?'

'No, I don't,' Eva retorted. 'And go easy on those things; you've poured far too many. And make sure you clean your teeth thoroughly afterwards. You weren't here when Jodie left yesterday, Laila, so how do you know that?'

'I was there when she told you the day before. Don't you remember?'

Eva felt she couldn't remember *anything* at the moment apart from the fact that bloody Joe Rosavina appeared to be back in their lives.

'She said she had a doctor's appointment this morning and *you* said, not a problem, *you'd* take me to school.'

Hell. It *was* a problem. Sylvia Faraday-Brown was her first patient in at nine and, if kept waiting, wasn't averse to being vocal in reception. She was one of their private patients and

Rayan had ordered that all private patients should be treated with reverence, and staff were to act accordingly. They were, after all, the bread and butter of the surgery after new NHS regulations had cut their income greatly. So much for the Labour-voting, staunchly anti-capitalist Rayan whom Eva had fallen in love with at university.

'Rayan!' Eva shouted through the open doors leading to the dining room. 'First of all, can you fix this damned clock? And then, you'll have to take Laila to school.'

'Me?' Rayan was involved in some strange bending and stretching exercises, prescribed by his physio, on the dining-room floor. 'I was going to cycle in. I've a race on Sunday and haven't put the miles in this week.'

'Well, I can't go on the back of *that*,' Laila shouted through a huge mouthful of cereal, spraying chocolate particles onto the butter.

'Don't talk with your mouth full,' Eva said automatically. 'Another race? On Sunday? Oh, for heaven's sake, Rayan.'

'My mother's here to help,' Rayan shouted, his legs pedalling and wheeling furiously above his head.

'Exactly.' Eva stopped herself expanding further as Azra appeared with Nora.

'She's done number twos beautifully,' Azra beamed. 'Bottom is all wiped and she's good to go.'

'Nanni, can you please not mention bottoms when I'm eating chocolate cereal.' Laila pulled a pained face.

'Daddy, I's going to *marry* you.' Nora took hold of Rayan's legs and he lifted her up on them towards the ceiling.

'Sorry, darling, I'm already married to Mummy.'

'She have to go. Is my turn now.' Nora shrieked with pleasure as Rayan continued to raise her vertically.

'Better than a gym session, this,' Rayan puffed, while Laila, not to be left out, launched herself at her father, knocking Nora to the floor where she landed with a hysterical squawk, before taking her sister's place on Rayan's legs.

'For heaven's sake,' Eva snapped. 'I'm off. I've got Sylvia FB waiting. If *she's* sick after all that chocolate and milk –' Eva grabbed her bag, using it to indicate Laila whooshing up and down in excited terror as Rayan determinedly pushed his legs to the limit '– *you* can wipe it up, Rayan. Give Mummy a kiss, Nora, darling. Oh, you've bumped your head? Let me see. Let me kiss it better.'

For once, Nora allowed herself to be picked up and administered to. Kneeling, Eva felt a ladder race triumphantly up the left leg of her brand-new pair of tights. She closed her eyes, swore under her breath and reached for the butter dish, dabbing a tiny, greasy amount onto Nora's smooth forehead. 'There was a big lump there,' she lied. 'All better now. All gone.' She turned from the table, placed her younger daughter back on the floor and bent to pick up her bag just as Laila vomited a chocolatey milky stream over her favourite Jimmy Choo suede shoes.

Eva knew she didn't want to be a dentist anymore. It wasn't that she wasn't good at it – she was often chosen over Rayan and the other two dentists at the surgery for her gentle hands, her careful aim with the anaesthetic needle and her calm, reassuring tone with, frankly, terrified patients. She knew this was all a total act. (Perhaps she should have been an actor – she'd been highly praised for her role as Lady Macbeth at sixth-form college after practising with the bread knife in the kitchen: '*Is this a dagger which I see before me?*' aping Macbeth himself and thrusting it towards a totally-over-the-top-in-love Rosa, once the latter had finally beaten the other two of them to Joe Rosavina.)

Yes, it was all one big act. As she soothed, reassured and complimented Sylvia FB on her beautiful skirt – was it Jaeger? – as well as the state of her gums, Eva hovered over the old harridan with the anaesthetic needle, wanting nothing more than to jab it painfully into the woman's mouth. 'Just a little prick,' she soothed, thinking, as always whenever she said the words, of Spike Overton's small appendage.

Apart from thinking up ways to make Nora love her as much as her younger daughter adored Rayan, Jodie, Hannah, Bill and now Azra – in fact everyone apart from herself – there were two other areas of her life where Eva constantly drifted off to while waiting for her patients' mouths to become fully numb. Firstly, there was her artwork to which she'd only recently returned, Bill allowing her access to his own studio up at the hall. After achieving an 'A' at A-level in the subject, she'd had the choice to either enrol on an art foundation course at Leeds College of Art or make full use of her other three As in the science subjects needed for dentistry. Rosa had sided with Susan, Richard and Virginia, advising Eva to take the prestigious place offered at Sheffield for dentistry, while Hannah was with Bill, urging her to make the most of the gifts endowed on her by their famous mother.

In the end, her head ruled her heart – rather than her art. Didn't dentists end up making lots of money and drive round in BMWs, their Mulberry bags on the front seat, while, unless very lucky, artists ended up at best in graphic design driving Ford Fiestas or, at worst, starving in a garret, their talent unrecognised until they were dead?

Eva had concentrated hard on achieving good results at Sheffield, as well as falling for the charismatic Rayan, a second-generation Pakistani immigrant from Bradford who she'd met after he stood to speak at *Justice for Silent Victims*, an intended peaceful protest in light of the Lozells riots going on in Birmingham at that time. The peaceful intention of the protest had unfortunately been sabotaged by others with a different agenda and, because of Rayan's ethnicity, he'd found himself a target of hate. Eva had found *herself* in the middle of a bottle-throwing fracas, separated from the boyfriend she'd accompanied to the meeting out of mild curiosity. Dodging an empty bottle of Stone Pale Ale, she'd found her wrist grabbed by Rayan and manhandled out of the hall. She never did see the former boyfriend again.

''An ooh mell omi?' Eva was broken from her thoughts of Rayan the activist by Mrs FB clutching none too gently at her arm.

'I'm sorry, Mrs Faraday Brown?'

'I ed, an ooh mell omi?' The woman endeavoured to sniff through her frozen lips and nostrils. At least the anaesthetic was working.

'Vomit? Can I smell vomit?' Eva glanced down at the shoes she'd changed into as well as yet another pair of new tights. There was a patch of undetected sick on her skirt that had gone unnoticed. The woman must have the olfactory senses of a sodding bloodhound.

'A side-effect of the anaesthetic, Sylvia,' Eva said smoothly. 'Things can begin to take on a strange, sickly smell sometimes. Ah, right, Gillian's back now,' she added thankfully as her dental nurse for the day reappeared from the x-ray room. 'Shall we make a start on this next root canal of yours?'

The other thing that took up so much of her thoughts these days was sex; she'd never felt so randy in all her life. Or so devoid of sex. She liked sex, usually really enjoyed it, especially with Rayan, who'd always been an ardent, if somewhat predictable, lover. But then, after sixteen years with the same partner and husband, wasn't sex bound to be a bit *samey*? A bit obvious? You know, the last thing she was going to do was start tearing off Rayan's jock strap with her teeth the minute he was in the garage oiling down his bike after he'd cycled up to Holme Moss and over the tops into Derbyshire – his favourite challenge at the moment.

Eva smiled as she began to clean Mrs FB's back molar once she'd removed the infected pulp and nerve in the root. Rayan's reaction to her having him up against the cans of motor oil, discarded bicycle tyres and half-full tins of magnolia paint while divesting him of his boxers with her teeth, would probably be to suggest it not the best thing for her incisors. She smiled again, sadly this time and Gillian, seeing this, mouthed in obvious concern: 'You OK?'

'Fine,' she mouthed back, concentrating totally on completing the perfect root canal instead of the fantasy of herself, still among the paint cans for some reason, dressed only in a balcony bra and split-crotch panties, being serviced by that new actor in *EastEnders*.

'Eva, don't forget Sam Burrows is coming here this evening.' Rayan popped his head around Eva's surgery door once she'd returned from accompanying Sylvia FB back down to reception and helping her on with her coat. It was these little niceties Rayan insisted upon in his quest to have MALIK & MALIK DENTAL SURGERY stand out as a beacon of all that was upmarket and professional in the care of teeth. There were bottles of Molton Brown handwash – regularly nicked by the patients – in the patients' bathroom adjacent to reception, and the staff had all been updated with racing-green and gold-embroidered scrubs to match the newly painted signage over the door. Eva sometimes felt she was working in Harrods. It wouldn't surprise her if Rayan was planning on offering a glass of fizz and maybe a nice little canapé – one of those little blini things with horseradish and smoked salmon – to those undergoing his newly acquired skills of administrating Botox and fillers, once he was fully operational with that side of things.

How Alice Parkes would scoff if she could see Eva now.

'Sam who?'

'Sam Burrows.' Rayan frowned, obviously harassed that he was already, by ten-thirty, behind with his list.

'Who's he?'

'Eva, for God's sake! The new guy we interviewed last month? He starts next week but I've invited him round this evening after five for a welcome drink and a "get to know the staff" sort of thing. I did tell you. Reminded you several times.'

'Did you?' Eva frowned. 'Listen, Rayan, Hannah and I had

arranged to go round to the vicarage after work. To let her know what's going on.'

'Going on?'

Eva tutted. 'You're not interested in anything apart from bloody molars, fillers and architectural plans, are you? I told you, Rayan, Joe Rosavina is back. Hannah and me have to break it to Rosa and I'm not sure of the best way to go about it. Plus, it means getting back really late for the girls.'

'Mum won't mind. You know that. She likes to help.'

And get her feet under the table, Eva thought somewhat sourly, the words left unspoken.

'Ten minutes, Rayan, to say hello and then I'm across to the vicarage.'

'Ask Rosa and Hannah round to our place. You know Mum will be more than happy to cook for everyone. Having twenty or so of Dad's Bradford councillor cronies round never fazed her in the past, and she really misses it.' Faisal Malik, Eva's now deceased father-in-law, had arrived in Bradford from the Mirpur district of Southern Azad in Kashmir and, fiercely ambitious, had worked his way up to management level in the textile mills and, eventually, been elected onto the local council. His dream of being mayor of the city had faded when he was diagnosed with lung cancer.

'But we won't be able to talk with you and your mum there.'

'We'll eat and *then* gossip.' Rayan was becoming irritable. 'We'll leave you alone for girl chat...'

'Girl chat? How bloody condescending is that, Rayan? In fact, fucking patronising... Ah...' Eva broke off her strident monologue as two little boys in the maroon striped blazer and cap of the local private school were ushered in by their Sweaty-Betty-clad mummy. 'Alfie and Wilfie?' Eva purred. 'How are we today? Do come in. Just a check-up, I think?'

'Where the hell *is* this Sam Burrows bloke?' Eva, glancing up at the clock in reception at 5.30 p.m., wanted nothing more than to get home to the girls, a huge glass of wine and to put her feet up. But Rosa and Hannah had both jumped at the unexpected treat of one of Azra's wonderful curries and, when she'd spoken to Jodie at lunchtime, her nanny said she was more than happy taking Nora out shopping for what was needed for a bonzer feast as well as having a cooking lesson from Azra, and had agreed to stay on until everyone got home.

'I'm here, Miss.'

Eva's head shot round. Sitting in the corner of reception, partially hidden by the huge aquarium of tropical fish, was the man she'd met for the first time a good month earlier. She and Rayan had interviewed several hopefuls for the new dentist to take over Rayan's present practice *operatory* (bloody silly name, Eva had argued – what was wrong with the word *room*?) when he moved himself into his new one, where, at present, the paint was still drying, in the adjoining former village shoe shop.

'Oh *hello*.' Eva replaced her irritable face with her practised patient welcome face. 'How lovely to see you again. Are you well? Do come up to the staff room. Rayan has a bottle of fizz waiting. Or would you prefer tea? Coffee?'

Sam Burrows stood, unfolding himself from the leatherette banquette and Eva was surprised to see how tall he was. And how good-looking. Had he been this attractive when she and Rayan had interviewed him? Or had she got herself into such a state of fantasising about men and sex that even the village traffic warden – Reg, whose one aim in life appeared to be to stick a triumphantly gleeful parking ticket on Malik & Malik's patients' cars – was fair game?

'Do come up,' Eva repeated, feeling the heat and energy of the man as he followed her up the narrow racing-green and gold carpeted stairs to the staff room. 'I'm afraid I can't stay long – I need to get home for my girls... And for my other girls as well... as well as a promised curry feast... my mother-in-law... my nanny, Jodie...' Eva found herself twittering inanely in very much the same way as when Joe Rosavina had first appeared in their life twenty years earlier. Sam Burrows, Eva realised, glancing back over her shoulder as the new dentist followed her along the corridor, had the same easy manner, the same fair hair as Joe.

'Your other girls?' Sam asked.

'My two sisters. We're triplets.' Even after almost forty years, Eva never uttered the 'T' word without a sense of pride, of achievement, of dealing a trump card amongst the mundane and ordinary.

'Triplets? Goodness, there are two more at home just like you?' Sam grinned down at her and Eva felt herself go pink.

'Well, not *totally* like me. We're trizygotic, and therefore as genetically alike – or unalike – as any other non-triplet siblings might be.'

'Don't you believe it,' Rayan breezed in, shaking Sam's hand cheerfully. 'They're as tight as ticks.'

Tight as ticks? Eva stared at Rayan who, full of male-bonding bonhomie and hail-fellow-well-met, was taking a bottle of champagne from the fridge. Was he implying that she, Rosa and Hannah were permanently pissed?

'Wrong idiom, I think, Rayan,' Eva frowned, as Sam Burrows smiled politely in her direction.

'As thick as thieves then,' Rayan added.

Now they were *pilfering* pissheads?

'All cut from the same cloth.' Rayan enjoyed showing off about the triplets as much as Eva did. 'Tell you what, Sam, my mother is cooking her famous Mirpur Bassar Masala this evening. She always does enough to feed the whole of West Yorkshire. You're more than welcome to join us.'

'I wouldn't dream—' Sam started.

'Eva's got *important things* to discuss with her sisters,' Rayan interrupted almost proudly. 'You'd be doing me a favour by coming along. In fact –' Rayan was obviously doing the sums '– I'm the only male amongst seven women. Even the cat's a girl,' he added somewhat gloomily.

Eva looked at her watch. 'I need to get home.' She was beginning to feel irritated by Rayan. He didn't half go on sometimes, especially when he was trying to impress new people or when he was, yet again, making out he found his all-female family intimidating to live with. 'I'll leave you two to discuss business,' she said and then, giving this rather lovely new dentist a long and meaningful look, added, 'You really are more than welcome to join us to eat if you're free, Sam. Follow Rayan back – we're only a few miles out of the village.'

11

Rosa had been looking forward to Azra's curry ever since Eva had texted her earlier that afternoon with the invitation; had been unable to think of anything else, even while discussing the forthcoming church jumble sale with those two fund-raising stalwarts, Hilary Makepeace and Pandora Boothroyd. She adored all food and, although she shouldn't boast, knew she was a pretty good cook. However, the three-ring upright cooker was on its last legs and she also knew, if she was going to get into being creative once again, she'd have to force herself to look inside it, which she kept putting off. Unbelievable that the lovely Sarah Carey, the previous vicar's wife, had created and tended the most fabulous kitchen garden and yet appeared happy with that damned Tricity cooker.

It was taking some doing, getting used to being back in the village in which she'd grown up. It wasn't that she didn't like Yorkshire. It was just that, after leaving for university and Durham when she was eighteen, then moving to the bright lights and hectic life of London before taking up her first post as curate and living in, in Nottingham for the last three years, it all now seemed a bit of a backward step. A mistake even. Which was a bit daft when she thought about it.

Her calling to the church was one giant leap forward. OK, not when it came to a career move and certainly not the meagre salary she now earned. She'd hit and gone through that glass ceiling dominated, as it was, by money and status-grabbing males in the City's world of finance. Rosa shuddered at the memory;

that part of her life was irrelevant, totally unimportant to how she felt now about her spiritual pathway in her new calling. It was just that the vicarage itself appeared overwhelming, cold and miserable, filled as it was with the ghosts of former vicars and especially of her grandfather, the Rev Cecil, of whom the triplets had all been wary, if not actually frightened.

Rosa remembered one particular visit to see Glenys with Susan and Virginia – she must have been about five and didn't recall either Hannah or Eva being with them – when the Rev Cecil had appeared from his study, greeting Virginia with kind words, a pat on the head and the proffered jar of humbugs that always resided on his desk to accompany his sermon writing.

He'd glared, actually glared, at Rosa, quoting Deuteronomy 23:2 – *A bastard shall not enter into the congregation of the Lord; even to his tenth generation shall he not enter into the congregation of the Lord* – and, while her little five-year-old self had had absolutely no idea what he was talking about, she'd never forgotten the words *Deuteronomy* and *bastard* directed with such venom towards her, as well as both her mum and Granny Glenys shouting – actually swearing – bad words at the old man before her mother had scooped up both herself and a reluctant Virginia, crashing out of the vicarage with such fury the memory had stayed with Rosa forever.

So it was that an evening eating Azra's wonderful food, as well as enjoying the company of Eva's hugely entertaining mother-in-law and seeing her two gorgeous nieces, was a treat she'd been looking forward to all day. The day itself had been quite exhausting: she'd helped with the jumble sale preparations before calling at the local hospice at the request of one of the villagers whose elderly mother was terminally ill. She'd sat with the woman, holding her hand, and listened while she talked as much as she was able. The woman had asked Rosa to pray for her and she'd done that willingly. Then, she'd spent an hour across at the church hall where she'd been invited – and willingly accepted – to jiggle babies and chat to toddlers at the Village Mother and Babies Club, as well as introduce herself to proud but exhausted new mums.

Rosa now acknowledged she didn't seem to have seen Eva's two for absolutely ages and she was dying to get her hands on them. She glanced at the clock on the Corsa dashboard as she pulled into Eva's drive. She did hope both little girls were still up.

They obviously were.

'Mummy,' Laila was wailing from upstairs, 'tell Nora to close her legs. I can see her *volvo*. She's rude, Mummy – I can see her *volvo*.'

'You've done half a job, Eva.' Hannah was laughing up the stairs from her position three steps up. 'It's absolutely no good going all right-on and yummy mummy with these two if you don't actually teach them the correct words for their womanly parts.'

'Womanly parts?' Eva's exasperated voice drifted down towards Rosa from another upstairs room. 'God, now you sound like Virginia.' Eva appeared on the landing. 'Either of you two seen her lately?'

'I bumped into Timothy at Mum's the other day,' Rosa said. 'He was picking up the kids. I'd have thought, at thirteen, Barty was old enough to pick himself up. We did all sorts at thirteen, didn't we? Anyway,' Rosa went on, 'Virginia herself made an appearance at the jumble sale committee meeting this afternoon after school finished. It was the first time I'd seen her since I took over. I can't say she was overfriendly.'

'Doesn't approve of women vicars,' Hannah said shortly. 'Especially a woman taking over what she still sees as her precious grandfather's domain.'

'Well, she didn't stay more than two minutes. Just long enough to give that bird-like on-off hug she always proffers – I longed to get hold of her and squeeze her properly. She did give advice about being careful of bedbugs in any duvet and pillow jumble we might be donated, before she was rushing off as usual.'

'Taking Barty and Bethany to: Kip McGrath, piano, gymnastics, cricket, Mandarin, Save the Whale, Young Conservatives, sudoku...'

'You do exaggerate, Eva,' Rosa laughed. 'And sudoku?'

'She's determined they won't end up with dementia.'

'What? At thirteen and ten?' Rosa frowned.

'You know Virginia: *Be Prepared* was always her motto.' Hannah lowered her voice. 'I bet she writes *Sex with Timothy Forester* in her diary every first Saturday in the month.' Hannah laughed out loud at the thought.

'So often?' Eva's voice was wistful and both Hannah and Rosa turned in surprise. Before either could comment, a wail of surprise went up behind them.

'Who that?' Nora cried, one arm grasped firmly onto each of her mother's and Hannah's leg, as she stared at Rosa's black vestment and dog collar, which she wore over a pair of Levi's.

'It's alright, Nora,' Laila said kindly from behind her. 'It's just Aunty Rosa who has become a nun. They marry monks...' Laila trailed off, thinking. 'They marry *Jesus*, so you'd better be a good girl and share your sweeties with me because, one day, Jesus will be your uncle when Aunty Rosa marries him. And Jesus will want to know that you've been a *good girl* when he comes to eat Nanni Azra's curry with Aunty Rosa.'

'*Allahu Akbar*,' Nora said, still gazing solemnly at Rosa.

'Oh good,' Rosa smiled, reaching out to pick Nora up, pressing her nose almost sensuously into the little girl's dark hair and the milk-chocolate skin of her neck, breathing her in and, as always, longing for a baby of her own. 'You're bringing her up to be multi-faithed.'

'Sorry, Rosa, we're absolutely *not*. You know neither Rayan nor I have *any* faith whatsoever. Having said that, with you batting for one side and Azra the other – as well as Richard's

Catholicism thrown into the pot – I guess these two will take some of it in and then make their own minds up eventually—' Eva broke off as the front door opened and two heads, one dark followed by one fair, came into view.

'Who that?' Nora asked once again, struggling to get out of Rosa's arms.

'I think it might be Jesus come for supper with Aunty Rosa,' Laila said importantly, stretching over the banister to see further.

'Jesus,' Hannah breathed as Sam Burrows turned dark brown eyes upwards and smiled up at the faces gazing down at him.

'Jesus,' Rosa breathed in unison.

'See, Nora, I was right.' Laila ran down the stairs, throwing herself onto Rayan as he pulled off his dark overcoat, shyly peeping at the stranger who'd accompanied him into the hall.

Hands off, you two, Eva breathed silently. I saw him first.

Sam Burrows was exceptionally good company, praising Azra's cooking to the hilt in between explaining how he'd ended up in the village, about to work for Rayan.

'I've been at sea for the last three years,' he smiled, looking directly at Rosa, Hannah and then Jodie who, with a good-looking single man on tap, had made sure she was invited for supper along with the others.

'Literally or metaphorically?' Hannah asked.

'Both, I suppose really.' Sam smiled again, his eyes never once leaving the face of whoever he was talking to. I signed up with P&O on the cruise ships...'

A girl in every port, Eva surmised.

'...as ship's dentist...'

A girl in every port as well as on every deck and dentist's chair, Eva guessed. A man as gorgeous and single as Sam Burrows must have been every cruising woman's fantasy.

'Until, after almost three years at sea, I'd had enough.'

'Not surprised.' Azra grimaced, passing more Kashmiri chicken down the table. 'I threw myself up six times that time on ferry across Mersey to Birkenhead. Do you remember, Rayan?'

'I can hardly forget it, Mum. We had to manhandle you back on again in readiness for the return trip. You said you'd rather swim across than get back on that godforsaken tub.'

'You can't swim, Azra, can you?' Rosa was laughing.

'Allah would have taken care of me,' Azra pouted.

'So why Westenbury?' Hannah asked turning back to Sam. 'Do you know anyone here?'

Sam Burrows shook his head. 'Nope. The world was my oyster. Literally. I did contemplate moving to maybe Australia, or back to Sheffield where I was born, but then saw Rayan's ad in the *BDJ* and decided to take a chance on Yorkshire again. I have to say it's very beautiful round here. I'm looking forward to doing a bit of exploring – you know, the Pennine Way, the Coast to Coast.'

'Oh, you're a walker?' Jodie said delightedly. 'So am I.'

Yeah, right, Jodie, Eva thought. *A five-minute walk to the pub and round Zara every Saturday*. Why was she feeling cross with Jodie flirting with Sam Burrows? Cross that both Rosa and Hannah appeared to be hanging on to his every word. Surely vicars shouldn't flirt? And Hannah had enough on her plate juggling her affair with Ben. But maybe this man was the answer for Hannah? Get her away from the adulterous relationship she didn't seem able to break away from? Oh hell, she and Hannah still had to tell Rosa about Joe Rosavina.

'You make sure you don't wear feet away,' Azra frowned. 'All this madness for walking all time. You'll end up as midgety as me – and I've never walked anywhere. Why you think Allah give us National Coach Bus, if he want us to walk everywhere?'

'Bit difficult walking anywhere when you're on a cruise ship?' Hannah put in.

'Yes, I was getting cabin fever,' Sam grinned, 'so that's why I jumped ship.'

'What, literally?' Jodie was fascinated. 'You went overboard?'

Sam laughed. 'No, I promise you, everything was *above* board – I gave my two months' notice. And here I am.'

'Here you are.' Jodie seemed unable to take her eyes from him.

'Well, you come here *anytime at all*,' Azra beamed. 'I feed you up. Fill you full of lovely Mirpur curry. So full you can't get off settee and set off on bloody silly long walk.'

Whose sodding house is this? Eva thought crossly. *And the word is sofa, not settee, Azra.*

'Right, ladies…' Rayan stood and pushed back his chair, draining his glass of beer.

'Ladies?' Eva snapped. 'We're *women*. Strong, independent *women*.' She frowned across at her sisters and Jodie and Azra, who all appeared under the spell of this good-looking new recruit of theirs.

'Right, *women*,' Rayan corrected good-naturedly.

Why was he always so bloody good-natured? Eva frowned again. And why was *she* so bad-tempered all the time? She must google 'perimenopause' when she got a moment.

'Sam and I need to dot a few i's and cross a few t's so we'll leave you to your important chat.' Rayan smiled and Sam rose from the table to follow him.

'Important chat?' Rosa frowned at Eva once the two men had made their way across the hall to the study. 'That sounds a bit ominous?'

'I'm off,' Jodie interrupted, obviously not interested in staying now that the main event had left the room. 'Fab, bonzer curry we made there, Azra. See you tomorrow.' She stood, high-fived Azra and pulled on her jacket. 'I'll just check on the girls before I go,' she added.

'So, important chat?' Rosa sat back in her chair at the dining table after the three of them had helped clear the plates, loaded the dishwasher and Hannah – big into Netflix – had shown Azra how to binge-watch every series of *Luther*.

'Thanks, Hannah,' Eva tutted crossly, pouring too much wine into each of their glasses and, in doing so, ignoring Rosa's question. 'Now she'll never go home until she's watched every single episode.'

'You're mad,' Hannah sniffed. 'Help with the girls and fabulous food into the bargain? I'd move her in permanently.'

'*You've* never had a mother-in-law,' Eva snapped back, 'so don't comment on mine, Hannah. And you'd hate living with *anyone*, so don't give me all this guff about family.'

'You're not half irritable at the moment,' Hannah said mildly. 'What's up?'

'Never mind *me*,' Eva said, downing her glass of wine in one, knowing she'd regret it in the morning. Luckily, she wasn't in the surgery until lunchtime. 'We need to tell you something, Rosa.'

'Oh?' Rosa sipped at her wine before placing it back on the white tablecloth. It left a red mark on the starched material and she rubbed at it absently with her little finger. It was her second glass and she knew, if she carried on drinking, she'd have to get a taxi. She could just see herself preaching the dangers of drink, when half the congregation knew she'd been done for being Over the Prescribed Limit earlier in the week.

'*You* tell her, Hannah,' Eva urged, suddenly losing her bottle. 'You were there.'

'You were *where*?' Rosa smiled.

'In the youth court,' Hannah said.

'You're always in the youth court.' Rosa frowned. 'It's your job, isn't it?'

'It's *who* was there.' Eva urged Hannah on with a glare.

'Well, who *was* there?' When the other two didn't appear to want to answer, Rosa added, 'Anyone I know?'

'A boy called Rhys Johnson,' Hannah finally said, leaning across the table and taking Rosa's hand in her own.

'Right. OK.' Rosa downed her glass of wine. That was a tenner from her housekeeping she'd have to fork out on a taxi. 'And is it... was it... you know, *the* Rhys Johnson?'

Hannah nodded. 'Joe was with him, Rosa. You need to know – he's back living in Westenbury. With his parents.'

'Permanently? Or just a visit?' Rosa felt an icy calm in the pit of her stomach. 'And with –' Rosa swallowed '– with *her*?'

'Long enough for the boy to have been out burgling houses and going equipped. And I really don't know about *her*...' Hannah hesitated and then, when the other two stared at her, she went on, 'The thing is, I shouldn't be looking into the boy's background for... for *personal gain*, as it were. You know I'm not allowed to discuss youth cases with anyone. We have to have regard for the welfare of kids who come to court as victims, witnesses or defendants. Section 49 of the Children and Young Persons Act places an automatic restriction on reporting information that identifies any child...'

'Alright, alright, Hannah,' Eva interrupted. 'Don't go all uppity on us. You know you tell us everything.'

'But not *work* stuff. And that includes me telling you this now. In fact, I really shouldn't have told you *any* of this. I'm going to end up in real trouble if it gets out that I've identified Joe's son to you two.' Hannah bit her lip.

'What about you telling us Joe Rosavina was there in the youth court?' Eva asked. 'Is that banned as well?'

'Dunno. By telling you Joe was there, it's pretty much identifying he was there with his family. Sorry, Rosa,' Hannah added when she saw Rosa blanch. 'It's pretty serious stuff to spill the beans about a child in court, especially by his YOT officer. In fact, it's reinforced in the European Convention of Human Rights...'

'Even though we're out of Europe?'

'Dunno. Oh God, and I told Bill. You know what a gossip *he* is.'

'You need to do your bloody homework, Hannah,' Eva

snapped. 'Look, forget the boy. It's *you*, Rosa. We need to know *you're* going to be OK?'

'OK?' Rosa frowned. 'No, for your information, I'm *not* OK.' She held up a trembling hand as evidence. 'I'm sorry, you two, I can't just put my vicar face on and say, you know, *God is with me and I'll be fine.* I loved Joe Rosavina from the minute I saw him with the alpacas. And I've never stopped loving him.'

12

In Eva's downstairs loo, Rosa painted a defiantly red colour onto her lips, which unfortunately emphasised the pallor of her face, leaching quite spookily into the white of her dog collar, but at least went some way to convincing her sisters that she was OK. Even though she, herself, knew she wasn't. Rosa needed to convince Hannah and Eva that the shock of Joe Rosavina being back in the village wasn't stopping her from heading back to the vicarage; that she didn't need to spend the night in Eva and Rayan's box room, the one remaining vacant bedroom in the house now that Azra appeared to have taken up residence indefinitely.

'You can't drive back,' Hannah warned, hugging Rosa to her, feeling how thin she'd become in recent years. It was always Rosa, out of the three of them, who'd loved her food; who'd been the one to have a piece of toast and peanut butter in her hand on the bus to sixth-form college, or tucking into a bag of crisps or a huge bun on the journey home. Who'd first met Joe Rosavina sporting a smeared red mouth after devouring a cheese and double beetroot teacake. 'I'll drive you – I've only had one small glass of wine.'

'It's the opposite direction,' Rosa smiled. 'Don't be silly. I'll get a taxi.'

'On a vicar's wages? Well at least let me pay for it.'

'On a YOT's wage?' Rosa smiled again.

They both turned to Eva. 'She'll pay – she's a rich dentist,' Hannah grinned.

'Get yourself an Uber, Rosa. Put it on my account.' Eva, in turn, went to put her arms round Rosa.

'Blimey, we now have Uber in the village?'

'And a Turkish massage. It doesn't all happen in London and Nottingham, you know.'

'Night, Eva. Thank you so much for having me.' Sam Burrows appeared in the kitchen. 'Can I give anyone a lift?'

'Oh, would you?' Hannah's eyes lit up. 'Our village vicar here is probably over the limit having knocked that last glass back too quickly.'

'Where are you staying?' Eva addressed Sam. 'Are you renting somewhere?'

'Hmm, fabulous little place. Got it for the next six months and then I'll decide. Holly Close Farm cottages?'

'Oh, has that come free again? Next to Daisy Maddison?'

'Yes, I believe it's her sister who rents it out?'

'Ooh, you lucky thing.' Hannah pulled a face of pure envy. 'I'd have rented it myself if I could have afforded it,' she smiled. 'Great, it's on the way back to the vicarage – you won't be going too far out of your way.'

'Leave your keys, Rosa,' Eva instructed. 'I'll drive your car down to you at lunchtime when I go to work and then get a lift back with Rayan.'

'Are you OK?' Sam Burrows asked as he put the car – a rather slinky, low-down little number which Rosa, not overly interested in cars, was unable to identify – into gear and shot out of Eva's drive.

'Yes, I'm fine thanks... Actually no, had a bit of a shock actually.'

'Oh?'

'It's fine, it's nothing.'

'How long have you been a vicar?' he continued when Rosa declined to elucidate.

'Here? In Westenbury?' Rosa smiled. 'Just a week. I was curate in Worksbrough in Nottingham previously.'

'And you wanted to come home?'

'I didn't really plan it as such. It wasn't my life's ambition to take over the church where my grandfather was once incumbent...' Rosa trailed off. 'It just seemed to happen,' she said finally. 'I missed my sisters, my family. I wanted to see my nieces grow up. When Ben Carey left the village church and the job came vacant back where I grew up, I applied for it. And got it.'

Sam turned to her but said nothing, encouraging her, Rosa realised, to tell her story. She clammed up, saying nothing more.

After a good few minutes Sam said casually, 'And Hannah? Does she have children?'

'Hannah? No, I'm not convinced she ever did want them. Or ever will have them. I think seeing all the quite damaged kids she often deals with has put her off.'

'And a partner?'

'Who? Me?'

'Well, yes, you... you know, if you want to tell me?'

Rosa smiled, turning towards him, taking in the short fairish hair, the tanned features, the large hands steady on the wheel of the car, understanding what he was asking. 'Hannah is sort of with someone. Probably shouldn't be with them, if that make sense?'

'Right, OK, I won't ask any more.'

They drove in silence for the rest of the way until they passed Malik & Malik on the right and Rosa gave instructions round the one-way system before Sam pulled up outside the vicarage.

'Are there no lights on?' Sam frowned. 'It looks a bit dark and gloomy. And is that a graveyard you have to walk through?'

'It's not the dead I'm afraid of,' Rosa replied. 'It's the living.' *And*, she wanted to add, *sometimes, myself*.

The large granite-stoned Victorian rectory stood bleakly stark against the cloudy skyline and Rosa's heart dropped somewhat at the thought of going into the sludge-coloured kitchen, and then into the high-ceilinged sitting room where the fire she'd laid earlier remained unlit and certainly unwelcoming. She'd be alone with her memories and she'd worked so hard these past six years or so, to keep them from bubbling up and taking over when she knew that going down that road was so utterly pointless.

'Well, I know where you are now,' Sam was saying as she opened the door, gave thanks for the lift and pulled up the hood of her jacket against the wet drizzle that had started to fall.

'Absolutely.' Rosa looked back at him. He really was rather lovely. Malik & Malik would soon be buzzing with women, young and old, eager to be administered to by this new dental surgeon.

'I hope,' Sam added, 'that whatever is making you so sad... you know...' He trailed off, obviously embarrassed.

'Thank you,' Rosa replied, somewhat stiffly. 'Maybe we'll see you in church on Sunday? The 10.30 a.m. communion or 6 p.m. for evensong?' She closed the car door and, head down, walked the few hundred yards through the Westenbury villagers' final resting place to her front door in darkness. The bulb in the lamp over the door had obviously had it – another job standing on a rickety stool in the morning – and she couldn't, for several minutes, remember where she'd put the single key that she'd retrieved from the bunch left behind on Eva's kitchen table.

Once she was in, she went straight to the sitting-room cupboard, poured herself a large Tia Maria and, with tears starting, took it up to her bedroom, unable to stem those bloody memories from crowding in.

After that first sighting of Joe Rosavina in the alpaca pen on the kids' petting farm at Heatherly Hall, all three of them constantly drifted over there to catch a glimpse of the boy they'd each fallen in love with. But to no avail. He seemed to have disappeared. Here one day mucking out the alpacas, and gone the next.

'Well, I don't know where he's bloody well gone,' Eva had said crossly after three days of volunteering for, rather than being assigned to, work on the farm.

'Do you reckon we made him up?' Hannah hypothesised. She was working her way through the job lot of *Man, Myth and Magic* magazines she'd bought for 50p at the village school car boot sale, as well as becoming really interested in Tarot and out-of-body experiences. (She'd yet to experience one herself, despite following instructions from Ian, the farmer down the road, who swore he'd found himself in a Paris brothel while still physically in his milking parlour.) 'You know, we were so desperate for Nick Carter to appear – *to be manifested* – he actually did.'

'Oh, don't be so daft, Hans,' Eva snapped. 'And you need to stop reading that stuff before you go to bed – you were talking in your sleep again last night. Anyway, *I* know his name – it's Joe Rosavina, and his mum and dad have just taken over the Italian restaurant down in Midhope.'

'So why was he here just for one day?' Rosa was convinced she, much more than the other two, had been dealt a more severe blow by Cupid's little arrows.

'I had a word with Mr Mitchell. I was very casual,' Eva grinned. 'You know, didn't want word getting back to JR that we were hunting him down? Stalking him?'

'And?' Hannah said, and she and Rosa leaned in.

'He's been doing some work with Bill's accountant in town. Apparently, he's a whizz at maths and has spent all the six-week summer holiday down there. The accountant went off for a couple of days and suggested, instead, Joe help out on the farm until he got back.'

'So, he's not coming back?' Hannah pulled a face.

'Doesn't look like it,' Eva agreed. 'But,' she added, 'we know where he lives. Or at least where he'll hang out.'

'Do we?'

'At the Italian place. I bet anything his parents will have him waiting tables. We could get Mum and Dad to take us there for Virginia's birthday.'

'But that's next month,' Rosa sighed. 'Ages away.'

'And don't go all New York on us,' Hannah added irritably. 'It's *being a waiter* here in good old Yorkshire, not *waiting tables*.'

'Well, we could go ourselves,' Eva said bossily, ignoring the objections of the other two. 'A celebration for me ending my days in the pigs.'

'Ending your days?' Hannah frowned. 'You're not dying, are you?'

'You know what I mean,' Eva tutted.

'It'll be expensive.' Hannah frowned again. 'It's not your usual pizza dive; it's pretty upmarket.'

'Do you want him to fall in love with me, or not? I need some help here.' Eva was getting cross.

'No, I bloody well *don't* want him falling in love with you.' Rosa, usually the shyest of the three of them, was adamant and folded her arms confrontationally against her chest.

'The thing is,' Eva went on, ignoring Rosa, 'he's only ever seen me in this awful polo shirt and stinking to high heaven; my hair needed washing and...' she paused, tutting at the outrageous memory '...I didn't even have *my lashes* on.'

Hannah started laughing at that. 'I bet Pinky and Perky were most offended you hadn't put on your slap for them.'

'How about next weekend?' Eva suggested. 'At the end of our first week at sixth-form college? We can tell Mum and Dad we're, oh I don't know, celebrating... celebrating...'

'Starting sixth-form college?' Hannah asked dryly. 'Actually, they might come with us and pay for us?'

'We don't want Susan and Richard with us.' Ever since the recent momentous trip to New York, Eva had pulled back from calling them *Mum and Dad* any longer. 'They're broke if you remember. And, for heaven's sake, I need him to see me as a bold woman of the world.'

'Even though you are, in actual fact, a bald-eyed child of the porkers?' Hannah started laughing and Rosa, despite usually taking Eva's side, joined in with her.

A week on, Rosa remembered as she hugged one hot water bottle to her pyjamaed tummy, caressed another with her freezing cold feet and savoured the comforting alcohol, it turned out there'd been no need for their making a reservation at Rosavina's, the expensive new restaurant in the town centre.

On their first day of A-level studies, the three of them had caught the bus into town before walking the short distance up to Midhope Sixth-Form College which, in its thirty-year history, had gained an impressive reputation for results and for sending more than its fair share of students on to Oxbridge. Rosa made a secret pact with her sixteen-year-old self that morning as she parted company with Hannah and Eva in the huge hall and refectory and made her way up a flight of stone steps to her first lecture (how important that sounded: lecture rather than lesson) in economics. While Eva had finally made the decision to take all sciences at A-level, and Hannah the arts, she, herself, had plumped for Maths, Business and Economics. She was going to work like mad and go to Oxford or Cambridge, be a top businesswoman like that Body Shop woman.

Slightly nervous, and hoping there'd be someone in the classroom who she'd know from school, Rosa tried to slip nonchalantly into a seat at the back of the room. Instead of the graffiti-decorated, lidded desks and, latterly, the grey Formica-topped tables of Westenbury Comp, the desk tops in this room were attached to their chair. Rosa placed her new bag full of shiny unblemished files and pencils onto the floor beside the chair and endeavoured to squeeze into the space between the chair and the desk. Blimey, she knew she enjoyed her food but surely she hadn't put on *so* much weight scoffing cream teas and cheese and beetroot teacakes in Tea and Cake, that she now couldn't actually get into the desk. Red-faced and sweating slightly, she tried going in from a different angle but only ended up getting her backside caught on the chair, unable to move. No one else seemed to be having a problem.

'You have to swing the desk bit out, sit down and then swing it back to wherever you want it,' a voice behind her advised.

'Oh, sorry, yes, thank you, I see.' Rosa, concentrating on doing as she'd been instructed, didn't look up and so didn't see Joe Rosavina until he carried on walking forwards, before expertly shifting his own desk from its chair and slipping smoothly into the seat three rows in front. Rosa's heart had started a mad gallop she was convinced the red-haired girl sitting next to her must be able to hear, and she dived into her new bag searching for a non-existent tissue, anything to have something to calm herself, desperate to do something other than having her eyes come back again and again to the beautiful blond-haired boy's denim-clad back; the broad shoulders; the tanned neck unwittingly revealed as he idly brought up a hand and ran it over the back of his head.

When the lesson was over, and Rosa realised she'd made three pages of beautifully written notes, but hadn't a clue to their content, or even what this introduction to economics had been about, she hovered in her seat as Joe Rosavina stood and turned towards the door with the others. As he walked past her, he frowned slightly, obviously trying to work out where he'd met her before but, seemingly unable to come to any conclusion, gave her a nod of his beautiful blond head and carried on walking.

Desperate to impart the amazing news that the Nick Carter lookalike was not only enrolled at the college but was, amazingly, in her economics class as well, Rosa set off to the refectory to find Hannah and Eva. Eva was already in the middle of a gang of sixteen-year-olds Rosa didn't recognise. But that was Eva for you; the confidence she'd generated over the years from being not only the marquess's daughter but also a world-renowned artist's daughter, bubbled up and over so that others were drawn to her like a moth to a flame. Like a fly to horseshit, Hannah had once suggested crossly when Eva had abandoned the other two and gone off with Josie Wadsworth's gang in Year 9. It hadn't lasted long and had never happened again, but there was always the unspoken notion between the three of them that Eva was top dog, the one who got first dibs at anything, who led while the other two followed. Well, not this time, Rosa vowed, seeing, and moving to, a table where a couple of girls from her maths class at school were now sitting. She wasn't going to tell either Hannah, but particularly not Eva, that Joe Rosavina was not only here, but that amazingly he was in her economics class and had rescued her – yes, actually rescued her – from that delinquent chair and desk.

Oh Lordy, he was in her pure maths class as well. Having lost their way up and down the flights of stairs and corridors that made up the west wing of the college, Rosa, accompanied by Ruth Dickinson and Maire McBride from the comp, eventually found where they should be. Embarrassed at their late arrival, they opened the door of the last room along the corridor in the maths department and, apologising as the lesson had already started, slid into the three remaining seats at the back of the room.

Oh heavens, how was she ever going to learn anything – become Businesswoman of the Year – if she appeared unable to take in the explanation to introductory exponentials the teacher was now writing on the whiteboard. Summoning all her concentration, Rosa moved her head so that Joe Rosavina was no longer in her line of vision and put everything into what the teacher was explaining. Oh, she knew this. She could do it – they'd already tackled something like it the previous year at school. With a sigh of relief, Rosa got stuck in.

'I *know* you, I know where I've seen you before.' Joe Rosavina headed directly for her as the class moved out for lunch. 'I've spent the last hour trying to work it out. It's Princess Triplet.'

'One of them,' Rosa stuttered and immediately wished she

hadn't. Why advertise that Eva – and Hannah – made up the three?' Rosa stared down at the new, carefully chosen short skirt and black tights she'd decided on for her first day here. Maybe they weren't sexy enough? Dull, even, compared to Eva's tight-fitting jeans and cleavage-revealing top.

'Do you fancy a coffee?'

'A coffee?' Rosa's head shot up.

'Only if you want to? Or are you meeting your sisters? Are you really triplets or were you having me on?'

'Yes, I mean no…' She broke off as Joe frowned at her seeming inability to get the truth out.

'Yes,' she breathed. 'We *are* triplets, but no, I'm not meeting up with them.'

'My dad, ever the Italian papa, has packed me off with enough food to feed the whole class.'

'Oh, thank you, but I've a sandwich with me.'

'Right.' He appeared uncertain, nervous even. 'Another time then.' He started to move away.

Jesus, what would Eva do? 'Why don't you show me yours and I'll show you mine?' Rosa managed to get out as he turned away.

'I beg your pardon?'

'Sandwiches,' Rosa gabbled, heat flooding her face in mortification. 'We could share them. Look, I think people are sitting on the lawn over there.'

Five minutes later, they were sitting on the grass, newly cut for the start of the autumn term. Rosa's palms were damp and she wiped them surreptitiously on her tights, wishing she had bare legs instead of what now appeared to be ridiculously dowdy Victorian schoolmarm ones. Joe passed her a doorstop focaccia laden with grilled Mediterranean vegetables and goat's cheese. Normally she'd have wolfed down such a glorious sandwich in no time, loving the headily bitter taste of the cheese in sharp contrast to the tomato and basil tones that were coming through. Now, she could only nibble in a ladylike manner, terrified that a piece of stray aubergine and courgette might land on her knee or, worse, get stuck in her teeth.

'Are you not keen?' Joe asked, smiling. 'It's not to everyone's taste.'

'Oh no, no. I mean, yes, I love it. It's wonderful.' Rosa kept the potted meat ('potted dog?' Eva had sniffed scornfully – 'we're going to college, Susan, not kindergarten') teacake her mum had prepared for each of them well hidden, and did hope it wouldn't begin to go off and smell before she could bin it. The early September sunshine was hot and Joe removed first his denim jacket and then, five minutes later, the navy sweatshirt. The white T-shirt made a startling contrast to the muscular brown arms, and Rosa continued to boil in her black tights and short woollen skirt that had seemed such a good idea when she hopped out of bed that morning.

'You're very brown,' Rosa said, once she'd managed to swallow a couple of mouthfuls of focaccia. She wished she could take it home and really get stuck into it in all its heady rosemary and olive deliciousness. Here, her throat was constricted with nerves as she took surreptitious glances at Joe Rosavina laid back in the sunshine, his eyes closed against the hot midday sun. Hair bleached to silver and gold, olive skin darkened almost black. Rosa longed to devour every single bit of him in much the same way she wanted to do with the sandwich.

'My grandparents live in Sicily,' Joe said once he'd made himself comfortable, his head pillowed on his rolled-up jacket and sweatshirt. 'I was there for a couple of months before we moved here to Yorkshire.'

'I thought Sicilians were small, dark and brown-eyed?' Rosa ventured. 'You're tall, blond and blue-eyed?'

'Ah.' He grinned. 'You've been looking? That's good.' When Rosa didn't know what to actually reply to that – so didn't – Joe went on: 'There are only a few of us, and we're allegedly throwbacks to Angevin rule, when Joanna, the sister of Richard the Lionheart, reigned over the island bringing with her a retinue of Norman knights. And –' he sat up and smiled '– the fact that my mum's as English as you are…' He broke off as two pairs of feet came running up towards them.

'Well, well, well.' Eva grinned, as Hannah glared meaningfully down at Rosa. 'Fancy meeting you here.' Ignoring Rosa, the pair of them shuffled down onto the grass, sitting down, like a pair of determined bookends, on either side of Joe Rosavina.

Pulling herself away from that bittersweet memory of her first day at sixth-form college, the now grown-up Reverend Rosa leaned over to switch off the bedside light and lay back, eyes screwed tight against the awful knowledge that Joe Rosavina appeared to have made the decision, for whatever reason, to move back to Westenbury. There was no way she could avoid seeing him again.

13

'Can I ask you something?' Joe had begun one afternoon when, wrapped around each other in Joe's single bed after what Rosa could only describe -- in Hilary Caldwell's terms -- as 'totally climaxic' sex, he suddenly sat up on the pillows, looking down at her, his beautiful blue eyes questioning.

'What?' Rosa felt herself redden. 'Did I, you know... come?' She still wasn't totally comfortable using the *come* word. Susan's own puritanical upbringing at the hands of the Rev Cecil Parkes spilling over into how she had brought up her own children, it had nibbled away at Rosa's own confidence with her body's needs and desires. Both Eva and Hannah appeared to be none the worse for Susan's moralistic, if not downright prudish, attitude to sex. In fact, now faced with a plethora of more than willing, bright and rather delicious, A-level students on whom to cut their sexual teeth as it were, the other two had just about forgiven Rosa for being the one Joe Rosavina had fallen in love with. Within weeks, Eva, followed closely by Hannah – determined not to be outdone by her sister – had lost their virginity, the one thing Susan had instilled into all her four girls that was not to be given away lightly.

'I think you did that. Without any question.' Joe grinned down at her. It had taken Rosa a while to achieve what it was everyone else seemed find easy, but Joe, having cut his own teeth on the – often older – North London girls more than willing to break in this Backstreet Boy lookalike, had brought both sexual experience, know-how and, having fallen head over heels in love with this marquess's daughter, a tenderness and care he'd hitherto not known with those others. 'Unless you were faking it?' he suddenly asked.

'Why would I do that?' Rosa had asked, puzzled. 'So, what? What are you asking me?'

'Well, knowing what *you've* told me, as well as reading that article in *The Sunday Times* last week about Alice Parkes and her many lovers, as well as now seeing your sisters in action, I just wondered, you know...'

'What? Wondered what?' Rosa pulled at the starched cotton sheet to cover her breasts, concerned that, while she knew Joe's parents were probably aware that their son entertained Rosa in his bedroom and that both Michelle and Roberto Rosavina were, at the moment, hard at work ten miles away in the town centre, serving lunchtime customers, they might suddenly be home, popping their head around Joe's bedroom door to see what their son was actually up to.

'Well, OK, how was Alice Parkes able to convince Bill Astley that you three were actually his?'

'Sorry?' Rosa turned to stare at Joe.

'You know, Rosa, if she had a one-night stand with Bill, what's to say she hadn't been having one-night stands with anyone else? How are you so convinced you're actually Bill's daughters?'

'That's an awful thing to say.'

'Oh, honestly, Rosa, I didn't mean it to be. I've not upset you, have I?' Joe moved to stroke Rosa's hair by way of apology. 'I suppose it was a bit of a rude question. It's just that I'm totally fascinated by it all. And surely you must have thought the same? Bill must have wondered?'

'Alice told him he was the father. Why would she lie? She never asked anything from Bill; never asked for maintenance or money.'

'Well, no, obviously she didn't. She gave you all away to your mum and dad.'

'Right, OK, I'll tell you now.'

'Tell me what?'

'When Dad...'

'Which dad? Richard or Bill?'

'*Dad.*' Rosa felt irritable as she always did whenever the circumstances of her birth were asked about or aired. 'I've got one dad. My *dad*. Dad. Richard.'

'OK.'

'So, when Dad had the awful accident a year ago – when he was knocked down after Keith ran into the road...'

'Keith?'

'His dog...'

'Right.'

'When he broke his pelvis and leg so badly...'

'Who? Keith?'

'No,' Rosa tutted. 'The bloody dog ran off unhurt. It was Dad who was in traction for six months and then, when he was physically able, he didn't seem actually mentally able to go back to his teaching commitment at the university, and had to carry on with sick leave.'

'And?'

'And recently, Mum has begun to get worried about money – she has the three of us to feed and clothe as well as subbing Virginia who's at teacher training college. Anyway, she didn't say anything to Dad, but went up to Heatherly Hall to see Bill to ask for help.'

'So had Bill never offered anything before that? You know, for the upkeep of you three?'

'Mum has always been really proud about not asking for handouts. As she said, she and Dad adopted us knowing the financial implications, and refused any help from Bill. She's always kept Bill at a distance, not really wanting to have him a part of our lives.'

'And from Alice?'

Rosa gave a humourless laugh. 'I don't think it ever occurred to Alice to offer anything towards our upkeep. She'd grown us – rented out her womb if you like – and that was that. If Susan and

Richard were basically daft enough to take us on when she'd been about to wash her hands of us through the adoption agencies in France, then on their heads be it. Mum certainly didn't want to ask Alice for anything – I suppose she thought it might allow more access to us three if Alice ever wanted that. She never has, and Mum never asked her. Anyway, Mum went cap in hand – or maybe begging bowl might be more appropriate – to see Bill and he was more than willing to give the three of us an allowance.'

'So, your mum told you all this? Or did Bill?'

'No, Bill certainly didn't. In the end, Mum *had* to tell us because Bill had to agree to a paternity test before his solicitors and accountants would allow money to be regularly taken from the estate for us. Bill's wealth is all tied up apparently and he's so generous and so liberal with his gifts and money, there was concern that, if it became public knowledge he was handing out cash willy-nilly, any number of bastard offspring...' Rosa flushed slightly at her use of the B word '...could end up putting in a claim.'

'Right. How interesting.' Joe folded his arms and leaned back, stroking Rosa's arm. 'Go on.'

'Blood-type testing between a child and an alleged parent has been around since the 1920s apparently, although it's not overly accurate. And then,' Rosa went on, 'highly accurate DNA parental testing became available about five years ago – PCR testing became the standard method. It's simple. We took the test; Bill took the test and we are his daughters. Easy as that.'

'Blimey, you seem to know a lot about it,' Joe frowned, wanting to know more.

'It was Eva and I who'd really looked into it. We'd studied genetics and DNA testing as part of a biology GCSE project when we were at school. We were just very interested. As well as pleased when it was proved Bill was our biological father and we were entitled to some help from the estate. To be fair to Bill, even if we hadn't been, I reckon he'd have sold a picture or two in order to help Mum out.'

'Well, Princess Rosie Posie,' Joe grinned, scooping Rosa up in his arms and rolling her over onto her back, 'I'd love you, whoever you were.' He trailed his open mouth down her body and Rosa closed her eyes, loving the moment, loving the feeling, loving Joe himself. 'I'll adore you forever, even if you turn into the kitchen maid at midnight.'

14

May 2015

London

'Gosh, Carys, I don't know how I'd have sorted all this lot without you.' Rosa stared round at the hotel conference room in central London she'd taken over for the weekend. 'You don't think this is all a bit, you know, over the top? A bit *more is less* sort of thing? *And* my birthday was actually four months ago, remember.'

'Oh, don't you be so daft,' Carys's sing-song voice drifted down from her position at the top of a stepladder where she was hanging yet more foil balloons. 'You can't celebrate all this lot with just a sausage on a stick in one hand and a pint of Cwtch Red Ale in the other.'

'I'm not convinced I *want* to celebrate being thirty.' Rosa pulled a face. 'Where did it all go?'

'In your case, ruling the world, I reckon.' Carys reached upwards and to her left in order to attach a glittering *Congratulations* banner above an architrave, and the stepladder wobbled slightly. Carys's pretty face was suffused with pink with the effort of the stretch involved, and her short skirt rode up her bare, bottled-St-Tropez-tanned legs.

'I can see your pants,' Rosa laughed. 'Come on, get down. I need some help with this seating list.'

'They're clean and paid for.' Carys grinned down at her. 'And there's nothing up there no one's not seen before. *And*,' she went on, 'that seating list is fine. I sorted it all yesterday. It's good to go.'

'Thirty years old though, Carys. Hell.' Rosa twisted the top from a bottle of Perrier, drank deeply of the contents and folded her arms, deep in thought.

Carys descended the steps and helped herself to Rosa's water.

'Get your own,' Rosa tutted. 'There's plenty.'

'You know we share everything.' Carys grinned again, draining the bottle before turning the bottle upside down as proof. 'I'm your right-hand woman from The Valleys, here to do your every bidding.'

And she was. Ever since Carys Powell had applied for and been given the job as her PA three years ago, she'd been there ready to do whatever Rosa asked of her. Rosa had made the momentous decision, after six years of working in the City and with the backing of an Investment Angel, at the ridiculously young age of twenty-seven, to set up her own investment fund management company and, with this new PA at her side, Rosa's ever-expanding life had never been so organised.

Carys had come highly recommended from her current position in the City, her CV and references immaculate and, at interview, she'd almost knocked Rosa sideways with her vivacious fervour. She was, she assured Rosa, discreet and trustworthy, flexible and adaptable, with the ability to be proactive and take the initiative. A good personal assistant, like herself, Carys had argued, when she suddenly appeared to realise she was, perhaps, being a bit over the top in her enthusiasm for the position, was always well organised and detail-oriented. From planning events, minute taking, scheduling people and organising and managing meetings, she would, she concluded, bring order to Rosa's chaos.

And she had. Carys had been on hand right from the start, when Rosa was at her desk at 5 a.m. and still there at midnight, determined that Scott Brannigan, the multi-millionaire who'd sought her out and invested in her, would never regret his decision.

Rosa continued to put in ridiculously long hours both in her office and out of it and although, with Scott's approval, she'd brought in two young up-and-coming hipsters to assist her, rather than relieve her workload, this had, she realised, only added to it and she still seemed unable to take her foot off the gas.

'Wow, looking good.' Joe nodded his approval as he appeared and stood in the doorway, surveying Carys's work.

'I always look good,' Carys teased, throwing another plastic-wrapped banner in Joe's direction. He caught it deftly and began to pull off the plastic.

And she did always look good, Rosa thought almost proudly – maternally even. Which was a bit daft seeing as she and Carys were about the same age. And it was Carys who carried the maternal advantage, being single mum to a now eight-year-old son. Carys had not mentioned the boy at her initial interview and, although Rosa knew it was against all ethical employment law to discriminate against a woman just because she had the sole responsibility for a young child, Rosa also knew that, had she been aware of the little boy, she wouldn't have taken Carys on. With a new business to get up and running, the last thing she needed was a PA ringing in to say her child was sick; she needed time off to attend sports day, assemblies, dental appointments; her son had broken his arm and she was up at A&E with him. And whatever else mothers were there for. Carys never had.

Carys Powell was a tiny, charismatically beautiful, organised firecracker of a woman who, Rosa had soon realised, she just couldn't do without. Together, they'd spent the last three years proving to Scott Brannigan he'd been correct in his appraisal of Rosa's potential to add hugely to his investment pot. As soon as she'd done just that, she'd been able to part company with Scott sooner than expected, sailing off into the national – and now international – world of business, Rosa Quinn Investments going from strength to strength here in London.

And Joe had been at her side all the way, her absolute strength and rock (*hell*, Eva had once grumbled, *you sound like the bloody Queen and the Duke of Edinburgh*) both at Durham where they'd each graduated with a first each in business management, and now here in the City where Joe was climbing his own ladder of business success as hedge fund manager for one of the bigger international banks.

She and Joe had recently spent hours and hours discussing whether he should revoke his present employment and be the one to head up the new Rosa Quinn Investment branch in New York. Or should they leave the London office in the hands of others more than capable of doing just that, now that her burgeoning business was both sound and flying, and both head off to New York together? Rosa knew she was already tired of living in London after almost eight years of the hurly burly, the squashed commuter rides when sometimes she felt she just couldn't breathe; even the constant wining and dining of potential investors in fabulous restaurants several evenings a week, where she could not only do business but also indulge her love of eating, had long begun to pall.

When a woman is tired of London, she's tired of life, Rosa often thought to herself as, misquoting Samuel Johnson, she'd found her nose buried yet again in someone's sweaty armpit on the tube. But she wasn't convinced New York was the answer. Out of the frying pan and all that, she'd argued with herself as, once more unable to sleep, she'd left Joe dead to the world (he'd always had the capacity to never worry about anything) and wandered through to the huge kitchen of the ultra-modern high-rise apartment they'd bought together in trendy Wandsworth, just six months earlier.

'Come on, Rosie Posie,' Joe was saying now, taking her arm,

'they'll all be getting into King's Cross any minute and I could murder a drink before they descend on us.'

'Descend on us?' Rosa repeated as Joe hailed a black cab outside the hotel. 'That sounds like you're not looking forward to seeing everyone?'

'Not at all. You know I adore your sisters – they're a part of you.' Joe kissed the top of Rosa's head and then frowned. 'Although your lot, when they're all out in force, are pretty overwhelming.'

'My lot?'

'Well, there's Bill and his latest mistress – or is he bringing more than one again? And then there's your dad, who will insist on bringing the dog with him, and I bet anything he won't have asked the hotel if he's allowed to have it in the room. Your mum will arrive with a whole load of corned-beef sandwiches no one will end up eating except the bloody dog and, I assume, Hannah's got some new man in tow? I just get used to one and then there's another one waiting in the wings.'

'You're being a bit...' Rosa glanced at Joe sitting back, arms folded almost crossly, next to her as the taxi left Grosvenor Street, heading through the Saturday lunchtime traffic for Chelsea, Wandsworth Bridge and, eventually, Wandsworth itself and home.

'A bit what?'

'Irritable.'

'I've a lot on at work.'

'Haven't we all?'

'Yes, Rosa, you always have,' Joe snapped. 'Will you slow down? A bit? If not for you, then for me? For us? Two years, Rosa, *over* two years and you've not had a day off. Not a weekend without working.'

'You know I can't...'

'Yes you *can*. You have to. And look, Rosa, this idea of yours about New York...' Joe broke off, shaking his head slightly.

'What, you've changed your mind?'

'No, well yes… well, I don't *know*, Rosa. I just think maybe it's all a bit much. And I like being here in London. I'm not convinced about New York; I wasn't overly impressed when we spent that week there with Alice.'

'That was over five years ago, for heaven's sake. And we were visitors. Tourists.'

'Exactly. It'll be even more New Yorkish now.'

'New Yorkish?' Rosa stared. 'I thought it was what you wanted?'

'No, it's what *you* wanted. I love London. Don't forget I was born here and lived here until I was forced up north when I was sixteen. It's in my blood.'

'I'm tired of it,' Rosa said, vocalising perhaps for the first time exactly what she was feeling. 'I'm tired of the whole thing. I *feel* tired. I'm thirty and I feel fifty…'

'Exactly.' Joe took Rosa's hand. 'And now we're having this conversation…'

'What conversation?'

'Children? Rosa, I want to marry you…'

'Are you proposing?'

'If that's what you want? Yes, marry me, Rosa. But children? You change the subject every time I mention children.'

'Joe, you know taking time off to get married… having children at the moment would be impossible. I can't… I don't…'

'Why does it take time to get married? We could just nip down to the registrar office.'

When Rosa didn't reply, unable to articulate what she was feeling, Joe attempted levity, obviously slightly embarrassed: 'Must be my Sicilian blood, this longing I have for children.'

'We'd probably end up with triplets,' Rosa interrupted. 'God, can you imagine?'

'Sounds wonderful.' Joe took Rosa's hand. 'Three more like you.'

'You're mad.' Rosa took back her hand, terrified at the very thought.

Joe, Rosa could see, was upset. He sat back in the taxi before coming out fighting. 'And Eva will be as bossy as always, ordering everyone about and, when she's had too much to drink, telling everyone she's a marquess's daughter. And, despite being a princess – as well as being the daughter of famous artist Alice Parkes – has deigned to marry a Pakistani immigrant from Bradford.'

'That's so unfair, Joe. Eva is neither a social climber nor a racist. And Rayan isn't an immigrant; he's as British as you and me.'

'I didn't say she was either of those things. Just sometimes she's, you know, a bit much. Both your sisters are – they always have been.'

Rosa took Joe's hand. 'What is it, Joe? Come on, out with it – don't blame it on this birthday party and my family, en masse, in one hotel.'

'Rosa, you know what's getting to me. We never spend any time together. You're out most evenings, wooing new clients. On the evenings you *are* in, you hit the sack at eight. But then you're back on your phone after midnight, catching the international trade.'

'I'm just so tired.'

'When was the last time we had a night out together?' Joe went on at full throttle, not listening to her response. 'Laughed at some daft film at the cinema? Sat in front of the fire with cheese on toast and a good book?'

'There is no fire in the flat.' Rosa attempted humour, but Joe was having none of it.

'Rosa,' he said finally, turning to her as the cab pulled up outside the apartment, 'when was the last time we had sex?'

She couldn't remember. Two months ago? Three? 'Oh, come on, Joe, it's not that long ago – a couple of weeks? Who's counting?'

'I am. I miss you, Rosa.' Joe, usually so mild-mannered, so *not* like he was being now, stamped off up the road, across the communal garden and, without waiting for her, went into the apartment, taking the stairs to their flat on the seventh floor rather than the lift.

'Pillock,' Rosa said under her breath. What the hell was matter with him? He was behaving like a spoilt child not getting his own way. Joe had never been a sulker, had never been one of those dreadful men prone to moodiness and resorting to petulance if they couldn't get their own way in an argument. Rosa set off after him up the stairs, but the effort seemed too much and, instead, she pressed the buttons on the second floor and was transported smoothly and quickly to their front door.

'Oh, you're all here and getting stuck in already?' Rosa's intention was that she and Joe would obviously be first at the subtly lighted and decorated conference room at the top of the hotel in Knightsbridge. Be first there to welcome the guests invited to celebrate not only her winning the Sunday Clarion's Future Management award three months earlier, but also her thirtieth birthday. But Joe had fallen asleep over a couple of beers while watching some important rugby final and Rosa had found herself cornered by phone calls from New York coming in thick and fast with questions that couldn't be put off.

'It's Saturday, for heaven's sake,' Joe had snapped crossly, bad-tempered both from actually missing the match and the unrefreshing kip on the sofa. 'And you're going to take ages to get ready now. And *I* need the shower as well.'

'Use the other one,' Rosa had yelled back from the shower room. 'We do have two, you know. And what's Saturday got to do with it?' she'd continued while hunting for, but unable to find, her conditioner. 'Have you been at my Sisley Restructuring?'

Her voice came through the open bathroom door as Joe, sitting yawning and irritable in his underpants and socks on the edge of the bed, scowled crossly.

'Chance'd be a fine thing. I can never get *in* the bloody shower. And working? Saturday evening? In New York?'

'It's lunchtime over there and yes, they're working. There's vital stuff we need to work out.'

'Oh, for God's sake, Rosa. Give it a rest,' Joe shouted. 'It can wait until Monday.'

'Not in my world it can't,' she'd yelled back, rubbing some cheap hotel conditioner she'd filched on one of her trips abroad into her shampooed and rinsed hair. (You could take the girl out of Yorkshire et cetera, et cetera. She'd smiled through the suds.) The smile was soon off her face as she tried to pull a comb through her badly conditioned hair. God, this was bloody awful stuff. Now she was going to look a mess and Hannah and Eva would be looking fabulous. They all still competed, Rosa acknowledged, to be the one looking the best out of the three of them, even at thirty.

The effort of holding the hairdryer and pulling the comb through her hair almost floored her and, reaching into the pocket of her dressing gown hanging behind the bedroom door, Rosa snapped open the foil covering before downing two of the little life savers Carys had recommended and found for her.

By the time Joe had managed to hail a cab, irritability wafting rife alongside his Creed's Aventus aftershave and her own Calvin Klein's Euphoria, they were already half an hour late for their own party.

'Hey, it's our party too, you know,' Hannah laughed. 'Whenever you celebrate adding another year, so do we. You can't escape us. Although I sometimes think you're trying to.' She beckoned a waiter over with a tray of champagne. 'Get stuck into this and loosen up a bit.'

'Loosen up?' Rosa frowned. 'And trying to escape you? What

are you on about…?' But Hannah was off, chatting up and flirting with the new twenty-five-year-old finance manager Rosa had taken on earlier that month.

'Darling girl.' Bill Astley appeared at Rosa's side. 'Hmm,' he said critically, hugging her before holding her out at arm's length while looking long and hard into her face, 'you've lost weight. You overdoing it? I know what London can do to you.'

'I'm fine. Really,' Rosa started as Bill clasped Joe's hand. The pair of them had always got on, ever since the days of working on the estate when she and Joe were kids. God, that seemed such a long time ago now. Heady days when they couldn't keep their hands off each other.

'Yes, she *is* overdoing it, Bill. Have a word with her, will you?' Joe clapped Bill on the arm before heading off to greet Virginia and Timothy, who'd driven down the night before with Barty and Bethany.

'We really couldn't face the *train*,' Rosa heard Virginia tell Joe in a pained voice. 'Not with two kiddies and all *their* paraphernalia. And Barty has been *desperate* to see the Rosetta Stone in the British Museum for absolutely ages.'

At seven years old? Rosa took a glass of proffered champagne and started to make her way over to her eldest sister. Barty didn't look as if he was desperate for anything except, maybe, the lavatory, his hand now firmly clasped onto his todger through the pocket of the somewhat strange-looking beige lederhosen shorts and long beige socks Virginia had put him into. Maybe Barty was also desperate to be part of the Hitler Youth?

'What the fuck has Virginia put that child into?' Eva whispered into Rosa's ear as she caught up with her, hugging her tightly while Virginia automatically wafted Barty's hand away from his nether regions with a curt: *hands off Mr Peepee, Barty*. 'How're you doing, sweetie pie? Continuing in your quest to rule the world?'

'Oh, you know – London today, New York tomorrow, the

world next week.' Rosa downed her champagne. 'God, I needed that,' she went on, scanning the room for a waiter and a refill. 'Do you want another? You've not touched that one yet?'

Eva smiled coyly, something Rosa had never seen before; Eva and coyness never went hand in hand.

'Oh my God, you're not? Are you? Are you really?' Rosa grabbed at Eva's arm and then at Rayan's who was standing talking to Susan and Richard.

'Yes,' Eva said, smiling but biting her lip. 'What the hell have we done? Twelve weeks now. I can tell everyone.'

'I can't believe you didn't ring me the minute you saw the double blue line.' Rosa felt ridiculously put out. And, she realised, envious. Jealous that Eva was going to be a mum and she wasn't. She hugged Eva, ashamed of her thoughts. 'This is *so* wonderful. Can I be godmother?'

'You can carry it and have it for me if you want?' Eva pulled the desperately horrified face again but her eyes, bright and excited, portrayed the true pride at her pregnancy.

'What, like Alice Growbag?' Rosa laughed.

'Do Mum and Dad know?'

'Yes, of course.'

'And Hannah?'

'Yes.'

'And Bill?'

'Yesssssss.'

'Why not me?' Rosa knew she sounded petulant.

'I didn't want to tell you on the phone. I was waiting for you to come home. You've not been back since Christmas, you know. And, anyway, I didn't really think you'd be that interested.'

'Not interested?' Rosa stared. 'Why on earth wouldn't I be interested?'

'An award-winning businesswoman probably hasn't got time for morning sickness and piles.'

'Piles already?'

'You know what I mean. And, actually, I've not been sick once,' Eva went on with obvious pride.

'Hang on.' Rosa caught at Carys's arm as she walked past. 'Listen to this, Carys, I'm going to be an aunty again – Aunty Rosa.'

'Oh, brilliant, Eva, that's wonderful.' Carys, who had been on more than one night out with the three of them when Hannah and Eva had been down in London for the weekend, gave Eva a congratulatory hug.

'*You'll* be having another, one of these days.' Eva laughed, kissing Carys.

'Why is it all pregnant women want everyone else to be in the same boat?' Carys grinned. 'I was just the same when *I* was expecting.' She chortled and Rosa realised Carys was already well stuck into the free alcohol despite continuing to see the party was running smoothly. 'You get over it,' she went on.

'Not another on the cards then?' Eva smiled.

'It would be the second immaculate conception.' Carys laughed again. 'And no, I'm not the mothering type. Looking after your wonderful sister here is more than enough for me right now. I absolutely love coming to work – I'm much more into the buzz of the office than the buzz of a baby monitor at two in the morning, dirty nappies and sleepless nights.' She shuddered slightly. 'And, to be honest –' she lowered her voice '– you've got to do that other thing with a man before you have babies.' She smiled and, seeing the waiting staff were awaiting instructions with the buffet, hugged Eva once more, winked at Rosa and set off in their direction.

'That *other thing*?' Eva raised an eyebrow once Carys was out of hearing. 'What other thing?'

'Sex, I think she means,' Rosa said dryly.

'Right. Is she a lesbian then?' Eva was mystified. 'She's a bloody attractive woman. I'd fancy her myself, you know, if I was gay.'

'Oy, hands off,' Rosa laughed, any remaining petulance at being the last to be told of Eva's pregnancy evaporating into the ether. 'I saw her first – I can't do without her.'

15

'Sweetheart, I know everyone has already been saying this to you, but I really do think you should slow down a bit; you're going to burn out.' Bill Astley took Rosa's hand across the starched white cloth in Simpsons in the Strand. Bill might be slightly bohemian, Rosa acknowledged as he squeezed her fingers, given to eccentricity when it suited him but, when it didn't, when it came to what he liked to eat, the twelfth Marquess of Heatherly favoured the more traditional English restaurants over those fashionably favoured places such as Ottolenghi's, where Rosa had recently been taking clients. Glancing across at Bill's face as he released her hand with obvious reluctance, Rosa wouldn't have been surprised to have him order brown Windsor soup and steak and kidney, followed by apple pie or Black Forest gateau. 'You've lost more weight than when we were all down for the party six weeks ago,' he said almost crossly. 'You're not looking after yourself. What does Joe think?'

'I'm not convinced Joe notices anything at the moment,' Rosa sighed. 'Unless it's to do with work.'

'The New York idea? He's busy with that?'

'No. Joe never wanted to really take that on. It was my idea, and I don't want to leave him here in London and go off across to the States by myself. He's got enough on with his own work. He's out of the apartment every morning at six and back late every night – you know how it is.'

'Well, *you* certainly must do. Are either of you ever *in* that beautiful flat of yours?'

'We manage weekends together. It's fine. I'm fine. Really,' Rosa argued for what seemed like the millionth time. She did wish people would get off her back and just let her get on with running her company, which was bursting at the seams with its own success. She had spent what seemed like hours the previous week looking at application forms and CVs of those Carys had already shortlisted in readiness for interview the following week.

'You do realise we're *already* totally all male here, Carys?' Rosa had frowned when Carys presented her with the five shortlisted male applicants. 'Surely there were some women candidates this time?'

'None that would come up to your exacting standards,' Carys had smiled. 'Really, I've whittled them down to the best possible ones. And the most important two of us here are women, of course,' she'd laughed.

'Two women out of twelve in top positions here isn't exactly healthy,' Rosa had said. 'I'm going to be shouted out for gender bias if I'm not careful. I'm going to go through them all again, Carys.'

'If that's what you really want,' Carys had smiled again. 'But I really do feel I've chosen the best...'

'Come back, Rosa,' Bill ordered across the table as Rosa continued to mull over the upcoming interviews. 'You're thinking about work again, aren't you? Now, what will you have to eat?'

'The Caesar salad, thank you. I've a dinner on this evening.'

'How about the steak and kidney pie?'

'The salad is fine.'

'Listen, Rosa, I've made an appointment,' Bill said, taking Rosa's hand once again and this time hanging on to it.

'Oh?'

'A check-up – a full MOT as it were. This afternoon at three. It's a twenty-minute taxi ride away in Harley Street.'

'Are you OK? You're not poorly, are you?' Rosa searched Bill's face for signs of ill health. 'And Harley Street? You're pushing the boat out? I thought you were broke?'

'My family, being total hypochondriacs, has always been seen by the top people,' Bill said a little huffily. 'But, anyway, I'm fine, Rosa. Blooming. It's for you, not me.' Bill gave her a determined stare.

'Oh no, no no...'

'Yes, Rosa. I promised Eva and Hannah I'd make the appointment and, if necessary, drag you there myself. I'm not taking no for an answer,' he went on and, as Rosa pushed back her chair, he took her arm and pulled her back down. 'He's a good bloke is Dr Robson. Put my mind at rest a couple of times when I was convinced I'd got a dicky heart... and when I had testicular cancer...' Bill frowned '...and sepsis...'

'You've had testicular cancer? *And* sepsis?' Rosa frowned. 'When was this, then?'

'No, I told you. He's a top bloke. He listens, does a battery of tests and then reassures you you haven't got it.'

'Oh, for heaven's sake, Bill, get over yourself. It's London. Everyone's knackered in London.'

'Just as a favour to me. And those two back at home? A half-hour when you'll have a few blood tests, all will be OK as you say, and I can then report back.'

'I really don't have time.'

'Make time,' Bill ordered. 'Right, OK, I'm having a large glass of wine now I've got that out of the way. My nerves need it.'

'So, tired all the time?' The private GP looked up from his desk, steepled his hands like all good doctors are probably trained to do at medical school and waited for Rosa's response.

'I'm very busy,' Rosa smiled. 'It's been a totally full-on few years.'

'Night sweats as well? Possibly hormonally related then.' The man made some notes, his expensive fountain pen flowing smoothly across the pristine white sheet in front of him.

'Oh God, I'm not going through the menopause, am I?' Rosa put a hand to her face, shocked.

The man smiled. 'I doubt it very much at…' he glanced at his notes once again '…thirty. Mind you, not beyond the realms of possibility. Irritable? Mood swings?'

Rosa frowned. 'Well yes, often bloody irritable. I am *now*, being forced by Bill to come here. But I'm in London… I'm busy.'

'How old was your mother when she went through the change?'

'My birth mother or my adopted mother?'

'You're adopted? Birth mother obviously, but I guess you won't know that then?' He smiled again. 'These things do tend to run in families.'

'She was actually my age when she had the three of us. And, if necessary, I can find out, you know, about her menopause.'

'Three of you?'

'I'm a triplet.'

'Goodness. That's fascinating.'

'So, am I, then? You know, old before my time? Going to sweat buckets – which to be honest, I *am* doing most nights. My partner had to move into the spare room last week; he said he was dreaming he was in St Mark's Square in Venice and it was flooding,' Rosa smiled, attempting levity. 'So, am I going to become a dried-up raisin?'

A prune instead of a plum? Wearing wee-leaking pads and too dry down there to ever have sex again? Big knickers and big cardigans; upholstered swimming costumes instead of bikinis? Rosa's heart missed a beat.

'Or you're pregnant?'

'Oh my God. Pregnant?'

'I don't know until we do some tests. I'm just surmising, raising a few possibilities here before we get down to really finding out the problem. If there is one. You're probably just overworked like the rest of us.'

'Pregnant?' And suddenly, Rosa knew – that was it. Pregnant. Eva had told her she was so fatigued when she was in between patients at the surgery, even before she'd had confirmation she was actually pregnant, she'd tipped back her dental chair fully horizontal, gratefully crawled on to it and fallen asleep. Dribbling, she'd added.

'Would that be a problem?'

'Yes! No! God, I don't know. Actually –' Rosa began to smile '– that would be OK. I think.'

'And could you be?'

'These things happen, don't they?' Rosa didn't like to admit to this professional she couldn't remember when she'd last had a period. Or, to be honest, when she'd last had sex. Goodness, she could be *months* pregnant. She and Eva could be having their babies together. She did hope Hannah wouldn't feel too left out. She'd take time off, persuade Joe to take over at the helm. Leave the business in Carys's more than capable hands, take on those two new recruits next week... be available at the end of a phone as a consultant while she took time off to have this baby...

'OK,' the GP was saying, 'my nurse will be in, in just two ticks. I'd like a full examination and a raft of blood tests in order to rule out – or confirm...' He broke off, smiling conspiratorially in Rosa's direction and she felt herself smiling shyly back. Coyly, even. God, all pregnant women must be visited with the coyness thing, even at this early stage.

A coy smile, a Madonna smile – a mother, a mummy.

'Ms Quinn?'

'Yes?'

'Dr Robson.'

'Goodness, that was quick.' Rosa looked at her watch. She was back in her office in St James, the early Friday evening commuter traffic already building up to a constantly steady buzz below her window.

'Well, I could have given you a few answers in my office, there and then, if you hadn't been in such a rush to get back to work.' He paused. 'So, we can rule out your being pregnant.'

'I'm not?' Rosa felt such a bolt of disappointment, she pushed her chair back from the computer and closed her eyes. No dark-haired little girl with Joe's incredible blue eyes? No trusting little hand in hers? No little soft-skinned being with that intoxicating vanilla smell, to call her Mummy? And Joe, Daddy?

'I think that was the result you were hoping for?' Rosa could almost see Dr Robson's smile down the phone.

Rosa shook her head but, realising the man was waiting for an answer, she took a deep breath and said, instead, 'So am I menopausal?'

'Possibly. Probably not. The blood test looking at your oestrogen, luteinising hormone and FSH levels won't be back until Monday, so I'm unable to give you the all-clear on that right now. Go home and enjoy the weekend. Have a lovely meal; enjoy your partner. And my advice, Rosa, is to take some time off work – even if it is just for the weekend. I really think you're doing too much.'

Two hours later and ignoring all the good doctor's advice, Rosa left her deserted office – even Carys had gone home – sprayed perfume, fluffed up her hair and added blusher to her too-pale face before hailing a cab to take her to her dinner reservation with four business associates in Holland Park.

Rosa woke when she heard Joe's keys rattling in the front door and knew he was home. She glanced at the illuminated digits on her bedside clock – 2 a.m. – and the awful realisation hit her immediately: she was going through an early menopause; she'd never be able to have a baby. Joe's baby. She needed to talk to him, cry, and have him tell her it would all be alright. Hearing the shower pump from the bathroom down the corridor cease its annoyingly monotonous whump and thump, she waited for Joe to join her in the bedroom. When, five minutes later, he still hadn't, she sat up in bed. What was he *doing*?

Rosa opened the bedroom door and tiptoed across the cream-carpeted corridor. The bathroom door was ajar, the light still on, any remaining steam that had escaped the automatic extraction fan drifting out towards her. She turned off the light and closed the bathroom door before crossing over to the second bedroom. Joe was in there, one bare arm thrust out above his head, his breathing heavy and steady. His navy suit, shirt and navy and burgundy spotted tie – the one she'd bought for him for his last birthday – were dropped in a pile on the floor and Rosa bent to pick them up, breathing in his Joe smell. God, she loved him. Fourteen years together, and Rosa knew she loved Joe Rosavina just as much now, standing here, gazing down at his beautiful, familiar face, as when she'd first set eyes on him at sixteen.

Rosa slipped in beside him, pulling his arm around her, breathing him in. Tomorrow she needed to talk to him; needed to make changes in their lives, tell him what was happening to her.

Saturday morning: the time for staying in bed, making love, eating toast dripping with honey, fingers sticky with sugar and love. Along with the wonderful freedom to have that second – and third – mug of coffee without having to drain the contents of the first down the kitchen sink because she was already late for the first of the meetings Carys had arranged at the office. Saturday morning: the time for having Joe take her in his arms, to make love before drifting off to sleep knowing it was the weekend and they were free to do whatever they wanted.

Rosa lay, still half asleep, knowing that the lovely picture of the two of them doing just that hadn't actually, in essence, manifested itself for what? Months? A year even? Saturday mornings, in reality, meant catching up with emails; sorting the problems that had appeared as she was leaving the office on the Friday evening; gathering up laundry, used mugs, plates and takeaway boxes that – to her utter shame – had remained just where they'd been left during the preceding days since Maria and her workers from the cleaning company had been in to weave their magic on the apartment.

Rosa turned to Joe, remembering why she was in the spare room rather than their own bedroom. He was already up and moving about in the kitchen and, as she called out to him, wanting him to come back to bed, she heard the click of the front door and then it closing behind him. Rosa sat up, taking in the sunlit roofs and chimney tops below, the communal gardens, Londoners and tourists alike already out to greet what was promising to be a hot sunny day; saw him appear down below in his running gear and set off in the direction of Hoxton Square Park where he usually started his run.

Rosa closed her eyes and drifted off. Tired. She was always so tired.

The next time she woke, over an hour had passed. Joe was obviously back in their en suite, shower going, his run over. Her head was pounding. She made her way to the kitchen, looking for juice, for paracetamol in her briefcase. The box she'd bought only a couple of days earlier along with her daily paper appeared empty. Surely, she hadn't chewed her way through that lot?

'Aren't you getting ready?' Joe came into the kitchen, expertly slotted a coffee capsule into the machine, poured juice and searched for bread that neither of them had had the time, thought or inclination to buy. 'Coffee?'

'Tea please.' The very thought of coffee made her feel sick. Maybe the good doctor had got it wrong and she was, in fact, pregnant? It had been a very basic urine test he'd carried out yesterday afternoon. Didn't the pee have to be an early morning sample? Hope flared, then evaporated, replaced by guilt as she realised the painkillers she'd obviously downed recently would have been passed on to any potential baby. 'Getting ready?' Rosa frowned. 'For what?'

Joe nodded towards the kitchen clock – a huge black wrought-iron affair that, with its balancing arrowhead, gave the impression of having three hands instead of the customary two, and which Rosa could never get to grips with – before looking back at her. 'My mum and dad? Yes? Here for the weekend? Their train will be just getting in to King's Cross.'

'Fuck.' Rosa's head pounded. 'Fuck it. Hell. Bugger. Fuck. Jesus.'

'For a vicar's granddaughter, you don't half know some choice words,' Joe said mildly, before upturning a box of some sort of cereal into a bowl and sniffing at the milk. 'I take it there isn't a welcoming cake in the tin? A bunch of flowers at their bedside?'

'Well, seeing as you slept *in* their bed, there's no clean sheets on it either.' Rosa folded her arms and went to sit down at the kitchen table. Three days' newspapers had accumulated there. 'Why *did* you sleep in there?' she asked.

'I didn't want to disturb you. The meeting carried on over dinner and then we went on to Annabel's; the Americans wanted to see what London nightlife has to offer.'

'And a shower? At 2am?' Rosa looked at Joe.

'Hot and sweaty in that club. The last thing you wanted, when you're having sweats yourself, was me getting into bed with you and adding more moisture.' He smiled in her direction.

It was the *first* thing I wanted, Rosa thought, but stayed quiet.

'Right, you get showered; I'll change the sheets.' Joe looked out of the window. 'And there's a bunch of dandelions and buttercups down there. Do we own such a thing as a vase?'

'You don't own a vase?' Michelle Rosavina clicked her tongue as Roberto decanted a load of goodies into the almost empty fridge. She handed over the huge bouquet of creamy white lilies. 'I don't know how these weren't squashed on the train. Goodness, it was packed. Some football or rugby final on down here, I think?' She laughed. 'Now, what we need, Rosa, is a *wedding*. You'd have a never-ending supply of vases, photo frames and other stuff then.' Michelle glanced round at the kitchen, taking in the top-of-the-range coffee-maker, the latest Kenwood Chef, the wine-cooler cabinet and the neatly stacked, but barely used, orange Le Creuset pans on their stand in the corner. 'Mind you, you appear to have everything else you need. I just adore this apartment.'

Rosa took the lilies, their heady scent immediately taking her back to when, as a little girl, she'd be holding on to Susan's hand in the front pew of her grandfather's church, her toes reaching for the embroidered hassock with her best Sunday patent shoes; feeling safe, knowing she was loved by her mummy and daddy, Virginia, Eva and Hannah. And Jesus.

'A wedding?' Roberto finally emerged from the fridge, which was now looking a good deal fuller than when they'd arrived. 'Are we planning wedding?' He smiled hopefully at Rosa before going in for his second hug in ten minutes. 'Rosa Rosavina. What a name to juggle with. We have to have wedding just for that.' He laughed loudly, his Sicilian generosity and bonhomie out in full force. 'A wedding reception up at Rosavina's – you don't want to be down here in London – and then honeymoon in Sicily like we had.' He glanced fondly across at Michelle and patted her cotton-trousered bottom, obviously remembering nights

– and afternoons – of love in the Sicilian-sun-warmed villa that had been in the Rosavina family for years. 'You need feeding up a bit first, Rosa,' Roberto added. 'You've lost weight. Right,' he went on, as Joe frowned in his direction, 'let's hit big city – I've booked Eye; got tickets for top of new Shard place; river trip and *Mousetrap* tonight.' He rubbed his hands in glee. 'Come on, let's go.'

16

After being hauled around what seemed to be every single bit of tourist London by Roberto Rosavina, Rosa woke up on the Monday morning knowing she just couldn't get on the tube and go to work as usual. But also knowing there was no way she couldn't. Carys had taken her little boy back to Wales to stay with her parents for the summer, and several of her staff were also out of the office on annual leave. The phones would be ringing, the emails pouring in regardless.

After another morning's exhausting tour of palaces – both Buckingham and Kensington – as well as a boat trip on the Thames (where, squashed between Roberto on one side and a huge German tourist on the other, Rosa had actually fallen asleep, embarrassed to find her head nodding and her mouth dribbling onto the latter's hairy muscular forearm), she'd made her excuses and hailed a taxi home, while the other three had left for lunch in Soho before Joe's parents took the train back north. She'd sat in the shade of the huge copper beech in the communal garden, answering emails, arranging meetings and generally making plans for the coming week.

When Joe came back from seeing his parents off, Rosa had planned to sit him down and tell him they needed – she needed – to put the brakes on the helter-skelter, the mad motorway fast-lane journey that her life had become. She suddenly wanted what Joe wanted. She wanted a baby. It wasn't just because Eva was pregnant – although, she knew, Joe would perhaps argue that it was. It was because, having opened up the *possibility* of being pregnant, having drawn back the Band-Aid she'd stuck over the very idea of having a baby, the lesion was now laid bare and, rather than cover it up again until some distant point in the future, she wanted to discuss this with Joe. Now. She knew he desperately wanted children, had even pointed this out against her plans to expand the business into the States. She thought she could do it all. Have it all. Now, not only did she know she couldn't have it all. She didn't *want* it all.

Joe hadn't returned until after 5 p.m. She called out to him from the tiny boxroom that acted as their home office, but he was back in the shower, emerging ten minutes later dressed in suit and briefcase to hand.

'Where are you going?' Rosa stared.

'I should have been gone two hours ago,' he said, checking his passport and placing it carefully into his briefcase. 'Mum and Dad missed their train home and I had to help them sort out another.'

'Yes, but where are you *going*?'

'Chicago.'

'Chicago?' Rosa had made to get up from her seat.

'Rosa, I told you this. I'm there for a good week. I've a meeting at 5 p.m., their time tomorrow, an hour's drive from O'Hare International.'

'You could go in the morning.'

'Hardly. I'd have actually gone this morning, or even yesterday, if we hadn't had Mum and Dad down.'

'Right.'

'Give you time to have an early night and catch up on some sleep. And then you'll be raring to go again: ready to carry on building that empire of yours once more.' Joe had stroked Rosa's hair, pulling her to him. 'I love you, Rosie Posie. Don't overdo it? Hmm? I'll phone when I get there.' And then he was gone.

And now it was Monday morning, and Rosa felt almost panic-stricken at the idea of going into the office, but especially knowing that Carys wasn't going to be there to field calls, to deal with the stuff she regularly sifted through before handing it on to her boss. Rosa put a hand to her neck, feeling the swelling that had been there ever since she'd contracted, and been ill with, glandular fever at the start of the long vacation after her first year at Durham.

'Who've you been kissing? Apart from me?' Joe had teased her. 'It's called the kissing disease, isn't it? How come you've got it and I haven't?' He'd called round to her mum and dad's every day after finishing his holiday job working at the company handling Heatherly Hall's accounts. Eva had gone out to India for six weeks, volunteering at a dental hospital in Mumbai while Hannah had gone interrailing with new friends from Manchester University and Rosa was feeling particularly left out and fed up with the bad luck of falling ill just as exams were over and the term had finished. Knowing this, Joe would come round bringing little presents: a tube of Love Hearts with *'Love You Forever'* stamped on every single sweet (he'd had to buy ten tubes and filch this particular message from all of them); a pomegranate and pack of pins to pick out the seeds; a cuddly toy (it was a bit like playing the *Generation Game* she wrote to Eva and Hannah); and, one afternoon, a pair of split-crotch panties (*for when you're up and running again*, he'd messaged on them and at which Susan, having found them peeping out from under Rosa's bed, had sniffed and warned, 'Just remember what happened to Alice.')

So now, having taken a taxi to her office rather than face the morning rush hour on the tube, Rosa was at her desk, her hand constantly straying to her neck, remembering Joe's little presents and wishing he was here with her now, instead of on the other side of the Atlantic.

She jumped when the phone rang. So often, calls went through to, and were fielded by, Carys.

'Rosa Quinn Investments. Rosa Quinn speaking.'

'Ah, Ms Quinn, Dr Robson here. Look, I have some test results that have come straight back from our lab. I hunted them down for you this morning.'

'That's private health for you,' Rosa said. For something to say. Her heart, for some reason was hammering.

'Can you come in this morning? I want to run more tests.'

'Oh? Is that necessary? Can they wait? I'm very busy...'

'Rosa, I'll see you at midday.'

'We're coming down, Rosa.' Hannah was adamant. 'Stop arguing.'

'You've both got work. Eva's five months pregnant.' Rosa's hand went automatically to her neck, as it had done every one of the five days since undergoing what seemed to be innumerable tests, and yet more tests. Scans, PET scans, ultrasounds and being poked about with and being sent off to different clinics and then off to King's College Hospital in Camberwell and waiting in queues and no one able or willing to tell her anything.

Until the votes were in and with it, the verdict. That's how Rosa saw it: the Verdict. A bit like on *The X Factor*. '*And the winner is...*' big pause for dramatic effect '...*Rosa Quinn with Stage 2B Hodgkinson's Lymphoma.*'

'We're booked on the 2 p.m. train. We'll be with you by teatime. Is Joe with you now?'

'Joe's in Chicago until next week.'

'You've gone through all this by yourself? Oh, for heaven's sake, Rosa. Get him to come straight back,' Hannah said bossily. 'You have told him?'

'I don't seem to be able to get hold of him.'

'Carys then? Carys is with you?'

'She's in Swansea with her parents. She's leaving her little boy there for the summer; saves on childcare.'

'Mum and Dad want to come down. And Bill too.'

'Please don't have them all coming down. Just you two. I want you two here.'

'We're coming. We're on our way.'

'I've been ringing Joe's number all the way down on the train,' Eva said. 'He's not answering.'

'It's early morning in Chicago.' Rosa shook her head. She didn't seem to be able to think straight. There was so much to sort out, so much to arrange. The business. Joe.

'So? Since when has Joe not had his phone clamped to his ear? We'd have rung Carys but neither of us have her number.'

'She'll be back in London in the next couple of days. It's her annual leave. I'm not ringing her to get her back early – she's gone off to Tenby, I think, with her parents. A caravan, she said. She'll take over at the office again as soon as she can.'

'So, come back home with us tomorrow. You can stay with me and Rayan. Or with Hannah? Or with Mum and Dad. You can have your old bed back.'

'I'm not a child, Eva. I live here in London. Why would I want to come back up to Yorkshire? I'm going to have all my treatment either at King's in Camberwell or there's talk of Parkside Hospital in Wimbledon. Still a load of stuff to arrange. This is only the very beginning.'

'So why, then?'

'Why what?'

'Why you?' Eva insisted, nursing a glass of milk while Hannah poured wine for herself and Rosa.

'What do you mean, *why me*?'

'Well, for heaven's sake, you're only thirty. I didn't think people our age got, you know…'

'Cancer?' Rosa tutted. 'You can say the word, you know. You especially, Eva, being a dentist.'

'What's my being a dentist got to do with anything?' Eva pulled a face.

'Oh, *I* don't know,' Rosa said irritably. 'You're medically trained, I suppose.'

'Well yes, actually we do check suspicious neck swellings. If you'd come to me and asked me about it, I'd have sent you off for further examination. Mind you, if you had, I'd have just thought it was a throwback to the glandular fever you had years ago.'

'That's what I thought,' Rosa nodded. 'Thought I was stressed and working too hard and I was having another bout of it. Apparently, according to the consultant I've been seeing, not only can this bloody Hodgkinson's thing affect younger women, but there is some thought, although tenuous, of a link between that and glandular fever.' Rosa drained her glass. 'Don't suppose I should be drinking really.'

'Blimey,' Hannah said, 'if it was me, I'd be downing a bottle a night.'

'For God's sake, Hannah.' Eva glared across at her.

'Sorry, Rosa, that was crass of me.' Hannah took one hand and Eva the other, the latter's bump snuggling in as if to comfort her aunt. 'We're here for you every bit of the way, day or night… Oh, Rosa…' Hannah broke off as Rosa, stroking Eva's abdomen, started to cry.

'It's just… it's just… I'm going to have chemo. And I might not be able to have a baby now. And Joe wants babies… And *I* want a baby… I didn't realise just how much. Until faced with the… the prospect… of… you know…'

'You'll have one,' Eva soothed. 'Of course you will.'

'One day.' Hannah stoked Rosa's fingers. 'When all this is over. One day.'

Joe returned from Chicago two hours after Eva and Hannah had taken the 11.30 a.m. train back north. Rosa had decided she needed to break the news to him face to face: she didn't want him on a nine-hour return flight in a state because he couldn't be with her, the minute she told him what was happening to her.

Rosa had had another appointment with her lovely consultant

– Mary Cooper – who had been assigned to her and, after laying all the cards on the table, and explaining in great detail what Rosa had in store, Rosa was feeling slightly more optimistic about what she was about to go through and the journey she'd have to embark on before being well once again. 'Not an easy trip,' Ms Cooper had warned, 'but you're young, we'll get you in the right frame of mind, and you'll come out the other end.'

So, when she let herself into the flat and, seeing Joe's case and briefcase in the hall, knew he was finally home, Rosa was determined to be upbeat, was going to reassure Joe all would be well.

He was sitting at the kitchen table, his phone in front of him, a beer to hand. When he looked up, his face was white, drained. Although usually clean-shaven, he looked as if he'd either been trying to grow a beard or just hadn't bothered with himself. There was a smell of fear on him – the tang of old sweat, of unwashed body. And Rosa knew he knew what was happening to her. Eva or Hannah had spoken to him; told him she might die.

'It's alright,' Rosa said, hurrying over to him. 'I'll be fine, really. I'm not going to die. Honestly. We'll still be together when I'm an old lady…' She broke off, drawing back as Joe appeared not to be taking in what she was saying. He stood up, his eyes haunted, real fear coming off him in palpable waves.

'I'm so, so, so sorry, Rosa.'

'I told you, it'll be fine.'

'It will be fine?' Joe stared at her.

And then she knew. Joe didn't know. This was something else. 'What is it you're sorry for, Joe?' Rosa sat down, picked up the salt and pepper pot, wiped at the sticky rim of the marmalade pot Hannah had put on the table just that morning.

'I'm sorry.'

'You said.'

Joe swallowed, pulled shaking fingers through his hair, wiped at his mouth with the same hand. 'She's pregnant.'

'Who's pregnant, Joe?'

'Carys.'

'Carys is pregnant?' The fridge hummed, the ridiculously overgrown clock ticked, a couple of starlings trilled and rattled harshly through the open window. There was still hope. 'OK, well that's not the end of the world. I can find someone else to run the business...'

'You don't get it.' Joe stood, almost angrily, and Rosa shut up. Shouldn't it be her, Rosa, who was angry? 'I am so sorry, Rosa. So terribly sorry.'

Rosa's own bombshell seemed inconsequential compared to this one: a Molotov cocktail compared to the nuclear holocaust Joe had just detonated.

'Right.' Rosa felt icily calm. 'I'm going back to the office. Leave your key on the table. Oh, and give Carys Powell a message from me – she's fired.'

Rosa walked into the bedroom, packed an overnight case and left the apartment, hailing a taxi for King's Cross, the north and the sanctuary of her sisters.

PART THREE

17

October 2021

'Now, children, we have a very special visitor who has joined us for our assembly this morning.' Cassie Beresford, head teacher of Little Acorns village school, beamed down at the children sitting cross-legged in front of her in the hall. 'Does anyone know who this is?'

'It's my Aunty Rosa,' a little voice called out confidently from the third row. 'She's going to marry Jesus.'

'Well now, how lovely is that, Laila?' Cassie continued. 'The Reverend Rosa *is*, of course, your aunty *as well as* our new vicar who has come to be with us in Westenbury.'

'She's not a vicar!' a little moppet from nursery shouted out from the front row. 'She's a *lady*. Vicars are daddies. And she's got jeans on and a pink dress. Vicars wear long black dresses. Even though they are daddies...' She trailed off, obviously confused.

'A bit of gender diversification and inclusion needed in PSHE I think, teachers.' Cassie grinned at her staff sitting down the length of both sides of the assembly hall and, pushing Rosa gently forwards with a whispered, 'All yours, Vicar,' Cassie took her seat at the front.

This was the one bit of *vicaring* – as Rosa had dubbed it – that she loved. She much preferred chatting to kids – had even enjoyed the older, bolshier kids at the couple of high schools she'd been allocated in Nottingham – than adults. She loved their innocence, their lack of guile, their ability to make her laugh and cry. Maybe, she thought, as she started on one of her stories, she should have retrained as a teacher rather than a servant of God.

'So...' Rosa smiled at the children while pulling a balloon from her jeans' pocket and attempting to blow it up. 'This is Benjamin,' she managed to get out before going in once again. Bloody hell, it was one of those balloons that was going nowhere. Red-faced with the effort, all she appeared to be achieving was an aching jaw, a few farty squeaks and a spit-covered bit of flaccid rubber.

'Mr Jamieson,' Cassie ordered, standing up. 'Come and put your muscles to good use. He's the student PE teacher,' she turned and whispered to Rosa. 'Biceps to die for.'

The young, exceptionally well-stacked, obviously rugby-playing student teacher made his way down to the front to cheers from the Year 6 girls at the back – he'd obviously made a big hit with the eleven-year-olds. Rosa handed him a second balloon from her pocket and, facing the children, he blew confidently into it. Nothing. The children began to laugh.

'I can do it, miss.' A tiny tot from nursery took Rosa's original balloon before she could stop him – hell, she and the school would be up for health and safety violations – and the balloon inflated triumphantly upwards.

The children and staff clapped, Rosa quickly tied a knot in the end of the balloon, took out a black felt pen and drew eyes and a nose, and, looking gratefully at the tot, said: 'So – finally – this is Benjamin.' She paused, smiling at the children, every eye upon her.

'Now Benjamin didn't like staying in his own bed at night. Mummy Balloon and Daddy Balloon would tuck him in and tell him they loved him, to sleep well and they'd see him in the morning but, every night, Benjamin would leave his own room and try and climb in between them and, every night, cross and tired, Mummy would take him back.'

'My daddy takes me back,' a little voice shouted from the front. 'He says I have my own bed and he wants to sleep with Mummy all to himself.'

'Right.' Rosa smiled and continued, 'So, every night for a week, this went on, with Benjamin coming into Mummy and Daddy's bed and Mummy or Daddy Balloon taking him back and getting crosser because they were being woken up and becoming more and more tired.' Rosa gave a big dramatic yawn. 'One night they were so tired, they didn't hear Benjamin creep in and try to get in between them in the bed.' Rosa wriggled her shoulders, acting out trying to squeeze the way in. 'Hmm, there was no room. So, do you know what he did? He let out some of the air in Mummy Balloon and snuggled down. How awful is that? Still not enough space, so he let out some of the air in Daddy Balloon. Can you imagine? Still not quite enough space for Benjamin Balloon, so what did he do? He let a bit of air out of himself.' Rosa pulled a shocked face but took hold of Benjamin and drew a big triumphant smile on the yellow rubber with her pen. 'He was in! Between them. Yes!' Rosa high-fived the kid sitting at her feet. 'Now, the next morning, when Mummy Balloon saw him there, in between her and Daddy Balloon – who were both looking a lot thinner and markedly wrinkled – she said, sadly: "Benjamin, you've let *me* down, you've let *Daddy* down, but, worse of all…"' Rosa's face and voice became sadder and sadder '"…you've let *yourself* down."'

Silence in the hall. Oh, holy moly, they hadn't got the punchline.

And then Grace Stevens, the Year 4 teacher sitting with her class halfway down the hall, let out a huge guffaw and started to laugh. And laugh. Until the infectious laughter spread like drifting smoke and the kids, whether they got the punchline or not, joined in and the whole hall was laughing.

'Now, there is a moral to this story,' Rosa eventually said, holding up a hand. 'Letting others down is bad enough, but letting yourself down is even worse. Think about that today, children, if you're about to do something you know you shouldn't...'

'My granny says Mummy's done something she shouldn't.' A little blonde-haired girl in the Year 1 row raised her hand.

Oops, dangerous ground. Rosa turned to Cassie as Cassie stood to deflect any response.

'But Daddy says she's just gone to *work* in Australia and she'll be back very soon. Or, I'm going to go and get on an aeroplane and fly out to see her in the summer holiday.'

'How lovely,' Rosa beamed. 'I'd love to go to Australia. To see the kangaroos and the koalas. I remember once...' She trailed off as she took in the blonde hair, the blue eyes – Joe's eyes – and the full mouth – Carys's mouth – and knew instantly who this little girl was: Joe's little girl. Rosa took a deep breath, realised the whole of the school was sort of frozen in time, suspended from reality as, waiting in anticipation, they geared themselves up for some story about Rosa wanting to visit the other side of the world. 'Children, it's been lovely coming to meet you all. I'm hoping Mrs Beresford will let me come into school a lot, to see you and work with you. And, I hope we'll see some of you in church...' Rosa breathed deeply, praying to God to stop the hammering of her heart '...and Sunday school.'

'Hans, I met Joe's little girl today.' Rosa tasted the vegetarian Bolognese sauce she'd spent the afternoon cooking.

'No! You're joking?' Hannah, in the process of pouring the wine she'd brought with her, stopped mid-pour. 'How did you know it was her?'

'I didn't at first, and then she started talking about her mummy who's working in Australia. Hannah, she's beautiful. A total mixture of Joe and Carys. And, I know this is absolutely stupid, and I know you'll think I'm crackers, but I miss her.'

'Who? Not Carys? Not the baggage from The Valleys? Not the Wicked Woman from Welsh Wales?'

'Stop it!'

'Stop it? Oh, come on, Rosa, get your vicar's head off for just five minutes and put back your poorly one of six years ago: ill with effing cancer and the pair of them do this to you.'

'Hannah, neither of them knew I was ill. You know that. And yes, I miss Carys. She took over from you two when you were both up here and I was in London. She was like another sister.'

'A sister who schemed to take over your business, your man and your life while professing to be your best friend? She was like that madwoman in that film – what was it? – *Single White Female* – you know with Bridget Fonda? At the end of the film, the faces of the Bridget Fonda character and the woman who adores her, and wants to *be her* have sort of merged into one.' Hannah shivered. 'Scary stuff. *And* calling Carys a *sister* is an insult to me and Eva.'

'I seem to remember the pair of you would have run off with Joe, given half the chance.' Rosa raised an eyebrow.

'For two or three weeks when we were sixteen,' Hannah tutted. 'He was still up for grabs then, even though you reckoned you'd nabbed him first because he was in your economics class.'

'Didn't the Carys character gouge the woman's boyfriend's eye out with her stiletto heel? Sam, he was called.' Rosa winced. 'You know, in the film?'

'Well,' Hannah sniffed, 'as far as I could see, when I saw Joe in court last week, he still had both of his. So, I guess the worst she's done is abandon both her children and gone off with some financier to Australia.'

Rosa turned and stared. 'Is that what she's done? How do you know? Did he tell you?'

'No. I read Rhys's file. Listen, Rosa, I really, really shouldn't be telling you any of this. Carys's son, Rhys, has pleaded not guilty to domestic burglary and been given bail until he's back in court after Christmas. He's only fourteen and, as far as I can see, was egged on by a group of older boys who are known to the youth service. I've had to tell them there's a conflict of interest; *I* can't deal with him. And I'm not supposed to be looking at any of his notes. Although I did. He was in trouble in London – took a mobile phone off another kid – and had already done a referral order down there.'

'It's funny, isn't it?' Rosa folded her arms, leaning against the table. 'Carys worked with me for almost three years, but I only ever met Rhys a couple of times. He was only seven or eight then and she had a succession of childminders and nannies and he went off back to his grandparents in Wales every school holiday. It was almost as if he didn't exist – she made sure she kept her home and work life totally separate. All I know, all she ever let slip, is that Rhys's father was some exceptionally wealthy, older married man who Carys had had an affair with and who shelled out a fortune every month to keep it quiet from his wife and family.'

'Scheming her way through other people's lives from before she came to work for you, then?'

'Suppose.'

'Talking of Sam...'

'Sam?'

'You just said the Bridget Fonda character's boyfriend – you know, eye on the end of her Jimmy Choos? – was called Sam.'

'So?'

'So, what did you think of Eva's Sam?'

'Eva's Sam?'

'Oh, don't pretend you don't know who I'm talking about.' Hannah waved her wineglass in Rosa's direction. 'Eva's new dentist. *Sam* the gorgeous dentist. I don't know how Eva's going to keep her periodontal probes off *him*.'

'She and Rayan are OK, aren't they?' Rosa pulled a face.

'She's bored, Rosa.'

'Bored? She's got a beautiful house, a fabulous job, two wonderful children…'

'And a husband who's turned into a cycling nerd. Have you *seen* the calf muscles on him lately? He's either pedalling for Britain or determined to have the biggest, most profitable dental surgery this side of Bradford. And *she* no longer wants to be a dentist.'

'Doesn't she? Why not?'

'Would you want to be gazing down the public's gobs all day?'

'Well, yes, if I was a trained dentist.'

'All that bad breath and bits of food stuck into people's back molars. She's – if you'll excuse the pun – fed up to the back teeth of it.'

'Does she want to be at home all day then? Get rid of Jodie and be a hands-on mummy?'

'I think she just wants to paint. You know she has a studio up at Bill's place? I think she sees herself as Alice's daughter.'

'She *is* Alice's daughter.'

'No, you know, she feels she's not fulfilled her destiny as an artist – or as a lover.'

'A *lover*?'

Hannah shook her head almost sadly. 'I just think Eva is ripe for plucking. Ripe for a bit of a knee-trembler up against the spittoon.'

'Jesus.'

'And no, *not* with your mate, Jesus, but with Sam Burrows. However –' Hannah's eyes twinkled mischievously '– not if I get in there first.'

'You're as bad as she is.'

Hannah agreed with a nod. 'While you, Rosie Posie, are the only saint around here.' Hannah grinned. 'Eva and I, it would appear, have both inherited Alice and Bill's genes.'

'OK,' Rosa said, once she'd boiled pasta, grated Parmesan and, with *oohs* and *ows* and other less demure oaths, unwrapped the steaming garlic bread from its foil covering. 'Come on, Hans, you might as well tell me about Ben. What's happening with him?'

'Oh, Rosa.' Hannah stopped twirling spaghetti against her spoon, laying it momentarily back on the bowl. 'I love him.'

'But, Hannah, he's not yours to love. You know that.'

'Please don't preach.'

'I'm not. I'm listening. I'm hurting for you. And for his wife.'

'Don't. I keep breaking it off. Honestly, I do. But it's like being on a diet when all you want is a great big slice of cheese on toast. You know, especially when it's Wensleydale cheese and there's Branston? And then, you've been really good for a week – eating nothing but sodding lettuce leaves and celery – and the cheese on toast – with Branston – appears on your doorstep saying it can't live without you.'

'What, the cheese on toast starts talking to you? I'm getting a bit lost here with this analogy.'

'You're not. You're not a bit lost. You know *exactly* what I mean.' Hannah chewed on a piece of garlic bread. 'I guess I'm either on a one-way trip to eternal damnation – you see, Rosa, those bloody sermons of Cecil's we had to sit through as kids made their mark after all – or I give Ben up and live out my life as a maiden aunt, knitting cardigans for my nephew and nieces, who will just throw them in a drawer in horror...'

'Barty and Bethany wouldn't do that,' Rosa laughed.

'...or, when I'm not clattering wool and needles together, dementedly getting in ten rows before I leave for work, I'll still be dealing with West Yorkshire's disaffected youth – which, to be honest, the way I'm supposed to work with them, I can't say I'm very good at. And then I'll die.' Hannah exhaled gloomily.

'Well at least, that way, you'll go to heaven instead of heading south.' Rosa grinned and sprinkled more Parmesan.

'And spend the rest of eternity sitting with Grandpa Cecil – who will definitely have bagged his spot next to God and St Peter – knitting leg warmers for the angels?' Hannah drained her glass of water. 'I think I'd rather take my chance with the flames.'

'Do it, Hannah, finish this thing with Ben. You know it's the right thing to do.'

'Oh, bloody hell, how've I ended up with *another* vicar in the family? And on my back? Right, I've got a great vicar joke for you.'

'One I can tell in church on Sunday?' Rosa's face lit up. 'Having a bit of a problem trying to work out the best way forward for my very first sermon here.'

'Hm, debatable.' Hannah grinned. 'So, a vicar is having a… you know… a private *pleasuring himself* session in his bathroom. Anyway, as he's finishing himself off, he turns around to see the window cleaner staring at him. Red-faced, he rushes downstairs when he hears a knock at the door.

'"I've done your windows, Vicar, that'll be £100," says the window cleaner with a smirk and a wink.

'Hurriedly, the vicar pays him and shuts the door. The vicar's wife, who's been listening, yells: "£100 for four small windows? He must've seen you coming!"'

Hannah drove home. As she passed Malik & Malik, she smiled to herself; Rosa might have portrayed nonchalance when it came to discussing Eva's new dentist, Sam Burrows, but she knew both her sisters inside out. How could she not? They'd shared a womb together; the same blood ran in their veins. Rosa might be a vicar, and Eva might be married, but all three had inherited Alice's genes when it came to fancying a good-looking man. And Sam Burrows was certainly that. May the best woman – or vicar – win. She smiled again as she turned into her street.

And then, heart thumping, all thoughts of Sam Burrows were immediately erased from her mind as Ben stepped out of his car, leaning against it until she drew up behind him and stepped onto the pavement.

'Oh, Hannah.' Ben reached warm fingers to her face, burying his hand into her long dark hair, drawing her to him and kissing the corner of her mouth. 'I've been waiting here for the last hour. I've been thinking about you all day.'

Hannah said nothing but, separating her door key from its mates, took Ben's hand and led her cheese on toast – Wensleydale with Branston – up the path and to her front door.

18

'Eva, love, you looking very…' Azra turned from wiping the kitchen surface, J-cloth held almost at ninety degrees as she tried, but failed, to reach an orange splash of something above the stove.

'Very?' Eva filled the kettle, pressed the red switch and hunted for coffee.

'You looking very… glamorous. Very very pizzaz.' Azra took a blatantly unsubtle sniff at the air around Eva. 'And patients must like coming to have teeth out with you rather than Rayan because you smell very delicious.' She paused and frowned. 'Maybe skirt just a little too near your bottom?'

'Don't worry, Azra, my patients usually have their eyes screwed shut tight in fear rather than open and looking at my bum.' Eva gave her an on/off smile – what was it about Azra that made her want to say rude words like *bum*? Quite possibly, having her mother-in-law still in situ after her unexpected – and uninvited – arrival two weeks earlier, had Eva reverting to being a child once more. A rebellious teenager answering back with more than rude words – she'd dared to say *fuck* a couple of times – at Susan, when her mother had challenged her for bleaching her dark hair blonde and wearing the nearest she could get to Ecko, Unltd. Fubu, and PNB Nation T-shirts and cargo pants, brands that incorporated spray paint and street art into their clothing, and which Eva knew brought her nearer to Alice and the world of art she felt she'd been denied.

'Anyway,' Eva went on, relenting, 'your son wants us all

looking and smelling wonderful in his ambition to rule the gleaming white world of choppers.'

'Choppers?' Azra beamed. 'Rayan such good boy. He always *was* such good boy. When we put him in for exam to go to Bradford Grammar, and he pass so well he get almost full scholarship, Dad come home with Raleigh Chopper for him.'

'I know, he told me.' Rayan had also told her how uncles and cousins had rallied round to help pay the remaining private school fees and that the said second-hand Chopper must have been ten years old at least. His mates, on their drop-handle, twenty-gear machines, had hooted with mirth as he sat astride the present his parents had been so proud to present him with. Rayan had soon 'had the bike pinched' and gone to work at his dad's cousin's corner shop and newsagent's in Little Horton, every Saturday and Sunday and school holidays. Despite Faisal Malik telling him he needed to stay at home to do his homework, to not squander this wonderful opportunity to make the very best of himself, Rayan had been up at 6 a.m. in order to earn and save up for a *proper* bike. And he still managed to come out with the highest number of GCSEs in his cohort, and the straight A's needed for dental school.

He'd always been so full of energy and ambition, had Rayan. That's what Eva had fallen in love with: his knowing just where he wanted to be and how to go about it. Whereas she, Eva, had deferred to what her family wanted, proud at her skill with maths and the sciences, and accepted the place at Sheffield rather than art college. She should have followed her instinct and taken a year off after A-levels, gone to stay with Alice in New York, but everyone – apart from Bill and Hannah – had been against it.

Eva glanced round at her beautiful modern kitchen: at Azra cleaning behind the fridge; at Jodie picking up scattered toys and jigsaw pieces in the room across the hall and knew, to her utter shame, that it wasn't enough. She picked up Nora who was running towards her, arms stretched out to be picked up, and reassured herself that this *was* enough. It was more than enough. It had to be.

'You're looking a bit dolled up.' Tamsin, one of the fleet of receptionists now needed to run the ever-expanding surgery, looked up from her computer and whistled. 'And get your scrubs on or the boss will be after you.' She grinned in Eva's direction. 'Oops, I forgot, you are the boss.'

'Absolutely,' Eva said tartly. 'And *don't* you forget it. And if you insist on eating sweets –' Eva indicated the corner of a packet of Haribo's peeking out from behind the computer '– can I suggest you keep them out of sight? And throw me a few too.'

Eva walked along the corridor to her room, chewing and enjoying the fruity-flavoured rubber.

'Oh, Eva, hi.' Sam Burrows appeared from Rayan's old practice room ahead of her, and Eva felt herself start to blush like a damned teenager.

'I thought you were coming in this afternoon to get yourself organised?' Eva hastily chewed and swallowed the four red Haribo she'd filched and crammed into her mouth, before bringing up her hand to contain the powerful smell of chemically formulated strawberry. God, she *was* acting like a teenager.

'Well, I was, but then I decided to come in this morning and get cracking. Move my stuff in, you know?' He held up framed certificates and a mug with *I want the tooth, the whole tooth and nothing but the tooth* emblazoned on the front. 'Any idea where I can find a couple of nails and a hammer?'

'You'll find we've moved on from hammers – we actually use drills, probes and mirrors here.'

Sam laughed, showing his own highly impressive set of beautifully white and straight teeth. Then he frowned. 'Can you smell strawberry?'

'Probably one of the new candles Rayan keeps lighting everywhere. He's trying to emulate a health spa. Either that or trying to set the place on fire to recoup the insurance...' Hell, what *was* she rabbiting on about? She swallowed the residue of the gummy sweets, ran her tongue over her teeth and smiled to show she was joking. Or had she just looked ridiculously suggestive, grinning while running her tongue over her lips like that? She'd totally forgotten the nuances of how to show a man she was interested. Totally out of practice. Maybe she should practise on her patients?

Bloody hell, she fancied him. She did hope she didn't have a red tongue.

'Right, OK.' Sam stared at her strangely as, almost mesmerised, she took in the golden hair and freckles on his tanned arms below the short-sleeved scrubs; his gorgeous dark eyes, his broad shoulders contained within the dark green cotton, his bare feet in a pair of crocs. 'Must get on...'

'If there's anything I can do to help you settle in, don't be afraid to ask.' Eva hoped her tone was somewhere between professional and friendly. Maybe with a slight hint of an *I fancy you like mad, big boy*. God, she really *was* out of practice. When, on Rayan's last birthday, she'd dressed in a black basque, suspenders, stockings and her one pair of red-soled black Louboutins, Rayan had asked, almost kindly, did she realise she'd still got her shoes on in the bedroom and, smoothing her side of the bed for her to get in as, still half undressed she must be chilly, continued reading *Cycling Weekly* until, with a chaste kiss, he'd turned off the light. And himself over.

Eva patted Sam's arm and walked past him into her own room. Oh hell, was she his mother now, patting his arm like that? Yes, she was definitely out of practice.

Across at Westenbury Vicarage, Rosa cleaned out the bath, threw Toilet Duck down the ancient wooden-seated loo before giving it a once-over with the toilet brush. She moved on to hoover the threadbare stair carpet with a feeble machine that must have been around when Methuselah was a lad, before setting off, Flash in hand, for the downstairs bathroom. The Church Young Wives Committee (CYWC) were round in half an hour, wanting to finalise preparations for some hoedown they'd arranged for a Saturday evening towards Christmas, and she didn't want Hilary Makepeace or, come to that – especially come to that – her sister, Virginia, inspecting her toilet and finding it wanting. *Cleanliness is next to godliness* and all that. She'd bet any money male vicars didn't clean their own lavatories or wash their own kitchen floors. Or maybe they did? Rosa wondered, not for the first time, whether she should use some of the money from the sale of the London apartment – guiltily invested instead of given to the poor and needy – for a new Dyson and toilet seat.

When she was training – she'd opted to go back to Durham – to become a vicar, Rosa had been quite shocked by the levels of financial hardship among some clergy who had mentored her. One lovely man, a fifty-year-old reverend whose wife had apparently run off a year earlier with a local Lottery winner with millions, had been quite dismissive about advising Rosa when, a year into her training, she began to have doubts about what the hell she was doing, questioning just why she was taking this path. Had she given up her former life because Joe had given up on her? Or was it because she'd been ill that she was now giving her life to God and the service of others? If either, or both of these, were the reason, then surely these were not reason enough?

It had taken a lot of soul-searching on Rosa's behalf for her to accept that both her cancer diagnosis, as well as losing Joe, had most certainly been the catalysts in her decision to become a vicar, but that these were by no means the main reason. She had, she finally accepted, through most of her life turned to God when times were both good and not so good. God, she acknowledged, had not only always been there for her, but she'd been there for *Him*. She believed in him. Believed in his presence, believed it was the reason they were all here.

Anyway, this lovely reverend hadn't been particularly

interested in *why* Rosa had taken her pathway to God. He was more determined to question her on the *how*? Did she think she was prepared, and willing – and able – to serve her community as well as she might if worrying about paying the bills, or shelling out for a new washer when the one left behind by the previous incumbent finally gave up the ghost? Would she be able to manage on the money, seemed to be all he was asking.

Rosa mulled all this over as she toasted a current teacake, smothered it in butter and Susan's homemade blackberry jam, and devoured it while standing at the chilly sitting-room window, watching a couple of squirrels race across the frost-rimmed lawn. *Sod it*, she thought. *Sorry, God, I'm having a new hoover*, and, shoving the remains of her breakfast into her mouth, chewed, swallowed and set off to put on some make-up.

Blimey, they *were* out in force. Rosa opened the heavy stained-glass windowed front door to the good women of Westenbury Young Wives. Bit of a misnomer, that one, Rosa mentally chortled, as she welcomed in six of the village church worthies, at least half of whom must have been drawing their pensions for years, and the other half possibly no longer married.

Virginia, obviously wanting to gain Brownie points by claiming sororal knowledge of the new vicar, was first over the threshold, uncharacteristically hugging Rosa to her bony chest while smiling importantly back at the others. 'Do come in and meet our new village vicar, girls – my sister, Rosa Quinn.'

'Hello, do come in, all of you. Kettle's boiled and I've even got custard creams.'

'Oh, never mind about them custard creams, lass; we've come fully organised.' The woman laughed, patted Rosa in a friendly manner and, placing her head on one side, winked conspiratorially in her direction.

'Maureen? Oh, Maureen?' Rosa's eyes widened as Maureen Hardcastle, last seen over a cheese and double beetroot sandwich in Tea and Cake, the café on the Heatherly estate, moved in for a hug.

'Hey up, love, how're you doing?' Maureen went in for a full motherly squeeze and Rosa hugged her back warmly. It felt so different to be hugging real squashy flesh than the half-hearted embrace allowed by Virginia. 'Now, are you alright, love? I heard you'd been poorly? Hmm, should have brought you some cheese and beetroot...' She broke off, laughing, and turned to the others. 'Rosa here couldn't get enough of a bit of cheddar and beetroot, could you, love?'

'You're not still at the café, are you, Maureen?'

'I am that. Don't you go putting me out to pasture just yet. Mind you, I only do two days now and I gave up my *managerial* role. Some young chef in there now who took over at the helm. Doing all sorts of fancy foreign carry-on – you know that couscous stuff and rocket leaves.' Maureen pulled out a tinfoil parcel. 'So, I've got a right grand quiche here and...' she delved once more, bringing out a Tupperware box '...and some nice roast beef and our Ron's horseradish sandwiches.' She turned to the others, expectantly. 'Right, come on, what have you lot brought?'

The others obediently emptied carrier bags and paper bags of goodies. Hilary Makepeace had a cheesecake, Pandora Boothroyd a beautifully presented plate of selected hors d'oeuvres and Virginia a bottle of non-alcoholic elderflower wine.

'You could have brought some of the hard stuff, Virginia.' Hilary grinned in Rosa's direction. 'I remember our vicar here knocking back more than her share of Liebfraumilch at some do when we were playing Spin the Bottle. Did you actually get off with Darren Crawshaw at that party?' Hilary asked the question as though it was still a current topic of conversation and she'd been biding her time, wanting to know the answer, for the past twenty years. 'Mind you, he's done alright for himself has Darren. Runs his dad's butcher's shop now. On Market Street, in the village. Got another two shops somewhere as well.'

'Lovely.' Rosa felt quite winded with all this information thrown at her at ten o'clock on a Wednesday morning. As well as the food and goodies that were now being unwrapped on her kitchen table, just as she'd eaten breakfast.

'So, this is *lovely*,' she managed to finally get out. 'Do you always make such a...' she wanted to say *performance* but thought better of it '...such a *party* of your meetings.'

'Oh aye, love.' Maureen was adamant. 'Gets us out of the house and up for a bit of a gossip. After we've done all the church stuff of course,' she added sternly. 'Oh sorry, everyone, this is Alexandra.' Maureen beckoned to the young pretty girl standing shyly behind the others. 'I've brought her along with me today, to see what she thinks. You know, whether she wants to join us on a permanent basis.'

'Oh, Alex please.' The girl blushed slightly. 'Alexandra is such a mouthful. And, I'm sorry, I've brought nothing to the feast; I thought it would be a coffee and a biscuit and a going through of a bit of an agenda.'

'Well, we certainly have an agenda,' Virginia said, giving Maureen a look. 'And we need to get on with it; decide who is doing what. It's only a month or so away, you know. Now, did you manage to get the cowboy hats, Hilary?'

'Of course. When I say I'll do something, I always deliver the goods. Make sure they come good and proper.'

Rosa wanted to laugh, remembering Eva's gossip about Hilary pleasuring the sixth-form boys down in the graveyard, as Hilary pulled another plastic carrier towards her. 'Now, they're a bit *pink*, but I got them as a job lot on eBay and, knowing you said we had to keep costs down, Virginia, I think they'll do the job. I mean, I think they're rather pretty.' Hilary gave an uncharacteristically nervous bark of laughter and passed a committee hat to each Young Wife, who dutifully tried them on.

'They're certainly *pink*, Hilary.' Pandora Boothroyd pulled hers onto her blonde bob somewhat gingerly.

'And a bit bloody – sorry, Vicar – rude as well.' Doreen Hirst, reading the back of Pandora's hat now perched somewhat jauntily over one eye, started to laugh. '*Learner Bride: Proficient Sex Goddess.*'

'Oh, we can ink the messages out with a bit of marker pen,' Hilary said airily. 'Although, to be honest, I quite like mine. It's a bit poetic… *Miss to Mrs with all my bitches…*'

'It only rhymes if you pronounce it *bitchies*,' Doreen sniffed, obviously slightly put out with *Mum of the Bride* etched onto the back of her own hat.

'*Boss Babe*,' Maureen pulled her own hat off and round to read. 'That'll do me.' She winked across at Rosa, who was beginning to wonder if she was in some sort of kaleidoscopically pink nightmare and that very soon, she'd wake up in her own bed. In London. Still with Joe.

'Here, love.' Maureen frisbeed a cowgirl hat in the direction of Alexandra, who lunged to one side – as if intercepting a pass from an opposition wing attack – and caught it deftly with one hand. '*Virgin on the Ridiculous*. Will that do you?'

'Er, yes, if I must.' Alexandra shot an anxious look towards Rosa, who grinned conspiratorially back. Here was someone her own age, Rosa thought. Someone maybe to be friends with. She *did* miss Carys; did miss the close female friendship they'd afforded each other. Of course, she had Eva and Hannah and, now that she'd moved back to the village, it was wonderful that she was going to be seeing them so much more but, at the end of the day, they were so involved in their own lives: Eva with work, the children and a marriage Rosa could now see was looking in need of some TLC. And Hannah had her own gang of girlfriends she met up with often. As well as being embroiled in an affair with a married man. Rosa smiled again at Alex. She didn't recognise her from school or college and she didn't have a local accent.

'Where are you from, Alex?' Rosa asked, heading off to find glasses for Virginia's elderflower wine which, once she'd opened it, smelled alarmingly like cat pee.

'Grantham, Lincolnshire,' she replied.

'Have you been in the village long?'

'We don't actually live here in Westenbury. We're a good twenty minutes at the other side of Midhope, but Little Acorns has such an amazing reputation, I want my own kids to go there.' She went slightly pink. 'I mean, I'm not here just to ingratiate myself, sucking up to the vicar in order to get an out of area place for my children...' Alex trailed off, embarrassed.

'You wouldn't be the first, love.' Doreen Hirst raised a somewhat cynical eyebrow. 'There's a queue a mile long trying to get in with Mrs Beresford; I had problems getting my own grandkids in there, even though I've been a regular churchgoer for years.'

'You're welcome here anytime, Alex.' Rosa smiled again, feeling for the obviously embarrassed girl in the pink cowboy hat in front of her. 'Lovely to have you here. I've only been here myself a week or so, so don't think I have much, if *any*, influence on who gets a place across at Little Acorns. But –' Rosa turned away from the others who were handing round plates and napkins and whispered '– even though I don't have kids myself, I can totally understand you doing anything –' Rosa laughed '– including wearing a rude pink hat, in order to do the best for them.' Rosa turned back to the other women who were calling order to the meeting, as well as tucking in to the food in front of them. 'OK, who's chair?'

'So, are you in contact with them other two?' Maureen had stayed behind once the others had left, clearing the kitchen table, wrapping up what was left and, despite Rosa's slight protestations that, really, she shouldn't, piling the remaining food into the vicarage fridge. 'Vicar's perks.' Maureen had grinned and, rolling her up her sleeves to reveal the powerful forearms Rosa recalled from her days in Tea and Cake, set to, attacking the washing up.

'What other two?' Rosa joined her at the sink, tea towel to hand. 'You mean Eva and Hannah?'

'No.' Maureen shook her head, frowning. 'Up at the hall. You *know*?'

Rosa shook her head. 'Who?'

'Oh, *I* don't know what they're called. Bill's second wife's two. You *know*.' Maureen handed Rosa a dish to dry. 'I suppose they're actually your brother and sister? Well, half-brother and sister, anyroad?'

'Henrietta and Jonny?'

Maureen nodded. 'I suppose this Jonny will inherit Heatherly Hall now?'

'I suppose he will,' Rosa smiled. 'But Bill's had very little to do with them as far as I know. You'll know better than me, Maureen. Diana, their mother, went off with someone called Roger McConville? All before my time, but I think he was the lead singer of the Screaming Eagles? After a big concert Bill decided to hold in the grounds to pay off a few more of his debts. He's always said it was the worst idea moneymaking idea he ever had. Not because Diana hopped it, but because the grounds were left in an awful mess. Anyway, according to Bill, Diana was fed up of not having the money and society she'd assumed she was marrying into. A famous rock star, living in Los Angeles, was apparently a lot better bet than a cold draughty hall in West Yorkshire,' Rosa laughed. 'Especially when it turned out the estate didn't have the money for all the shoes, bags and holidays in St Tropez she hankered after.'

'Bill and her weren't married long, were they?'

'No, she was a model from London—'

'Aye, I know. I remember. They were married the same year as the Queen's Silver Jubilee. I remember, because it was the same year Ron and I got married. It were a right cold miserable summer was 1977; we all thought it was going to be another scorcher like 1976, but we brides all shivered in our thin wedding dresses.'

'Bill doesn't talk about her *or* Henrietta and Jonny much.' Rosa smiled. 'I think from actually meeting Diana in London, to her divorcing him on grounds of cruelty, was no more than five years or so.'

'Cruelty?' Maureen looked shocked. 'Bill Astley doesn't have a cruel bone in his body. He's a right grand lad is Bill. No airs and graces at all, gives me a hug whenever he sees me and always comes into the café for a chat and a mug of tea.'

Rosa laughed again. 'I think the cruelty involved having to live up here in Yorkshire rather than back in London, and not having the funds to live the lavish lifestyle Diana was convinced she'd bought into. Anyway, she ran off with Roger McConville, taking the children with her and, I think, Bill was a bit relieved all round. He's had little to do with the two children and, now they're adults, with what Bill calls *bloody awful Californian accents and ideas*, he's not had much to do with any part of their lives.'

'They must be well into their forties now – they'll be after their inheritance once Bill kicks it.' Maureen sniffed and nodded her head knowledgably.

'I'm not convinced there is much.' Rosa smiled again. 'Seriously.'

'Don't you believe it.' Maureen elbowed Rosa before hanging up the dishcloth over the tap. 'The hall is doing pretty well at the moment, particularly as a wedding venue.'

'Well, I suppose, as the only son and heir, Jonny's in line to become the thirteenth Marquess of Heatherly.'

'It was a right tragedy when Elizabeth, Bill's first wife, died in that fire in Scotland.' Maureen shook her head. 'It was terrible. I don't think Bill ever got over it, or ever loved anyone like he loved her. And poor Henry, Bill's first son, was only five or so when his mum died. He were a right grand lad as well. Just like his dad, he was. And then even more tragedy for Bill when Henry himself died. And that lad was only eighteen or so, you know, Rosa.'

Rosa nodded. 'He died a couple of years before we three were born,' she said, 'so we never knew him. I don't think

Bill – or Henry – ever got over Elizabeth dying in Scotland in such horrible circumstances.'

'Probably why Henry turned to drugs. Overdose, was it?'

'Hmm.' Rosa folded her arms and leaned against the sink. 'Terribly sad. Bill won't talk about it much – you know, losing his wife and then his son.'

'Aye, well, I reckon Henry would have made a much better marquess than this American son no one really knows. Shame all round, really. Right, love, must get off and stop this gossiping and get our Ron's dinner ready. Lovely to see you back here. I reckon you'll make a right good vicar. Just what the village needs.'

19

Sunday morning and Eva was feeling a sense of anticipation; a frisson of excitement even. A feeling of there being something rather lovely in her life at the moment. She was taking her girls to church to watch Aunty Rosa's inaugural speech. Or was that title only for incoming American presidents? Aunty Rosa was making her *maiden speech*? Was that any better, or was that only given by new and nervous MPs? What was the very first Sunday sermon given by a new village vicar actually called? Eva, standing at her mirror, towelled herself down and sprayed perfume liberally. The First Sunday Sermon more than likely. Eva selected her favourite cream Lepel bra and matching briefs, almost caressing the flimsy cloud of lace as she slipped them seductively onto her body, pouting at her reflection before closing her eyes and wishing they were being slipped slowly *off it*...

'Why are you pulling silly faces in the mirror? And why are your eyes closed?' Laila, still in her *Frozen* nightie, was standing behind her. 'Are you tired?'

'Laila, why are you not dressed yet?' Embarrassment at being caught out fantasising about Sam Burrows removing her pants – oh so slowly – made Eva's tone sharper than she'd intended. 'We're leaving in half an hour,' she relented, smiling, before reaching down to plant a kiss on Laila's dark head. 'I want you and Nora looking lovely. We're Aunty Rosa's family and we're going to sit right at the front and sing our hearts out to welcome her to her new church.'

'*You* can't sing.' Laila was dismissive. 'You weren't very good when we had that karaoke machine at Daddy's birthday party.'

I wasn't very good at seducing Daddy in my suspenders and Louboutins on the said man's birthday, either, Kiddo, Eva was very tempted to reply. But, instead, the sense of anticipation wrapping seductively around her like a warm shawl, she smiled beatifically, kissed Laila once more and sent her off to get dressed.

'We're going to be late,' Eva shouted crossly, any sense of anticipation evaporating at seeing Nora still in pyjama bottoms at the top of the stairs. 'Nora, I laid out all your lovely Sunday clothes for you. Your new tights, your new shiny black shoes. Laila was supposed to be helping you get dressed. Laila?'

'Laila is here with me,' Azra shouted from the bedroom she'd moved into over two weeks earlier. 'She's helping *me* get dressed.'

'Are you going out?' Eva called back, surprised. Azra rarely set foot out of the house unless it was to go to Aldi, where she'd recently discovered, and become slightly obsessed with, the lure of the middle aisle, galvanising first her daughter and now Eva, Rayan or Jodie to drive her and leave her there for a good hour, emerging triumphant with a two-kilo pack of smoked salmon, disposable coffee cups, a football-jersey-shaped peanut dispenser and, last week, a marine safety kit.

Azra's head appeared round the bedroom door. 'Of course, I come to your church with you to cheer on your sister. To sing songs and support her.'

'It's not a football match, Azra. There's not much cheering to be had in a C of E church.' Hell, this was all she needed. 'Laila, please go and help your sister.'

'But, Mummy, I'm helping Nanni Azra to look beautiful for God...' her voice trailed off '...but I don't know where the end of all this glittery material is.'

Eva peeled off her leather gloves and, regardless of her black suede high-heeled boots, took the stairs two at a time. 'You go and help Nora, please, Laila, and I'll sort Nanni.'

'Right,' Eva finally said two minutes later, as she pinned the ends of the gorgeous pink fabric onto Azra's shalwar kameez. 'There you go. Now, are you sure about this, Azra? Does your God allow you in a Christian church? I mean I don't want you getting his back up...' She trailed off, not sure what to say without giving offence.

'Now, Eva, love, both Pope and Archbishop of Canterbury have prayed with Muslims before, and done it in open public. It perfectly possibly to do so without... without *compromising*... own faith. And,' she went on, 'we live in multicultural place. I wouldn't miss this *jamboree* for nothing. Allah be very pleased I'm cheering Rosa on. And finding out what goes on with your lot. It's what families do. Allah will be...'

'OK, OK.' Eva put up a hand in Azra's direction before checking her own lipstick in the hallway mirror. 'Let's go. Are we all ready?'

Eva took Laila's hand who took Nora's hand who dutifully took Azra's hand and they trooped off, in line, down the drive to the car.

Once in the Evoque, Eva's thoughts turned once more to Sam. How eager had he appeared when she'd suggested he might like to join them all in the village church this morning? Get to know his new village? Eva smiled at her own reflection in the mirror, checked her lipstick once more and put the car into gear as she answered her own question – *Very*.

Hannah rolled over, opened one bleary eye and, lifting Ben's arm from its position across her middle, squinted at his watch before uttering a silent oath. And then, when Ben made no response to her kicking at his leg, uttered the curse aloud. 'Ben, it's six o'clock. For heaven's sake, wake up. Get up and go home.

Your emergency aneurysm would have been done and dusted hours ago.'

'You can't hurry an op,' Ben sang sleepily, aping Diana Ross. 'Five hours at least if you're going for a complex craniotomy. It's dark out there, Hans; it's the middle of the night still.' He pulled Hannah towards him, reaching for her breast, moving his mouth towards it and then south.

'I mean it,' Hannah said, loving what he was doing to her body, but terrified he was pushing his luck with the amount of time he was spending with her lately. 'And *of course* it's dark out there – it's 6 a.m. on a November morning.' Hannah sat up in bed, peering behind the Laura Ashley curtains she'd chosen for her bedroom, and which she now wasn't so sure about. They appeared a bit girly, a bit frothy when she was trying to be a sophisticated woman of the world. When she was, in fact, a mistress, aiding and abetting this man to cheat on his wife and children. Shame engulfed her like a cold shower as it always did when, in the cold light of day, she assessed what she'd been doing.

Again.

Indigestion following the devouring of too much cheese on toast. With Branston.

Ben jumped out of bed, headed for the shower, obliterating, Hannah thought sadly, all trace of herself from his body. Off for breakfast with his wife and children; Sunday lunch – roast beef and Yorkshire pudding and all the trimmings – followed by a walk, his younger child on his shoulders. His cheating daddy's shoulders.

Once her front door had banged closed on her married lover, Hannah tried to catch up on another hour's sleep, but found she couldn't drift off. Before 7 a.m., she was up herself, cleaning the flat from top to bottom – the best way, she'd found, to overcome any lingering indigestion – and by 9 a.m. was showered, made up and in her favourite dress, black coat and boots, the very picture of pious sobriety, and on her way to church to celebrate Rosa's first sermon in her new church.

Rosa woke up feeling sick. *This is ridiculous*, she scolded herself. *You are a vicar of three years' standing. You're not a novice; this isn't your very first time standing in the pulpit.* She supposed it was because this was a home game with all her family out in front ready to cheer her on. Oh God, what if she dried up? What if she fluffed her lines? What if she fainted? *You've never fainted once in your life*, she reminded herself. *Now, get a grip, girl – God is with you.*

She'd already been across to the church that morning, sitting in the front pew where she always used to sit with Susan and her sisters when she was a little girl. She was instantly back thirty years, where she would be sitting quietly and attentively, reverentially even, on one side of Susan, Virginia on the other, while Eva and Hannah, further down the pew, drummed their heels against the wood, kneeled when they shouldn't, picked at scabs on their knees, turned round, whispered and giggled (*just like Alice used to do*, Susan sighed to Richard, on their return) before leaning over to Susan and asking in a loud whisper: *Is it finished yet? Is it over? Can we go home? I want to wee...* Anything to get away from the Reverend Cecil's long-winded and sanctimonious sermons.

In the end, Susan had left the other two at home with Richard and the dog, taking only Virginia and Rosa. The church had continued to play a big part in Virginia's life but, by the age of ten, Rosa too had had enough and joined Eva and Hannah in voting with their feet.

So, early that morning, as she so often had during the past couple of weeks, she'd unlocked the heavy outer doors with the huge key, drawn back the bolts and walked down the chilly aisle, loving the fact that this was her church; that she was responsible for its smooth running, for inviting and encouraging the villagers into its hallowed space. She'd sat in the front pew she knew so well and bowed her head, giving thanks for the calm she felt here, asking for assurance that she'd made the correct decision in actually returning here. For the ability to forgive and forget; giving thanks for the wonderful team who had saved her life six years previously; for strength to live the life she now had, rather than the life – and with the man – she'd once taken for granted would be hers forever.

The church began to fill up, parishioners moving towards their preferred pews, some stopping in the nave to greet and introduce themselves to Rosa, others ushering elderly relatives to their seats and hushing small offspring. Rosa looked round. It was all going to be alright – she wasn't going to be talking to just a handful of worshippers on this, her first Sunday as the village vicar.

'OK, sweetheart? Nervous?' Bill was at her side, patting her arm before joining Eva and her two, and – Rosa smiled – a waving Azra at the very front. She watched as Bill leaned on his stick, wheezing slightly, his arthritic knee and hip obviously bothering him again and then actually laughed as Nora broke free from Laila's hand, her little legs in their white tights, running towards Rosa while shouting in glee at seeing her aunty, but then halting, unsure, as Rosa turned in her full white liturgical surplice. Rosa picked her up and kissed her, swinging her round before walking back down the nave to return her to Eva.

'You OK?' Eva whispered.

And she was. Susan and Richard had arrived, followed by Hannah, who was looking particularly stunning in full make-up, black coat and boots. Cassie Beresford from Little Acorns was soon joined by the teacher – Grace Stevens, was it? – who had laughed out loud at the Benjamin Balloon punchline, accompanied by two small children and a rather striking older dark-haired man.

The Young Wives who had shared their goodies with her only

a couple of days earlier were out in force and, as Rosa turned to walk down the aisle to stand at the back of the church, she saw the newcomer – Alexandra – making her way through the congregation. She seemed nervous, unsure where to sit and, as she lifted the smaller of her two children onto her hip, Rosa greeted her warmly. 'Come on down.' Rosa smiled in what she hoped was encouragement and then, conscious she sounded like some TV game show host added, 'Look, why don't you join my sister, Hannah? She's sitting by herself behind the rest of my family. I'm sure she'd like some company.'

The girl's pale face coloured slightly, and she was obviously ill at ease. 'Thank you,' she said somewhat stiffly and made her way down to the front, seating herself and the two children next to Hannah.

As the church clock struck ten-thirty, the organist, Daphne Merton, turned in anticipation towards Rosa who mouthed, 'Go for it, Daphne,' and the church was filled with the first – vivacissimo and exceptionally fortissimo – notes of 'At the Name of Jesus' as Daphne, full of breathless enthusiasm, pulled out all the stops – quite literally – and did just that.

'Welcome. Welcome all,' Rosa started. 'How lovely to see so many of you here for my very first Sunday service in Westenbury. What a brilliant turnout.' Rosa beamed at the congregation in front of her. 'I do hope you'll all join us *every* Sunday and not just today to see if I'm going to be any good at this. I'm sure many of you know I grew up here in Westenbury and, although I've been away for the last twenty years or so, I can't tell you how good it is to be home…' Rosa trailed off, realising that what she was saying was the truth and not just the spiel she'd practised in front of the mirror in the chilly vicarage bathroom mirror earlier that morning.

She suddenly stopped talking, her eyes arrested by her family and those she loved gazing encouragingly back at her: her adored sisters, Eva and Hannah; Susan and Richard who had sacrificed so much to bring the three of them up with an abundance of love and acceptance; Bill, her birth father who loved the three of them unconditionally. Rosa felt tears threaten and had to shake herself mentally. That would go down well – the new vicar sobbing uncontrollably at the pulpit like some sort of loon.

'Let's get this show on the road with a jolly good sing,' she finally managed to blurt out, nodding towards Daphne who, quivering with expectation at the organ like a fired-up meercat, turned back to the keys. 'Oh and –' Rosa paused '– there are two more *just like me* down in the cheap seats –' she waved a hand, grinning, towards Eva and Hannah '– who'll sprag you up if you don't.'

The whole congregation laughed, none louder than Hannah, who closed her eyes briefly in relief, loving Rosa, loving that she appeared to be confidently making such a great start to her new job. Nora, already fidgeting at Eva's side, took the opportunity, while everyone was standing to sing, to climb and position herself on the wooden pew before turning to stare at the two children belonging to the woman who had slid into the seat behind her. Nora, having made eye contact with the little girl who must have been around her own age, obviously decided, as formal little girl introductions had apparently been made, to up the ante, and did a sort of round off over the pew to land on Hannah's quickly seated knee.

'That one's going to be a gymnast,' the elderly woman behind Hannah laughed between verses three and four of 'Fight the Good Fight', and Hannah started to giggle.

'How old is your little girl?' Hannah whispered, smiling at the woman at her side once they were all seated again.

'She's just two and, this one here –' the woman stroked the blond hair of the little boy on her other side '– is five.'

'Lovely,' Hannah whispered, smiling. 'You're very lucky.'

'Well yes, I am,' the woman whispered back as her little girl and Nora began some silent sort of Follow my Leader game involving kneeling, and then sitting on, the hassocks. 'But unfortunately, they're a bit sad because they're not seeing their daddy as much as they should.'

'Oh?' Hannah whispered back, even though Rosa was in full throttle at the pulpit and Virginia was turning to give the pair of them a silent admonishment to shut up whispering. 'Is he away a lot?'

'Working too hard.' The woman appeared to be giving full attention to Rosa's sermon, which, going by the congregation laughing along with their new vicar, was obviously a funny one.

'Oh?'

'Hmm, he's a brain surgeon at Midhope General and called in to do a lot of emergencies, particularly at night.'

'Right.' Hannah felt her heart pound, her pulse race.

'Mind you –' the woman leaned towards Hannah and whispered confidentially '– I reckon that's all a bit of a cover. I think he's actually having an affair.'

'Right.' Hannah thought she might hyperventilate, and considered telling the woman she felt faint and needed air. She did actually feel faint and need air, she acknowledged, her mouth dry, her armpits wet. But she was rooted to the spot. Nora, obviously bored with the game she'd just initiated with the woman's daughter, climbed onto Hannah's knee, popped her thumb in her mouth and stared at the woman instead.

'I think this harlot who's –' she lowered her voice and leaned once more into Hannah, disregarding Nora's presence '– *fucking* my husband is a youth worker.'

Hannah said nothing but stared woodenly ahead, shame and mortification flooding through her in equal measures.

'And, I even know her name.' The woman leaned back a little, appraising Hannah fully now. 'It's Hannah. Hannah Quinn. I believe she's the new vicar's sister. I don't suppose *you* know who the bitch is? Mind you, after a night spent whoring with my husband, I don't suppose she'd have the gall to come and sit in church. In her sister's church…'

White-faced and trembling with fear, guilt and mortification, Hannah found she couldn't speak. As Rosa intoned, 'Let us pray,' and the congregation closed its collective eyes and knelt, the woman – Alexandra – patted Hannah, almost comfortingly on the back and said, 'I think we're done here, don't you?' She stood and, as Rosa said a final amen, beaming round at her parishioners, gathered her two children to her, took their hands and walked slowly – almost regally – past the seated and kneeling churchgoers. She turned slowly at the end of the red-carpeted nave, resting her large Mulberry handbag on the font before facing the pulpit and uttering one sentence in a loud and clear, measured voice: 'I suggest, Reverend Quinn, you remind your sister of the Sixth Commandment…' before taking her children's hands and walking towards the heavy door at the back, closing it quietly behind her.

20

'OK, you're all coming back with me.' Bill laid a restraining arm on Hannah's own as she made for the car park, seeking the sanctuary of her car. Of her flat. Of her own shame and misery.

'No, no, Bill, I need to go home.'

'You're in no fit state to go home by yourself, Hannah. Mrs Sykes is making lunch for all of us. Had you forgotten?'

'Bill, you saw – and heard – what happened in there.'

'Of course,' Bill said calmly. 'And if you continue to play with fire, Hannah, you must expect to get your fingers burnt *and* for it to finally blow up in your face at some point.'

'Oh, for heaven's sake, Hannah. How *could you*?' Virginia was speaking before she'd even reached Bill and Hannah standing at the far end of the churchyard. 'Have you no *shame*? And me a part-time teacher at Little Acorns. And on Rosa's big day too... *And* in front of Barty and Bethany as well... They're asking to be reminded of the Sixth Commandment.'

'I'm sure you've already filled them in on that, Virginia.' Bill had never found this older sister of theirs easy, and turned away as her two pre-adolescents, lumpy with awkwardness, spots and hormones, followed Tim, their father, towards the car park. But then, obviously annoyed at Virginia's sanctimonious outpourings, Bill turned towards her once more. 'I'm amazed you've managed to keep the pair of them following you to church, Virginia. What's Barty now? Fourteen? I think I was smoking twenty a day and desperate to get my leg over when I was fourteen.'

'Stop it, Bill.' Hannah laid a warning hand on Bill's arm. 'This isn't necessary. I'm sorry, Virginia.'

Two pinpricks of colour had appeared in Virginia's cheeks. 'There really is no need for *smut*, Bill. And, with what Hannah has apparently, been up to, you've obviously had a far greater influence on her than Mum and Dad would ever have hoped for. She's *obviously* got Alice's genes in her veins and we know where *she* ended up. I'd have thought better of you, a man in your position.'

'Oh, get off your effing high horse, Virginia.' Bill actually started to laugh, moving a hand to the now thin and grey ponytail the triplets had spent years trying to persuade him to cut off. 'And smut? A little smut does no one any harm every now and again – ask your husband.'

'I beg your pardon?' Virginia wheeled round, glaring at Bill. 'I need to go. Mum and Dad are coming for their Sunday dinner and I need to get the rice pudding in.' She glared at both Bill and Hannah once more, turning in the direction of her waiting offspring, and then, obviously trying to work out Bill's insinuations re her husband, retorted, with some degree of triumph, over her shoulder, 'You do know what they say about a man with a ponytail?'

'I don't, Virginia, but I'm sure you're about to enlighten me.' Bill was still grinning, one eyebrow raised.

'Under every ponytail there's a horse's *ass*.' Virginia spat the final word before setting off at speed towards her family.

'What's up with her?' Eva, walking towards Hannah and Bill, daughters and mother-in-law in tow, stopped as Virginia stormed past her.

'Bill winding Virginia up as usual.' Hannah, distraught at the trouble she was causing and was continuing to cause, rubbed a hand over her eyes. 'I'm going home.'

'She was being unpleasant, Eva,' Bill said. 'I just intimated that the oh so virtuous Timothy might have a little hidden penchant for girly magazines.'

'And does he?' Eva leaned in towards Bill, eyes wide.

'He likes a bit of titillation as does any man,' Bill grinned. 'He bought four magazines off the top shelf in WHSmith in the middle of Leeds last week. I happened to be in there, buying a birthday card, as he paid for them before furtively hiding them in his *Telegraph*.'

'There's been enough unpleasantness this morning, Bill. There really was no need for all that.' Hannah fished for a non-existent tissue in her coat pocket. 'You know how Virginia always wants to ingratiate herself with you; feels left out when we all get together with you and she's not a part of it. You should have invited her for lunch along with us lot.' Hannah's voice broke as the full impact of what had gone on in church that morning really hit her. 'I'm going.'

'Oh no, you're *not*.' Eva took hold of her arm. 'You need to say something to Mum and Dad. They deserve at least that. They'd no idea that the man you've been keeping to yourself is married. You need to put them in the picture. Before Virginia does just that. *And* you need to apologise to Rosa.'

'Now *you're* beginning to sound like Virginia, Eva.' Hannah rubbed at the smudged mascara underneath her eyes, crying even more at the traces of black on her new pink gloves.

'What do you want me to say, Hannah? Well done?' Eva wasn't happy. 'You totally sabotaged Rosa's first sermon,' she added crossly.

'Azra? You're joining us for lunch, aren't you?' Bill was obviously making an effort to defuse the situation and, when Hannah set off back towards the now-empty church in search of Rosa – as well as Susan and Richard, who she knew would still be with her sister – Bill turned back to Eva. 'Who rocked your boat?'

'Sorry?'

'You're being slightly sanctimonious yourself, Eva. What's up?'

Eva was hardly going to admit, even to Bill, that she'd spent hours tarting herself up that morning, knowing Sam Burrows had said he was going to be in church for the service. And he *was* there, sitting towards the back of the church in a pew all by himself. Eva had craned her neck round several times to get a good look – as well as his attention – her heart doing that little dippy thing when she saw he'd arrived, dressed soberly in shirt and tie underneath a heavy navy overcoat buttoned high against the November cold. God, but he was gorgeous.

Every time she'd peered round – and at one point even told a protesting Nora she must need a wee in order to get up and walk past him – he'd smiled pleasantly, raised a hand in greeting, but immediately turned back to what Rosa was saying or inviting the congregation to do. Oh well, Eva told herself, he was obviously shy. There'd be ample opportunity at work...

Eva was getting cold and the girls were becoming hungry and fractious. 'Bill, why don't you take Azra and the girls back to Heatherly Hall and I'll go and rally Hannah and Rosa. And stop Hannah from slinking off, tail between her legs, back home. She needs gin,' she added. 'And lots of it. I think we all do.'

There was just a handful of people left in the church when Eva made her way back through the doors. There was no sign of Rosa herself, and Daphne Merton, never one to leave the scene of a bit of potential gossip, was still hovering at the organ, giving it what appeared to be several spurts of Pledge and a more than leisurely dust around.

Susan and Richard were making their way down the aisle, Richard holding on to an obviously upset Susan. 'It's fine, it's fine,' he mouthed over Susan's blonde bob. 'Hannah is fine and Rosa's gone to get changed, ready for lunch.'

'It's not Hannah I'm upset about,' Susan said crossly, obviously getting the gist of what Richard was indicating to Eva. 'I *wondered* why we'd never been allowed to meet this mysterious man of hers. Married! A married man! And outed like that in church. In Rosa's church. It's not on, you know.'

'It'll be all over now, Mum,' Eva soothed. 'His wife has found a way to make sure of that.' Eva was secretly impressed with Alexandra Pennington. Ten out of ten for ingenuity and having the balls to do what she did. She needed to remember this little method of outing the other woman if ever she found out Rayan was up to no good in his sweaty cycling Lycra. Eva grinned inwardly at the ridiculous thought of Rayan doing just that. 'Don't worry, Mum, I'll make sure Hannah and Rosa are both alright. You get off and have a lovely lunch with Virginia and Tim.'

And if Timothy disappears for fifteen minutes or so, don't ask where he's been. And make sure he's washed his hands before he carves the Sunday roast.

Eva smiled, feeling quite perky once more. After all, even though Sam Burrows had left church without saying goodbye, he had actually turned up as he'd said he would. And seen her looking her best in her Sunday glad rags. She gave herself a mental high-five.

Eva stopped short as she took in the remaining four people left in church and couldn't quite work out who to be more pissed off with: the older couple sitting right at the back behind the central column of the main vault, presumably keeping out of sight of Rosa until they could get her alone, or the much younger couple deep in conversation, sitting in the pew she'd only recently vacated at the front of the church.

She thought, on balance, it was probably Hannah, returning a pristine handkerchief – after giving a good blow into it – to a smilingly attentive Sam Burrows that was having the effect of making Eva's blood boil.

Once they'd all eaten and drunk far more than was necessary or advisable, Azra had taken Laila and Nora into the little snug off the huge sitting room where both Azra and Nora had fallen fast asleep in front of an ancient black and white video of something called *Bill and Ben the Flowerpot Men*, and Laila had been allowed access to Bill's – not the flowerpot man's – iPad. They'd all then helped Mrs Sykes, Bill's part-time housekeeper, to clear the table and load the dishwasher so she could get off and see to her own family's Sunday dinner before returning to the table with cheese, fruit and a huge cafetière of fresh coffee.

'Come on,' Bill said, brandishing a full bottle of Fonseca vintage port. 'Let's really go for it.' He closed the door on Azra and the girls and poured glasses that were guaranteed to have heads aching the following morning. Rosa passed round plates and a Brie that was on the point of galloping off the cheeseboard. 'And don't any of you girls cut off the nose of that Brie,' he admonished, serving himself a large wedge of mature Cheddar. 'If I've taught you anything about how to behave in society,' he added almost crossly, 'let that be it.'

'Since when have *you* cared about what society thinks? And *you* need to watch it.' Eva frowned. 'All that cheese and port at your age, Bill. I thought your cholesterol wasn't good?'

'Eva, darling, I'm eighty-three years old—'

'Exactly,' Eva sniffed, removing both the cheeseboard and the port from his reach.

'—and if I drop down dead tomorrow, so be it. I've had a good life. I can't complain.'

'Maureen Hardcastle was asking me about Jonny and Henrietta the other day?' Rosa raised a questioning eye in Bill's direction, any talk about Bill's demise resurrecting the question of his successor.

'Maureen Hardcastle is a gossip. Always was and always will be.' Bill drained his glass and, despite Eva shifting the cut-glass decanter nearer to herself, took possession of it once more, filling his glass to the top. 'Forget Henrietta and Jonny – *I'm* trying to – and let's have the low-down and a full analysis on everything that went on in church this morning.' He held up a hand as Hannah started to object, but Bill was determined to have his say.

'So, were the Rosavinas there all along then?' Bill moved from his position at the end of the long table in the huge dining room in order to be nearer to the triplets and thus engage fully in what had happened earlier in church. 'Or did they sneak in at the end, in order to catch you before you left church?'

'I don't think they were sneaking around as you put it,' Rosa frowned. It had been such a shock to see Michelle and Roberto Rosavina sitting there at the back of church. Normally she'd have exited the nave from the side door and would have missed them, but Denis Butterworth, the verger she'd inherited, was tucked up at home with pleurisy and she'd needed to lock up the main doors herself. 'I think they didn't want me to see them and be put off my stride, if that makes sense? Do you know, I'd not seen them for over six years? The last time was the weekend they came to stay with Joe and me in the flat in Wandsworth, just before I became ill. And before Joe went off with Carys.'

'What did they want? Or is that a daft question?' Eva shook her head slightly and poured more port, knowing she needed to get hold of Rayan soon and ask him to pick the four of them up.

'They missed me, they loved me; they didn't want to be in the same town and feel they were unable to come and see me.'

'So did you absolve them from all guilt at what their son had put you through?' Eva laughed mirthlessly. 'And did you bless them and say a prayer over them and send them on their way?'

Rosa smiled. 'Something like that. I mean,' she went on as the other three tutted in her direction, 'it wasn't their fault Joe did what he did.'

'Suppose.' All four mulled this over for a few seconds until Bill said, 'And?'

'And?' Rosa glared back at Bill, knowing exactly what he was aiming at.

'What's Joe Rosavina doing back here? And are you going to see him?'

'What's happened to the Welsh Piece of Work?' Eva interrupted before Rosa could reply. 'Did they say?'

Rosa took a deep breath, recalling the ten-minute chat she'd had with the Rosavinas before saying she really must go, Hannah and Eva were waiting for her in the car park – she was going out for lunch. 'Basically, Carys has done a bunk to Sydney. Fallen in love with some wealthy Australian seconded to a bank she was working with. Left her son and their little girl with Joe and done a runner. Joe spent almost a year in London trying to keep it all together with nannies and the like and then decided to quit the south and come back here where Michelle and Roberto can help out.'

'Aren't they still running the Italian place in town?' Hannah asked. 'I've purposely avoided it for the past six years. You know, on principle. Even though,' she added wistfully, 'their aubergine caponata was to die for.'

'I went further than that,' Eva said darkly. 'Told everyone I knew to avoid the place like the plague: health and safety issues with the spaghetti... possible mouse droppings in the pasta puttanesca...'

'You didn't!' Rosa and Hannah spoke as one while Bill just laughed.

'You're your father's daughter, Eva,' he said simply. 'Loyal to those you love but watch out any who cross you.'

'That really is not on, Eva.' Rosa fingered her dog collar. 'Not on at all. It wasn't Michelle and Roberto's fault Joe ended up where he did. If you want to blame anyone, blame Carys.'

'Oh, does she run a restaurant we can blacklist as well?' Eva smirked.

'Oh, for heaven's sake, Rosa, why must you always blame Carys? Joe saw what was on offer, decided he wanted a piece and took it.' Hannah folded her arms crossly.

'Ah,' Bill put in before Rosa could speak, 'so we shouldn't blame you, Hannah, for pinching this brain surgeon of yours? We should blame Ben?'

When Hannah didn't respond, but simply gazed crossly at the tablecloth, Eva said, 'Oh, come on, Hannah, Carys schemed and lied and had Rosa for a fool. I reckon she knew what she wanted from the very start. She wanted Rosa's business and Rosa's man.'

'Well, she didn't *get* the business, did she?' Rosa frowned remembering how, despite feeling so ill and undergoing treatment, she'd worked with her lawyers and contacts to break up Rosa Quinn Investments and sell the different aspects of it for a good price. That money, together with her share of the apartment in Wandsworth was now, apparently, working for her in stocks and shares. She never asked; not only was she not interested, she didn't feel it had any part in her new life. One day, she was sure, she'd know exactly what to do with it, but for the moment, apart from maybe spending a little of it on doing up the vicarage, it was sitting somewhere offshore, minding its own business.

'She got a lot of your contacts though, didn't she?' Hannah said. 'And Joe went along with it.'

'That's what hurts the most. You know?' Rosa gave a little smile. 'That even though Joe knew what she'd done – to me – he still went off with her. Mind you, there was a baby; Joe just couldn't abandon a baby. Couldn't abandon any child – I suppose that's why he's taken on the responsibility for Carys's fourteen-year-old son rather than pack him off to his grandparents in Wales. If Carys hadn't got herself pregnant…'

'Oh, for heaven's sake, Rosa, we've been down this road before. You don't just *get yourself pregnant*.' Eva was cross. 'It takes two to get pregnant. This isn't the 1950s – women are on the pill, use contraception, know their own bodies.'

'I'm sorry, Eva,' Bill said equally crossly, 'Carys did *just that*. She'd done it before when she was having an affair with that wealthy married man. *He* certainly paid for it, monetarily anyway. And Joe paid for it by losing Rosa.'

'And that was one hell of a loss, Rosa,' Eva said, almost in triumph. 'Joe Rosavina *loved* you, Rosa, from the minute he set eyes on you.'

'Not enough to leave Carys though, was it?' Hannah sniffed.

'He did try.' Rosa, fiddling with the cheese knife, didn't look up.

'Did he? When? You've never told us this.' The other three stared.

'A few weeks after it all blew up. He came back to the flat just as I was packing up a few things to come back to stay with Mum and Dad. You know, before the treatment started back in London. He'd found out *somehow* I'd been diagnosed with Hodgkin's.' Rosa looked straight at Eva, and then across to Hannah.

'Not guilty, m'lud.' Eva held up her two hands and both she and Rosa looked directly across at Hannah.

'It wasn't *me*. I didn't tell him. You'd made us promise not to. Didn't want him coming back to you out of pity, you said. Mind you, I think I picked up the phone a couple of times.'

'It was me,' Bill said calmly, draining his glass. '*I* told him. Told him to boot the Welsh hussy out the door and get back where he belonged. With you, Rosa. You needed him.'

'It was *you*?' Rosa glared at Bill. 'I might have known. Yes, well, I told him no. He had a child on the way.'

'Oh, for heaven's sake, Rosa, *Carys* had a child on the way – her choice, her decision.'

'The thing is, Joe was always going on about us having children. He loves kids. And, I knew then – I'd been told – there was a big possibility the chemo would wreck my fertility. I'd probably never have children.'

'Joe didn't have to *end up with* Carys,' Eva said crossly. 'There wasn't an angry father standing over him with a gun forcing him down the aisle. He could have had shared custody with the child without going off with her. Look at Bill, here.'

'What about me?'

'You didn't marry Alice.'

'Alice didn't *want* to marry me,' Bill protested. 'She didn't want to marry *anyone*. Whereas Carys certainly did want to get her claws into Joe.'

'I heard later that Carys told Joe straight: that if they weren't going to be together then she was going to have… an abortion… I so hate that word… She was planning a termination of his child. I'd said no to him coming back, couldn't forgive him for what he'd done, so she got what she wanted.' Rosa looked at her watch. 'Gosh, look at the time. Your girls need to be in bed, Eva. And all that we've been talking about is a long, long time ago. All water under the bridge. We've all moved on.'

Eva tucked up her sleepy girls, made Azra and Rayan a cup of tea and left them in front of some TV drama they were both into. She did the usual Sunday evening jobs of laying Laila's uniform out in her bedroom, and packing her costume and towel in her sports bag ready for the Monday afternoon swimming lesson. She emptied and refilled the dishwasher, picked up Barbie dolls, AWOL Lego and jigsaw pieces and spent half an hour on her laptop sorting a couple of work things Rayan had asked her to go over. With all the boring but necessary jobs done, she poured herself a glass of wine to top up what she'd got through at Bill's, then settled down at the kitchen table to write and send a text to Hannah:

You OK?

Has Ben been in touch?

Did you have a good chat with Sam Burrows?

Nice, isn't he? What do you think????

Hannah paid the lugubriously silent driver and fell out of the taxi, fumbled with the key in the lock, dragged herself up the stairs and, without taking off her make-up, pulled off her lovely Sunday clothes and boots and fell into the bed that still smelled of Ben. She pulled the duvet over her head and, with the room spinning slightly, sobbed into the pillow.

There was no way she was going to work in the morning.

Bill checked the main doors of the hall were locked, bolted and alarmed and, for some reason he couldn't quite decipher, made his way slowly and stiffly up the four flights of stone stairs to the huge, elongated gallery he'd taken Alice to show his artwork all those years ago. Nearly forty now, for heaven's sake. He'd not been up here for months, but had a need, after being with them all afternoon, to see, one more time, where these three beautiful daughters of his had been conceived. He'd fancied Alice Parkes, yes of course he had, been fascinated by her obvious artistic knowledge and ability and the wanton desire awoken in her by his own artwork.

But Rosa, Hannah and Eva – they were something different. His somewhat selfish part in these lovely girls' creation, and how they'd turned out as human beings, had to be the best act he'd ever been a part of. How he loved them. How they'd helped soften that dreadful blow of losing Henry. Bill gazed around him for a good ten minutes and then switched off the lights and went wearily back down the stairs.

He was tired. He'd had enough.

Totally wiped out with the nervous excitement of taking her first Sunday sermon, the awful outburst from Alexandra Pennington and the unexpected arrival in church of Joe's parents – as well as far too much alcohol consumed – Rosa slipped beneath her duvet, said a much- abbreviated prayer to thank God for a day well spent and slept.

21

Rosa woke with a start, not knowing what it was that had pulled her from sleep. All that cheese and port, she assumed, turning over and thumping her pillow slightly before searching for the comfort of her hot water bottle once more. She must be getting old. It was Richard who always said, once you got past the age of forty, you couldn't take too much rich food before bed. She glanced across at her bedside clock. Not yet 1 a.m. – she'd only been asleep a couple of hours at the most.

She found her thoughts wandering again and again to the lovely new dentist Eva and Rayan had just taken on. She'd been really surprised to see him sitting in the congregation that morning. Certainly, Rosa hadn't taken him for a man in need of spirituality, but he'd knelt and prayed, joined in with the singing and had surprised her by making his way to the front of the church to accept the confirmation wafer and wine.

And then, she understood.

Once she'd seen everyone out of church, shaking hands and accepting really quite lovely compliments from those who'd sat through and joined in with the service, Rosa had slipped back across to the vicarage to change out of her working clothes and back into her jeans. She'd been expecting a massive fallout from the bombshell Alexandra Pennington had decided to detonate halfway through the service but, really, on reflection, she'd got away with it pretty lightly. There'd been a couple of acerbic, quite unpleasant comments from two elderly women who told her they'd been utterly *disgusted* with the carry-on in what was the Lord's house and they certainly wouldn't be returning *next*

Sunday, and would be going back to worship at St Luke's up in Heath Green where the toilets were better and you got a cup of tea and a Garibaldi biscuit after the service. Making a mental note to get in some custard creams for the following Sunday– no currants to get stuck behind old codgers' dental work – she'd continued to smile and chat, patting babies' heads like some sycophantic politician and laughing like a drain at a random joke she didn't actually get, from a six-year-old who whispered the – obviously rude – punchline into her ear.

And then there'd been Virginia, slightly hysterical, grabbing at Rosa's arm as she continued to shake hands with the queue of parishioners and asking what she, as vicar of All Hallows, was going to do about it?

When Rosa had replied, 'About what? The toilet facilities and the lack of a Garibaldi?' Virginia had narrowed her eyes and hissed, what did Hannah think she was *up to*, bringing her *married lover's wife* into church, as well as the good name of Grandpa Cecil's church into total disrepute?

Rosa had patted her eldest sister's arm and said, 'Nothing. Not really my business, Virginia,' and Virginia had stormed off in the direction of an obviously utterly mortified Hannah, standing at what she'd assumed to be a safe distance, with Bill.

And then, fifteen minutes later, coming back through church to lock up, she understood. Understood why Sam Burrows had been in church. He and Hannah were now sitting in the front pew, the only ones remaining in the building as Susan and Richard made their way out, her mum obviously upset. Sam was handing Hannah his handkerchief, his attention all on what she was saying; comforting her, listening. And Rosa had felt a sharp – totally unchristian – stab of envy that it was Hannah he'd dressed up in his Sunday finery to see. *Stop it, Rosa*, she'd admonished herself firmly as she walked up towards the font feeling a mixture of emotions. How wonderful if this rather lovely man – and he did seem, from only a couple of conversations with him, somewhat special – could be the one to counter the tangled web of deceit into which Hannah had allowed herself to be drawn.

Rosa wasn't sure if she'd fallen back to sleep and the noise was part of the dream where both Virginia and Grandpa Cecil were lobbing hymnbooks and Garibaldi biscuits at her head, shouting that she, Rosa and Hannah – and yes, Eva as well – were an utter disgrace, bastards all of them…

Rosa sat up in bed, her pulse racing. She really would have to give the port a miss next time she was up at Heatherly Hall. And then the noise came again: scratching, a door opening; footsteps.

Someone was in the vicarage. In her house. Her home.

She might have God on her side when she eventually walked, yea, through the valley of death, but Rosa wasn't convinced he was going to be at her side as she crept along the gloomy upstairs corridor, past the lavatory and downstairs to the kitchen where whispering, and the occasional sound of drawers being pulled out and cupboard doors opened, appeared to be coming from. Rosa leaned over the banister, heart pounding and then, for some reason she couldn't quite fathom, turned back to pull on her dog collar over the red and blue Spider-Man pyjamas Laila and Nora had given her the previous Christmas.

What was she? A minister or a mouse? She needed to get in there and show them she had the Almighty on her side. Surely they'd respect that? With her heart pounding so hard against her ribcage she felt it was about to leap out of her body and scuttle for safety back upstairs – what she herself should, in fact, be doing – Rosa opened the kitchen door really quickly and, again for some reason, she couldn't quite work out, barged through it, shouting, 'Aggggggghhhhhhh,' at the top of her voice and sort of kung fu-ing her way in, her pyjama bottoms – man-size rather than the petite size eight she actually was – dropping and flapping dangerously towards her nether regions as she flew across the kitchen.

'Fuckin' hell!' A being – boy, man, girl – Rosa couldn't tell which it was, under the disguise of a smiling, but decidedly creepy, Duke of Edinburgh mask – dropped the one remaining piece of Maureen Hardcastle's quiche onto the blue Formica kitchen unit and headed, in a panic, for the locked kitchen door.

There were three of them in her kitchen, all fairly pint-sized in stature but, as she herself was only just a good five foot in height, Rosa didn't feel to have any particular advantage in that regard.

'Kitchen door's locked,' Rosa said, trying to speak calmly. 'And to be honest, I don't have a clue where the key is. If you come across it while you're going through my drawers, I'd be grateful.'

'Your *drawers* are the last thing we'd be going through, you lezzer.' The middle one of the three sneered behind his own mask – Prince Andrew this time – before adding: 'All women vicars are lezzers because they're doing what men normally do. They want to *be* men.'

'Is that right?' Rosa buried her hands into her armpits so they wouldn't see their trembling. 'Well look, lads – I'm assuming you are lads? – you're welcome to share my quiche, what's left of it – and then I suggest you leave the same way you got in. I tell you now, there's nothing of any value in here – unless you fancy humping that old cooker over there…'

'Better than humping *you*, you old lezzer.' The mouthpiece was on a roll, smirking behind his royal alter ego.

'…off my hands.'

'Just give us your phone. And your car keys. And your purse.' The third boy, the smallest, spoke for the first time from behind his Lady Di covering.

'Well, giving you my keys wouldn't help you – my car isn't here. And, to be honest, my phone is so old, you'd probably have to pay someone to take it off you.'

'You're just saying that,' Prince Philip snarled. 'Give us what you've got.'

Rosa had suddenly had enough. 'Just get out. All of you. Go on. Piss off.'

'Ooh, fuckin' hell, I didn't know vicars were allowed to swear. Your boss'll be after *you*.'

Rosa never got to work out if the little toerag was referring to the Archbishop of Canterbury or the Main Man Above, because, before she could respond, there was a loud knocking on the heavy Victorian vicarage front door and the three intruders leapt as one towards the locked kitchen door, furiously grabbing at and turning the handle in vain, while the one who appeared to be the ringleader snarled once more at Rosa for the key.

'Back through the window,' Lady Di shouted and the three of them exited the door leading to the corridor and the sitting room, where a blast of cold January night air and blowing curtains lay testament – if proof were needed – to the forced entry through a jemmied side window.

'I got the little sod!' A man's voice from the front garden could be heard competing with furious shouts of: 'Gerroff. Gerroff me.'

Rosa ran to the front door, unlocking it and pulling it open, expecting to see a panda car – blue lights blazing – and a couple of burly policemen at least. Instead, there were two men and one scowling, kicking child. For, despite, all of his fourteen years and the bravado manufactured from hiding his true identity behind the former Princess of Wales, Rhys Johnson was just that – a child.

'I'm so sorry, Rosa, you'd better call the police.' Joe Rosavina pulled a hand through his thick blond hair in a gesture redolent of both anger and despair while Roberto Rosavina, still in the same aubergine sweater and dark blue overcoat he'd been wearing in church just twelve or so hours earlier, sat at her kitchen table and momentarily rubbed his large, dependable hands up and down his face. He eventually stilled them in steepled fingers and stared across at Rosa with raised eyebrows, awaiting her response.

'Police is best peoples to deal with this, Joe,' Roberto said eventually. 'We can't carry on like this. With *him*.' Joe's father glared across at the boy who was still struggling somewhat in Joe's grasp.

'Don't get the fucking police.' Rhys turned angry eyes – Carys's eyes – towards Rosa, and Roberto leaned across the table to shake his arm angrily.

'Shut that foul mouth, Rhys,' Roberto snapped. 'You in house of God here.'

'Well, *my* house, really, Roberto.' Rosa attempted levity, although she was still trembling and had to sit down at the table herself. 'I don't think the Almighty has had much to do with the décor in this place, do you?' The others all glanced round, taking in the Seventies' kitchen, so badly in need of an upgrade, before returning their gaze back in her direction.

The whole thing was totally and utterly surreal. She'd had no contact with Joe – apart from what was necessary in order to sell the apartment once she'd left London for Durham – in over six years. And yet, here he was, standing in her kitchen, talking as if those intervening years, and what had caused the break-up, had never actually happened. As if the last time she'd seen him was a couple of days ago in the village pub or buying a paper at the local newsagent.

But it *was* six years. After just a month or so, she'd gone home to stay with Susan and Richard once they'd driven down, packed a few essentials and taken her back with them for a couple of weeks before her treatment was to start. In a state of utter shock both at Joe's betrayal as well as her cancer diagnosis, it hadn't seemed to occur to her to plead with him, make him see, as well as her accept, he'd made one hell of a big mistake and tell him to kick Carys into touch and come home. To be with her, Rosa, as she went through the radiotherapy, the chemo, the sickness and her hair dropping out.

'I'm not having Joe stay with me out of pity,' she'd told Eva and Hannah when they'd urged her to tell Joe what was happening to her.

'You're effing crackers,' Eva had fumed. 'What on earth's the matter with you? You've given him to her on a plate.'

'Bonkers,' Hannah had agreed. 'For heaven's sake, give him a call and get him back where he belongs. With you.'

But she'd refused. And eventually the only contact she had with Joe Rosavina was through her solicitors when she finally wound up her business, the apartment was put on the market and she signed for Joe to receive his share of the life they'd had together and which was now over.

Joe was looking at her, staring at her, but appeared unable to get any words out apart from *sorry*. Again and again, he kept saying, 'I'm sorry, Rosa, I'm so sorry,' repeating himself like some strange automaton until Rhys, tutting, flung himself onto the chair opposite.

'You've said sorry, for God's sake, Joe. We didn't take nothing – there was nothing to take. Can we go home now?' He shoved his hands into his jacket pocket, and slumped down almost horizontal in the chair, his eyes closed.

'What do you want to do, Rosa?'

'How on earth did you know he was here?' Rosa asked, frowning.

'Joe's car has tracker,' Roberto sniffed. 'Rhys know he can't take and drive that one anymore.'

'Anymore? At *fourteen*?' Rosa stared. 'I'm assuming he's not passed his test?'

'*Fottuto piccolo stronzo*,' Roberto spat angrily. 'He not know I put tracker in my *own* car. And in Michelle's car too. Just in case. He take Joe's momma's car and we follow him here.'

'I want to go home,' Rhys muttered. 'If you can call it home with *him* there.' He nodded towards Roberto, his eyes still closed.

'Why don't you all just go?' Rosa finally said, shaking her head. 'Go on, go home.' She felt drained, empty.

'But what about window?' Roberto frowned. 'You going get burglars.'

'I think I've already had them.' Rosa managed a smile. 'I've got some thick garden twine somewhere. I'll tie it up for now and get Bill to send someone down from the estate to mend it tomorrow. A couple of the estate workers are driving my car back down in the morning.'

'I want the bill,' Joe said, rubbing at his face, dark stubble rasping under his hands. 'You'll need a new window...'

'OK, OK.' Rosa put up her hands in acquiescence; she needed them gone.

'Are you going to tell the cops?' Rhys was staring at her in turn, any bravado evaporating as he realised his fate was in Rosa's hands. Rosa was aware, because Hannah had explained, this child had been bailed – rather than remanded – at his last court appearance. There'd be no second chances once the police knew he'd been out burgling again while on bail.

'I don't know what I'm going to do yet. Apart from refilling my hot water bottle and going back to bed.'

'I'll be in touch. I'll come round tomorrow.' Joe's voice was pleading. 'I need to talk to you, Rosa... you know...'

'It's really not necessary,' Rosa said stiffly. 'Now, if you don't mind, all of you, I've a funeral at nine-thirty in the morning. I'd appreciate being able to look half decent as I send Beryl Waterhouse to meet her maker.'

22

'Hannah!'
Hannah opened her eyes, sticky with sleep, tears, yesterday's mascara and definitely too much alcohol, before quickly closing them once more in an attempt to block out yet again the pictures of Ben's wife sliding into the pew beside her. Images of the woman whispering and pouring her contemptuous allegations into Hannah's ear as the rest of the congregation were led by Rosa to give thanks to God for all his mercies. And then, the final coup d'état as Alexandra Pennington walked calmly back up the aisle before turning and regaling the whole church with what she, Hannah, the adulterous husband stealer, had been up to.

'Hannah!' The shouting underneath her bedroom window was becoming more insistent and Hannah suddenly knew it was Ben down below who had come to be with her; to tell her he'd left Alexandra and was going to be with *her*. She slid out of bed, holding her head as pain rocketed through it and gingerly made her way over to the window, drawing back the curtains on a miserably cold, damp and still insistently dark November morning. Ben was no longer down below. Had she dreamt her name being called?

A loud knocking on the front door, echoing painfully through her skull, had her reaching for her dressing gown and descending the stairs which, since she'd climbed them the night before, had turned into a penance worthy of the twelve tasks of Hercules.

'Hannah!' The voice again, accompanied by more banging and shouting through the letterbox.

Hannah closed one eye to alleviate the throbbing that felt like the dinner gong the triplets had loved to wallop when they were kids up at Heatherly Hall. She searched for the key, opened the door, ready to tell Ben not to look at her like this, she was a total mess...

'Oh, you're alive.' Eva pushed crossly past her and stood in the hallway, eyebrows raised.

'Sorry?' The anti-climax of it not being Ben standing at her door had the effect of almost winding her and she immediately sat down on the hall chair, head in her hands.

'Here.' Eva thrust a pack of painkillers in Hannah's direction. 'Industrial strength for gum boils – thought you could do with them this morning...' Eva trailed off and then said, still apparently cross, 'Actually, Hans, I suddenly got *really* worried and thought you might have... you know...'

'What?' Hannah lifted her head.

'Well, you had such a shock yesterday. You were in a bad way when you went off in that taxi – you'd drunk almost a bottle of port, you know.'

'Must be why my head feels like a boiled egg being cracked open. Actually, Eva...' Hannah ran for the tiny downstairs loo '...I think I'm going to be sick.'

And she was, several times, throwing up all her unhappiness, the guilt, the utter mortification she'd tried to alleviate with alcohol. She should have known it always came back to bite you. Eva held her head, drawing back her hair as she retched.

'Jesus, Hannah, is there anything left inside you?' Eva pulled a face of distaste, handing Hannah a glass of water as she slowly got to her feet from her knees on the cold tiled floor.

'Thought you'd be used to it, having two kids.'

'They vomit hot chocolate and Ribena, not expensive twenty-year-old vintage port.' Eva frowned before continuing, accusingly: 'You said you'd text me as soon as you got out of the taxi. I kept ringing you and texting you but you didn't answer – I spent all night thinking you'd either topped yourself or been murdered and thrown into the canal.'

'You have an overactive imagination.' Hannah made her way into the kitchen for coffee and several of Eva's painkillers. 'I'm going back to bed. What time is it, anyway?'

'Nearly 6 a.m.'

'What? Not six o'clock yet? What is the *matter* with you?'

'As I said, I was worried about you. I've come to drive you back to Heatherly Hall to get your car. You can't get to work without it.'

'I'm not going to work.' Hannah was mulish. 'I'm not well.'

'Yes, you *are* going to work; you're a professional, like me.'

'Well, I might be a professional – although to be honest I'd question that – but I'm also a drunk. I've seen enough people in court done for drink-driving after a skinful the night before, thinking they've slept it off and are safe, to know there's no way I'm getting in my car.'

'Actually, you're right.' Eva conceded the point. 'Look, why don't you ring work?'

'At six in the morning? On a Monday morning? People with any sense are still fast asleep.'

'OK, go back to bed, have a couple of hours' more sleep, get showered and I'll come back and drive you up to Bill's when I've finished at the surgery at lunchtime. How's that?'

Hannah squinted across at Eva suspiciously. 'You're very jolly this morning?' Hannah opened both eyes. 'Something – or *someone* – at Malik & Malik keeping you awake? And having you in full make-up and...' Hannah assessed what her sister was wearing '...short skirt and favourite long boots at 6 a.m. on a Monday morning?'

'As I said,' Eva returned primly, 'I am a professional. Now, get back to bed and if you give me the necessary phone number to ring, I'll inform your work colleagues you'll be in at lunchtime – you're not at all well, but should have got over it by this afternoon.'

'What are you: my mother, writing a note to get me out of Games? They'll know I've been drinking,' Hannah protested, but nevertheless making her way back up the stairs.

'Better than knowing you've topped yourself,' Eva sniffed, heading for the door.

Half past six. Eva knew she should be driving home, helping Rayan and Azra organise the girls before Jodie arrived to take over at eight. Instead, she texted Rayan:

Needed to make sure Hannah was OK after yesterday's little bombshell. Are you OK if I go straight into work, rather than driving back home? Can you manage? Jodie will take over at 8.

Was she going to appear a bit too keen if she was at the dental practice, cafetière and a box of M&S shortbread biscuits to hand, ready to casually bump into Sam when he arrived? Would it be over the top to find croissants somewhere? Eva dithered before making a decision, putting the car into gear and setting off in the direction of Westenbury village centre.

'What are you doing up and full of it at seven in the morning?' Eva was surprised to find Rosa not only up and dressed, but looking as stunning as ever. Eva sometimes forgot how bloody gorgeous Rosa was, the stark black of her vestment and dog collar only adding a sort of sexy glamour to her thick, curly dark hair and pink lipstick.

'I could ask the same?' Rosa frowned, peering behind Eva on the doorstep. 'What's happening? Are you by yourself?'

'Who else would I have with me?' Eva said almost crossly,

and then relented: 'I just needed to go round and check Hannah was OK...'

'She is,' Rosa interrupted, leading the way into the kitchen, which appeared surprisingly warm for once. 'I've just spoken to her – well, texted her. She says she's not feeling wonderful and is staying in bed. You don't need to go round there.'

'Already been over,' Eva grinned. 'Held her head while she called for God – oops sorry, Reverend – down the loo. Totally hungover with a thumping head and obviously in a state of depression and mortification over Ben. Anyway, I thought I'd come here for a coffee before going over to open up the surgery. Or, I've time to drive you over to Bill's to get your car?'

'It's OK, a couple of Bill's estate workers are bringing it over later this morning. And hopefully going to mend my broken window.'

'Broken window? The graveyard ghouls been playing football again?'

Rosa smiled at that. 'I had visitors last night. Jemmied a side window to get in.'

'Shit.' Eva stared. 'You OK? You *look* OK? In fact, you look gorgeous. Wonder if I could get away with wearing black and white without looking like a nun? Or a penguin? But, you're OK? Did you catch them at it? God, I'd have been terrified. What have the police said?'

'Yes, I'm fine. Yes, I caught them at it. Yes, I was terrified. No, I didn't ring the police.'

'Why on earth not? Ring them now? Fingerprints – don't go disturbing the evidence.'

'I don't need any evidence.' Rosa turned to feed slices of wholemeal bread into the toaster. 'Want some toast?'

'Yes, I will actually.' Eva went to sit at the kitchen table. 'You didn't go all *vicary* on them, did you? Let them get away with all your jewellery while turning the other cheek?'

'*God has the sole power to punish those who sin,*' Rosa smiled, buttering toast lavishly and handing a plate to Eva. 'Samuel 1:26 – or thereabouts.'

'*Don't let the little bastards get away with it.*' Eva bit into her toast, offering up, through a large mouthful: 'Eva 11:21.'

Rosa started to laugh at that. 'They were little and one certainly was a bastard – like us, don't forget.'

'Sorry?'

'One of them, when he finally took off his Lady Diana Spencer mask and I could see him, was Carys Powell's son.'

'What?' Eva was so stunned she didn't notice when a globule of butter dripped down her chin and onto her best cream cashmere sweater.

'You heard. So, yes, fun and games all round.'

'And?'

'And Joe and his dad appeared in my kitchen ten minutes later.'

'What?' This time, Eva actually replaced her toast on the plate. 'You *are* joking.'

Rosa shook her head. 'They'd tracked Michelle's car.'

'What, Michelle was in on it too? I don't know what you mean?'

'Oh Eva, long story, but apparently, Rhys has a penchant for driving cars.'

'He's not seventeen. He's not allowed to drive.'

'He's not allowed to go breaking and entering either, but he did both, taking Michelle's car, which he didn't know Roberto had put a tracker on.'

'Shit.'

'I know. Anyway, it was pretty weird having Joe in my kitchen as if he'd just dropped in for a cup of tea.'

Eva shook her head, utterly speechless.

'The other two ran off, back through the window, but Joe and Roberto had hold of Rhys. Up to me, apparently, what I do now.'

Rosa paused, not looking at Eva. 'Joe said he was coming round to talk to me later on today.'

'Don't let him in.' Eva was adamant. 'Don't have *anything* to do with any of the Rosavinas. And shop Carys's little scumbag – he's obviously as much a thief as his mother is.'

'He's fourteen, Eva. His mother has abandoned him.'

'Not surprised if he behaves like this. And don't go all bleeding-heart liberal and… and *nice* on me.'

'I'm a vicar. Vicars *have* to be nice. It's part of our job spec. Look at the Reverend Richard Coles. He's *very* nice.'

'Only after he'd had some fun playing in The Communards,' Eva sniffed. 'And Grandpa Cecil wasn't one bit nice.'

They both mulled this over, nodding in agreement. 'You must *not* tell Hannah, 'Rosa said eventually.

'Why not?' Eva frowned.

'Why do you *think*? She has a professional interest in Rhys. She *can't* know.'

'I don't see how you can keep it from her.'

'Well, I'm not going to tell her, and neither must you. If I'd thought you were going to run straight back to Hannah, I wouldn't have told you.'

'What about the next house they burgle?' Eva insisted. 'Just think about *those* poor people; it could be some little old lady next time. The Princess of Wales popping up at your bedside in the middle of the night when you're ninety is enough to finish anyone off. You could stop them doing it again if you get the police involved.'

'I'll just have to live with that possibility. I do have some idea what I'm going to do. I've been thinking about it all night. I'm actually shattered – that's why I've got so much make-up on, to hide the bags.'

'Oh?' Eva paused, holding Rosa's eye. 'Not because Joe Rosavina is coming back round? And what are you planning?'

'I'll let you know, if Joe and Rhys agree to it.'

'Look, Rosa, you may be a vicar and think you're pretty near to God, but that doesn't mean you can play at being God Almighty himself. *You* can't start making the decisions about how to deal with the boy. Hannah's lot, the police, his school, all have to be involved, not just you.'

Her eyes gritty through lack of sleep, Rosa made her way back through the churchyard after leading the service of thanks for the life of Beryl Waterhouse then accompanying the cortège to the crematorium. It was a simple service, with few family or friends left to send the ninety-eight-year-old former village postmistress on her final journey, and Rosa was back – having begged a lift from the current postmaster rather than a regal ride back in the funeral hearse – at the vicarage by 11.30 a.m.

She needed coffee. She'd just filled the kettle and was reaching for the jar of instant when there was a knock on the front door. Leaving the kettle to boil, her heart thumping at the thought of seeing Joe once again, Rosa headed down the corridor, examined her face in the hall mirror and added lipstick. She ran fingers through her hair and, as the knock on the door came a second time, reverberating down the hallway, she went to open it.

'Oh?' Rosa stepped back, opening the door wider. A sudden draught of the sneaky east wind that had been hanging around for days had the man on the doorstep reaching for his scarf, which was trying its best to leave his neck.

'I'm sorry, I didn't mean to disturb you, Rosa,' Sam Burrows smiled. 'Although, isn't Monday a much less busy day for you than the weekend?'

'Well, I've been up half the night with burglars, and half the morning giving Beryl Waterhouse as good a send-off as possible, given there were only a handful of people at the party.'

'Sorry?' Sam stared while trying once again to control his scarf.

'I'm sorry, I'm sorry, come in before we're both blown away.'

'Are you OK? Have the police been involved? Is that where they got in?' Sam nodded towards the sitting-room side window, which was now tied up with bright red garden twine.

Rosa nodded. 'It's fine; *I'm* fine. Really.'

'You sure? Look, I just wondered if you'd come across a pair of gloves?' Sam followed Rosa down into the kitchen. 'Black leather? I appear to have lost them – I think possibly in church yesterday?'

'I didn't see any when I was over there just now. We're a bit short-staffed at the moment.' Rosa laughed at that. 'Listen to me – short-staffed – duh, I sometimes think I'm still running my business in London. We have *no* staff here – never mind short-staffed. Denis, our verger, is off at the moment, but Sandra, his wife, has the key and comes in to help Daphne the organist to have a bit of a dust round the pews every now and again. You know, shake the old hassocks out a bit... And I'm not averse to throwing a bit of Toilet Duck down the loo myself...' *Shut up, Rosa, for God's sake stop wittering and going on about bloody Toilet Duck,* she admonished herself, turning round and handing Sam a mug of coffee.

'Right. OK.'

'So, what I was trying to say was, your gloves might well be where you left them. The church will be open if you want to go over there? You know, they might be still in the pew. Either at the back, in the pew where you started off, or at the front where you ended up when you moved down there with Hannah.' Oh heavens, now she was making him out to be a pew tart. *A pew tart?* Was there such a thing? She turned away to hide a nervous giggle that was bubbling up and threatening its exit. Nerves at having this rather lovely – *rather lovely? Get a grip,*

Rosa, he's bloody gorgeous – man in her kitchen was making her act like a red-faced teenager again. In fact, she obviously hadn't grown up at all, hadn't progressed from sitting on the lawn on that first day at sixth-form college, trying to eat the unexpected gift of an unwieldy focaccia sandwich in front of Joe Rosavina.

'How is Hannah?' Sam's casual query had Rosa down to earth with a bump. Of course, that was why he was here – he wanted Hannah's number. Probably didn't dare ask Eva for it, but Rosa the vicar would be far more accommodating. 'Is she OK? That was an awful experience for her to have to go through yesterday.'

'Would you like her phone number?' Rosa smiled, reaching for her own mobile on the table.

'Her number? Erm, no, not particularly.' Sam was embarrassed. 'Unless you'd like to give it to me?'

Before she could respond, there was another loud knocking on the front door. Blimey, was *this* Joe? Rosa thought she might just fall into a heap on the kitchen floor if she didn't get a grip of her jitters. Too much coffee, obviously.

'Rosa, love, we've brought your car back.' Stuart, who'd been an estate worker up at Heatherly Hall for ever and a day, had let himself in, large bag of tools to hand. 'And keep this bloody door locked, love – you'll have burglars.' He laughed at his own wit. 'Right, lad –' he turned to the youth hovering behind him '– let's have a look at this window. See if we can fix it, or if we need to get a joiner in. I hope you've had the police round?' he added, not waiting for an answer, but pushing Damien unceremoniously into the sitting room with the help of his big leather bag.

'I need to go.' Sam wound his scarf round his neck. 'I only slipped across to get my gloves.' He paused before looking Rosa fully in the eye. 'No, that's a lie. And, I guess, I shouldn't lie to a vicar. I came to ask, would you come to the theatre with me, Rosa?'

'The theatre? With you?' Rosa stared.

'Yes,' he said firmly. 'The theatre. With me. Next Wednesday evening.'

'Oh, I wasn't expecting that.' Rosa found she was grinning, a somewhat asinine grin. 'Yes, please. That would be lovely. Thank you.'

23

Eva, no need to come round to pick me up. Am going to walk up to Bill's with Brian to get my car. Told the office am working from home for rest of day. Am OK.

Hannah finished texting, drained her mug of tea and, wrapping up against the ridiculously blustery wind, set off in the direction of Heatherly Hall, her intention to call in at Richard and Susan's on the way in order to collect the dog for the walk up there. Richard hadn't been well again and her mum was no great dog lover. Or walker.

She needed to walk, needed to push her limbs to the limit across the fields and up the steep roads to Bill's place. She needed physical pain to wipe out the mental pain of losing Ben. And she had lost him. He'd simply texted a single: 'So sorry, Hannah,' an hour or so ago and that was it. That was it? After nine months of borrowing him, taking him without permission from his wife and children, she was left with one line of apology? Well, it was all she deserved. She had, as Bill had pointed out, played with fire and got her fingers burnt. But it wasn't just her fingers that were hurting. Every single bit of her was in pain.

She walked the two miles to her parents' house, her legs and arms pumping along at a ridiculously co-ordinated speed until her heart had joined in with their maniacal rhythm and she had to bend over in the road, convinced she was about to throw up once more. She wiped the sweat from her brow and set off, once she was able, at a more leisurely speed. This unfortunately allowed her to think and, determined not to, resolute in trying to take away the images that were crashing into her brain, she set off once again at speed.

'What on earth are you *doing*, Hannah? Why aren't you at work?' Virginia, kerb crawling behind her, pulled up at her side and peered at her through the open car window.

Oh God, that was all she needed: Virginia catching her for another telling-off.

'Just getting some practice in. Have taken up speed walking. Hoping to represent England in Paris.' Hannah wheezed to a standstill, hands on knees.

'Oh, don't be so ridiculous, Hannah.' And then, not entirely convinced Hannah wasn't telling the truth, added, 'You're not thin enough to be a speed walker.'

'Thanks for that, Virginia. The diet starts tonight.'

'I'm just going up to see Dad. He's got a bout of his bronchitis again.' Virginia's tone was accusatory. 'And that little outburst you provoked in church yesterday hasn't helped, you know. He and Mum left before they'd even had their rice pudding.'

'So I hear – that he's not so good, I mean – didn't know about the rice pud. That's where I'm heading too. Going to take Brian for a walk up to Bill's place to pick up my car.'

'Oh? Too much to drink as usual?' Virginia sniffed disapprovingly. 'And why aren't you at work?'

'Virginia, you're not my mum. Now, if you don't mind, I'm timing myself.' Hannah set off once again at such a cracking pace she began to seriously wonder if training for Paris was actually not a bad idea; maybe the solution to getting over Ben.

'Oh.' Susan raised an eyebrow as Hannah walked through the door, holding on to her galloping – but broken – heart. 'I'm *surprised* at you, Hannah. A married man, for heaven's sake. And with those two beautiful children.' Susan was obviously going straight for the jugular, egged on by the self-righteous Virginia who had arrived five minutes before her and had already had a good stir of the gossip pot.

'Mum, honestly, I'm not proud of my behaviour.' Hannah found she was actually crying. 'All you're about to say is absolutely what I deserve, but just do me a favour would you and not go on and on at me? I'm thoroughly ashamed of what I've been doing, but you and Virginia having a go at me isn't going to make things right. How's Dad? I've come to take Brian for a walk. I need to pick up my car from Bill's.'

'Oh, drinking again, were you all?' Susan, who'd never been able to maintain her displeasure with any of her four daughters for long, shook her head disapprovingly, but patted Hannah's arm with some modicum of sympathy. 'Your dad's on the mend, I think, but still in bed; don't disturb him. The dog is desperate for a walk.'

'Right, I'm off. I'll see Dad when I bring Brian back.' Hannah whistled for the dog who eyed her warily from his basket by the Aga. Desperate for a walk, Brian clearly wasn't. She hooked the lead onto his collar and, grudgingly, he shook out his arthritic back legs and followed her outside.

After walking for a good hour, the bitter east wind appeared to have dropped somewhat and, tired, she slowed her pace to match Brian's up the steepest gradient of the seemingly never-ending meadow towards Heatherly Hall. *Misery Hill*, Eva had once dubbed it when, as kids, Richard had insisted they troop out for 'a quick walk to blow away the cobwebs' when all they wanted was to stop at home watching *Top of the Pops* or *The Royle Family* – which Susan regularly turned off, saying it gave a poor impression of the North – or *EastEnders* – which presumably didn't.

'Oy, get that dog on a lead.' Hannah was pulled from the reverie of TV programmes she had known and loved by a tall, well-set man, arms folded, watching her from the summit of the hill.

'Why?'

'What do you mean, *why*? There are sheep back there.' The man raised a hand indicating blobs of white some distance away.

'Yes, *back there*,' Hannah shouted back. She knew she was being obstreperous but she was feeling that way out now. She might as well go the whole hog and become totally objectionable.

'And you've a dog there.'

'Well, that's debatable,' Hannah shouted into the wind. 'He's more of a geriatric pussy cat. And your sheep...' she raised a hand to her eyes in the manner of Little Bo Peep looking for said animals '...are so far away, even *I* can't even make them out, never mind a myopic, arthritic dog on his last legs.'

'Oh, just do as you're told, for God's sake,' the man shouted. 'You townies make me sick with your aversion to the rules of the countryside. I bet you leave gates open and drop litter too.'

'Yeah, yeah, yeah,' Hannah muttered, putting Brian on his lead and heading for the woods that bordered Heatherly Hall. 'Yeah, yeah, effing yeah.' At least these were Bill's woods and, as Bill's daughter, surely her woods too? Hell, she was making enemies daily. At this rate, she was going to be run out of town by the sheriff. This little thought made her giggle and then, for some reason, start to cry. Hannah tugged on the dog's lead, waved at a couple of estate workers and limped in the direction of Bill's private apartment. 'Come on, Brian, let's find my car keys.'

Bill was sitting in his favourite armchair, his back to her, but in front of the huge diamond-paned baronial window overlooking the gardens to the south.

'Gosh, why are you sitting there in the dark?' Hannah moved to switch on a variety of overhead lights and table lamps. 'And draw the curtains, for heaven's sake – it's really quite dark and gloomy out there now.' Brian made his towards the huge open fireplace, immediately lying down with a grateful sigh in anticipation of rest and warmth.

'Don't make yourself comfortable, dog, we're not stopping. And that fire's no use to man nor ornament. Bill? You need to put some more logs on... I've just met the most objectionable farmer. He really told me off…' Hannah trailed off. 'Bill?' She made her way over to the chair, standing in front of Bill, looking down at him. She shook his arm. 'Bill? Bill?'

Hannah put out a tentative hand to Bill's much-loved face. It was quite cold. She gently closed his open eyes because, wasn't that what people did in all good films whenever they found someone unexpectedly dead? William, twelfth Marquess of Heatherly, had come to rest, not on the battlefields of England as had so many of his forebears, but sat in his favourite armchair, looking out at his favourite view, with one of his favourite children to hand.

The enormity of the last couple of minutes suddenly hit her and, in a panic, Hannah ran down the red-carpeted stairs, running and running until, breathless, she burst out of the side door of Heatherly Hall, hurrying awkwardly along the badly lit paths and through the door of the manager's office where three of the estate groundsmen were drinking coffee and laughing over something or other.

Could this day get any worse?

'It's Bill,' Hannah managed to get out, before bursting into tears. 'I think he's dead.'

24

While Hannah was getting into trouble with the local farmer, and Eva extracting a back molar from the mouth of one Geoffrey Shaw while contemplating her next move re Sam Burrows, Rosa was up a ladder. With a surfeit of nervous energy fizzing round her body from too much coffee – she really was going to have to go decaf – Sam Burrow's utterly unexpected but rather lovely invitation to the theatre the following evening and, predominantly, anticipating Joe's return at her front door, she'd decided to paint the vicarage kitchen.

Cocking a snook at the warning of Luke 12:15 that: *'a man's life does not consist in the abundance of his possessions,'* Rosa had spent the next hour online at Argos, in a wonderful orgy of delight, temptation and guilt, drooling over and ordering the most up-to-the-minute Dyson vacuum cleaner, a state-of-the-art Rangemaster (bright red) kitchen stove and a lovely set of pans and dishes. She was going to start cooking and baking again, something she'd not had much enthusiasm for over the past few years. The task of cooking, just for herself, had become somewhat onerous, but she was going to find her old cookbooks, unpack her cake tins and utensils from the box in the back bedroom and get into it again. Just think of those flapjacks, that millionaire's shortbread and other baked goodies she was going to get back into making. And eating. As well as fulfilling the promise to herself to sit down and really enjoy the meals she was going to create, with lovely cutlery and a starched napkin, as she always used to before Rosa Quinn Investments really took off, even though, now, she'd be laying the table just for one.

Next job was a quick trip down to B&Q for paint, decorating materials and a ladder – if she wasn't in when Joe called, so be it; she wasn't planning on waiting around for anyone. Offering up a silent 'sorry' to God, as well as the poor and homeless who didn't actually *have* a kitchen, never mind one to decorate and kit out with expensive fripperies, she arrived back, fizzing with anticipation and good intentions. She was shattered from her sleepless night, but adrenaline was shooting through her veins and, by the time she actually set to, she felt capable of giving the Sistine Chapel ceiling a once-over, never mind the vicarage kitchen one.

A Day-Glo yellow shower cap was in place on her tied-up dark brown hair, and she'd pulled on her old pair of denim dungarees, resurrected from the charity shop bag to take the brunt of the enthusiastic rolling on of white emulsion to the kitchen ceiling. Stopping only to insert a CD of House of Pain's 'Jump Around' and sing along to the beat, she was off, obliterating decades of nicotine-stained Anaglypta (Rev Cecil had been a heavy smoker) with a beautiful creamy Jasmine White.

After a good two hours of non-stop reaching and rolling, when every muscle in her right arm was screaming out for surrender, she knew she'd had enough. She also knew she'd gone at it like a roadrunner on speed, as well as put on the loudest, punchiest music, so as not to allow herself to think thoughts of Joe. It had been a shock seeing him standing there, in her kitchen, as if the six years since she'd seen him, and the awful hurt and despair caused by his defection, had somehow been gobbled up by a black hole, and everything that had gone on after that hadn't really happened. But Rhys, growing from a nice little eight-year-old lad into the adolescent scowling and sulking before her last night, had certainly happened. What turned a perfectly ordinary little boy like Rhys Johnson into a miscreant? A thief? A juvenile delinquent? That was an outmoded handle, she chided herself, one the Rev Cecil would have had no compunction about using, and Virginia – and possibly Susan as well – would still bandy around.

Rosa glanced at her wristwatch, but since it was covered in dots of white emulsion, she was unable to make out the time. She shifted decorating paraphernalia from her favourite chair and sat down, closing her eyes for a few minutes...

She woke with a start, seeing a face at the window.

Joe.

Still half asleep, dreaming of homemade chocolate brownies and blueberry frangipane tart, Rosa jumped up, pulse racing as she tried to get her brain into gear and work out just why Joe Rosavina was staring in at her through the vicarage kitchen window.

'I've been knocking,' he mouthed. 'Shall I go back round to the front door?'

Rosa nodded, tried to run a hand through her hair and found the paint-splatted yellow shower cap still on her head. Bugger. What must she look like? Sod it, she told herself mentally, she'd looked a hell of a lot worse when she'd lost all her hair after the chemo. Not that Joe had ever seen her like that. She walked determinedly down the corridor, refusing to check what she looked like in the hall mirror, but pulling off the shower cap nevertheless.

'Sorry, Joe, come in. I was just in the middle of decorating. Actually, as I'm sure you saw through the kitchen window, I was fast asleep.' Rosa looked directly at Joe. 'Something kept me up most of the night.' Joe followed her into the kitchen and, turning away from him, she asked, 'Coffee? Tea? Something stronger?'

'Tea would be good, thank you. I'm sorry.'

'Yes, you kept saying, last night.' Rosa searched for the teabags. 'You look pretty knackered yourself. I'm going to have wine. I think I deserve it.' Rosa poured herself a glass while the kettle boiled.

'Well, you certainly didn't deserve those little bastards breaking in. I'm sorry... really sorry.'

'Joe, if you've come for me to hear your confession and hope three Hail Marys will absolve you from all sin, then you've come to the wrong place; St Augustine's is five miles away in the next village.'

'I've come to say sorry.'

'You did that last night, Joe.'

'And to explain.'

'What, that you've ended up being responsible for Carys's son? I know all about that.'

'I don't know what to do with him, Rosa.'

Seeing Joe, now seated at the kitchen table, his face grey with worry, Rosa relented and, switching off the kettle, poured him a glass of wine instead. 'Small one,' she said, handing it to him. 'You can still drive on that.'

Joe took it gratefully and took a mouthful before placing the glass on the table in front of him. 'I know I have no right to ask, Rosa, but if you inform the police about last night, there's no doubt Rhys will end up with a DTO.'

'A DTO?'

'Detention and training order. Basically, the nick.'

'At fourteen?'

'Yep.'

'Maybe the best place for him.' Rosa knew she was playing devil's advocate but she didn't care. 'You know, maybe sort him out a bit?'

'I think it would finish him off. He's got problems.'

'Well, that's pretty obvious.' Rosa stared at Joe.

'Carys didn't have much time for him.'

'That's pretty obvious as well, Joe.'

Joe sighed. 'She was very good at hiding it all.'

'Hiding Rhys as well. We hardly ever *saw* him. She managed to keep the very distinct parts of her life quite separate. I should have suspected her motives then.'

'She took us both in, Rosa. You were as mesmerised by her as...'

'As *you* were, Joe? Is that what you were going to say?'

Joe nodded miserably but seemed unable to add anything

further until he said, 'She walked out on us, Rosa and, to be honest, it was a total relief.'

'A relief? Oh, for heaven's sake, Joe.'

'Just hear me out, Rosa,' Joe pleaded. 'Carys walked out on me, which I had no problem with whatsoever. As I say, it was a relief after five turbulent years. But she left her *kids*. How could *anyone* do that to a vulnerable, already unhappy adolescent as well as to a little girl who adored her mummy? We'd been heading for separation for years, but we'd have shared custody with the kids – Rhys too. I might not be his biological father but he's come to see me as his dad. He'd got used to having a father figure round after not having one for the first eight years of his life. But no, typical Carys, she does nothing by halves – when she jumps, she bloody well leaps.'

Rosa folded her arms and stared at the man she'd loved unconditionally for years. Still loved. You don't stop loving someone for mistakes they've made in the past. Didn't Jesus teach that? Although she couldn't quite recall chapter and verse, she was sure the good man had said it, and preached it, somewhere along the line. And then she started to laugh, but it was a mirthless laugh, one that so very easily could turn to tears. How *on earth* had she and Joe come to this?

'Who'd have thought, Joe, sitting on that lawn outside sixth-form college, me struggling with that focaccia, all those years ago, that one day we'd be here, me with a dog collar round my neck and a bloody paint-spattered yellow shower cap on my head and you pleading for your wife's...' Rosa hesitated and then repeated: '*your wife's* son's future. You couldn't make it up.'

'Rosa,' Joe said levelly, 'Carys was never my wife. I didn't marry her, didn't *want* to marry her despite her insistence that it was what she deserved, her *right* as the mother of my little girl.' Joe drained his glass of wine and Rosa knew he'd have welcomed more. 'I'm sorry. Rosa, I made the biggest mistake of my life... Carys...'

'Oh, do NOT blame Carys.'

'I don't,' Joe said bleakly. 'I blame myself. Every bit of the way. The only good thing to come out of this whole fucking mess...' Joe paused, suddenly embarrassed. 'I'm sorry, am I allowed to say that in front of you?'

Rosa simply looked at him as she pulled a face of pained exasperation.

'Anyway,' he continued, smiling slightly at her expression before becoming totally serious once more, 'the only good thing to come out of this mess is Chiara.'

'Your little girl?' Oh, heavens that hurt. Rosa felt a piercing pain, as though she'd been stabbed and winded in her solar plexus, and had to look away before Joe saw the blatant need in her eyes for a child of her own.

'She's my absolute life. She's lovely.'

'I know she is.'

'You know?' Joe stared. 'Ah, you met her the other day? At school assembly? She said the new vicar had been in. We've had to sit through that balloon story again and again. It always makes her laugh.'

'And *Chiara*?' Rosa said, trying to smile. 'Chiara Rosavina? I bet your dad was pleased with that. You got your way with an Italian name rather than another Welsh one? How did you manage that?'

Ignoring the implication that what Carys wanted, Carys got, Joe said, shrugging slightly, 'I don't think she cared one way or another.' He paused, rubbing a hand over his face. 'Look, Rosa, you must know there's never been a single day when I've not regretted what I did. Or, over the past six years, when I've not thought of you.'

Rosa put up an angry hand to stop him right there, before dashing away an angry, traitorous tear. She scratched at the dried emulsion on her cheek, watching it fall like confetti onto her dungarees. 'So,' she sniffed. 'I've been thinking about this.'

'Oh?' Joe stared at Rosa in turn, his face hopeful.

'How about if we say to Rhys, he has a choice?'

'What sort of choice?'

'Well basically to carry on like he *is* doing. *Or not.*' Rosa tutted, then relented. 'How about, you bring him back here and give him the choice. He either helps me here, in the vicarage...'

'I tell you now, Rosa,' Joe interrupted, shaking his head, 'Rhys won't accept being turned into a choirboy, if that's what you're thinking. There's no way you can turn him into that kid who sang "The Snowman".'

'Aled Jones?'

Joe nodded. 'That's the one. Just because Rhys has Welsh heritage doesn't mean he can sing. And even if he *could* sing – which, as far as I know, he can't – you'd never get him within spitting distance of a church.'

'He didn't appear to have any problem being here last night.'

'You know what I mean, Rosa.'

'But you obviously have no idea what *I* mean, Joe. What I'm suggesting is that Rhys comes over to the vicarage and helps with the gardening and a spot of decorating – I intend doing the whole place over the next few months.'

'Oh right, yes, sure.' Joe put up both hands almost in protest. 'I can really see Rhys going along with that.' He dropped his hands. 'I'd never get him here.'

'His choice, Joe. You either tell him to get himself over here or I go to the police and they'd have him back in court and probably remand him. I've done some work in a couple of youth offending institutions in Nottinghamshire; they're not the most pleasant places in the world. It'd be a bit like doing community service but without being sentenced first. You know, a sort of out-of-court order.' When Joe shook his head slightly, Rosa went on, 'His choice, Joe. He's almost fifteen, for heaven's sake. Time to stand up to him and show him who's boss.'

'My dad does that regularly,' Joe sighed. 'It seems to send Rhys in the opposite direction.'

'Well, totally up to you. If he's not back here by, shall we say, Thursday afternoon...?'

'He's got school, Rosa.'

'Yes, and the bus for Westenbury High – I'm assuming he's at the comp? – drops in the village. If he's not been back here by Thursday afternoon after school, then I *will* go to the police. You tell him that, Joe. And don't bring him yourself – he's fourteen. Old enough to sort himself out.'

'You sound just like you did when you were setting up Rosa Quinn Investments.' Joe smiled slightly. 'You know, when nothing would stand in your way.'

'Yes, well, something did stand in my way, didn't it?' Rosa glanced at the kitchen clock. 'I've a meeting of the parish council in... oh hell, half an hour. I really need to get in the shower, Joe.' She stood, her arms folded; her stance, she knew, defensive.

'Look, Rosa, can I just...?'

'Sorry, Joe. I need to get on.' Rosa took Joe's old university scarf from the arm of the kitchen chair where he'd left it after unwinding it from around his neck. It took her all her willpower not to bury her nose in its purple and black stripy depths. Instead, she handed it to him before determinedly ushering him towards the front door.

25

'Rosa?'

Rosa stopped in her tracks as she ushered down the vicarage steps the nice elderly couple with whom she'd spent the last hour discussing their forthcoming nuptials. Both in their mid- seventies, the marriage was apparently a first for both of them and Rosa had laughed, joking there was still hope for herself then.

'Hope for *you*?' Barbara Shufflebottom had chortled. 'A lovely young thing like *you*?' She'd patted Rosa's hand and added confidentially, 'I'm only giving up my independence so's I can finally get rid of this surname of mine. Can you imagine, all the forty or so years I carried this damned name as a teacher? I've been called every name under the sun by the kids I've taught, from ShuffleBum, to ShovelArse to Backside Barbara.' She'd grinned across at her betrothed, who'd smiled adoringly back. 'And now I'm going to be Barbara Bellingham. How fabulous is that?'

Rosa had joined in the banter, not wanting to rain on their forthcoming wedding parade when all she wanted to do was bury her head in her pillow and sob. How could Bill be dead? Died all alone in his armchair, the fire long gone out, with no one there with him as he exited this world. Surely everyone should have a hand to hold as they shake off this mortal coil and go off to meet their maker?

Oh, but she was going to miss Bill. He'd loved the three of them as much as – no more than – his legitimate offspring, Jonny and Henrietta. He'd once confided to her that if it hadn't been for herself, Eva and Hannah being there once Henry, his beloved son had died from a drug overdose, he couldn't have carried on. His love for the girls, he'd said, had kept him sane, kept him going when all was dark and hopeless.

'Rosa?'

Rosa said her final goodbyes to Barbara and Alan on the drive before walking over to Sam Burrows, who was standing at the vicarage garden's side gate.

'I'm sorry, Rosa, I don't have your phone number. Eva's just told me about your… your father. I'm so sorry. Would you rather cancel next week? I totally understand if you would.' Sam patted Rosa's arm sympathetically.

Rosa realised she was actually crying now, tears rolling down her face unbidden. 'Have to say, Sam,' she sobbed, 'I'm not convinced I'm going to be the best company.' She reached into her pocket for an already sodden tissue. 'You know, if it's, if it's… some stand-up comedy you've tickets for, then you might be better taking someone else.' As she spoke the words, despite the shock of learning of Bill's sudden death, Rosa realised she really hoped he wasn't going to cancel on her, wasn't going to accept she might not be the best company.

'Actually, it's a dress rehearsal of *The Nutcracker*.'

'The ballet?' Rosa sniffed once more and stared. 'And a dress rehearsal?'

'Before I joined the cruise ships as their dental officer, we lived in Sheffield.'

We? Who was *we*? Rosa automatically glanced towards Sam's left hand which, unfortunately, was encased in its black leather glove.

'Ah, you found them then?'

'Found them?'

'Your leather gloves?'

'They were in my car along.' Sam smiled, going slightly pink. 'Anyway, we had a lot to do with the South Yorkshire Ballet

Company there.' Sam paused but didn't elicit further, apart from adding that the company was putting on its traditional performance of Tchaikovsky's Christmas ballet for which, over the years, it had been both lauded and become actually quite famous. 'A friend of mine asked, now that I was back in Yorkshire, whether I'd like tickets for a pre-opening night performance. They're like gold dust apparently and, although it's still only November, they're well into rehearsals.' He paused once more. 'I thought it might be up your street?'

'Absolutely,' Rosa beamed, rubbing at the mascara she knew must now be heading down her cheek. 'I adore ballet.' She paused, feeling her nose grow longer. 'Actually, I'm telling great stonking fibs. I've never been to a ballet.'

'Even when you lived in London? All that opportunity to go to the Royal Opera House in Covent Garden or Sadler's Wells?'

'Guilty as charged, I'm afraid. Eva, Hannah and me were more Backstreet Boys' girls. But, there's always a first time for everything and yes, I'd still love to come.' *Especially if you wear that charcoal grey sweater, which is doing wonderful things for your eyes, not to mention my nether regions. Hell, get a grip, girl,* Rosa warned herself as she managed to tear her own eyes from those deep dark ones of his, *you're a vicar, not some sort of Jezebel.*

'You sure? You know, with your... with your father dying?'

'Please.' Rosa smiled. She'd save any excuses and explanations for when Hannah and Eva knew what she was up to.

'You're doing *what*?' Eva was livid. 'You're going to *a ballet*?' Eva spat the words as if Rosa had said she was going to *a brothel*. 'With my – our – new dentist? And Bill not been dead forty-eight hours yet?'

'You don't actually know that, Eva,' Hannah said mildly, glancing up at Rosa's kitchen clock now hanging proudly on the newly painted Jasmine walls onto which Rosa had spent the last couple of days rolling emulsion. 'By my reckoning, it's possibly longer. He was quite—'

'Alright, alright, Hannah, we don't need the full lurid details.' Eva's eyes narrowed as she glared across the table at Rosa. 'I really do think the three of us should be up at the hall, sorting things, being mindful of our father's passing, rather than you gallivanting off to some… some *ballet* with someone you don't know. And you, as a vicar, Rosa, should know this. You should know better.'

'Eva, I don't know what your problem is.' Rosa refilled Eva's mug with the last of the tea in the pot. 'You're beginning to sound like Virginia.'

'Now you're being insulting. I just think a bit of decorum, some decency, some propriety, protocol, good form…'

'Did you swallow a Roget along with your cheese sandwich for lunch?' Rosa began to laugh. 'And you know Hannah took another day off work today. She's been up there sorting things all day, Eva. I went up at lunchtime to join her there for a couple of hours before I came back to get on with my decorating and, really, we've probably done as much as we can at the moment.'

Hannah nodded in agreement. 'I was there all last night with the hall staff and the estate management team and went back up there this morning. Bill's solicitors know what his wishes are re funeral and burial and they've already informed his next of kin.'

'We're his next of kin,' Eva said hotly. '*We* are.'

'Not really, Eva,' Rosa said gently. 'We're not legitimately his next of kin.'

'Of course we are. We're his daughters. He loved us the most.'

'I'm not disputing that, but Bill's name isn't on our birth certificates. I once asked Dad about it and you can only put the birth father's name on a child's birth certificate if you are married to him or if he goes along with the mother to register the birth. Mum persuaded Alice not to go down that route. Alice's name is down of course, but not Bill's. And then within weeks of Mum and Dad adopting the three of us, the new adoption certification shows them as our parents.'

'And,' Hannah put in, 'even if Bill *had* put his name to our original birth certificates, Jonny and Henrietta are his legal offspring, were born before us, and are his true next of kin. Apparently, the pair of them are flying in from California tomorrow or the day after.'

'Vultures,' Eva said crossly. 'Just coming to claim their inheritance.'

'Of course they are. What do you expect, Eva?' Rosa smiled. 'Jonny Astley will inherit the title and everything that goes with Heatherly Hall.'

'They've no right to any of it,' Eva went on. 'How often have the pair of them been back from the States to see Bill?' When Rosa and Hannah both shook their heads, not knowing the answer, Eva snapped, 'Exactly – never. And now they'll be swanning in, getting all their ducks in a row.'

'Swans *and* ducks, Eva?' Rosa smiled. 'You can't blame the pair of them. Jonny will always have known he's next in line and, possibly, like Bill himself who didn't really want to leave London and move up to a crumbling draughty hall in cold windy West Yorkshire, it might be the last thing Jonny wants as well. Meanwhile, I've said I'll help arrange the funeral. I think we're looking at least ten days from now. Could be more.'

'So, do you fancy Sam, then?' Eva suddenly asked, her tone truculent.

'Ah, this is what's put your nose out of joint, isn't it?' Hannah grinned across at Eva who scowled back.

'I am a married woman,' Eva snapped.

'Exactly,' Hannah retorted. 'So keep your mitts off and let Rosa have a nice evening out with a rather gorgeous young man.' Hannah turned back to Rosa. 'Is this your first date since that doctor chap you went out with from Mansfield?'

'No, there have been others,' Rosa admitted. 'I may be a woman of the cloth but I have *a woman's needs*.' She mimed quotation marks around the words, while giving a slightly nervous laugh.

'And does your boss approve? You know of a vicar having carnal knowledge before marriage?' Hannah leaned forwards. 'Come on, Rosa, you've never admitted anything.'

'Who mentioned carnal knowledge?' Rosa went slightly pink. 'And the last thing I'm going to do is discuss with anyone, even you two, whether I end up in bed with anyone I go out with. That is between me and my date...' she paused '...and God.'

'Oh heavens, Rosa, when did you become so *good*?' Hannah elbowed Rosa in the ribs and then turned it into a full-blown hug. 'And Joe's been round, you know, Eva.'

'Sniffing round?' Eva said in exasperation. 'I hope you told him where to get off.'

'No,' Rosa went on calmly. 'I told him to send Rhys to do some little jobs around the church and the vicarage. Community Service as it were. Or, I'd have the police after him.'

'Really?' Hannah and Eva stared. 'Hmm, feisty, Rosa. So, how do you feel?'

'Feel? Well, at the moment, seeing as I've not really eaten all day, I'm suddenly feeling rather hungry. I could murder a crumpet.'

'No,' Hannah tutted. 'About, you know, Joe. Come on, Rosa, tell all.'

Rosa ran a hand through her long dark hair, sighed deeply and walked over to the breadbin on the blue Formica-topped kitchen unit. 'Sorry,' she apologised. 'It does seem a bit awful eating and enjoying crumpets when we've lost our father. Oh and I do miss him, you know. He wasn't always there for us when we were kids, but appeared to sort of grow into us and accept us as we became more interesting.' She posted two crumpets into the toaster and stood at the window, looking out over the vicarage garden. 'I'm going to extend Sarah Carey's herb garden, you know. Make a fabulous proper kitchen garden out here. Every herb and vegetable known to man. Woman.'

'Joe?' Hannah insisted.

'I love Joe. You know, you don't stop loving someone because they've made a mistake.'

'One bloody big mistake,' Eva sniffed, shaking her head at Rosa's back as her sister continued to survey the huge garden pots left behind by the former vicar's wife.

'I know, I know,' Rosa sighed again. 'Crumpets, either of you?'

'You look lovely.' Sam Burrows opened the car door for Rosa and she climbed into its showy, plush depths.

'Thank you. So does this car.'

Sam grinned. 'My one vice – always been a bit of a petrolhead. So,' he went on, once he was belted up and manoeuvring the car down the narrow vicarage drive, 'I really know very little about female vicars.'

'Not much different from male ones really,' Rosa smiled. 'Apart from the usual stuff.'

'You're not wearing your dog collar.'

'There's no law laid down by God or the Archbishop of Canterbury that says C of E clergy must never take off their working uniform. Think of vicaring being a bit like my day job and wearing overalls, and when I'm invited out to lovely things like this, I'm allowed to get dressed up like any other person off out for the evening.'

'I didn't realise.'

'No, people don't. Of course, there are some vicars who wear their dog collar constantly, and, to be honest, I rather like wearing mine, but just occasionally, it's nice not to stand out. You know, be seen as a woman rather than a vicar...' Rosa trailed off, embarrassed. Oh hell, was she pushing *I am a woman with a woman's needs* once again? 'In fact,' she quickly went on, 'there was advice handed down from the top a few years ago when it appeared vicars were being singled out for a quick mugging – you know, I suppose the idea being that a servant of God is less likely to turn round and thump the perpetrator back – that we should only be wearing the collar when we're actually working.'

'That's so interesting.' Sam smiled across at Rosa, once they'd entered the motorway slip road and were headed out towards Sheffield at speed. 'My parents brought me up a churchgoer and, as you know, I can take communion, but once I'd hit the age of eleven, I'd had enough; I wanted to be out on my bike, playing with my mates. Just Christmas Eve and Easter Sundays, christenings and marriages from then on. Sorry.'

Rosa laughed at that. 'You really don't need to apologise. I was the same. I soon joined Hannah and Eva who, after being forced to sit through hours of my grandfather droning on, had voted with their feet before I did. I think your church attendance probably fits into the same category as 90 per cent of people who write down C of E when they're asked what religion they are. For many years I wrote "none".'

'Really?'

'Hmm.' Here it comes, Rosa thought, the million-dollar question: *Why on earth did you become a vicar?* But, instead, Sam started asking about her time in London, the business that she'd created and she, in turn, found herself fascinated by his work as a dental officer on board huge liners including a short spell on the *Regent, Seven Seas Explorer* dubbed the most luxurious cruise ship in the world.

By the time Sam had explained how after several years it had all become too much for him – too exotic, spoilt rich people with nothing better to do than eat far too much, drink too much and follow guides with little orange markers on umbrellas round too obvious amazing places ruined by crowds of sightseers – he had parked the car and Rosa was following him into the theatre.

'If you've never been to a ballet,' Sam said, once they were settled in the theatre in rather good seats, '*The Nutcracker* is a great one to cut your teeth on.'

'Or crack your nuts on?'

'I beg your pardon?'

'Oh sorry, that just slipped out.' Rosa gave a nervous titter. *Bloody hell, Rosa, you'll be wittering on about Toilet Duck down the vicarage lavatory again if you don't shut up*. She gave another little involuntary giggle and was relieved to see Sam not only smiling but actually laughing, his shoulders heaving with mirth. Oh, thank goodness, a man with a sense of humour. She'd always been able to make Joe laugh and he her. For just a split second, Rosa longed for it to be Joe sitting next to her.

'So, as I was saying,' Sam finally managed to get out, '*The Nutcracker* is a great introduction to ballet appreciation. You'll recognise half the hits.'

'The hits?' Rosa started to laugh again.

'Yes, *the Pas de Deux, The Dance of the Sugar Plum…*'

'Sam! Darling, I'm so glad you felt able to come.' Sam stood up and was immediately embraced by a middle-aged, somewhat flamboyantly dressed man. 'How are you? I hear you've finally left the cruise liners?'

Sam nodded, slightly ill at ease, Rosa felt, as he turned to introduce the man. 'Rosa, this is Tristan Sinclair. He's been allowed to bring Peter Wright's fabulous production of this particular ballet to the North for years.'

'Ten actually, darling. This is the tenth year we've put it on.' The man held out a hand and shook Rosa's own. 'Now, must get backstage and make sure everything is going to plan. Don't forget this is a dress rehearsal. I may have to stop the performers mid-jeté if they're not up to scratch. But then, you'll know all about that, Sam, won't you?'

'You're obviously big into ballet? Know a lot about it…?' Rosa started to whisper, but the lights were dimming and the orchestra tuning up and within the first few minutes she was hooked, absorbed fully in the wonderful introductory *Miniature Overture* leading to *The Decoration of The Christmas Tree*. 'This is fabulous,' Rosa eventually whispered in Sam's direction and, obviously gratified that bringing her here had been a success, Sam took her hand and squeezed it.

Oh hell, she was *so* out of practice. Did she actually *acknowledge* the hand in hers? Squeeze it back in encouragement or simply hold it there, wrapped in his? Hope against hope he would continue to hold it? Rosa suddenly knew, more than anything, she wanted Sam to keep on holding her hand. It felt so right; so wonderful to have her hand held in another. She looked down at the large, tanned hand with its clean fingernails and, without thinking further, stroked the sensitive area between finger and thumb with her own thumb. Sam smiled down at her, his large, dark eyes full of warmth and Rosa's heart did that little flippy turnover thing that anyone who has suddenly and unexpectedly fallen in love can recognise.

She was basking being in the moment, simultaneously intoxicated by the music while exhilarated by the dance and then amused but cross as Fritz, Clara's brother, runs off with and breaks the Nutcracker doll at the Stahlbaum household Christmas Eve party. She turned to say something to Sam, but was horrified to see tears rolling down his face. 'Sam?' she whispered. 'Are you OK?'

Sam seemed unable to say anything, but attempted to smile, dashing crossly at the tears with the hand that had previously been in her own.

'Do you want to go? Leave?'

Sam shook his head, whispering in a low voice, 'It's just... you know... this is the first time I've been back... and I thought I'd be OK... It's hard... I loved him so much.'

Oh heavens. Rosa felt the bubble she'd been floating on since Sam held her hand burst in a wet soggy splat around her. Of course, of course, it was all falling into place: Sam was gay and had been in love with one of the male dancers and something had happened to their relationship. What had that producer bloke said? *I'm so glad you felt able to come.* And working on cruise liners? Did gay men find themselves working on cruise ships in the same way that, stereotypically, one thought of airlines attracting gay men? And had Sam reasoned that she, Rosa, as a vicar and therefore presumably not about to jump on him, was a safer bet to accompany him back to this theatre than either Eva – particularly Eva – or Hannah who, in some respects, had both been fairly blatant in their fancying of the new village dentist.

Rosa felt a cold shiver of disappointment go through her knowing that, from the minute she's seen Sam Burrows at the bottom of Eva's stairs when invited to Azra's curry supper, she'd been immediately drawn to him. Rearranging her face in its best caring vicar's look, Rosa patted Sam's arm sympathetically and he nodded towards her gratefully. When, twenty minutes later, the curtain came down on half-time, he took her hand, leading her up the aisle to the back of the theatre and the bar.

'It'll be a longer half-time because it's a dress rehearsal,' Sam said, turning his head to face her. 'Come on, let's get a drink.'

Once they were seated, each with a gin and tonic to hand, Rosa asked, 'Something upset you? Or are you always moved to tears by Tchaikovsky?'

Sam said nothing for a while but stirred the ice round his drink with the black plastic straw. Eventually he took a deep breath. 'I've not been able to bring myself to come back to this theatre. You know, to watch this production.'

'I'm so sorry,' Rosa said. 'You were really hurting back there. You said you loved him very much. Had you been with him a long time?'

'With him?' Sam looked surprised and then nodded. 'Hmm, twelve years. It's a long time to have someone in your life and then lose them. Ollie was such a superb dancer. It was funny really, because, a bit like me, football and rugby were his big thing until we took him to see *Billy Elliot* in the West End. After that, he changed direction completely. And you know, he never cared that the kids at school teased him about being a ballet dancer – he just got on with it.'

'Right.' Kids at school? Rosa wasn't quite understanding.

'So,' she finally asked, taking the bull by the horns, 'you were in a relationship with Ollie?'

'In a relationship with him?' Sam stared. 'I was his dad. I *am* his dad. You don't stop being someone's dad because they die and are no longer with you.'

'Oh heavens, Jesus, I'm so sorry, Sam. You lost your son?'

'Hmm. I'm sorry, for some reason I thought you knew. I don't know why.' Sam ran a hand through his fair hair and looked across at Rosa. 'Er, who did you think I'd lost?'

'I thought you loved some man. Some fabulous dancer who'd you been with for twelve years.'

'You thought I was gay?' Sam looked horrified for a couple of seconds and then began to laugh, seemingly unable to stop.

'Hmm.'

'Rosa, sitting next to you in my car and then in the theatre, I can assure you my thoughts and feelings were entirely and utterly those of a red-blooded, absolutely heterosexual male...'

'Oh.' Rosa felt the splatted, wet bubble of disappointment reform into a light airy-fairy thing that was in the process of lifting her up off her seat and floating her up somewhere in the region of heaven and a band of grinning, whooping, cheering angels.

26

With the wonderful knowledge that Sam had invited her along to the theatre because he actually fancied her and hadn't sought her out as someone trained to support others in their time of need, Rosa sat through the second half of the performance in a slight daze. Only the stunning *Dance of the Sugar Plum Fairy* finally brought her back to concentrating on the story and the dancers, rather than the presence of the man sitting beside her.

'Let's make a quick exit,' Sam urged, abruptly standing once the curtain came down for the third and last time. 'Much as I love people I still know here, I really don't want to find myself backstage, dealing with their questions and sympathy. I'll come back to an actual performance nearer Christmas and see everyone then. Let's find somewhere for a quick drink.'

Once ensconced in a rather lovely country pub on the way back to Midhope, Rosa warmed her hands at the blazing open fire and took a sip of her wine.

'Soon be Christmas,' Sam smiled. 'I can't believe it's almost December already. I guess it's a busy time for you – you know, Christmas?'

'It can be.' Rosa looked directly at Sam. 'Sam, are you able to talk about Ollie?'

'Yes of course. It's been three years since he died and, while it doesn't really get a great deal easier, especially at Christmas, I find with time I'm more able to come to terms with his death. I can now look at photographs of him, watch videos of him when he was little, not get too upset if I come across his teddy or the first baby tooth he lost – you know things like that. This evening was a big test. I nearly went to see the performance of *Nutcracker* last year when I was home with my parents for Christmas. They were going to come with me, but it was snowing heavily and a jolly good excuse not to actually go.' Sam turned to Rosa. 'Thank you so much for coming with me, Rosa… and, you know, apologies for the emotional outburst.' Sam looked away, obviously embarrassed.

'Why would you apologise for showing emotion? Was there something in that scene, particularly, that triggered it?'

'Ollie had only been dancing three years – he was twelve when he died – but he'd auditioned for and been given the part of Fritz – you know, Clara's brother who runs off with and breaks the nutcracker doll? – and seeing the boy this evening dancing the part of Fritz and giving it everything he'd got, just like Ollie did…'

'All a bit much, I guess?'

Sam nodded. 'Ollie's mother, Penny, and I had split up a year before that and we had shared custody of Ollie here in Sheffield which, although I obviously wanted to have him with me all the time, was, I suppose, working as well as it could. Penny is an interior designer and spends a lot of time both in London and New York, which was good for me as I had him living with me those weeks as well.'

'Not easy sharing a child.' Rosa knew, if she and Joe had had children, she would have absolutely hated sharing her child with anyone else.

'Penny fell in love with someone else. Always hurts when their new partner becomes a part of your child's life. Anyway, Penny's new man was big into skiing and the three of them went off to Courmayeur in Italy just as soon as they could after Christmas. I've always loved skiing myself and Ollie had been on the slopes with me and Penny since he was tiny so, although it hurts seeing your son eager to be off with your ex-wife's new man, you just have to go along with it.'

'Ollie died in Italy?' Rosa reached for Sam's hand.

'Yes. An avalanche. Penny's partner possibly ignored the warnings and they got caught in the middle of it. He and Ollie died, but Penny, apparently some way behind the two of them, was caught on the periphery of it and survived.'

'I am sorry. So very sorry. I've never heard of anyone dying in an avalanche.'

'On average, a hundred lives a year are lost in avalanches. And that's just Europe.'

Rosa mulled this over in silence, unable to contemplate Sam's loss of his son, so far from home.

'So, after months of flying to and from Italy, of burying my twelve-year-old son and obviously trying to comfort Penny – who blamed herself – as well as my parents, who were distraught, I just wanted to get away.'

'Running away?'

'Yes, I did. I ran away. I ran away to sea and to see the world. I reckon I've seen every major tourist attraction – the Statue of Liberty, Sydney Harbour, the Pyramids, both the Aurora Borealis and the Aurora Australis, Table Mountain – you name it, I've seen it several times over.'

'And did it help?'

'To begin with, yes, I think it did. The challenge of a new job, as well as having to make people believe I was emotionally stable when there were times I just wanted to throw in the towel and walk the plank, as it were.' Sam smiled. 'I suppose I'd always wanted to travel, but Ollie came along when we weren't really expecting it, and… you know…' Sam sighed. 'Anyway, three years on and I'd really had enough of being on board. I happened to be home on leave at the end of the summer and saw Rayan's advert for Malik & Malik, wanting an additional dentist, but not until the extensions to the new surgery were completed. And so, I had a long phone call with Rayan from very near the Panama Canal; he asked me to apply and here I am.'

'Here you are.' Rosa smiled across at Sam, taking in the dark eyes, the fair hair and the full mouth which, when he smiled, showed perfect teeth. Well, he was a dentist, Rosa reminded herself.

'I'm sorry, I've talked all about myself and you've just lost your father.'

'One of them. I have two.'

'Ah yes, Azra told me the whole story of you and your birth mother and father. Wow, Alice Parkes *and* the Marquess of Heatherly. You couldn't make it up, could you?'

'Azra told you?'

'Hmm, on curry night. I helped her make coffee once I'd finished sorting a few things with Rayan. She obviously loves your story and all it entails.'

Rosa laughed. 'She's great, is Azra. Drives Eva mad, but then I guess that's what in-laws do.'

'Was your father's death unexpected?'

'Bill's death? I always think of him just as Bill and my dad as my father. If that makes sense?'

'I think so.'

'So, in some ways it wasn't unexpected. Bill was eighty-three and always lived a fairly sybaritic lifestyle. Smoked like a chimney, ate what he shouldn't and drank far too much red wine and port. To be honest, I'm amazed he made it to eighty.'

'And who will take over the hall and be the next marquess?'

'John Astley, Bill's only remaining son. It will all be very different up there when Jonny takes over, I guess, but absolutely nothing to do with us three girls.'

Sam glanced at his watch. 'I'd better get you home.' He paused. 'I've really enjoyed being with you this evening, Rosa. Can we do it again?'

'Please.' Rosa heard the angels' harps tuning up once more. 'Yes please.'

'Kitchen's looking good.' Eva paused to survey the new decorating. 'You've missed a bit. Up there.' She pointed to a small patch, still Sludge Green beneath an ocean of Jasmine White, towards the left of the battered and rusting Tricity three-ringed cooker.

'Not a problem,' Rosa said cheerfully. 'My lovely new red stove is being delivered next week and it will hide it. How come you're not working?' Rosa handed Nora one of the tiny gingerbread reindeers she'd made that morning, its nose and antlers marked out with white and red icing.

'Don't give her sugar.' Eva frowned and then relented. 'I don't suppose one will hurt. We're off to family assembly across at Little Acorns. It's the last Thursday in the month and it's Laila's class's turn to take it. She's a Victorian workhouse kid and has spent the last week practising her lines with one hand pressed dramatically to her forehead: "Oh, my poor little brother, Bobby – what's to become of us now that Ma and Pa and all our ten brothers and sisters have died of the cholera and we have to go into the workhouse?" while unravelling rope.'

'Unravelling rope?'

'According to Laila, that's what you do all day in a workhouse – unravel rope. Oh, and eat thin porridge made with water. Jolly glad the three of *us* weren't born a hundred and fifty years ago or that's where Alice would have put us. We foundlings would have ended up in the workhouse and I really can't eat porridge without brown sugar and double cream. I thought you'd have been going over to the school yourself?'

'I'm booked in for the religious, not the family stuff. Anyway, if I've time I'm going back up to Heatherly Hall to see if I can do anything to help up there. Hannah's now actually taken over a week off work – using up any holiday period she has left this year.'

'Right.' Eva looked slightly put out. 'I've not been up there yet myself. I don't seem to be involved in what's going on. I mean, shouldn't we be writing letters, you know, telling people, inviting people to the funeral?'

'Hannah seems to be doing all that with the solicitors and the estate management team. I think she's thrown herself into all the arrangements, trying to take her mind off Ben.'

'She's not heard anything from him then?' Eva glanced across at Nora who was licking thoughtfully at the icing. 'He's not, you know, arrived on her doorstep with a suitcase and all his worldly goods in two black bin liners?'

Rosa shook her head. 'No. She's had one miserable text from Ben saying "Sorry".'

'Sorry? Sorry for what? Sorry for being an adulterous wa...' Eva, aware of Nora's presence whispered the *nker*. 'Or, sorry for Hannah being outed in church? Or, sorry, he's just having his tea with his kids and his wife, and he'll be round as usual later on once he's helped clear the table?'

'Just be thankful it's all over. Ben appears to be staying with his wife and Hannah will just have to get over it.' Rosa pulled a face. 'Hell, that makes me sound as sanctimonious as Grandpa Cecil; sorry, it came out wrongly.' She folded her arms. 'So, I don't suppose you dropped in just to tell me about the goings-on in Victorian workhouses?'

'As opposed to what?' Eva looked shifty.

'As opposed to how did my date go last night?'

'Your *date*? So, it was a date? With Sam?'

'Yes, Eva, it turned out to be a date,' Rosa grinned. 'And it was lovely.'

'And are you seeing him again?'

'I do hope so. I'm going to invite him over for supper once the funeral's over and the kitchen's up and running again.'

'Do you think it's a good idea you having a relationship with one of my staff?'

'A relationship?' Rosa burst out laughing. 'I don't think one date constitutes a relationship. Do you?'

'But you're hoping for more?'

'Oh, listen to yourself, Eva.' Rosa was laughing more as she went to wipe Nora's sticky fingers. 'I'm sorry if I've come between you and your little fantasies.'

'Fantasies? I don't know what you're talking about.'

'You know exactly what I'm talking about, you baggage. Now, take this glorious little girl you and Rayan have produced together, go across to school to see your other miracle – unravelling rope' – Rosa laughed out loud at this – 'and then go home with them both and book a surprise romantic weekend away for you and your husband. I'll have Nora and Laila to stay here if Azra isn't around when you get off somewhere.'

'Hmmph.' Eva pulled a face. 'Hannah was right, Rosa – when *did* you become so bloody *good*?' She picked up her bag and coat, marched over to Rosa and glared at her before enveloping her in a bone-crushing hug. 'And wise?'

'Hello, Rhys. You decided to go along with my idea then?' Rosa led Carys's son down the corridor and into the kitchen. 'Cup of tea? A Coke?' Rhys glared at Rosa but said nothing. He glanced round at the newly painted kitchen but, if he was surprised at how different it looked from when he was there before, declined to comment. 'Coke?' Rosa asked again.

Rhys nodded but still didn't speak.

'So, come on, Rhys, what do you think of this idea of mine? You come and help me here and in the church, and I won't go to the police. 'It will be a sort of payback to the local community. The vicarage is in need of some tarting up.'

'Tarting up?' Rhys gave Rosa a look.

'You know, a bit of decorating?'

Rhys shrugged. 'I've no choice, have I? But I'm telling you now, I've no idea how to decorate. And I don't want you praying over me. Or having me on my knees, praying with you.'

Rosa laughed out loud at that. She was surprised to hear a voice that was well spoken, almost accent-less, and had to remind herself that Rhys was a Southerner, brought up in London and, from what she recalled of Carys telling her, educated at private schools paid for by his wealthy but absent birth father. She wondered how much input this father of his still had now that Carys had abandoned him and Joe had taken on his upbringing.

'We could sing "Onward Christian Soldiers" together instead of praying?'

'You *are* joking?' Rhys looked at Rosa in horror.

'Yep, I'm joking. You put on whatever music you want. And we can learn together. I'm not so hot at it myself.' They both stared at the missed patch of Sludge Green.

'That manky old cooker is spoiling your paint job.'

'I know. That's why it's going. So, I've just about finished in here. What I want to do is the sitting room next. There's years of wallpaper on the walls that has to come off.'

'Well, I've no idea how to do *that*.' Rhys was truculent once more. 'Why don't you just paper over the old stuff?'

'Because every other incumbent here appears to have done just that...'

'Incumbent?'

'Every vicar. So, let's learn together.'

'Oh, God, do I have to?'

'Your choice, Rhys. Look,' she went on, leading him into the sitting room, 'I've hired this steam machine. As far as I can see, we just spray the walls with steam and scrape.'

'Come on then, let's get it over with. How long do I have to stay? And how often do I have to come?'

'Let's see how we get on, shall we? Right, help me get these curtains down and then we'll get steaming.'

Two hours later when the layers of old wallpaper were coming off in surprisingly gratifying strips, and Rhys had stopped only a couple of times to check his phone and plug himself into his music, Rosa tapped the boy on his shoulder, making him jump.

'Cup of tea? And a chicken sandwich?'

Rhys merely nodded but downed his tools and took the mug and plate Rosa offered him.

'How are you finding the high school?' she asked as she sipped at her own hot tea.

'S'OK.'

'Made any friends?'

'A few,' he offered once he'd swallowed the first bite of the sandwich and was going in for a second.

'What subjects do you like?'

'Art, maths, DT.'

'Oh, art? My sisters and I were pretty good at art ourselves.'

'Well, you would be, wouldn't you?'

'Would we?'

'You know, being Alice Parkes' daughters and all that.'

Rosa looked up from her tea. 'Oh, you know that?'

'Yeah, course. I know it all. We're actually studying Alice Parkes' stuff at school. You know, with her being an ex-pupil of Westenbury Comprehensive and a local celebrity. I also know that Mum used to work with you and that she pinched Joe from you.'

'You can only pinch someone if they want to be pinched. It's not like pinching a mobile phone that has no say in the matter.' *Oh bugger*. Rosa mentally kicked herself. Hadn't Hannah told her Rhys had been up for robbing a mobile phone from someone when he was in London? 'So, who told you all this?' she added quickly when Rhys's face was beginning to close down once more.

'Roberto, Joe's dad.'

'Right.'

'He doesn't like me. Blames me for all the stuff Mum got up to.'

'Surely not. Roberto is lovely.'

'He might be to you and he is to Chiara, but he's always trying to catch me out. If he can't find his watch or his cufflinks or something, he looks at me as if I've nicked them.'

'I'm sorry.'

'Yeah well...' Rhys trailed off and then added: 'I asked him if I could work in the restaurant, you know, earn some money on Saturdays but he won't let me. Says I might end up pinching things from the place. Or from the customers.'

'What do you want money for?'

'What do I *want* it for?' Rhys gave her such a look, Rosa wanted to laugh. 'You know, the usual stuff: trainers, music, smokes...' He scowled up at her before demolishing the remains of the sandwich in one huge final bite. 'And,' he added through the mouthful, 'I want to go and live with Mum.'

'Sorry?'

'I want to go to Sydney. I want to go and live with my mum.'

'I can understand that.'

'Can you? No one else can, although Roberto would have me off and out of his hair in a flash if he could. Mum says I have to wait, she'll send me a ticket soon. But she hasn't, so I need money to get one myself.'

'You know, Rhys,' Rosa said gently, standing up to gather the dirty mugs and plates, 'you'll need to have a clean record before they let you into Australia.'

'Why do you think I'm here?'

Before she could reply, Joe had appeared in the room, making them both jump. 'You need to lock that door, Rosa.'

'I'd have dropped him back home,' Rosa said as he followed her into the kitchen. 'I have to say, Joe, Rhys has done a good job.'

'I need to talk to you. Rosa, please, have dinner with me? Just let me talk to you. *Please*? On neutral ground.'

'Neutral ground?' Rosa pulled a face. 'You sound like Switzerland during the war.'

'You know what I mean. Please? Tomorrow night?'

'Fine, fine.' She put up her hands in acquiescence. 'I'm always happy to have my dinner bought for me,' she said breezily, although her pulse was racing and she was already planning what she would wear.

27

Rosa had been doggedly determined in her decision to drive herself to the restaurant, telling Joe she'd meet him there and didn't need picking up. She didn't trust herself, or her emotions, to be sat at dinner alongside Joe Rosavina with several glasses of Merlot inside her. Who knew what she might end up doing? Far better to take her car and not be tempted to rely on alcohol to prop her up, as well as not be fully in control of herself. She'd also been about to don her vicar's robes (albeit her best pink one, which she knew complemented her dark hair and brown eyes) but a natural vanity – for which she apologised profusely to the Almighty for having – had her choosing her favourite pink figure-hugging dress, a Christmas present from Hannah the previous year.

She made up her face carefully, defiantly outlined her full mouth in the brightest of pink and slipped on a pair of black high heels which, after months of flatties, were guaranteed to have her with aching toes and calf muscles by the end of the evening.

'Hey up, Vicar, you look grand. Are you off somewhere nice?' Denis Butterworth, the verger, recently risen, like Lazarus from his sickbed, was unlocking the church hall door as Rosa hobbled somewhat precariously down the cobbled path towards her car on the too-high heels.

'Denis? What are you doing out of bed? Are you feeling better?'

'Much,' he nodded. 'But don't tell our Sandra I'm up and about or she'll have a fit. She's gone to a final meeting of the

Young Wives up at Maureen Hardcastle's place before this hey-up do next Saturday night.'

'Hoedown, Denis. It's a hoedown not a hey-up.' Rosa laughed at the verger's words.

'Whatever, love. I just wanted to make sure everything in the church hall was OK; didn't want to leave it all up to you to sort out. It's my job.' He paused. 'I were right sorry to hear about your dad, lass.' He paused, and gave her another once-over, his eyebrows raised. 'But you seem to be coping alright.'

Oh hell, that was all she needed. The whole village knowing she'd been out on the town dressed in vibrant pink when, presumably, the accepted thing was to stay at home in black funereal weeds, praying for the soul of the twelfth Marquess of Heatherly.

'Just going to visit my mum and dad,' Rosa called sweetly. *Sorry, God,* she offered up a silent apology, for telling fibs once more.

'What, dressed up like a chocolate box?'

A chocolate box? Rosa hesitated. Had she overdone it? Should she go back and change into her black cassock? 'Mum's just gone into her... er... *pink phase* and is cooking a pink dinner: you know, everything pink: er prawns, salmon, er...' *oh hell, what other food was pink?* '...beetroot and radish salad, then pink blancmange... you know... a bit of fun... she's told us we actually have to wear pink as well.'

'A pink fun dinner? And not ten days since the marquess passed over?' Denis stared and then shook his head slightly. 'Right, fair enough, love, Bill Astley wouldn't have wanted you miserable.' He gave a short bark of laughter. 'Hey, you could do with one of them there rude pink cowboy hats they're all going to be wearing a week on Saturday.'

'Oh, silly me. Duh,' Rosa tinkled. 'Why didn't I think of that? Right, must go; glad you're feeling better, Denis.' She gave a final wave of farewell and slipped into the driving seat, adjusting the mirror as she did so. Hell, *had* she overdone it? She dithered slightly, on the point of going back to the vicarage to change her dress and tone down her make-up but, chastising herself instead with the admonishment: *What are you doing, you devastated one? Why dress yourself in scarlet and put on jewels of gold? Why highlight your eyes with make-up? You adorn yourself in vain*, while simultaneously trying to remember which bit of the Bible the censure originated from while putting the car into gear.

Rosa hovered uncertainly both on her too-high heels and the periphery of the restaurant, trying to locate Joe in the dimly lit and already crowded room. Then he rose from a table to her right and made to come forward to greet her but, instead she walked towards him on legs of jelly. Oh, but he was still so gorgeous; still, after all this time, so Joe. Was she ever going to stop loving him?

He was nervous, she could tell, his hands shaking slightly around the glass of wine he immediately put down on the table as she sat on the chair he pulled from the table.

'Rosa, you look absolutely stunning.' Joe kissed her cheek. 'I'm so glad you felt able to come.' He hesitated. 'Let me get you a drink. What's your tipple these days?'

'Just a sparkling water, please.'

'You don't drink anymore? Is that with your being in charge of a church?'

'No, it's with my being in charge of a Corsa.' Rosa shook her car keys in his direction before dropping them into her bag and turning to look at Joe as he endeavoured to get the attention of the waiter. Every bit of him was as she remembered: the thick fair hair and the amazing blue eyes she'd, over the years, nightly conjured up, unable to let him go in her dreams as she'd had to let him go in the flesh. He'd aged well: there was still a tightness of the jaw, his hairline still well forward, a lack of the fine lines and wrinkles one might expect in a man about to enter his fourth decade.

Joe's eyes met her own as she drank in every aspect of him and, embarrassed, she quickly turned away, reaching for the menu the waiter had placed in front of her.

'Rosa, I know I don't deserve for you to sit here and listen to me but please, please hear me out? You'll never ever know how much I regret what I did. How I hurt you so badly; how there's not been one day in the last six years when I've not wished I could put back the clock.'

Rosa nodded her thanks to the waiter as he placed the tall glass of carbonated water clinking with ice, lemon and bubbles in front of her.

'Rosa, I swear to you,' Joe went on, 'it was one drunken night. A total and utter mistake that I will regret for the rest of my life.' Joe sighed deeply, ran his hand through his thick blond hair and looked Rosa directly in the eye. 'It was the evening of our annual staff do at the Grosvenor on Mayfair. I'd bought you that dress…? Remember?'

Rosa did. The most beautiful midnight blue dress that Joe had known instantly was so right for her.

'And then, at the last minute, you didn't come with me. You took a flight to Japan instead…'

'And I suggested you take Carys along in my place.'

'You did. And I didn't want to. I wanted you with me, Rosa. But you were off to Heathrow without a backward glance. And Carys and I both drank too much and then…' Joe's face was pale, his blue eyes dull as he remembered. 'And then…'

'Spare me the details, Joe. I'm really not interested in hearing this.' Rosa glared at him. 'Actually, no, I do want details. Do you remember the weekend Michelle and Roberto came down to stay with us?'

Joe nodded.

'The night before, you slept in the spare room.'

Joe nodded. 'I remember.'

'You had a shower at 2 a.m.' Rosa glared once more. 'You'd been with her, hadn't you? Carys? You were washing off the sex.'

'No!' Joe gave a bark of astonishment 'No! Is that what you've always thought, Rosa? As far as I remember, I'd been to some club with some Chinese clients. Or possibly Americans... I honestly don't recall. It was a hot night; I was sweaty and tired. Didn't want to disturb you when you weren't sleeping well and having all those hot sweats yourself.'

'Right.'

'Rosa, I've never lied to you about what happened.'

'What? It was all one big lie. Would you have told me what you'd been up to with Carys if she hadn't got pregnant?'

'Yes.' Joe looked Rosa straight in the eye. 'Yes, I would.' He sighed deeply. 'You've never let me tell you what happened, Rosa.' Joe rubbed at his face, his eyes haunted, but never once took his gaze from her own. 'For almost two years I'd felt I couldn't get through to you, Rosa. You were flying high and that was absolutely brilliant. I loved your ambition, your energy; wanted to share it all with you. But you were exhausted. Some evenings when you came home at midnight – and there were a couple of evenings you never even made it home, when you were still talking to the States at four in the morning – you were drip white. You couldn't even eat you were so wiped out. It was almost as though you were addicted. You know, an adrenaline junkie.'

'But...'

'Rosa, please just hear me out. I tried talking to you, telling you to slow down. Trying to get you to take time off. Remember the weekend away in Dublin I'd organised for both of us? And then you cancelled at the very last minute? Hannah and Eva had a go at you; Bill did too. But you were on a mission. I'd lost you, Rosa...'

'Oh, don't be so ridiculous,' Rosa snapped. 'You hadn't "*lost me*"' – she drew furious quotation marks in the air – 'at all.'

'You weren't there, Rosa. And I don't mean, you weren't there just for *me*. I don't mean that at all. Both physically, but more importantly in spirit, you'd changed. You were off wheeler-dealing, determined not to let anyone else get that deal you wanted.'

'You were happy with me making money and getting in there first. You encouraged me...'

'I was. I did. I was so proud of you, Rosa. But then I lost you. You'd become a totally different person. You just wouldn't *give up*. Even though you'd promise not to think about work and have some time just for yourself or for us, I'd find you on your phone, at your laptop...' Joe shook his head. 'And then you started on stuff to keep yourself awake. Instead of sleeping, coming to bed, you'd fill yourself with strong coffee and Red Bull at one in the morning just so you could pull off deals in America.'

'That was only a couple of times, Joe...' Rosa broke off, unable to meet his eyes.

'Rosa, you know it wasn't. And don't tell me you didn't carry on taking Provigil after I'd found them in your bag and thrown them out.'

'They were in my bag. Just in case...'

'Rosa, we'd already been through all this at Durham when it was finals. You took the stuff to keep yourself awake so you could keep working through the night in the library. You were so determined to get your first. So determined to be the triplet out on top.'

'It wasn't like that; that's not why I did it...'

'No? What was it then?'

'Everyone took stuff...' Rosa reached for her drink, her hand shaking slightly.

'They didn't, Rosa. *I* didn't,' Joe said gently.

'Exams were easy for you. It all was easy for you.'

'Not an argument, Rosa. Not an excuse for you to take uppers. And to keep on taking them again when we were in London.'

'You're making me out to be a drug addict,' Rosa protested.

'I seriously thought you were addicted. Carys was worried too.'

'Carys?' Rosa snapped. 'Carys was worried? Ha, it was her who went out and got me the stuff.' Rosa felt herself redden as she remembered how she'd confided to Carys she needed to keep awake to pull off a couple of deals over the phone in New York.

'I didn't know.' Joe stared.

'No.' Rosa held Joe's eye. 'We trusted her.'

There was silence again as they both contemplated what had just been revealed and then Joe said, 'Rosa, when it all blew up, when the Carys thing happened, you didn't give me a chance. I know, absolutely, I didn't deserve it, but we could have sorted it, talked about what to do, where to go. You were straight off, back up north, like a rat up a drainpipe, the troops descending, whisked away by Eva and Hannah instead of us sitting down and trying to work a way forward out of the mess.' Joe took Rosa's hand once more. 'The mess of my making – I know that, Rosa.'

'Joe, I'd just been diagnosed with Stage 2 cancer.'

'I know, I *know.*' Joe closed his eyes at the memory. 'It was all so terrible for you. I loved you, Rosa. I've always loved you.'

'And,' Rosa interrupted, 'I hate to remind you of this, Joe, but Carys was pregnant. You knew how much *I* wanted a baby.'

Joe stared. 'Sorry, mate, can you give us another five minutes?' He nodded at the waiter who was hovering, and drained his glass of wine. 'Actually, sorry, could I get another of these?' He turned back to Rosa. 'Hang on a minute,' Joe continued to stare, his eyebrows raised, 'I was with you for almost *fifteen years* and you never *once* mentioned wanting kids. You *never* gave me the impression you wanted children, Rosa. Ever. When I brought up the subject, you closed down completely...'

'When we were kids ourselves, yes OK, you're right,' Rosa interrupted hotly. 'The last thing *either* of us wanted was domesticity. We were going to travel, see the world, *conquer* the world...'

'Exactly.' Joe was angry. 'So why on earth are you now saying you *did* want children?'

Rosa felt herself lost for words. Joe was right – she'd never wanted to be a mother. Not until Eva was pregnant. Not until Carys was having Joe's child. Not until the cancer had stripped away a good chance of her ever having her own baby in her arms.

When she finally looked across at Joe, he was still staring at her, but shaking his head. 'Rosa, I remember you telling me categorically you couldn't see yourself ever having children. You were terrified you'd end up with triplets. I remember exactly where we were...'

'I'm sorry.' Rosa felt tears start.

'You were the totally driven businesswoman, going through the glass ceiling like there was no tomorrow. To be absolutely brutal, when *would* you have fitted in having *children*?'

When Rosa didn't reply, guiltily remembering how much Joe had wanted them to have children of their own and how she'd constantly put him off when he'd approached the subject, he went on, 'I couldn't come to terms with Carys terminating a child. My child.' He paused, reached for his glass of water. 'Chiara is my life, Rosa. The one – the *only* – good thing to come out of this whole terrible mess of my doing.'

'Of course she is. I wouldn't expect anything less from you. She's beautiful.'

Joe glanced behind him at the hovering waiter. 'Look, we need to order. What will you have?'

Rosa felt any food would turn to ashes in her mouth, but she quickly scanned the menu for something that would slip down easily. 'The gazpacho please...' (she loathed gazpacho) '...and... erm... the salmon.' Pink food.

'You appear to have been a bit of a hit with Rhys,' Joe smiled, once the waiter (the most obsequious Rosa thought she'd ever encountered and who, had she been there with Eva and Hannah instead of with Joe, they'd all have ended up teasing) had almost bowed double in his sycophancy as he left the table once more.

'A bit of a hit?' Rosa frowned. 'With Rhys? We hardly exchange more than a few words.'

'Any words elicited at all from Rhys is progress. He shuts himself in his room and doesn't communicate with us at all.'

'He's not happy, Joe. And he's fourteen.'

'Nearly fifteen.'

'Nearly fifteen then. Didn't *you* hate the world and his wife when you were that age? I think we three did.'

'Ah yes, how are the Shadows?' Joe smiled; the wonderful smile Rosa thought had gone forever. 'I never thought I'd miss them as much as I do.'

'The Shadows?' Rosa frowned. 'You make me sound like Cliff Richard.'

Joe actually laughed out loud at that. 'They always came first in your life. I don't suppose they'll ever forgive me...?'

'I don't imagine they ever will.' Rosa knew she wanted to hurt Joe badly and, in doing so, felt quite terrible herself that she felt unable to forgive. She was a vicar, for heaven's sake – it was part of her job description to forgive people. Especially those she loved. She'd forgive Hannah and Eva if they let her down. Wouldn't she? Rosa shook her head slightly, trying to sort out her feelings but, instead, hearing Eva's scornful furious voice: *Forgive the bastard? He fucking well slept with your best friend. Got her pregnant.*

'Rosa, can we at least be friends?' Joe's eyes held her own.

How many times had she fantasised about this moment? Of Joe asking to come back into her life? But, suddenly confused, she found she was looking at him objectively for the first time, maybe ever. She could never deny the attractiveness of him, the sheer sexual masculinity of him, but she also thought, feeling terribly sad at the idea, it was a bit like looking through her old *Teen* magazines featuring the Backstreet Boys. Looking at Joe was like looking at an adult version of her idol, Nick Carter. In the same way she might take down her old scrapbooks and magazines from where she'd left them in Susan and Richard's loft, spend perhaps half an hour nostalgically reclaiming her lost youth and forgotten fantasy before laughingly closing them and relegating them back to the past where they belonged, so, perhaps she should do the same with Joe. You couldn't go back. People changed. *She'd* changed. Joe had another family...

And then Rosa asked, quite calmly, even though her heart was pounding, 'Joe, when she was supposed to be in Wales with her parents and her eight-year-old son, was Carys in the States with you?'

'You knew?'

'Knew what?'

'That... you know...' Joe's face was ashen. 'Carys had been with me in the States?'

'I didn't actually know that, Joe. You've just confirmed what I've always *wondered* about. You never admitted she was there with you in Chicago. All these years I just assumed you'd had a bit of a fling with her. Maybe a one-night stand when I was away myself and the pair of you had drunk too much. Or something like that? I could possibly have understood that. But with you in Chicago?'

'It really, really wasn't like that, Rosa. It wasn't what you think... I *promise* you that...'

Standing and calmly pushing back her chair, Rosa replaced the starched napkin on the table, picked up her bag and turned back to Joe.

'I've forgiven you, Joe. And that's not just me speaking as a vicar absolving you from sin. I loved you and will always love you. Problem is, it's all too late. Too much has happened... I shouldn't be here. I can't do this...' She broke off as the waiter, unsure what was going on, hovered with her plate of soup. 'And, I'm sorry, but I absolutely loathe gazpacho.'

Although her legs were even more of a tremble than when she'd walked in – she'd never been any good at confrontations, always been the first to back down in any argument with Eva and Hannah – Rosa concentrated on putting one high-heeled shoe in front of the other, determined that she would bow out of the restaurant as gracefully as was humanly possible.

Once she'd escaped the main dining area, she continued to walk loftily towards the entrance, head held high, toes screaming to be let out of the pinching leather. 'Sod it,' she muttered, freeing her feet from their incarceration and heading, in her stockinged feet, to the door. Rosa hesitated when she saw it was now pouring, the rain bucketing down as only it can in early December. Some sixth sense had her turning her head to the right where a loved-up couple were seated, clinking glasses together.

Sam Burrows' eyes left those of the blonde-haired woman he was with and latched onto Rosa's as she stood deliberating and, as her already racing heart plunged southwards somewhere in the region of her left big toe, which had broken through a hole in her stockings, she did the first thing that came into her head and waved her shoes gaily in his direction shouting, 'Halloo there,' which not only rent the air several decibels louder than she'd intended but, for some reason she was never able to fathom, came out in a broad Southern Irish accent, before she dashed out into the dark, the rain, and the safety of the night.

'I've never even *been* to bloody Ireland,' Rosa sobbed as Hannah towelled her down and Eva pulled one of Bill's huge sweaters over her head. 'And the whole restaurant turned as I stood waving my shoes and carrying on like a sodding leprechaun on speed. And I wouldn't mind, but not one drop of alcohol had passed my lips. And,' she went on, 'I'm sure I spotted Hilary Makepeace and half the parish council in there, getting stuck into their Christmas do.'

'Begorrah,' Hannah hooted. 'That's brilliant.'

Knowing both her sisters had said they were going to be up at Heatherly Hall, helping the estate management committee with Bill's affairs any way they could, Rosa had rung to confirm they were both still there and, mortified at how the evening had played out, had driven like a bat out of hell, cringing with embarrassment as she recalled the look of sheer surprise on both Sam Burrows' and his gorgeous, upmarket dinner partner's face, only to be stopped for speeding on the country lane leading up to the hall.

'And when the policeman had me wind down my window, saw my lovely pink dress all soaked and dripping, my laddered tights and looking like some pink blancmanged Alice Cooper –' Rosa rubbed at the rivulets of black mascara down her cheeks '– and he asked me for identity and I said, "I'm Reverend Rosa Quinn, the village vicar. I'm just on the way up to my father's place at Heatherly Hall," he replied with: "Yes, sweetheart, and I'm the Archbishop of Canterbury and later on, I'll be off to my mother's place at Buckingham Palace." And he made me get out of the car in the rain and breathalysed me.'

'And were you still speaking in tongues?' Eva giggled.

'Tongues?'

'You know, in Irish?'

'No, I just sobbed over him. And, when he saw my driver's licence, and that I *was* the village vicar, he let me off the speeding and said he realised I really was one of Bill's daughters. Even escorted me up here in his panda.'

'Let you off?' Eva tutted. 'That's the luck of the Irish for you,' and she started laughing. 'Here, get that down you. You deserve a drink.' She poured a glass of Bill's port and the three of them each raised a hand in silent tribute to their birth father.

'You seem very bubbly, the pair of you,' Rosa said, sipping at her drink. 'In a celebratory mood almost? When we're actually here on Bill's behalf?'

'Well, I would imagine Eva's over the moon that her new dentist hasn't fallen in love with you after all.' Hannah arched a brow in Eva's direction and Eva scowled in return. 'Not the done thing to carry on a flirtatious work relationship with your sister's new man. Totally different if he's involved with someone she doesn't know. Eva can now carry on her little fantasies to get her through the next root canal without the fear that it might actually lead somewhere she doesn't really want to go.'

'Excuse me,' Eva snapped, giving Hannah a sharp dig in the ribs. 'What about you?'

'What about me?'

'I bet Ben Pennington's been sniffing round again. Telling you he can't be without you?' Eva glared in Hannah's direction.

'I don't know what you're talking about,' Hannah said, avoiding both her sisters' accusing looks. 'I'm putting all my energy into being up here at the hall. You know, trying to help with the smooth running of the place until Jonny Astley moves in and takes over. There are two big weddings on this weekend and Tiffany, the wedding organiser, has been off with flu for the past few days. I'm merely doing my bit to help.'

'Have you seen Jonny? Has he arrived from California?'

'Flies in to Manchester tomorrow, apparently. Mrs Sykes has been getting rooms ready for them the last couple of days. I guess we ought to make the most of just swanning in here and helping ourselves to Bill's port while we can. I don't suppose Jonny will want anything to do with us once he inherits.'

'Sad. End of an era, I guess.'

The three of them nodded, lost in their own thoughts. 'Maybe we should suck up to him a bit,' Hannah suggested. 'I mean, he is our half-brother after all. Don't we have any rights to the place? Can't we just drop in here, like we do now?'

'Nope.' Eva shook her head. 'I can't see it; you know he and Henrietta have never acknowledged any familial relationship or contact with the three of us. And I can't see him letting me carry on with my art studio here. Can you? Really?'

'Maybe Bill's put something in his will to say we can have access to the place for the period of our lifetimes?' Hannah said hopefully. 'You know, you can carry on with your artwork, Eva; and Rosa and I can come and drink Bill's port.'

'Forget it,' Eva sniffed. 'Right, Rosa, have you stopped crying and shivering now? Are you going to tell us how you left it with Joe Rosavina?'

'It really is all over,' Rosa said, wiping at her eyes. 'It really is. You just can't go back to how things were. Too much water under the bridge and all that...'

'So why are you crying again?' Eva asked, handing her a tissue. 'Sorry, that's a bit used.'

'Why do you think, you idiot?' Hannah glared at Eva and patted at Rosa's arm. 'She's finally fallen out of love with Joe Rosavina, only to fall in love with some man who appears to be involved with someone else.'

28

Rosa lay in her bed in her vicarage bedroom and couldn't sleep. One dinner date out with Joe when, as she'd fully anticipated, he'd tried to apologise; when, as she'd expected, his one aim had been to try to put things right. What she hadn't anticipated was the awful realisation that it was, more than likely, all too late. You couldn't go back. They'd both moved on. It was quite a revelation considering that only weeks earlier, on her first night back in the village, she'd still been crying herself to sleep over him.

Rosa sat up in bed and turned on the light, then set off downstairs to heat up some milk.

What also was a revelation, she told herself as she climbed the stairs once more, was the fact that she'd felt so bad, in fact actually quite angry that Sam Burrows had invited *her*, taken *her* to something so special, so terribly poignant for him as his deceased son's ballet company's performance and then, just a few days later was out, all dolled up in a fancy restaurant with another woman. An exceptionally attractive woman at that.

For heaven's sake, Rosa, she censured herself, as she sat up in bed sipping at the too-hot milk and contemplated reading some new psychological thriller Eva had said was unputdownable, *dating has totally changed since you were first at it over twenty years ago*. Then, in the bygone halcyon days of Westenbury Comp, you let it be known you fancied someone, they got their mate to ask you out and you went for an illicit Bulmers cider at the Jolly Sailor or down into town to see a film (the word *movie* was still in its place of origin, firmly across the Atlantic and hadn't yet quite reached Westenbury village).

You had a first-date necking session at the bus stop once they'd walked you there, slapped down any wandering hands and then you went home and wrote in your diary either: '*Awful kisser*' or '*Am in love*' with the added enjoyment of artistically embroidering their names in gel pen all over your diary and school jotter. As well as experimenting the coupling of their name with your own – Rosa Rosavina was a dream come true – while planning which of your mates would look good together as your bridesmaids. The bloke of the moment was your *boyfriend* – if just for a month or so – you didn't *two-time* him with anyone else and, eventually, one or the other '*was stood up*' or '*finished with you*' and you then legitimately moved on to the next. Like chess, the rules were laid down.

When she thought about it, she'd really had little practice at the whole dating game because, apart from probably five or six earlier boyfriends who'd lasted no more than a couple of weeks each, once she'd met Joe, she'd known she didn't ever want anyone else.

And now, apparently, the current rules of dating were vastly different, influenced once again by what was laid down in New York. According to Hannah, who'd been firmly enmeshed in the dating game until her affair with a married man – and presumably was about to launch herself back out there once more – as well as almost-seven-year-old Laila (who'd assured her Aunty Rosa that Archie Kaye who she sat next to in PSHE, was on the point of asking her, Laila, for her exclusivity), there was a strict guidance to which one must adhere. This, in a nutshell, boiled down to the understood fact that you must be prepared to accept that your date will be dating many others (including presumably having sex with them) as well as yourself until, after several months or even a year, you will be invited to go *exclusive*.

At the end of the day, she, Rosa, had absolutely no excuse for feeling upset that Sam Burrows was wining and dining another woman, clinking glasses chummily with her across the table. And, she thought, lying down and hiding her head under the pillow in mortification, she had no excuse for addressing him like a banshee with a foghorn in a Southern Irish accent.

Had she cried and ignored the speed limit because of Sam? Or was it still Joe? Or was she crying for Bill? All three, she reckoned.

'I'll never be able to have babies of my own now,' Rosa had sobbed over Hannah and the pregnant Eva when she'd been told chemotherapy was her only way forward. She'd stroked Eva's seven-month-pregnant belly as tears fell down her face, and the other two had reached for a hand each, silent for once as they acknowledged the enormity of the treatment she was about to undergo. Until Eva had determinedly stood and made her way from the hospital room, returning fifteen minutes later not only with a cardboard tray of Costa coffee, but also with an impressively senior consultant oncologist in tow.

'Right, Ms Bailey,' Eva had said to the doctor somewhat bossily, 'I've got you a coffee. Now would you please sit down just for ten minutes – I know how terribly busy you are – and reassure my sister that having chemo isn't the end of her chances of having children in the future?'

'I thought my colleague had talked to you about this, Rosa?' Ms Bailey, although obviously overworked and harassed, sat down beside Rosa, sipped gratefully at the proffered coffee and proceeded to explain what could be done to maximise any chances she might have in the future to have a child of her own.

'There are options available for women undergoing chemo to preserve their fertility. This should have been discussed with you, Rosa, and you should have been put in touch with the fertility clinic or assisted conception unit. It's important to understand that these methods aren't always successful or suitable for everyone. So, the possible options for preserving fertility include –' Ms Bailey broke off to enumerate each method on her fingers '– freezing embryos, freezing eggs and, a fairly new idea of freezing the ovarian tissue which, at this moment in time, I wouldn't be advising you to go for.'

'When does she do this?' Eva interrupted. 'Can she do it now? This minute?'

'If you choose to go down this road, Rosa, it must be done before starting chemotherapy. Basically, you have fertility drugs to stimulate your ovaries to produce a number of eggs. These are then harvested and your partner's sperm used to fertilise them in a laboratory, creating embryos...'

'But I don't *have* a partner anymore.' Rosa felt tears run unheeded down her face and Hannah, on the point of tears herself, passed a tissue. 'He's left me for my closest friend.'

'Let me explain the process, Rosa,' the consultant went on, patting her hand. 'The embryos are then frozen until you want to have a baby, when the embryo is returned to your womb by IVF. It's quite a complicated process and isn't always successful. It is important to understand that the embryos are the joint property of you and your partner.'

'She doesn't *have* a partner,' Eva said crossly. 'Rosa's just told you that. I mean, there's no way she's going to accost the bastard and say: "Please can I have what's rightfully mine? Just get in that room with a stack of magazines and a petri dish and do the deed..."'

'For heaven's sake, Eva, calm down,' Hannah snapped, glaring at Eva. 'This isn't being a bit helpful. Just hear the doctor out.'

Ms Bailey gave a little obvious smile in Hannah's direction before continuing. 'Both of you would need to *agree* to use these embryos at a later date. Now, Rosa, what I *was* going on to say –' she raised an eyebrow in Eva's direction '– was that you may not have a partner at the moment. If that's the case, you can have just your *eggs* frozen until you're ready to have a baby; you'll be given drugs to stimulate your ovaries to make mature eggs, which are then collected and frozen until you are ready for them to be fertilised.' She smiled at Rosa reassuringly. 'You're young, Rosa, just thirty. Women under thirty-five have the highest degree of success in harvesting a good number of high-quality eggs. We'll do everything we can to ensure you have every chance of becoming a mummy at some point in the future. But,' she warned, 'don't put it off too long to get pregnant after the two years or so we advise leaving it once your chemo treatment is over. And,' she added, 'you need to know, from the start, that UK regulation only permits human eggs to be frozen for ten years.'

Which was why there were now thirteen of Rosa's eggs snugly protected in a cryoprotectant freezing solution and stored in tanks of liquid nitrogen in a clinic in London. And why, although she'd learned that under some circumstances, particularly for women who, like herself, had undergone egg freezing because of chemotherapy, this ten-year lifespan could be extended, she thought constantly, and worried excessively, about these potential babies of hers. Which, unfortunately, whenever she brought them to mind, she could only visualise underneath a great ticking clock, the years and months ticking off her babies' sell-by date, as in some avant-garde, dystopian Sunday night TV drama.

One of the perks of owning and building up a company like Rosa Quinn Investments was that Rosa had been coaxed by the company accountants to contribute into a private health pot for herself and her staff and, as a result, had been persuaded not only by Bill but, despite his left-wing leanings, also by Richard, to book into, and take advantage of, the private Parkside Hospital in Wimbledon for her treatment. She might be, apparently, making lots of money, but in her heart she knew it wasn't the money that was driving her forever onwards and upwards. And when she tried to reason with herself, ask herself just *what* it was that was making her relentlessly want to be the best, she didn't have any answers. Surely it wasn't just an innate desire to be Top Triplet? How shameful if that's what it was. Or, maybe, she'd just become addicted to the adrenaline rush of the chase and capture? She was seemingly a capitalist in socialist clothing. Or was it the other way round...?

'There are times, Rosa, sweetheart,' Richard had reassured her when she'd demurred about occupying a private health room with all its trappings, 'when your principles are put on the back boiler in order that you have the best possible chance of surviving some unexpected thing that's knocked you sideways. We'd much rather you came back to Yorkshire where we can keep an eye on you but, if you insist on staying in London, make sure you're in the best place possible.'

Those words over the phone from Richard had shaken her; while she herself, in yet another walking round the London kitchen flat at 4 a.m., wide awake, alone and frightened, might worry that her days were numbered, she didn't want Richard and Susan, Eva and Hannah also awake and worrying that she might not actually survive. As such, she acquiesced to their urging that she submit to what was ahead of her in the most pleasant and comfortable of surroundings.

It was a beautiful but chilly Friday morning in late October, and Rosa had taken her customary taxi ride from the apartment in Wandsworth over to the hospital in Wimbledon in order to get her bloods checked before another chemo session after the weekend. Wincing as usual at the extravagance, but accepting a journey on public transport was not the most sensible of ways to travel when her immune system was being bashed about and she was possibly neutropenic from the previous chemotherapy sessions, she sent up a silent prayer – to a God she wasn't convinced about – that two more sessions after the six she'd already endured would have killed the interloper in her body.

Eva, despite being pregnant and working with Rayan at the dental surgery, had organised what she dubbed the *Yorkshire Chemo Assistance Committee*, making sure either herself, Hannah, Susan, Richard and even Bill were on the rota to train it down to King's Cross, stay with Rosa at the flat (or, in Bill's case, when it was his turn, at some Knightsbridge hotel) and accompany her over to the hospital in Wimbledon.

One Friday morning, she was alone and missing the comfort of having one or other of her family with her. Virginia had offered to be an extra body if needed but, when called on to be there this particular weekend, she'd had to pull out, a prior engagement taking precedence. And for that, Rosa felt guiltily relieved. Much as she loved her eldest sister, in the way that one *has* to love an elder sibling, Rosa wasn't quite sure she could have coped with Virginia's humourless fussing, her constantly asking if she wanted to rest, to lie down, some Lucozade, some of the homemade lemon drizzle cake she'd bought at the church Bring and Buy sale? As well as another session of Joe-and-Carys-bashing, in which Virginia appeared to take great pleasure.

It felt strange to be walking into and through the hospital grounds alone, having always been accompanied previously by one of the YCAC, as the committee was now called. Rosa glanced up at the four-storey red-brick building and, as she made her way to outpatients, sent up another silent prayer that the medical panel, which would review her progress after the set eight sessions, would make the decision that no more would be necessary.

At reception, she was told that because of circumstances beyond their control, there was going to be a delay of a couple of hours or so before they could get started and would she wait until called?

'I can't bear to be inside on such a glorious day.' Rosa smiled at the receptionist. 'I'm going to wander down the street.'

'Don't go too far,' the girl warned. 'And we've not checked your immunity status so don't go talking to anyone who looks as if they might have a cold or something worse.'

Rosa was relieved to be outside in the gloriously golden morning, wanting to hang on to every vestige of the season before winter spread his pernicious fingers and took away the wonderful light and colour of autumn. Funny how she attributed the male gender to winter, while thinking of the other seasons as definitely female. Maybe it was because Joe, being male, had stripped bare the joy and light she'd once had for every new day, leaving her, as winter so often did, in a sunless wilderness of seemingly unending dark.

Blimey, you're being a bit heavy there, girl, Rosa censored herself. A bit Ted Hughes at his darkest. No wonder Sylvia Plath had put her head in that gas oven if she'd had to live with her husband spouting stuff like that at her. She decided to cheer herself up by treating herself to a big blueberry muffin and a hot chocolate but then remembered that refined carbs and sugar were the worst thing to put inside her, either before her bloods were taken or especially before a session of chemo. Instead, she wandered up to Wimbledon High Street, window-shopping as she went and then, when nothing caught her attention, when there wasn't one single thing she felt she remotely needed, apart from her previous good health – and, of course, Joe willingly returned to her once more – she turned and made her way back the way she'd come.

Rosa's eye was caught by a sign for a Buddhapadipa Temple and, intrigued, she set off in the direction of Calonne Road as instructed.

'Oh!' She actually spoke the word out loud as the temple was suddenly in front of her, its white exterior a stark but calming contrast to the red and gold roof and decorations. 'That is so beautiful,' she breathed, unable to do anything but stare. She walked further into the beautiful grounds, taking in everything from the tiny house to the pond and bridges.

Wisdom Springs from Meditation. She read the words out loud from one of the signs on a bridge. Moving forward she found: *Without Meditation, Wisdom Wanes* and, then: *One Should so Conduct Oneself that Wisdom Increases*.

Sitting herself down on a wooden bench opposite the actual

temple, Rosa closed her eyes and found that she was crying. Crying for Joe, for Carys, for those eggs of hers that she'd had taken from her body but wasn't convinced would come to fruition. For some strange reason, she found herself crying for Alice, her birth mother who'd missed out on so much by giving away her three daughters. Funnily enough, though, she wasn't crying for her old life: the mad world of London and Rosa Quinn Investments. She didn't want it anymore. She didn't want to be in the centre of this great city anymore. She wanted to go home.

'Are you alright, my dear?' A gentle hand was on her arm. 'This place has the ability to make one look into oneself, I know.'

Rosa's eyes flew open and, embarrassed at being found in this state, she fumbled for a tissue in her bag. An elderly man was smiling at her, his black robes and dog collar informing her of his status as a Catholic priest. 'I'm fine, really, thank you. So, are you, you know…?' She trailed off, embarrassed.

'What? Am I a priest?' The man actually laughed. 'I think that's pretty obvious.'

'No, I'm sorry, I'm being nosy.'

'Are you asking whether, as a man who follows and preaches the work of God and Jesus, I'm *allowed* in here? Am I not in the wrong spot? Is it like a Manchester United fan sitting in the Manchester City stadium?' He roared with laughter at his analogy. 'Why am I sitting in a Buddhist place of worship rather than a Catholic one?' He laughed again.

'I'm sorry, yes,' Rosa apologised. 'That's what I was asking.'

'If you were to speak to a Sikh who might also find himself taking advantage of the quiet, calm spirituality found in this beautiful place, he would assure you that all religions, all roads lead to one God.' The priest's accent was pure Southern Irish, and Rosa felt she could listen to his melodic timbre forever.

'And do *you* believe that?'

'Yes, I think I do.' The priest held out a hand to introduce himself. 'Michael Carrol.' He smiled. 'I've sort of been put out to grass a bit now – I help out the current Apostolic Nuncio to Great Britain with the smooth running of the Apostolic Nunciature down the road there.' The man pointed in the direction Rosa had walked from the hospital.

'Right?' Rosa had no idea what he was talking about.

'Basically, the place is the Pope's home from home in the UK. We keep it running for him if he should need it. It's at number 54.' He pointed vaguely over his shoulder once again.

'Oh, I'm at number 53.'

'Ah, you're having treatment at the hospital?'

Rosa nodded.

'Chemo?'

'How did you know that?' Rosa asked and then when he didn't reply, she put up a hand to her head. 'Oh, the wig? A bit of a giveaway?'

'It's a very good wig.'

'It's jolly hot even on a chilly day like today,' she smiled. 'I'm a brunette really. I was going for the Britney Spears look today. I was a redhead last week.'

'And why not?' He smiled again.

'My grandad was a C of E vicar.' Rosa had no idea why she suddenly came out with that.

'I can sense a certain belief in you,' Michael Carrol said. 'A certain spirituality.'

'Well, it certainly wasn't passed down to me through Grandpa Cecil. I'm not convinced he even believed in God. Or in what he was doing. He was a totally miserable, sarcastically irascible old man whom his congregation couldn't wait to get rid of. The more they wanted him gone, the more he was determined to hang on in there.' They both smiled at this.

'You've not got this old man's genes.' The priest patted her arm. 'I can always tell when someone is turning to God. Certainly, you have a need to know more.'

'Are you trying to get me to join the Catholic church?' Rosa laughed. 'You know, knocking on my door like the Jehovah Witnesses?'

'I think your church might give you solace. You're looking for something.'

'I'm looking to get better, is all. I don't want to die.'

'Have faith,' the man said, standing up and handing her handbag to Rosa. 'Come on, I'll walk back with you.' They walked in silence back to the hospital.

'May your god be with you.' The priest smiled once more as they parted at the respective buildings. 'If you look into your heart, Rosa, I believe you'll find he already is.'

'You *are* joking?' Eva, attempting to encourage some beige mush down seven-month-old Laila had looked across at Rosa in absolute horror. 'A vicar? You're going to train to be a *vicar*? Hang on, is it April Fool's Day? Good joke, Rosa – getting the six-month all-clear on your cancer has obviously gone to your head.'

'Yes,' Rosa had said calmly. 'I've spent the last four months persuading myself it would be wrong; that I'm not the right person to be a vicar.'

'Well, good. Listen to yourself, then. You're *not* the right person. You're a businesswoman.'

'I don't want to be a businesswoman anymore.'

'This is because Joe left you, isn't it? And you became ill?'

'Well, yes, I'm sure those two things together have gone some way in pointing me in that direction.'

'Well, that's your first mistake then. You sound like Catherine of Aragon when Henry the Eighth was chasing after Anne Boleyn. She put herself into a convent rather than have her head chopped off. Can't you find some nunnery to take yourself off to for a couple of months? You'd soon be getting over this bloody silly idea when you've shaved all your hair off... Oh, sorry, sorry, I'm sorry, Rosa.' Eva threw out the arm that wasn't holding the plastic spoon towards Rosa in apology. 'It is growing back now, isn't it? You know, under that scarf? Anyway, when you're on your knees on a stone floor, at 3 a.m., praying, you'll soon find you want to be back in London in your lovely flat, wheeling and dealing once more.'

She prodded the mush towards her daughter's mouth again as Laila grinned but kept her mouth firmly shut. 'I've been on my knees every morning at 3 a.m. and 6 a.m. with this one and, let me tell you, now, Rosa, you don't want to be *voluntarily* on your knees, when you could be fast asleep in a lovely bed.'

'What *are* you wittering about, Eva?' Rosa laughed. 'I'm going to train to be a vicar, not a nun.'

'Hannah,' Eva shouted crossly towards the kitchen where Hannah was making tea. 'Come in here this minute and listen to what your mad sister is suggesting.'

'Which one?' Hannah shouted back over the boiling kettle. 'I have *two* mad sisters.'

'Which *one*?' Eva, tired and grumpy from sleepless nights with an equally sleepless baby closed her eyes in exasperation. 'Do I *look* as if *I'm* going to be the one to train as a damned vicar? Come and tell her she can't do it. We won't allow it.'

'I already know,' Hannah said, coming into Eva's sitting room with the tea tray.

'Oh, you know? You two have discussed all this without consulting me?' Eva snapped.

'I knew this would be your reaction,' Rosa smiled, stroking Laila's cereal-encrusted fingers as they reached for her own.

'I think if that's what Rosa wants, she should follow her dream. As long as she doesn't turn into Grandpa Cecil, I think she'll make a great vicar.'

'You're not going to stop drinking, are you?' Eva's eyes narrowed suspiciously as she regarded the requested cup of tea now in Rosa's hands.

'Why would I do that?'

'Well, you won't be able to go on the lash.'

'We went on the lash as teenagers. I would hope we'd be beyond all that by now.'

'See?' Eva frowned. 'You've gone all prissy and vicary already and you haven't even started yet.' She shook her head. 'Bonkers,' she went on, dropping a kiss on Laila's dark head, 'your Aunty Rosa is absolutely, utterly *bonkers*.'

29

Hannah didn't want to go into work after two weeks away from it; couldn't bear the thought of joining the daily madness that was the eastbound M62 and then, once in court, dealing with unhappy, disaffected youths and their worried or, as was more often the case, angry parents. While most parents and carers were extremely grateful for her input, happy to listen to her advice, asking her to tell them where they'd gone wrong when their teen had gone off the rails and ended up in youth court, there were some who were confrontational, furious that they'd been forced to take time off from their daily lives in order to accompany their kids who were – in their words, not Hannah's – 'a waste of bloody space,' 'totally out of control', 'an idle little bastard who spends all his time smoking skunk with his mates and, when he is at home, glued to his phone or PlayStation'.

Hannah had enough experience of working with kids who ended up in court, particularly the abused and Looked After Children, to know that the majority needed guidance, understanding and help rather than censure, which was why it was her job to try and avoid at all costs their ending up with a detention order rather than a youth rehabilitation order to be undertaken in the community.

She was also convinced society had got it all wrong. Exams were fine for academic kids like herself, Eva and Rosa, but she wanted to see schools equally geared up for teaching practical skills, particularly cooking, building, engineering and computing. Gardening, farming, art, learning to play a musical instrument, childcare... the list was endless. These were kids lured by the excitement and instant gratification of being part of a turf territory, experiencing, for the first time, being a member of a community with its own set of rules and hierarchy – however dodgy that might be – rather than on the periphery of conventional society for which there appeared little access. No wonder the County Lines gangs had a constant turnover of teen recruits, eager to do their bidding.

If she had *her* way – Hannah scowled angrily at the huge white van in the process of undertaking her in the slow lane and forcing her to almost miss her exit into the city centre – she'd have one big agricultural farm where kids in trouble would have to grow their own organic fresh food and cook it themselves in order to eat. There'd be no TV, no phones, no social media and definitely no weed or alcohol, but, instead, the learning of new practical skills.

Hannah hadn't said anything to Rosa or Eva, but she knew that, despite the shock and sadness of Bill's death, the past couple of weeks spent every day up at Heatherly Hall, rather than at work, had been the most productive she'd ever experienced, marred only by one awful, sickening incident.

After that initial text of apology from Ben, she hadn't expected to hear from him again, but, after a week's silence, he'd started to ring and message her once more, promising her he would *definitely* leave Alexandra. He just needed time. And, addict that she was, she'd fallen off the wagon. And her heart had raced in excitement when, two evenings previously, she'd returned from Heatherly Hall just after 10 p.m. to find Ben's car pulled up outside her front door. She exited the car, ready to fall into his arms, wanting him so much, but another vehicle had come racing round the corner, tyres squealing, and she'd jumped back in alarm. The car had come to an abrupt standstill at Hannah's side, the front window wound down and, to an accompaniment of frightened cries from the rear seat, the liquid contents from a glass jar was thrown into her face. Her immediate thought was acid and, in total and utter panic, she'd clawed at her face, rubbing at the wet with her scarf and gloves.

Ben had jumped out of the car in a similar panic, uncertain whether to see to his wife and children or to a shocked Hannah standing dripping in front of her ceanothus.

'You promised,' Alexandra Pennington had shouted furiously through her window. 'You promised you'd never see her again, you bastard.'

An icy calm had taken hold of Hannah as, realising the liquid was the contents of Alexandra's child's potty, and not something that was going to disfigure her for life, she walked over to the car and spoke directly to the children.

'Shh, shh, it's all alright, really. Everything's going to be alright. Mummy's just having a bit of a silly game,' and then, turning to Ben's wife she'd said, 'I am *so* sorry, Alexandra. I can only apologise for all the pain I've caused. I accept that I *am* responsible and all I can do, Alexandra, is apologise from the bottom of my heart once again for what I'm continuing to put you and your children through.'

Hannah had turned to Ben who was standing, white-faced at her side. 'Take your family home, Ben.' She'd walked as calmly as she could despite a couple of twitching curtains from the houses on either side of her own – found her door key, unlocked and closed the front door and immediately rung a number in her phone.

'I'm so sorry for ringing at this late hour,' Hannah had managed to say, 'but, Rosa, I need you.'

'I'm a terrible person,' she wept as Rosa made them both tea and listened while she told her that, despite telling her and Eva to the contrary, she'd continued to see Ben even after the outing in church. 'I can't believe I've had an affair with a married man. I know he loves me, Rosa. I know he wants to be with me. Over eight months, Rosa. I knew he was married, knew he had children, and now I deserve everything I've had thrown at me – including a potty full of pee.' Hannah had taken off her coat immediately she'd come into the house and rung Rosa, but she now realised her jumper was also wet, and she pulled it off in disgust, shivering in just her T-shirt.

'You've no heat on,' Rosa frowned, feeling at the radiator in Hannah's little kitchen. 'Here.' She took off her own sweater that Virginia had knitted and given to her a couple of Christmases previously, passing it to Hannah who, shaking with shock and cold, took it gratefully. Until she read what was knitted into the front of the white wool in bright orange letters:

JESUS IS MY ROCK AND THAT'S HOW I ROLL

'Oh blimey? Really?'

'Really. I suggest you wear this always,' Rosa added piously. 'To, you know, remind you of your sins.'

'What like a hair shirt?'

'No, like you wear it so *I* don't have to wear the fecking thing a minute longer!'

Rosa started to laugh and, through her tears, Hannah joined in until they were almost comatose with giggles.

'Oh but, Rosa…' Hannah finally sobered up first. 'What must poor Alexandra Pennington have been going through to belt her kids up in the car at ten at night, before setting off with the sole purpose of throwing urine over me? Not that I blame her,' she hastily added. 'I know I'm a terrible person.'

'Stop beating yourself up,' Rosa said seriously. 'We've all done things we wish we hadn't.'

'I bet *you* haven't.' Hannah managed to smile.

'I let Joe go without listening to his side of the story.' Rosa sighed heavily. 'I should have let him explain.'

'Explain? Explain?' Hannah threw Rosa a look of utter disbelief. 'We all *knew* his side of the story. He was a cheating bastard…'

'Like Ben?' Rosa asked gently.

'Suppose. Listen, Rosa, what do you do when you love someone but can't have them because they belong to someone else?'

'You give them up,' Rosa smiled, listening but never preaching. Never accusatory, never judgemental. 'You give them up and get on with your life the best way you can.'

Hannah should have returned to work the next day but instead explained there'd been a death in the family and she was taking the holiday owed to help sort it all out. For the last couple of weeks she'd worked with the management committee and staff at the hall, helping out where she could, calling in at Tea and Cake, the wedding venue, the Airbnb cottages and even at the petting zoo – all bringing back memories from twenty years earlier – while the staff awaited – somewhat nervously – the arrival of Jonny Astley from California. Then, on the morning of his expected arrival, an email to Bill's solicitors confirmed that, owing to a variety of circumstances, Jonny and his wife wouldn't be flying in until the funeral at the start of the following week.

While an almost party atmosphere had ensued in the knowledge that Heatherly Hall's new boss was not actually arriving for another few days, all the staff had got on with their tasks as usual, determined to show Jonny Astley how much they loved their work and how he would need them to carry on with it, without making any changes, once he was actually in West Yorkshire and running the place. Rumour and gossip abounded in the staff restroom and, while Hannah wasn't quite sure why or how she'd taken on the role, she found that she was thoroughly enjoying helping allay any fears, but was unable to confirm what would be happening in the future. Besides, thinking of others stopped her thinking of Ben and the misery and embarrassment of the pee-throwing drama the other night.

Hannah pulled into her car-parking spot, loath to actually get out into the rain and explain to her line manager why she'd felt it her right to take the extra days off that she'd ended up taking, when the youth service was so busy and other people had had to do her work for her. Trying out the different excuses in her head as she ran across the car park, rain and wind battering down on her head (supporting my family after our bereavement; stress caused by the bereavement; went down with a virus after taking my holiday period... actually *had* a debilitating period), Hannah knew the truth: that the main reason she hadn't wanted to return to work was because she would *much* rather be up working at Heatherly Hall where she could still feel close to Bill.

Before its new owners arrived and, more than likely, she, Eva and Rosa – the embarrassing illegitimate daughters of the eleventh Marquess of Heatherly (deceased) – would no longer be welcome there or have any reason whatsoever to be there.

30

The following Sunday, the second week in December, Eva woke to the sound of movement and banging downstairs. It was only 8 a.m., but Rayan had already been gone an hour, showered, shaved and dressed in his Lycra, attaching his bike to the back of the car and setting off for yet another Tour de Something competition or other, over Glossop way, while both Laila and Nora – as well as a plethora of dolls, cuddly toys and some sort of rubber dinosaur – or was it an alien? – had climbed into their bed to take his place.

'What's all that racket going on downstairs?' Eva, surveying one daughter fast asleep, face squashed onto Rayan's vacated pillow, her bum in the air, and the other daughter plugged into Rayan's iPad watching some Disney cartoon, realised the question was more than likely rhetorical.

Throwing her bathrobe over her nightie, Eva descended the stairs where more banging was coming from the kitchen. Azra's battered suitcase, together with four Aldi carrier bags, sat waiting at the front door.

'What are you *doing*, Azra?'

'Hello, love, I'm off now. I've cleaned out cupboard beneath sink and high up one that I had to climb on chair to get to. All grand and shiny clean now. And I've cleaned kitchen floor – all grand and shiny clean too.'

'But where are you going? You didn't say? You didn't say you were off? I thought you were going back in the new year. You know, spending Christmas with us?'

'Hadhira need me back now, love. Sabir coming to pick me up this morning.'

'But it's only 8 a.m., Azra. Sabir won't be driving over from Bradford at this time of the day.'

'Oh, he is. Hadhira and Sabir going off to Ten-er-ee-fe for dirty week.'

'Dirty week?'

'You *know*.' Azra elbowed Eva suggestively in the ribs and grinned. 'Hadhira booked it just yesterday. A week of love and *how's your father* in Ten-er-ee-fe without kids. I am needed *immediately* in Bradford to look after Sharjeel and Usaid,' she added importantly. 'Make sure they go to bed on time and do homework. And I do cooking and housework.'

For some reason, Eva felt slightly put out; she'd got used to having Azra in situ and now she appeared to be leaving at the drop of a hat, without her or Rayan informing her of this. She wasn't sure what she was going to do all Sunday without Jodie, Azra or Rayan around to help. 'Right, OK. Have you got everything?'

'Bed all stripped and in washing machine,' Azra said proudly. 'I clean up after myself.'

'I know you do, Azra. You've been so helpful.'

'Ah,' Azra beamed. '*Though you be guest, you are not dead man*.'

'Right?' Eva said, frowning.

Azra reached for her coat and scarf and actually placed a hand, somewhat comically, behind her ear as a vehicle pulled up on the drive and the metronome ticking of a diesel engine was silenced. 'Car, I think for me. Bye, love, be good.' She turned back to Eva. '*You* need dirty week away too, Eva. You tell Rayan to get off bloody bike and take you to Ten-er-ee-fee. I come back to look after girls. Jodie and me, together we manage. And, don't forget, love: *a cock makes a great to-do whether you catch hold of it tightly or gently*. My ammi used to say that all time to me.' Azra beamed her farewells.

I wish I could tell your ammi: chance would be a fine thing. Eva sighed as she helped Azra out with her bags. And, it would have to be somewhere a lot more exotic than a week in Tenerife, Eva thought, as Sabir, waving and refusing the offer of a coffee, reversed at speed and set off back down the road, Azra already chatting ten to the dozen in the passenger seat. Barbados at least. And for ten days as well. Bloody cheek of Hadhira, demanding her mother return at the drop of a hat just so she and Sabir could have a week of luuuurve without their kids.

Eva climbed the stairs slowly and headed for the shower, planning the day that appeared to be stretching out ahead of her, now that she would be unable to spend a couple of hours at her artwork up at the hall, as she'd hoped. She'd take Laila and Nora to Rosa's 10.30 a.m. sermon (show Rosa they weren't just fair-weather churchgoers as well as letting the girls see the church decorated for the Nativity) and say a prayer for Bill, who she was actually beginning to miss more than she'd ever thought she would. She wasn't looking forward to the funeral in the coming week, or of seeing Jonny Astley stepping into Bill's shoes and make the changes she was sure he'd probably have been planning for years.

And then, a great idea came into her head: she'd take the girls and drive out towards the moors and Glossop, go over the top into Derbyshire and find Rayan with a picnic.

'You can't have a picnic in December.' Laila was scornful. 'Picnics are for summer.'

'This will be an alpine picnic,' Eva laughed, warming to her theme. 'We'll go and find Daddy on his bike, follow him round the moorland roads and, when he's finished, we'll have a lovely surprise picnic ready for him.'

'Why?' Laila was doubtful. 'It'll be cold sitting down on the wet grass.'

'Come on, live a little. Let's get a picnic ready. You can help me.'

'I think we need to go to M&S,' Laila said, as – head in the fridge – she appeared to be taking on the role of mother. 'There's just a load of Nanni Azra's curry stuff in here, and I don't think that will be very nice when it's cold.'

'OK. Church first to see Aunty Rosa and the Nativity she's hopefully put up; then M&S for picnic stuff and then, *Hunt the Daddy*. Look,' Eva went on, opening Rayan's *Cycle Weekly* magazine and drawing a finger down the announcements for cycle races, 'this is today's race: starting at Holmfirth and up to Holme Moss, Glossop and Sheffield and back to Holmfirth. Register at 9 a.m., set off at 10 a.m. and a four-hour hard hill climb to the finish back at Holmfirth. We can be there at two o'clock to cheer Daddy on to the finish and then have our picnic with him.'

'What if he does it in three hours and we miss him?'

'We'll find him,' Eva smiled.

'Or what if he takes five hours and we have to wait in the cold? And Nora gets fed up and starts to cry? Or has one of her tantrums?'

'Then we'll have a little wander and talk to the sheep.' Eva smiled again, somewhat impatiently this time.

'I don't like sheep.'

'I thought you were a sheep in your class Nativity?'

'That's why I don't like them. I wanted to be Mary.' Laila shook back her dark hair scornfully. 'I said to Miss Worthington: "Is it 'cos I is black I can't be Mary?"'

'What?' Eva spun round in alarm, staring at Laila. 'You didn't say that? Where've you heard that?'

'Matilda's daddy was watching something called *Ali G* on TV. Matilda and I were behind the sofa laughing at the man saying it. People were laughing, so I thought it must be a funny thing to say.' Laila looked suddenly worried. 'Is it rude, Mummy? Am I in trouble? I am black, aren't I?'

'Darling, you and Nora are both beautiful girls of colour. You are dual heritage, of mixed race, and that's something to be really, really proud of, and pleased about.' Eva paused. 'What did Miss Worthington say? What did she reply?'

'She sort of looked at me as if she didn't know whether to laugh. Or cry. And then, she just said: "No, Laila, I didn't choose you to be Mary because not everyone *can* be Mary, unfortunately. You are such a strong leader, I wanted you as Chief Sheep, to lead the other sheep. You can either be a white sheep or a black sheep. Up to you, sweetheart." That's what she said, Mummy.'

Rosa, Eva acknowledged, as she sat objectively taking in everything about her sister as she stood before her congregation, was going from strength to strength in her role as the village vicar. There was an inner confidence and happiness shining out of her as she stood, up at the front of the church, dressed this morning in her trendy pink cassock and Converse boots, the ever expanding congregation almost eating out of her hand as she took them through another of her funny stories before leading them in prayer.

Rosa had blossomed, found her niche, in a way that, although supremely confident of her abilities when running Rosa Quinn Investments, Eva didn't think had been really there when boss of her own London-based empire. She'd so often been stressed then, worried about where she was heading as well as always endeavouring to juggle her relationship with Joe. Not listening when Joe tried to make her slow down, take some time out just for the pair of them. Well, she'd certainly bloomed now, appeared happy in her own skin which, back when they were kids, Eva didn't think had always been the case. It was always her, Eva, the other two had followed, playing the games *she'd* suggested or made up, while Hannah, but particularly Rosa, had brought up the rear.

Eva envied this rightness, this *right here and now, happy with her lot* air that Rosa carried and which appeared to come off her in waves. She glanced over her shoulder where, several pews back, Hannah was sitting peacefully, her head bowed. Had she, Eva mused, finally come to terms with not having the man she loved? Or was she still seeing Ben Pennington?

Eva glanced down at her beautiful girls beside her and knew

she needed to sort out her own relationship with Rayan. Needed to ask him to spend more time with her and the girls rather than shooting off every Sunday to prove himself on that damned bike. Marriage and kids, domesticity and everyday life had got in the way of love and romance. She supposed it was par for the course – fifteen years on and they just took each other for granted.

Date nights – wasn't that what was prescribed for reviving floundering relationships in *Grazia* and *The Sunday Times Magazine*? Eva almost chortled out loud as she imagined getting all dolled up to meet her own husband in some seductively dim-lit bar. This, after she'd just seen him in the bedroom rubbing Daktarin into his athlete's foot, and he'd complained about the amount of her long dark hair he'd once again had to remove from the shower plughole.

Rather than having fantasies about other men and, particularly, Sam Burrows – Eva glanced round once more; the man himself didn't look to have put in an appearance again this particular Sunday morning – she would make an effort with the man she had. The man who, years ago, she had fallen in love with and married.

'Mummy, where *is* he?' Laila shivered dramatically, huddling into the warmth of her best red winter coat to make her point.

'I don't think we've missed him. Hang on, here's another load of cyclists. Let's see if he's amongst this little lot.' The three of them stood back from the moorside road as five bikes sped by in single file.

'Am 'ungry,' Nora wailed. 'Want my *picernic* now. Want my Percy Pigs from M&S.'

'You know you can't have sweeties until you've had your picnic,' Laila said bossily and then, turning to Eva asked, 'Can we have it now, Mum?'

'Sheeps,' Nora shouted in delight, momentarily distracted

from her desire for pigs. 'Sheeps, Mummy…' She pulled at Eva's hand, running towards the moorland animals who eyed her balefully from their ovine, devil's eyes. 'Got dirty botties,' Nora went on, her enthusiasm waning somewhat as she took in the dags hanging unceremoniously from the sheep's back ends.

'Eva?' A man dressed in official-looking cycling gear veered off the road, pulling up beside them in a black Evoque. 'I thought it was you. What are *you* doing here?'

'Having *picernic*,' Nora shouted. 'With sheeps with dirty botties. And pigs.'

'Pigs?' The man stared. 'No pigs up here, sweetheart.'

'Percy Pigs from M&S,' Laila explained kindly. 'We can have them after we've had our picnic.'

'We're waiting for Rayan,' Eva smiled. She knew she'd met this man somewhere before, been introduced to him as something to do with cycle competitions but, not overly interested, hadn't taken much notice at the time. 'Any idea if he's near the finishing line?'

'Well, if he is, he's cycling without registering.'

'Oh?'

'I registered them all in at 9 a.m., Eva, and Rayan wasn't among them.'

'Oh?' Eva stared. 'Oh, well that's strange. He set off at eight this morning with his bike.'

'Not seen anything of him.' The man turned to his companion. 'Did you see Rayan Malik this morning, Rob? Have you seen him at all?' The man leaned further out of the car window. 'No, not been racing this morning, love. In fact, come to think of it, not seen him for a while. Is he OK?'

'Are there any other races going on? You know, somewhere else?'

'There's a big one going on down in Somerset and another up in Newcastle that Rayan might be interested in. Somerset, do you think?'

'Somerset?' Eva shook her head. 'Leaving at eight this morning? I don't think so, do you?'

The man shrugged and started to move off. 'Hope you find him, love.'

'Let's go and have our picnic back at home on the sitting-room floor,' Eva suggested to her girls, as she tried to work out just where Rayan might be. 'I think December is too cold to be sitting outside eating, and Daddy is probably home by now.'

'I did say that, Mummy,' Laila said with an affected little sigh. 'I did tell you that, you know.'

Rayan didn't put in an appearance until after 3 p.m. when the December evening was already drawing in and the girls were firmly ensconced in yet another rerun of *Shrek* in the sitting room. Eva had sat with the girls on the floor, eaten the picnic and then played seemingly endless games of Snap and Snakes and Ladders with Laila and, when Nora had demanded her turn, had built a whole village out of Mega Bloks before lying down as a patient and been administered to by both girls dressed in their nurses' outfits.

Eventually, Eva had sent both girls off to watch TV with a saucer of Percy Pigs while she surreptitiously rang every A&E department – like in some bloody Sunday night drama, she'd later told Hannah and Rosa – in both West and South Yorkshire, to see if a man by the name of Malik had been admitted, after being knocked off his cycle somewhere.

And then Rayan had walked in through the front door, shouting, 'Hello, I'm back, I'm desperate for a shower, won't be long,' and gone straight upstairs, peeling off his gear as he went and, by the time Eva had followed him, was already under the running water.

Eva closed the bedroom door and sat on the bed, waiting until Rayan came out of the en suite, towelling himself down, rubbing at his hair and smiling.

308

'Good day?' he asked. 'Sorry I'm a bit late back.'

'How was the race?' Eva asked.

'Good. Yes, good one.'

'Where were you? Where did you end up? I can't remember where you said?'

Rayan faltered for only a split second. 'The Glossop Hill Climb? Starts at Holmfirth and you end up in Sheffield and then back through Glossop and Holme Moss. Bloody hard hills, I can tell you.' Rayan went towards his underwear drawer, seeking clean boxers, and Eva took in the beautiful coffee-coloured skin moving imperceptibly over well-toned muscle as he searched for socks. 'Has Mum left?' Rayan turned slightly when Eva appeared unable to speak.

'Hmm, Sabir picked her up this morning. You didn't say she was going.'

'Sorry.'

'Other things on your mind? The race maybe?'

'You know what I'm like on race days.'

'I thought I did.'

'Sorry?' Rayan still didn't turn but, instead, made a great performance of looking for socks and underwear.

'I said, Rayan, I thought I knew what you were up to on race days.' Eva suddenly jumped up and went directly to the linen basket, taking out Rayan's discarded shorts and singlet, sniffing at them with some deliberation. They smelt only of Persil and the rather expensive fabric conditioner she liked to use on the family's clothes. 'Not worked up much of a sweat then?'

'What the hell are you doing?' Rayan glared, red-faced.

'Wondering why your kit isn't stinking of sweat after all those bloody hills you've cycled up. And why the bloke – can't remember his name; bloke in a black Evoque – who registered all the racers this morning, said you hadn't.'

'Hadn't what?'

'Stop playing for time, Rayan. *Registered*,' Eva spat. 'Registered for the race you said you've been at all day, but clearly haven't.'

'Just leave it out, Eva.'

'Leave it out? Where've you been all day? We came up to find you; to reward you with a picnic at the finishing line.'

'A picnic?'

'A picnic,' Eva snapped. 'You know, ham sandwiches, quiche, M&S pâté, Percy Pigs? You're having an affair, aren't you?'

When Rayan didn't say anything, Eva gave a bark of laughter. 'Unbelievable. There's me, having fantasies about sex with other men because you and I never do it anymore, because all I want is affection and some bloody good sex...'

'Daddy!' Laila flung herself on Rayan, followed almost immediately by Nora. 'Where've you been? We saved you some Percy Pigs.'

'Thanks, sweetie.' Rayan hugged both the girls to him and tried to smile. He turned away from Eva, but not before she saw him wipe surreptitiously at his face with the back of his hand.

31

The day before Bill Astley's funeral, Rosa was surprised to see Rhys Johnson back on her doorstep.

'I'm here again,' Rhys finally grunted by way of greeting, once he'd followed her in silence down the corridor and into the kitchen. 'You know, like you said I had to.'

'Yes, absolutely, of course.' Rosa looked around her in a slight panic trying to work out what little jobs she might give Rhys to do.

'Only, you don't seem to have been expecting me.' Rhys gazed round at the now neat and tidy kitchen where, earlier that day, Rosa's beautiful new red stove had been delivered and fitted. He glanced over to the sitting room where the walls were now liberated from their former layers of wallpaper. 'You don't look to have got anything out and ready for me to do.'

Rosa hadn't. After the disastrous night out at the restaurant with Joe Rosavina the previous week, she'd not expected to see either Joe or Rhys or, for that matter, Sam Burrows. While seeing Joe in the restaurant had brought up all sorts of feelings – regret, anger, but also acceptance and, yes, OK, still love for the man – she'd accepted that in all probability Joe had told Rhys to keep away as well, that his stepson wouldn't be welcome at the vicarage. And, while she wanted to see Sam again, had come to the conclusion after she'd caught him, *all loved up* (wasn't that the wording used in the tabloids?) with the attractive blonde in the restaurant, he'd obviously only invited her out to the ballet for her support. Like some sort of damned counsellor or social worker or, she'd smiled ruefully to herself, like some village vicar.

'How many times do I have to come?' Rhys now asked. 'You know, so you don't go to the police about the other night.'

Rosa turned to Rhys. 'So, what do *you* think is fair?'

Rhys shrugged. 'Dunno...' He looked away and then, as if suddenly remembering, added, 'Roberto's going to ask you something when he comes to pick me up.'

'Oh?'

'I phoned him when I knew I was coming here – Joe's gone to London for a couple of days – and asked him to pick me up.' Rhys paused, seemingly embarrassed. 'I've got to go back to court again after Christmas. For a trial. I've pleaded not guilty to breaking into a house with the others and taking a mobile phone, a laptop and a bike. I gave a "no comment" interview to the police.' He added the last sentence almost proudly.

'Oh?' Rosa looked at him full in the face. 'Who told you to do that?'

'My solicitor. And my mates.'

'Really? These are the mates you were with the other night?'

Rhys nodded but didn't say anything for a while, his bravado evaporating slightly. He stared out of the kitchen window, his back towards her. He suddenly appeared terribly vulnerable.

'And are they *still* your mates?'

Rhys shrugged and, still turned away from her, muttered, 'I don't really like them much, but they sometimes wait for me outside school or when I get off the school bus. They followed me today, and that's why I came here.'

'Ah, you hadn't *intended* coming here then? You know, to help me again?'

'Yes, I did, honest...'

'Right.' Rosa smiled to herself. 'So, these *mates*, they're not actually at your school then?'

'No, they've all left, or are at other schools.'

'Rhys, are you frightened of them?'

'Frightened? No, course not. I'm not frightened of nobody, me.'

'You can tell me, you know.'

'Because you're a vicar?'

'Because I'm a grown-up and might be able to help.'

'They keep wanting me to go with them again.' Rhys's voice faltered. 'They were out on our road last night. Roberto and Joe saw them hanging about, shouting up at my bedroom window, but they ran off.'

Hell, Rosa thought, this was like something out of *Oliver Twist* when Sikes is wanting a small boy to burgle houses. 'Joe should be telling the police this is going on. I assume your bail conditions specify no contact with this little gang?'

Rhys nodded, but added, 'They'll have me, if I grass them up.' Rhys's educated London accent appeared at odds with the words.

'So, what is it Roberto's going to ask me?'

'Will you come to court with me? You know, dressed like a vicar?'

'I *am* a vicar.' Rosa wanted to laugh but, one glance at Rhys's serious face and she kept her own likewise.

'You know, tell the magistrates how I'm working with you. That I need another chance and not be sent to prison. How I'm going straight.'

Rosa didn't know whether to laugh or cry at this; all she could picture now was Ronnie Barker in *Porridge*.

'Otherwise, I'll end up in Wetherby. I don't want to go to prison... and I... you know... like you said... I won't be able to go... and I want to –' Rhys rubbed furiously at his face '– I want to go to Australia to see my mum.'

'Rhys, of course I'll do that. I'll come with you and put my best vicar's outfit on. Right, look, how about a cup of tea and a biscuit? And then the garden could do with a bit of tidying up.'

'Not the graves?' Rhys finally turned round, a look of horror on his face. 'You don't want me to weed round the graves?'

Rosa laughed. 'No, you daft thing. The Friends of Westenbury Church do that. There's a whole load of fallen leaves still to brush up, just outside the back door, and the herb garden could do with a good weed.'

'It's dark out there now,' Rhys protested. 'And I don't know which is a herb and what's a weed. And your garden's *very near* those graves.'

'The porch light is on so you can see to sweep up the leaves. And then –' Rosa handed the boy a bucket and sponge '– the paintwork on the front door needs washing down before the decorators come tomorrow.'

'*I'll* paint it for you,' Rhys said. 'I like painting; I told you, I'm good at art. And it'll save you some money too. I know you're really poor.'

'How do you know that?' Rosa gave a fleetingly guilty thought to the money from the sale of her flat and business, apparently accruing healthy interest in various – albeit ethically sound – accounts.

Rhys gave her one of his looks. ''Cos you had nothing to rob when we broke in the other week.'

Almost an hour later, Rosa heard voices coming from the garden through the open kitchen door and assumed it was Roberto Rosavina arrived to pick up Rhys. It was dark and cold in the vicarage garden and, feeling slightly guilty that she'd had the boy working out there so long, went out to bring them both in.

Rhys was deep in conversation with the man who was helping him carry the pile of autumn leaves out to the compost heap at the bottom of the garden. Rosa squinted against the dark and shadows and, with racing pulse, saw it was Joe. He waved a hand in greeting as she stood illuminated in the light of the doorway, before he and Rhys collected up the long-handled brooms and spades and made their way back up the garden path.

'Oh, Sam?' Not Joe then.

'Hi, thought I'd just call in and see you.' Sam appeared oblivious to the fact that the last time she'd seen him he'd been wrapped round some other woman. *Modern dating rules, Rosa,* she reminded herself once again. 'I've been away in Southampton this last week. Some course Rayan insisted I go on before taking on my own patients. There are new UK regulations I needed bringing up to date with.'

'Right.' Rosa took in Sam's dark brown eyes and beautiful full mouth and felt her knees give way slightly. Blimey, he wasn't half gorgeous. No wonder the blonde had been launching herself almost halfway across the starched white tablecloth in his direction, the other night.

'Er, I bet you're hungry, aren't you?' Rosa asked, addressing Rhys.

'Absolutely starving,' both of them said in unison before heading for the kitchen.

'Eggs?' Rosa asked from the fridge, wishing she could climb in there herself. Anything to get rid of the heat suffusing her face Sam's unexpected presence was causing. 'Cheese?'

'Can I make an omelette?' Rhys asked. 'I'm a whizz at omelettes. Do you want one, Sam?'

'Do you know, I can't think of anything better,' Sam smiled. 'Shall I help you?'

'You can grate the cheese if you like. I always end up grating my fingernails.'

'No problem, although I've often found a *soupçon* of grated finger and the accompanying nail can add a certain *je ne sais quoi* to an omelette. Oh look, new stove, Rhys. Are you OK christening that?' Sam turned to smile behind him at Rosa who was still, apparently, finding something of interest in the fridge.

'Yes, course, I told you.'

'You alright in there, Rosa?' Sam moved behind her, and she could feel him, sense him, smell his citrus aftershave. Her pulse raced some more. 'Right,' he went on, 'omelettes are a great idea because I called in at my mum's in Sheffield on the way back up and she, as always, loaded me up with stuff.' He walked over to the door before holding up a brown carrier he'd brought in from the garden. 'Homemade focaccia studded with rosemary and baby tomatoes, some chutney and a rather nice bottle of Malbec.'

'I'll have a glass of that with you,' Rhys called over his shoulder and Rosa was amazed how relaxed and smiley he'd become in Sam's presence.

'You'll have a Coke and like it,' Rosa laughed, her eyes meeting Sam's in one long glance that neither seemed able to break.

'Are you going out with this dude, Rosa?' Rhys asked, as he slipped two finished cheese omelettes onto warm plates and back into the new stove, before starting on a third. 'Is he your boyfriend?'

'I hope so,' Sam grinned, slicing the focaccia into large, olive-oil-saturated salted pieces and, with a start, Rosa realised this was the first time in over twenty years she'd been about to devour this type of bread without instantly thinking of Joe.

'This is a brilliant omelette, Rhys,' Rosa grinned, the large glass of Malbec, together with Sam's words, making her light-headed with happiness as she tucked into the food with relish. 'I thought you wanted to be an artist, not a chef.'

'An artistic chef,' Rhys said seriously between mouthfuls. 'That's why I want to help in Rosavina's – Roberto's restaurant. If he'd just let me without... you know... thinking...' He glanced across at Sam, obviously not wanting to carry on.

Rosa patted Rhys's hand. 'I know, Rhys. How about I have a word with him? Ask him to let you spend some time in Rosavina's?'

And when Roberto did arrive to collect Rhys half an hour later, having taken in the three of them getting stuck into big pieces of Sam's mum's Christmas cake and crumbly Wensleydale, he shook his head sadly and, lowering his voice, said to Rosa, 'That son of mine such a fool. I met new dentist last week, at your sister's surgery. Had filling and not a bit of pain. Nice chap. You do well there. That son of mine a fool…'

Once Roberto and Rhys had left, Rosa having confirmed not only that she'd be more than happy to accompany Rhys to court to speak on his behalf, but suggesting Roberto might give the boy a chance to show what he could do in the restaurant, Sam poured more wine and loaded up the new dishwasher that had also been fitted that week.

'What was with the Irish accent the other evening?' Sam asked, grinning. 'You sounded like a stand in for Mrs Doubtfire. And, can I just say, you looked absolutely stunning in that pink dress. I wanted to introduce you, but you scuttled off before I could come over to you.'

'I didn't scuttle,' Rosa said with as much dignity as she could muster. 'You make me sound like some sort of crab. Anyway, you were obviously well entrenched.'

'Entrenched?' Sam started to laugh.

'You know exactly what I mean. 'You were all… all… loved up with your… your… guest.'

'*Loved up?* Hell, Rosa, don't tell me I've fallen in love with a *Daily Express* reader.' He was laughing across at her, enjoying himself.

Rosa's head shot up. Had he just said what she thought he'd said? 'You're perfectly entitled,' she said primly, 'to take to dinner whomever so you wish… so whom you wish… so you wish whom…' The red wine and Sam's beautiful brown eyes, laughingly gentle as he teased her, were making her fall over her words. 'Oh hell, Sam, you know what I'm getting at.'

'Whomever you so wish?'

'That's the one.'

Sam took her hand, stroking her fingertips, the soft skin of her wrist, trailing cool, lazy fingers up to, and then inside the cuff of her sweater until she heard Gabriel and his mates cooing with delight once more, and knew this was utter heaven.

'I was saying goodbye to Penny.'

'Penny?'

'My wife. My *ex-wife*.' He paused. 'Ollie's mum.'

'Saying goodbye?'

'She's been trying to get a green card to live and work in New York permanently. It's finally come through, and I said I'd take her out to celebrate. And obviously say goodbye. We'd been together to Ollie's grave in Sheffield to lay flowers. She needed to know that one of us is going to be here in the UK with him.'

'Right.'

'I suppose you thought I was some sort of Lothario – out with you one night and then her a couple of evenings later?'

'Not at all,' Rosa lied. 'Never gave it a thought.'

'I'd just been telling Penny all about you, about how I'd met this wonderful vicar, and she was holding my hand, saying how pleased she was for me. And then the very next minute, this sultry vision in pink shakes her Louboutins at me and does a very good impression of having been born and bred in County Mayo. *Hello dere*.' Sam started laughing again and putting on a terrible Irish accent. '*How're you doing?* Oh, Rosa, you were wonderful. I fell in love with you there and then – that very minute. Penny said: "Go and get her, go after her so I can meet her," but you'd run off into the rain in your stockinged feet.'

'Heavens, how embarrassing. I'd just left my ex-partner – Rhys's stepfather – in the other half of the restaurant, and finally realised, and it's taken me a hell of a long time *to* realise, that we've both moved on. We've had to move on. I suppose I was running away from him again.'

Sam kissed her fingers. 'Eva told me the whole story.'

'Eva did?'

'Hmm. I sat and had a coffee with her when I reported back in to the surgery. She told me about Joe, about your falling ill… Gosh, Rosa, you've been through so much. I didn't realise. I'm sorry.'

'Nothing to be sorry about, Sam. Really, nothing at all.'

'So, are there any rules about kissing vicars? You know, does God approve?'

'Absolutely.' Rosa smiled before closing her eyes and feeling Sam's mouth on her own, teasing gently and then with such expertise she wondered how anyone could be so good at such a simple thing as kissing. 'Absolutely, he does,' she murmured, mentally writing in her diary:

Best kisser ever.

32

It had been a total and utter shock for the triplets to turn round, as they sat in the tiny chapel on the Heatherly estate, and see Susan and Richard, themselves invited to the private but simple humanist service for Bill, walk in accompanied by none other than Alice Parkes. Richard, who had been ill for a week or so with a chest infection, seemed much improved, but Alice – Eva calculated she must be almost seventy now – appeared frail. She walked slowly to a seat, aided both by a stick as well as by Susan who, in comparison, was upright and sprightly, looking years younger than her sister.

'Alice!' Rosa, who had been asked to officiate at the short but strictly not religious ceremony, smiled, walking to greet the three of them and hugging each in turn. 'How lovely to see you. You didn't say...' She trailed off, looking towards Susan for some sort of confirmation.

'I was in Paris,' Alice rasped, her voice thick and hoarse from years of smoking her signature cigarillos. 'Seem to spend an awful lot of time there at the moment. My spiritual home, I suppose. Anyway, made the decision, at the very last moment – history repeating itself I guess,' she added with a little laugh that ended up in a long and worrying cough, 'to, you know, get myself to Orly Airport and a flight over for Bill's funeral.' Her accent was New York mixed with West Yorkshire undertones. 'And look at you – a daughter of mine a vicar, for heaven's sake. I do hope you're a much kinder one than that old sod, Cecil...' She broke off, obviously struggling for breath, and Susan searched for, and then handed over, an inhaler from the pocket of Alice's voluminous bright yellow and turquoise cloak she'd apparently thought fitting for Bill's funeral.

'Well, it's so wonderful to see you. Hannah and Eva will be with you once the service is over – Jonny Astley and Henrietta are going to be the only two accompanying Bill to the crematorium.'

Alice turned, gazing long and intently at her other two daughters who were staring back just as hard at this birth mother of theirs whom they'd not seen for at least fifteen years and then, as two women and one man walked in, all eyes swivelled to them instead. Jonny Astley, his wife, Billy-Jo, and sister Henrietta, walked in single file and in silence to the front of the chapel, and took up the seats reserved for them earlier that morning.

'Ah, Bill's *legitimate* heirs, I suppose?' Alice Parkes' voice, at once both hoarse and strident, drifted unceremoniously around the chapel accompanied by a series of, 'Shh, shhh, Alice,' from Susan.

'Those two never had any time for Bill,' Alice was saying. 'And Bill had much more time for *my* girls. I was always in touch with him, you know, Rosa. He often came out to see me in New York, and when I was over in Paris. Maybe, you know, I should have worked a bit harder with him – I could have become the marchioness of bloody Westenbury. Ha, that would have been one in the eye for old Reverend Cecil, hey?' Alice hooted with mirth at the very thought. 'And then you girls would have been legitimate and inherited the hall. How would that have worked? Suze?' Alice turned, frowning to Susan. 'Which of the three came out first? Oh, *I* don't remember. You'd have had to fight it out amongst yourselves, you girls, as to who inherited the lot.'

'Hell, she's a nightmare.' Hannah pulled a face, turning from where Alice was holding court, back to Eva. 'Do you think she's on something?'

'I hear she likes a gin or three,' Eva smirked. 'Good for her.

She's a feisty old broad, isn't she? Can you believe she's our mother?'

'I can believe she's *yours*.' Hannah dug Eva in the ribs. 'But don't say that about her being our mother. She was Alice Growbag, remember, and gave up all rights to us when she gave us away. Mum – *Susan* – is our mother.'

Eva turned once more, glancing across at Henrietta Heatherly and Jonny before whispering to Hannah, 'So, you've not told me what Jonny Astley said to you last night?'

'Well, they'd arrived half an hour or so earlier when I got there after work, but were already demanding electric blankets on the beds, adapters for all their US plugs, and tea and cucumber sandwiches.'

'Cucumber sandwiches?' Eva stared. 'Really?'

'Hmm,' Hannah giggled. 'Now that Billy-Jo is the thirteenth Marchioness of Heatherly and a paid-up member of the English aristocracy, she must think that's what she should be eating every afternoon.'

'She'll soon be back on burgers, fries and doughnuts.'

'I doubt it. She's from California; they don't do any sinful stuff there, do they? Anyway, Lachlan Buchanan had a long chat with Jonny and Billy-Jo while Henrietta took herself off with a notepad.'

'Lachlan Buchanan?' Eva frowned. 'Who's he when he's at home?'

'New estate manager. Bill took him on just a week before he died. I thought he was another of the local farmers when I first met him, telling me off for not having Brian on a lead. Not sure there'll be a job for him here now. Everything's up in the air.' Hannah shook her head.

'And a notepad? What was she doing? Sizing up the joint?'

Hannah pulled a face. 'Well, making an inventory, anyway. I had a ten-minute chat with Jonny, who wanted to know all about us three, what our relationship with Bill had been like and why I was actually there at the hall that evening. What business I had there. And, cheek of the man, how had we ever been sure we were actually Bill's daughters?'

'What a pillock. I know, you should have told him you were shagging the estate manager and, as such, had every right in the world to be there.'

'Shhh, for heaven's sake, Eva,' Hannah whispered crossly. 'You *are* just like Alice. And, as I've only just become acquainted with Lachlan Buchanan – and he's not my type *whatsoever* – that is highly unlikely. And I really dislike the "sh" word. I can't even *say* it.'

'So, which one is he? This Lachlan Buchanan?' Eva peered round at the gathering crowd of mourners to where a tall, auburn-haired man was greeting and showing people to their places. 'That him? Over there?'

Hannah turned in the direction of Eva's gaze and nodded.

'Goodness. He's rather splendid in a Liam Neeson sort of way.'

'Liam Neeson?' Hannah tutted. 'Liam Neeson's Irish, not Scottish.'

'Not when he's playing Rob Roy in a kilt. When he goes all sexy, in the way only Liam Neeson can, and says something about Mary McGregor being *so fine* to him?' Eva adopted a – terrible – Scottish accent. 'Blimey. And then whatsername...?'

'Mary McGregor?'

'Played by Jessica Lange, then has her hands up his kilt. I've thought about that scene often when...'

'Do you mind, Eva? We're at one of our fathers' wake,' Hannah hissed. 'And when are you going to tell us what's going on with you and—'

'I will tell you. Once we're out of here. I need to talk to someone about it all.'

'Where is he?'

'Someone has to hold the fort at the surgery. Hopefully he'll make it on time.'

'Go on, tell me now.'

'Shh, Bill's arrived.' The pair of them stood as Rosa walked to the front of the chapel and Bill, carried in a simple wicker casket, followed behind on the shoulders of the pallbearers. 'Exercise a little decorum, Hannah, would you, please?' Eva said piously, reaching for her tissues.

'I thought we, as beneficiaries, would be called in together by the solicitor for the will reading, after the funeral.' Hannah wiped away the tears that she didn't seem able to arrest now that Bill, twelfth Marquess of Heatherly, had been laid to rest. The first instruction in his will had been, apparently, that he wasn't to be buried in the family's plot alongside his ancestors in the mouldering graveyard of Midhope's town centre parish church but, instead, his ashes were to be scattered, by his three daughters – Eva Malik, Rosa Quinn and Hannah Quinn – at Norman's Meadow, a local beauty spot on the outskirts of Westenbury village.

'Will readings, when all the family troop into the solicitor's office after the funeral and end up arguing and fighting when they don't get what they think is their right, are pure Hollywood,' Eva sniffed, wiping at her own eyes with a thoroughly damp tissue. 'The estate can take years to sort out and, knowing Bill, he'll have left it all to chance, letting others fight it out amongst themselves.'

'Miss Quinn? Miss Quinn? Mrs Malik?' All three of them turned as Rodney Bowman, the main man from Bowman, Bowman and Foley – Bill's solicitors – ran out from Heatherly Hall to join them. He was a diminutive man, his greying hair combed over his head from a parting just above his left ear in an unsuccessful attempt to hide his quite extensive bald patch. He reminded Rosa of a hysterically efficient mouse that wouldn't be out of place in a Lewis Carroll storybook.

'Ladies, I know that you're aware, from the letters I sent out to you this week, that the three of you are all beneficiaries in the late Marquess of Heatherly's estate.'

'Well,' Eva interrupted, 'we know we've been asked to scatter Bill's ashes. I don't know how we go about that, not having done it before.'

'I'll take you through *that* later this afternoon,' Rodney Bowman said almost irritably. 'Now, while the day of the funeral isn't perhaps the most apt to be sorting a few things out, the Marquess of Heatherly has asked us to get straight down to business, as it were.'

'The Marquess of Heatherly?' Hannah turned in surprise and then, understanding, felt tears start once more.

'I'd be obliged if you three ladies would reconvene with myself and the marquess and marchioness at –' the solicitor shrugged at his cuff to reveal his wristwatch '– shall we say 4 p.m.? In the late marquess's apartment? Hmm? Does that suit all parties?'

'Let's go and have a drink,' Eva suggested. 'Let's get wasted and celebrate Bill's life. That's what he'd have suggested we do, you know. If he was here.'

'We're expected at the main hall for sherry and a sit-down lunch at 2 p.m.,' Rosa reminded the other two. 'And we really need to be there to help with Alice. She really is a bit of a liability, isn't she?'

'OK. Look, it's only one,' Eva said. 'Why don't we tell Mum we're just popping over to the pub across the road for twenty minutes and then we'll join them at the hall for sherry and lunch. I think coffee's being served over there first and they can have a comfortable seat and catch up with Alice before we do the same with her later. *I* really need to talk to you two.'

She ran off towards Susan, Richard and Alice, hugged the three of them and then accompanied them into the hall where coffee and biscuits were being served. Hannah and Rosa walked slowly across the road to the Heatherly Arms pub and ordered gin and tonics for the three of them.

'Is something going on?' Rosa asked as the two of them sat down. 'With Eva and Rayan?'

'What makes you say that?'

'Just something Sam said. He got the impression there was some friction between them. Oh, she's here now.'

'What's up, Eva?'

Eva took a long drink from the proffered gin glass, ice and a large piece of lemon bumping unceremoniously against her nose as she did so.

'Rayan is frightened of me.'

'*We're* frightened of you, Eva.'

'He says I'm the cause of him needing help.'

'What sort of help?' Hannah and Rosa leaned forwards as one.

Eva hesitated. 'I promised I wouldn't discuss it with you two.'

'Well then, you mustn't,' Rosa advised.

'It's us. You can tell us; we're a part of each other,' Hannah simultaneously advised.

'I'm sorry, Rosa, if you don't want to be a party to this, then move away now.'

'Oh, stop being so dramatic,' Rosa tutted.

'Rayan and I haven't had sex for ages,' Eva said almost defiantly.

'What's ages? A day? A week? A month?'

'A year.' Eva went slightly pink.

'A year?' Hannah stared. 'Is it just, after having Nora, you've not been interested? It happens, you know.'

'*How* do you know?' Eva glared across at Hannah.

'It's in all the magazines,' Hannah soothed. 'You can get some help, some counselling.'

'It's not me who doesn't want it. It's Rayan.'

'Right.' Hannah and Rosa exchanged glances but didn't say anything.

'That's very normal as well, you know,' Hannah said. 'It's a well-known fact – men have busy lives, trying to run a business and a young family. They're under a lot of pressure to succeed in every aspect of their life.'

'He says I've emasculated him.' Eva drained her glass and looked hopefully towards the bar.

'Well, you are a bit, you know...' Hannah was trying hard to choose her words with care.

'What? A bit what?'

'A bit full-on. And Rayan is very sensitive; a really nice bloke.'

'He says he's *surrounded* by strong, strident women: me, you two, the girls, Azra, Jodie, the dental nurses at work, the cat, the Barbie dolls...'

'Blimey.'

'...and, as such, feels his very masculinity is being drained out of him.'

'I thought it would be the other way round,' Hannah pondered. 'You know, in a harem, when there's just one man and a load of women, all waiting their turn, he's always at it. And,' she went on, 'look at that ram, on Clarkson's Farm. One ram and a fieldful of sheep and it's *wahey, and off we go*.'

'Hannah, Rayan is not a *ram*,' Eva said in exasperation before taking out the lemon from her drink in order to suck out any remaining alcohol. 'I thought it must be all that cycling he's been doing. All that testosterone going into his legs to pedal so that there's not enough, you know, going to... you know...'

Rosa and Hannah nodded sympathetically.

'Anyway, last Sunday I took the girls to meet him on the bike ride he was supposed to be doing. He wasn't there; hadn't apparently been there for the past few Sundays, even though he'd set off with his bike and in his cycling gear, telling me that's where he was going.'

'And where *was* he going?'

'Leicester.'

'Leicester?' Rosa frowned. 'What was he doing there?'

'Paying a lot of money to a woman who is supposed to be the UK's top psychosexual expert. She is so busy, and apparently so feted at what she does, she's booked up for months ahead. Anyway, she agreed to see him on a course of six Sundays if he would drive down to her place in Leicester and, presumably, pay her double time. He won't tell me how much he's been shelling out.'

'I'm not surprised, Eva. Why would he tell you all this, especially if he knew that your reaction would be one of derision? You know, erectile dysfunction is a really common problem,' Hannah went on. 'I remember reading that 52 per cent of men between the ages of forty and seventy suffer from it at some stage in their life.'

'Hannah, Rayan is thirty-eight. I don't get what the problem is. There I am, in my sexy outfits, in my high heels and stockings, and he doesn't want to know.'

'Gosh, I bet you do frighten him,' Rosa said sympathetically. 'Poor bloke.'

'Scare the bejesus – sorry, Rosa – out of him, when you jump on him, your nipple tassels twirling, expecting him to perform.' Hannah threw up her hands.

'Have you got *nipple tassels*?' Rosa stared.

'Figure of speech, Vicar,' Eva retorted. 'Do you both think it's all my fault then? Is that what you think? Is that the general consensus?'

'Well, I don't think you're helping.'

'I try every which way *to help*,' Eva replied crossly. 'I don't just lie there and think of England.'

'Might be better if you did,' Rosa smiled. 'You know, just occasionally,' she added hastily. 'Rather than making a huge performance of it all when he's afraid he's going to get stage fright.'

'Which obviously puts him under pressure and then nothing happens. It must be like trying to sneeze when you can't! You know, you gaze up at the light, desperate to sneeze...'

'Are you suggesting I tell Rayan to look up at the light in order to… you know…?' Eva was visibly upset.

'No, Eva,' Rosie said gently. 'You accept that this is both your problem, you go with him to counselling sessions and you stop frightening the poor bloke into trying to give the performance of his life.'

'I'm a terrible person.' Eva started to cry.

'Not always.' Rosa patted Eva's arm. 'Not always.'

33

'So, now that the main beneficiaries of the will of the twelfth Marquess of Heatherly are gathered here...' Rodney Bowman glanced around the dining table in Bill's apartment where Jonny and Billy-Jo, Henrietta and the triplets were seated '...I can formally inform you all of the contents – signed in my presence just a year ago. These were Bill Astley's wishes.' The solicitor took off his glasses and spoke directly to the six of them. 'There are other, smaller bequests of course, and the beneficiaries of those will be informed in due course.' He cleared his throat, replaced his spectacles and started reading:

'This is the last will and testament of me, William Henry Astley, and I hereby revoke all former wills and testamentary dispositions made by me...' Bowman removed his glasses once more and smiled across at Jonny and Billy-Jo. 'The title of Marquess of Heatherly, which as I'm sure you are aware, is a hereditary title in the peerage of Great Britain, created for one William Astley, third Viscount Heatherly back in 1623 – goes to the eldest living legitimate male heir, John William Rufus Astley. His legal wife, Billy-Jo' – Rodney Bowman gave a little cough – 'will inherit the title of the thirteenth Marchioness of Heatherly.'

Rosa saw Jonny pat his wife's arm and exchange congratulatory glances.

'The late marquess added the following codicil: *if they want it...*'

'If we *want* it? What's that supposed to mean?' Billy-Jo's voice was pure West Coast, and she threw up her hands before pointing a slim tanned finger almost rudely in the solicitor's direction.

'Just that. While Bill Astley was in no position to do so, he suggests, in the will, that the title be made extinct.'

'Oh, alright for him to carry the title,' Billy-Jo drawled indignantly, 'but once he's dead and buried, he wants the title buried with him? I don't *think* so.' She leaned across to Jonny, taking his hand.

'And that is your hereditary right and, as such, my congratulations go to both of you, My Lord and Lady Heatherly.' Bowman bowed his head slightly in Jonny and Billy-Jo's direction.

'Now,' the solicitor went on, warming to his theme, 'Britain's aristocracy is a somewhat quaint historical curiosity, you know. Going back in time, land and estates – such as this one – were either given under some royal jurisdiction, possibly as a reward for services to the monarch, or actually taken illegally under the pretence of piety or with the excuse that land had to be enclosed for agricultural reasons...'

'Do we really need the history lesson, Bowman?' Jonny interrupted, his top lip curled in irritation. 'Can we just get on?'

'Apologies, apologies, I'm just trying to point out to all parties here a little of Heatherly Hall's backstory and to inform you, if you were of the opinion otherwise, that the Heatherly estate has never owned large chunks of land and real estate in Mayfair or Scottish estate, as so many other big estates in England have. Now, as I'm sure you're fully aware, the hall and the estate no longer belong, per se, to the current marquess...'

'What do you mean? *No longer belong?*' Jonny Astley interrupted the solicitor once again.

'Just that, My Lord. The hall and the estate are both owned and managed by Heatherly Hall Estates Limited with the deceased being 51 per cent shareholder, as well as holding the position and title of Chairman of the Board.'

'Your dad didn't actually *own* this place?' Billy-Jo turned to Jonny.

'Of course he did. Been in the Astley family since... since... years back. And it's passed to me now. *I* own it.'

'Well, sir, that's not strictly true.' Rodney gave a little impatient smile. 'Now, if I may continue?'

Rosa glanced across at the new titleholders and then at Eva and Hannah, who were obviously trying to work out what was going on.

'I, William Astley, being of sound mind, bequeath my 51 per cent shareholding of the Heatherly Hall Estate to my three daughters, Rosa Quinn, Hannah Quinn and Eva Malik to share equally, and in the knowledge that they will do the very best for the hall and the estate, however they think fit and whatever that may be.'

'*Whatever that may be?* What are you talking about, man?' Jonny was now actually standing, pointing his own finger at Rodney Bowman.

'I am merely reading out the will, sir, and will attempt, in time, to explain exactly what that means for all of you here this afternoon.'

'What about the pictures? The artwork? The silver? The tapestries? The... the...'

'Jewellery,' Billy-Jo reminded her husband. 'You know, that priceless jet set studded with diamonds everyone knows and talks about?'

'The jewellery?' Jonny repeated.

'All part of the Heatherly estate and held in trust by, and for, the management of the estate alongside everything else. Now –' Rodney held up a hand as Jonny started to speak '– there is, of course, Bill Astley's personal wealth and assets and again – once death duties and inheritance tax have been paid – these are to be divided equally amongst Bill's three daughters.'

'*I'm* his daughter.' Henrietta Astley spoke for the first time, pinpoints of red in her tanned, unlined face. 'The marquess's *legal* daughter. He can't leave everything to these three... these three illegitimate...' Henrietta waved a furious arm at the triplets who were sitting in stunned silence '...*interlopers*. He can't legally do it.'

'OK, stop right there.' Jonny jumped up, pushing back his chair with such force it actually toppled over. 'I want blood tests...'

'DNA...' Billy-Jo was shouting now.

'...paternity tests first of all to make sure these three women are who they purport to be. Looking at that old broad, Alice Parkes, in the chapel this morning, I'd put her up to anything. She's got a reputation for having *hundreds* of lovers; my father, the marquess, was one of many.'

'Hundreds? Really?' Eva spoke for the first time.

'Can I just say, Jonny and Henrietta' – Rosa tried to calm the waters – 'that this has all come as big a shock to my sisters and me, as it must have to you? We genuinely *never* expected this outcome and, to be honest, I'm not sure – and I'm speaking for myself here – we want to be put in the position of holding such a responsibility.'

Eva and Hannah, faces pale with the shock of the last few minutes, merely nodded.

'Oh, come on,' Jonny sneered, 'you three were always up here. That one –' Jonny shook a hand dismissively at Hannah '– just about *lived* here. She certainly must have known what the old man was planning.'

'No, truly, I didn't.' Hannah was almost in tears at the implication.

'Anyway, you can stop right there,' Jonny repeated. 'We want details of my father's full medical history. He obviously wasn't of sound mind.' Jonny turned to his wife. 'Mental instability can totally reverse a decision like this. And paternity tests for these three. This minute.'

'We were actually asked to prove Bill's paternity when we were sixteen or so, Jonny,' Rosa said. 'My father – Richard – had an accident and couldn't work for about a year and my mother – Susan – came up to the hall to see Bill to ask for help. Bill's solicitors at the time – and certainly not instigated by Bill, who would have given us anything he had – insisted on the tests as proof of paternity. We *are* Bill's daughters.'

'Handouts,' Jonny sneered. 'Charity. Well, that was years ago when these tests weren't that accurate. I want the best, up-to-date tests available so that when we go to the highest court in the UK and contest this damned will, we will have the judge on our side.'

'Absolutely,' Rosa said calmly, spokesperson once again when, before, it had always been Eva. 'I can totally see why you'd want that. Let's put your mind at rest on that score and prove that we three all have the same Astley blood as yourself.'

'But how do we do that, you know, now that Bill has passed away?' Hannah frowned across at Rosa.

'Oh, there are ways and means,' Eva said, put out that her relationship to Bill Astley was being questioned, as well as the morals of their birth mother being dug up and aired by the legitimate offspring. 'It's obviously more problematic now that Bill is no longer with us, but there will still be his DNA present in his hairbrush, on his toothbrush...'

'Isn't that all a bit ghoulish?' Hannah winced. 'I hate the idea of us scratting about, trying to find traces of Bill, now that he's gone.'

'Is it really *necessary*?' Eva was cross. 'There will be evidence of the tests we all did over twenty years ago somewhere. Mum will have the results, or they'll be in some files of Bill's or held in the vaults of the former solicitors. Somewhere.'

'Exactly. *Somewhere*.' Jonny Astley was triumphant. 'You've no idea where they are – if they ever existed at all. We need new ones. Now.'

'Really not a problem as far as I can see, if you insist on having the Ms Quinns and Mrs Malik's proof of paternity.' Rodney Bowman spoke calmly. 'Twenty years ago, Bill Astley's affairs were not dealt with by my company – he moved everything over to us only five years ago when he made the big decision to put the ownership of the estate into a public limited company – and, to be honest, I have no knowledge of this proof of paternity asked for by the original solicitors before apparently setting up some funding for the girls.'

'It wasn't a huge amount,' Eva protested. 'It got us through sixth form and university and, once Dad – Richard – was back at work, Mum insisted that it stopped. She hated going begging for charity.'

'I bet she did,' Henrietta sneered.

'Although, you know,' Rodney interrupted, seeing the discussion was becoming heated, if not downright unpleasant, 'to be honest, the twelfth marquess had every right to leave his shares of the Heatherly estate, as well as his personal wealth, to whomsoever he pleased. He could have left it to the cats' home...'

'Oh, don't roll out the cats' home argument.' Billy-Jo actually snarled the words. 'This is aristocratic, landed estate, passed down from royalty. You Brits wouldn't allow Queen Elizabeth the Second...'

(Rosa smiled at Jonny's wife's deference to the monarch in giving her the full handle, as if there were any *other* Queen Elizabeth just hanging about.)

'...to hand over Buck House to some mangy cats. It *has* to stay within the family it was given to originally.'

'Things move on, you know, Billy-Jo.' Hannah tried her best to appease the woman whose slender neck was now flushed with a mottled red. 'Social nuances and accepted norms and traditions change. Look at how the United States has changed and moved on – just over one hundred and fifty years ago, black slavery was accepted and now you've voted in the first black president…'

'Hannah,' Rosa soothed, interrupting and smiling across at Jonny, Billy-Jo and Henrietta, who were becoming angrier by the minute, 'I really don't think any reference to Barack Obama has any relevance to what's happening here this afternoon.'

'Oh, but I think it has. I was merely…' Hannah ran a hand through her hair.

'As I was saying,' Rodney interrupted, 'Bill Astley had every legal right to leave his personal wealth to the three ladies present. But, as far as I can see, all you need to do, My Lord –' he nodded in Jonny's direction '– if you feel that it will help your contesting of the will, is to simply match your own DNA with that of the ladies.'

'Of course. Absolutely. And I will do just that.' Jonny Heatherly stood, adding, as though delivering lines on some second-rate radio drama, 'You've not heard the last of this.'

'I don't believe this. Do you? Did you have any idea at all what Bill was planning?' Hannah's voice followed the other two back across the road to the Heatherly Arms where they'd decided to reconvene rather than going back into Heatherly Hall where the last of the mourners were still lingering.

'Let's get inside, Hannah, before we start talking. I can't take it in without a drink inside me.' Eva turned as Hannah continued to pull at her coat in order to get her attention.

'I'm going to order coffee,' Rosa said. 'We have to drive home.'

'You're such a goody-goody, Vicar,' Eva tutted. 'Rayan's still at the wake with Mum and Dad and Virginia. He'll drive us home.'

'Coffee for me,' Rosa insisted.

'And me,' Hannah agreed.

'OK, OK.' Eva held up her hands in acquiescence.

Once they were settled, Rosa frowned. 'Do you actually *want* all this? I mean, it's a total change of lifestyle. And responsibility.'

'*Yes.*' Hannah spoke firmly. 'I can't think of anything I want more. You know, to be up at the hall every day, working there, managing the place. I can leave the youth service – you can't imagine how I was beginning to really dislike going in. Panicky almost, once I hit the traffic on the motorway.'

'And yes,' Eva added, her eyes gleaming, 'I can help with it all – as long as you don't put me back in with the damned pigs – and I'll be able to paint whenever I want.'

'You're not spending all day floating about in an artist smock, painting, while I'm back cleaning toilets in the holiday cottages.' Hannah raised an eyebrow as she sipped at her coffee.

'Ha, you'll be too busy being chased along the ancestral corridors by that Lachlan Buchanan bloke to be chasing dust with a feather duster. I think there's something about him – haughty, distant, noble, laird-like...' Eva and Hannah grinned at each other inanely as the implications of the will reading began to sink in.

'You see,' Rosa shook her head, 'you're arguing already. It's too much for us; you'd need to give up your dental work, Eva, and how can I continue to be the village vicar if I'm inheriting a share of Bill's personal wealth?'

'Isn't the Pope pretty rich?' Eva frowned. 'And the Queen, as head of the Church of England, isn't without a bob or two, you know. Don't worry about being a rich vicar, Rosa. And, if it bothers you that much, you can give your share to charity. Or *us* if it comes to that.' Eva grinned. 'And there can only be one chairman, so you don't have to put yourself up for that if you don't want.'

'I think you're both getting totally ahead of yourselves,' Rosa sighed. 'Although I do, I have to admit, feel a certain excitement at how the hall could be developed in the future.'

'Well, the wedding venue business is thriving,' Hannah said.

'We could extend Tea and Cake and turn it into a fabulous fine dining restaurant...'

'There's already Clementine's in the village.' Rosa shook her head. 'You'd be competing with that.'

'People always want to eat posh food,' Eva grinned excitedly. 'And we could have an art retreat, charge an absolute fortune.'

'And a cooking retreat,' Rosa added.

'A cooking retreat?' The other two stared.

'Yes, absolutely. Like Prue Leith's place in London. There's nothing like that round here. I might even take some of the classes myself.'

'What? *Cook Vegan with the Village Vicar?*'

'Why not?' Rosa's eyes lit up at the thought. 'Or we could get Azra in to do a few days of Indian cookery.'

'Oh, I know,' Hannah said excitedly, 'instead of packing kids off to Wetherby with a detention order, they could come and work the farm. I've always wanted to do something like that with kids who've got themselves into trouble.'

'I don't know about *that*,' Eva frowned. 'I don't want your naughty kids mixing with my art retreaters. Especially after they've paid a fortune to be there. Hey, maybe we can get Alice to be artist in residence?'

'Or, listen, we could become the Glastonbury of the north. How about that? That would be brilliant.' Hannah's eyes shone at the thought.

'If you think there's mud down there in the south, there'll be twice as much up here with all the rain we get coming off the Pennines.'

'It's a thought, though, isn't it?'

'We could get the Backstreet Boys to come over and do a reunion concert. Whoa, what about that?' Eva and Hannah actually high-fived, before giggling at the very idea.

'Look, let's get Mum and Dad over and tell them what's happened,' Rosa said. 'But we don't want anyone else to know just yet.' She paused, thinking. 'Although, I suppose, the estate management team will know soon enough and, if Rayan is actually speaking to you, Eva, you need to tell him, obviously. And, if it's OK by you two, I'd like to share it with Sam.'

'Woohoo, you've fallen big time, haven't you?' Hannah squeezed Rosa's arm, delighted that her sister appeared happier than she had for years.

'Might have,' Rosa grinned. 'Might just have.'

34

'He's insisting we do the paternity tests all together and witnessed by Rodney Bowman at the solicitor's office.' A week after Bill Astley's funeral, Rosa had dropped in to her parents' place to keep them up to date with any developments regarding Heatherly Hall. 'I really miss Bill, Mum. He was always sort of there in the background, never interfering – apart from when I was ill and he insisted I get checked out – but you know, always there. But, we could often go for months without actually seeing him, particularly when we were younger. I suppose we've been in touch with him more as he's got older, but I'm still surprised I'm missing him as much as I do.'

'He was your father, Rosa. What do you expect?' Alice, who, in the last couple of weeks since the funeral, appeared to have taken up residence with Susan and Richard, pulled painfully at her arthritic fingers in an attempt to ease, if not alleviate, their stiffness.

'He was *not* their father, Alice. Richard was – *is* – the girls' father. Don't you go thinking anything different.' Susan was irritable; had probably had enough of Alice, Rosa thought.

Rosa glanced round the sitting room. Every surface appeared cluttered with Alice's magazines, newspapers and medication, as well as myriad ashtrays overflowing with butt ends of her cigarillos. Susan, who was naturally – even obsessively – neat and tidy, was in the process of tidying up after her sister once more. 'What are your plans, Alice?'

'Well, I shall go back to New York eventually.'

'Not Paris?'

'Not in December. The low cloud and drizzle there is as bad as here. At least in New York, it might be bloody freezing right now, but there's generally some sunshine. This awful low cloud here affects my mood and my arthritis.'

'So, you'll be off soon then?'

'Trying to get rid of me?'

'Not at all. I think Mum's hoping you'll stay for Christmas.'

Susan's head came up and she frowned meaningfully at Rosa. 'Don't give her ideas,' she hissed as Alice moved slowly off to the kitchen to pour her first gin of the day.

'I actually can't bear the thought of a ten-hour flight at the moment and, anyway, I can't do a great deal of painting with my fingers in this condition,' Alice shouted crossly from where she appeared to be struggling to open a bottle of tonic. 'So,' she went on as she reappeared, glass in hand, 'you're going ahead with these paternity tests then?'

'Absolutely. No reason not to.'

'Well, I wouldn't give that little weasel *any* help in his claim to Heatherly Hall. Bill used to tell me how he tried to see the pair of them, have a relationship with them, but neither he nor that sister of his – Henrietta is it? – were the least bit interested. Bill wanted them back from California during their school holidays, but they preferred to be off to the Caribbean or up to the Hamptons or Martha's Vineyard where Roger McConville has a place.' She pulled on her cigarillo, closing one eye against the smoke. 'Don't blame them really.'

'So, yes,' Rosa nodded, 'the three of us are meeting up with Jonny at the solicitor's place in the town centre in the morning. You know, I can't remember a great deal about doing the tests the last time. Did we do them here in the kitchen, Mum?'

'Hmm,' Susan nodded. 'Bill's solicitors at the time sent over three tests for me to administer to you girls. I did the cheek swab tests, named them and took them into the solicitor's office so that he could send them off as a job lot with Bill's sample. As far as I remember, it took a good couple of weeks to say, yes, Bill was your natural father, and then money was put into my bank account for your education.' Susan frowned. 'It was all very embarrassing.'

'Why?'

'Having to beg for money.'

'You should have asked me for help,' Alice sniffed. 'I'd have seen you right.'

'I didn't want *any* handouts,' Susan snapped, 'but when all three of them needed new shoes and stuff for sixth-form college, and Virginia was on a grant at university, well I just had to swallow my pride and ask.'

'Hey, I've just had a thought.' Alice blew a series of professional smoke rings towards the ceiling and Susan wafted at them crossly. 'What if Jonny's test comes back and he's got nothing to do with you three? You know, because his mother – Diana, is it? – had been having it off with one of the estate gardeners or someone?' Alice cackled throatily, which led to a long bout of coughing.

'For heaven's sake, Alice, stop tarring everyone with the same brush as yourself,' Susan snapped, flapping at the furniture with a duster.

'If that were to happen –' Rosa smiled '– then we'd insist on doing more tests using Bill's hair from his brush and DNA from his dentures. Or something like that.'

'Gross.' Alice pulled a face of distaste before knocking back the contents of her glass.

At the end of the second week in December, Rosa was across in the church hall helping Hilary Makepeace to recover the church's Nativity statues from the large dusty cupboards at the back of the hall itself.

'Is this it?' Rosa frowned as Hilary, her bleached blonde hair collecting a bounty of cobwebs, shuffled backwards from the depths of the cupboard with a large cardboard box.

'This is it,' Hilary confirmed as they both pondered the contents.

'Bit battered, aren't they? Poor old Mary's only got one eye and this shepherd looks somewhat randy and the other one –' Rosa held up another '– looks half cut. And Joseph just looks thoroughly fed up. Do you know, I think this is the same Nativity scene we had when I was a kid and Grandpa Cecil was here.' Rosa frowned. 'I'm not putting this up. We deserve better.'

'Not sure how much is in the coffers.' Hilary pulled a face. 'I suppose you can have some of the money we made at the hoedown, although I think Pandora Boothroyd's got her eyes on that for the flower rota.' Hilary turned and frowned. 'You didn't turn up for it   you know, the hoedown?'

'Sorry, sorry, something came up.'

'A certain new village dentist?' Hilary nudged Rosa in the ribs. 'Did he come up – you know, *come up* to scratch?'

'Mind your own business, Hilary. And you're talking to your parish vicar, not your mates in the sixth-form common room.' Rosa wanted to laugh, but didn't want Hilary spreading rumours about what the village vicar had got up to on a weekend away in a cosy barn in the Peak District of Derbyshire.

'Good for you, Vicar. You might have been called to do God's work, but you have a woman's needs like any other.'

And that's when Rosa did laugh, giggling until she couldn't stop. 'Right,' she said eventually, replacing the tatty Nativity statues back in their box. 'I'm going back home now to order some new ones – my Christmas present to my church.'

'Ah, spending some of your inheritance, are you?' Hilary nudged Rosa once more. *Hell*, Rosa thought, if she carried on like this, she was going to be covered in bruises.

'Inheritance? What inheritance is that then, Hilary?'

'Oh, come on, Vicar, the whole village is talking – that you, Eva and Hannah have been left all of Heatherly Hall and everything in it. And that you're going to be in charge up there. Turning the place into a monastic retreat, I heard? And that you've got

Ed Sheeran – or was it Elton John? – lined up for a concert there. Or, according to the verger, and he seems to know, there's going to be a whole load of tigers like at Longleat. You'll have to mend some of them fences up there before you do that, you know.' Hilary frowned. 'Or the villagers won't be too happy when they've had one too many at the Jolly Sailor, and there's a big stripy pussy cat waiting for them in the car park.'

'Hilary, I promise you – and you can pass this on – there's going to be no marauding wild animals up at Heatherly Hall. Having said that...' Rosa paused '...a couple of elephants wouldn't go amiss. You know, to keep the grass down?'

'Elephants?' Hilary nodded speculatively. 'Right, I'll pass that on.'

Grinning to herself, Rosa made her way back across to the vicarage. The heady smell of the lamb tagine she'd put in earlier hit her as she walked into the kitchen. Sam was popping round from the surgery for an early supper, and Rhys was joining them, presumably starving as usual, from the school bus. Rhys's visits had become a twice-weekly occurrence and, although she'd told him and Roberto (Joe hadn't come near since she'd walked out of the restaurant on him) that she felt Rhys had now paid his dues, he continued to call in, usually ending up eating with her and Sam and, later, playing chess with Sam or her helping him with his English homework, which appeared to be the only subject with which he struggled. While the court case was still hanging over him, Rhys was keeping to his bail conditions and Rosa knew she'd have no problem being truthful in her verbal assessment of him, when she accompanied him to youth court at some point after Christmas.

There was a formal-looking letter waiting for her behind the door, the thick creamy vellum standing out amongst the less upmarket brown envelopes and the free papers sporting advertisements for local tradesmen.

Dear Ms Quinn, Rosa read,

I'd be grateful if you'd attend for appointment, at your convenience, on Tuesday December 14th at 10 a.m., with myself and your sisters regarding the paternity tests you undertook under my supervision last week. This request has been sent to Ms Quinn and Mrs Malik as well as yourself.
Rodney Bowman
Bowman, Bowman and Foley (Solicitors)

'Bit formal, that, isn't it?' Sam said, reading the letter once he'd arrived to eat and Rosa had poured a glass of the wine he'd brought. 'I'd have thought this solicitor could have just rung you.'

'Solicitors are always formal, aren't they? That's their business.'

'Are you nervous?'

'Nervous? Of what?'

'That you might not be Bill's daughters after all.'

'But we *are*. We did tests years ago and, actually, you only have to look at my eyes to see Bill's eyes.' Rosa smiled across at Sam.

'All a bit of a waste of time then?'

'Suppose. Although it makes me feel better, you know, puts *us* in a better position when Jonny Astley is trying to argue that we shouldn't be inheriting anything from his father.'

'And have you come round to all that? Do you want to take on the running of the place between the three of you?'

'If I can help by being on the management committee, then yes. If I find it's going to interfere with my work here in the church, then no.'

'As long as you're not worked too hard and won't have any time to see me.' Sam pulled Rosa to him, his chin resting on her head. 'Because, as you may have gathered, I want to see you all the time. Every minute. Every second.'

Rosa laughed. 'Can I just have time to get this tagine out of the oven?'

'Oh God, yes, I'm starving.' He kissed Rosa and released her from his arms. 'And,' he added, grinning as they heard the front door bang and a bag of sports gear and one of school books dumped audibly in the hallway, 'I would imagine that's Rhys and he'll be even more starving than me. I'm becoming quite fond of the kid, you know.'

'I know you are. He'll be about the age Ollie would have been now, I suppose?' Rosa asked gently.

Sam nodded. 'Yes, he would. But, don't go thinking I'm looking for a substitute child for the one I've lost, Rosa. I genuinely like Rhys and, while he may be a good little chess player, I can tell you now, he'd never been any good in a pair of tights.'

'Shall we go straight in?' Hannah and Eva were waiting impatiently as Rosa joined them on the steps of the solicitor's office.

Rosa nodded. 'Sorry I'm late. I was chatting to Denis the verger about the Nativity stuff I've ordered.'

'Right.' Eva was impatient. 'Come on, I've got to get back – got three fillings and two extractions before lunch. Jonny and Billy-Jo are already in there.'

The three of them made their way up a dusty flight of stairs to an equally dusty-looking set of offices and Rosa wouldn't have been surprised to see Ebenezer Scrooge in attendance on the front desk. Once inside, however, she was pleasantly surprised to see a hub of quiet, exceptionally modern, glass and chrome efficiency and they were immediately shown into Rodney Bowman's office.

'Ah, do come in,' he smiled, standing and offering a limp handshake. 'I believe all parties are acquainted?'

That made Rosa want to laugh and, glancing across at Eva, she could see her sister was equally amused.

'Now,' the solicitor said, 'I think we're all agreed as to why we are here...?' He trailed off, seemingly hesitant. 'I'm just wondering, at this juncture, as this whole thing is extremely personal to all the individual parties involved, whether I should just hand over to each of you the envelope with your relevant paternity test result in it?'

'A bit like when you're handed your A-level results?' Hannah smiled.

'Well, no, not really, no... I'm not sure the two are really the same? Ah, I see you're jesting, Ms Quinn?' Rodney Bowman smiled nervously. 'Would you prefer I do that? Hand each of you the envelope?'

'Just tell us, Mr Bowman,' Eva smiled, but her words held impatience.

'Just get on with it, Mr Bowman, if you would.' Jonny Astley was obviously keyed up.

'Very well.' He coughed, removed his glasses, shuffled papers and replaced the spectacles once more. 'So, there is no doubt whatsoever that you, Mr John Astley, are the son of William Astley, deceased. At your request, sir, as well as comparing your own DNA with the ladies' here, a good sample of DNA was able to be extracted from both the deceased's hairbrush and from bone fragments after cremation.'

'Really?' All three girls stared, quite shocked at the marvels of science.

'Hmm. I was surprised myself by that but yes, there is absolutely no doubt *whatsoever* that not only is Mr Astley here the deceased's son, but also shares a very large percentage of DNA with *you*, ladies...' Mr Bowman looked up from his desk, staring long and hard at the triplets.

'Our half-brother then?' Eva smiled, flashing a triumphant glance in the direction of Jonny Astley, who scowled back furiously. 'Welcome to the family, Jonny.'

'Well...' Bowman peered over his spectacles, hesitating '...of *two* of you. Mr Astley, here, is most definitely the half-brother of *two* of you.'

'Sorry?' Rosa, Eva and Hannah stared across the desk at the solicitor who was now dabbing at his forehead with a large clean white handkerchief.

'While, most certainly, *two* of you ladies are the daughter of William Astley, and hence the half-brother of Mr John Astley, *one* of you, it seems...' he coughed nervously '...it appears... is not.'

35

'**R**ight, here we are, this is what we need – this should tell us something.' Eva sat with the laptop open on her kitchen table as Rosa and Hannah peered over her shoulder. 'OK, blah, blah, blah, yes... triplets... different fathers... this is it:

'*Can triplets born to one mother have different fathers?*'

'What does it say, Eva?' Hannah pushed Rosa slightly to one side in order to get a better view but Rosa, herself impatient to read, pushed her back.

'I don't know why you two are so desperate to read this,' Eva snapped crossly. 'You know who *your* effing father is. Just wait until I see that slut, Alice.'

'Eva, stop it. Calling Alice horrid names like that doesn't help one bit.'

'Maybe not, but it makes *me* feel better,' Eva almost snarled. 'And alcohol would go down well at this juncture too. Hannah, get some wine out, will you?' She waved an angry arm towards the fridge behind her.

'A glass of wine at eleven in the morning?' Jodie, coming in from the utility room with a pile of washing to be ironed, pulled a face. 'Mind you,' she added hopefully, 'I won't say no if one's on offer. Your daughter, much as I love her, has been jolly hard work this morning.'

'Jodie, will you just get on with looking after Nora?' Eva said through gritted teeth. 'Something awful has happened.'

'Oh?' Jodie's eyes gleamed. 'Someone else died now? You've

finally given Mrs Faraday-Brown too much laughing gas and she's carked it? Well, don't you come asking me for help disposing of the body if I'm not being offered a glass…'

'Jodie!' Eva exploded. 'Just go and see what Nora's up to. Please?'

'Right,' Hannah read out, over Eva's shoulder: *'Although rare, the phenomenon of twins or triplets having different fathers can occur when a woman, having ovulated at least twice in the same cycle, sleeps with more than one man within twenty-four hours and conceives children by them. Superfecundation is the fertilisation of two or more ova from the same cycle by sperm from separate acts of sexual intercourse, which can lead to twin or triplet babies from two separate biological fathers…'*

'Right, that's it then,' Eva said, slamming down the lid of the laptop and pulling on the coat she'd discarded ten minutes earlier.

'Where are you going now?' Rosa and Hannah stared.

'Where the hell do you think? Off to see that piece of work, Alice, and find out who my father is, if it's not Bill.'

'Hang on, hang on,' Hannah said, the bottle of Pinot Grigio in one hand. 'I thought you wanted a drink?'

'A *drink*? At this time of day?' Eva's eyes flashed. 'What's the matter with you two? I need to keep a clear head so I don't miss a trick when I confront Mommy Dearest.'

'Right, hang on,' Rosa said, pulling on her jacket and throwing Hannah's coat in her direction. 'We're coming with you.'

'Mum? Mum? Where is she?' Eva raced into the house, coat buttoned up haphazardly, her mud-encrusted down-at-heel gardening boots, for want of any others to hand, on her feet. Her eyes were blazing and Rosa recalled only ever seeing Eva in this state once before: when she heard that Joe Rosavina had upped and left with a pregnant Carys.

'Where's who?' Susan looked up in surprise as Eva, followed closely behind by Hannah and Rosa, stormed into the kitchen. 'What on earth is the matter?'

'Bill Astley wasn't my dad, Mum.' Eva gulped a little over the words and dashed away an angry tear that was threatening.

'What do you mean, he wasn't your dad? Bill *wasn't*. Richard's your dad.'

'Mum, you *know* what I mean. We've just come back from having the results of new paternity tests at the solicitor's. Bill Astley was Rosa and Hannah's biological father. But not mine.'

'Of course he was. You can't be triplets and have different fathers. It's not possible.' Susan looked at each of the triplets in turn. 'Is it?'

'Apparently it is,' Eva snapped. 'So where is she? Where *is* the bed-hopper from Brooklyn Bridge when we need her?'

'She's somewhere about. Oh, here. Here she is.' All four turned as Alice, in a flowing luminous green kaftan, made her way slowly down the stairs and towards them in the kitchen.

'Does no one work round here?' Alice sniffed. 'Have you no jobs to go to?' She nodded towards Rosa. 'Mind you, I suppose once Sundays are over, you live the life of Riley the other six days? I don't seem to remember the Reverend Cecil working his bollocks off during the week – too busy complaining about his lot in life, I suppose.' Alice glanced at the girls. 'Or have you come for a little lunchtime snifter? I'll join you if you are?'

'Alice, can we have a word?' Rosa smiled at the older woman whose eyes were narrowing suspiciously at the apparent confrontation.

'A word?'

'So, Alice,' Rosa said slowly, as if talking to a recalcitrant child, 'you know the three of us had an appointment this morning to prove a paternal link between ourselves and Bill Astley? We were just…'

'Cut the crap, Rosa,' Eva demanded, squaring up to Alice. 'Bill Astley was Rosa and Hannah's father. He *wasn't* mine. OK, Alice, who *was*?'

'Who was what?' Alice frowned, not understanding.

'Alice, what Eva's trying to tell you –' Hannah put a calming hand on Eva's arm '– is that it's just been proved—'

'Proven,' Alice interjected.

'Sorry?' Hannah tutted.

'I believe the term is *proven.*'

'You've been living in the States too long,' Eva snapped. 'Either is correct.'

'OK,' Hannah continued, 'this morning we've had *proof* that Bill Astley was not Eva's biological father.'

'Of course he was.' Alice pulled a face. 'You can't have *two* of you girls with one father, and *one* of you with *another.*'

'Apparently you can,' Rosa said gently. 'Look, can you think back, Alice? I mean, I don't want to rake over old…'

'Well, *I* certainly do.' Eva folded her arms and glared at her birth mother. 'Alice, at the time you were involved with Bill, were you sleeping with someone else as well?'

'Sleeping with them? Oh Eva, you're the last person I'd accuse of being so provincial.'

'Alright, shagging.'

'Eva!' Susan, Hannah and Rosa simultaneously tutted in Eva's direction.

Alice, despite her apparent bravado, had gone slightly pale and moved towards the kitchen table where she sat down painfully, rubbing at her right hip as she did so.

'Alice,' Susan said, frowning as she tried to remember an event almost forty years in the past. 'Wasn't there a reason you'd come back to Westenbury that weekend?'

'Yes, it was the Rev Cecil's' birthday as I recall.'

'Can't you call him *Dad*?' Susan snapped. 'Anyway, I'm sure you didn't come home for that. You *said* you did, but it was just a coincidence. You'd no idea it was his birthday.'

'Suze, you're going back nearly forty years. You girls *are* heading for the big four-oh anytime soon, aren't you?' Alice glanced up from the table. 'How do you expect me to remember who I was *sleeping with* forty years ago?'

'Alice.' Eva took a deep breath in an effort to speak the words calmly. 'Please try and remember if you can. Were you involved with someone, in a relationship with someone, around that time?' When Alice didn't say anything, Eva sat at the table, her eyes concentrated on her birth mother, as she felt any composure fly out of the window once more. 'Actually, never mind *around that time*, Alice. According to what we googled on superfecundity – was that the word? – having sex with someone else, other than Bill, within a *twenty-four-hour window*?'

'Oh, Alice. Really?' Susan was shocked.

'So, girls,' Alice finally drawled, 'if I remember correctly, I was having a bit of a thing with an artist in Paris. I seem to remember his wife...'

'His wife? Oh Alice. Really?' Susan raised her eyes to the ceiling.

'...I seem to remember his wife, barging into my apartment with a knife.'

'A knife?' Susan closed her eyes. 'Can this get any worse?'

'Well, yes, it apparently can,' Eva snapped. 'I appear to be the offspring of a mad, knife-wielding woman's adulterous husband. Great stuff. Absolutely fucking great.'

'Language, Eva,' Susan tutted.

'Well, at least you're half-French,' Hannah soothed. 'How exciting is that?'

Eva gave Hannah a withering look. 'Oh, I suppose my right to apply for, and now own, a French passport is meant to compensate for not knowing where I've come from? Who I am?'

'Well, I'd say it goes *some* way, you know, now that we're out of Europe? You'll have the right—' Hannah broke off mid-sentence as she saw Eva's face. 'Well, maybe not.'

'Eva, darling.' Alice took hold of Eva's hand. 'You might not be so disappointed at not being the Marquess of Heatherly's daughter when I tell you who that artist – the man I was having an affair with – actually is.'

36

'Hello, Mum? What's the matter?' Rosa opened the vicarage front door to Susan, and Sam, catching sight of Susan's distressed face as she stepped into the hall, reached for his jacket where he'd left it at the bottom of the stairs, and made to leave.

'Hello, Mrs Quinn,' Sam smiled. 'I was just leaving. I'll get off, Rosa.' He picked up his car keys and headed for the still-open door.

'You don't have to go, Sam.' Rosa pulled a face; she'd been so looking forward to his staying over with her, to having his arms and legs wrapped round her in her chilly bed instead of hers around the hot water bottle which, until meeting Sam, had been her usual companion.

'I think it's best if I go.' Sam indicated Susan, who had walked past the pair of them and was headed into the newly painted and decorated sitting room where the last vestige of a log fire was continuing to throw out a welcome warmth. 'Is it because *I'm* here she's come round at eleven o'clock at night?' Sam whispered. 'Wouldn't she approve?'

'I don't know,' Rosa frowned, looking back over her shoulder. 'I've never seen her like this before. I can't imagine she's driven all the way over here just to catch me in the sack with you. It's obviously about what we found out this afternoon.'

'I'll go.' Sam kissed the corner of Rosa's mouth, winding her long dark curly hair between his fingers.

'You sure?' Rosa felt her nether regions jump to attention and she kissed him back.

'Absolutely. Go on, your mum's waiting.'

Rosa closed the door reluctantly on Sam and made her way back to the sitting room where Susan was sat, staring at the wall, her coat buttoned up, scarf still in place, despite the warmth of the room.

'Mum? What on earth's the matter?' Rosa kneeled down on the floor beside Susan. 'Is it what we found out this afternoon from Alice? Has that upset you?'

Susan shook her head. 'I've come to tell you something.'

'Oh?'

'I've come to confess something.'

'Confess? What have you done?' Rosa smiled. 'Oh hell, Mum, you haven't murdered Alice and hidden her under the floorboards, have you?'

'I did something years ago.'

'Did you?'

'And, while I'm very ashamed of what I did, I don't regret doing it *for one single moment*.' Susan stared defiantly down at Rosa.

'Right, OK. Look, do you want some tea? Cocoa? Glass of wine?'

Susan shook her head.

'Come on then, what's so bad you feel you have to come and tell me about it at nearly midnight? Do Dad and Alice know you're here?'

Susan shook her head. 'Alice drank rather a lot of gin and took herself off to bed, and Dad went up about nine. Anyway, after what happened at the solicitor's this afternoon, I knew the writing was on the wall.'

'Blimey, Mum, that's a bit dramatic.'

'So...' Susan paused and then sighed heavily. 'So,' she continued, 'do you remember when you three all did those original paternity tests when you were sixteen, when the solicitors said they'd only put a little money into trust for you if there was definite proof you were Bill Astley's daughters?'

'Yes, of course.'

'So, three tests were sent over. I helped all three of you take a swab from your cheeks.'

'Yes, I remember.'

'Well, one of them wasn't an actual part of a test.'

'What do you mean?' Rosa frowned.

'I didn't want to *use* one of them. I assumed, with you being triplets, that if two of you – or, come to that, just *one* of you – was proven to be Bill's daughter, then obviously all of you would be.'

'Mum, I don't know what on earth you're talking about. Start again, would you?'

'So,' Susan sighed again. 'As far as *I* could see, we only had to do a test on *one* of you girls. If that proved a match with Bill, then obviously you were *all* his. But they insisted on all three of you being tested.'

'Right.' Rosa still didn't have a clue where Susan was going with all this. 'You wanted to save money, was that it? Just do one test? But the tests had all been paid for by Bill's solicitors, hadn't they? *You* hadn't had to shell out any money?'

'Yes, they sent three over. So, I did two of the tests on two of you.'

'You *didn't*, Mum. You did all three – I distinctly remember us all standing there in a row.'

'I did two *proper* tests.' Susan was adamant. 'The third was a cotton bud that I pretended was a test. I threw it in the bin once you'd gone to college.'

'But why? Were you hoping to send the third test back and get a refund? Were we so broke?'

'No, of course not. I would *never* have done such a thing.'

'Why then?'

'*I* needed the third.'

'Did you? Why?' When Susan seemed unable to continue, Rosa took her hand. 'Mum?'

'I wanted to know who Virginia's father was.'

'Virginia?' Rosa stared. Was Susan losing it? 'Why on earth did you hold back one of the tests in order to prove that Dad – Richard – was Virginia's father? You *knew* he was her dad.'

'No, I didn't. And he isn't. Bill Astley is. There, I've confessed it now. I've got it off my chest. I can go home.' Susan made to stand.

'Whoa, whoa, hang on, Mum.' Rosa sat back on the floor. 'Are you saying Virginia isn't our birth cousin, but our actual half-sister? Well, mine and Hannah's, anyway?'

'Yes, that's right. You heard right.'

'You had an affair with Bill as well? As well as Alice?'

'Neither of us had *an affair* with Bill Astley.' Susan spat out the words. 'We both had… you know… sex with him.'

'Right.'

'And you were married to Dad?'

'Of course, I was married to Dad.' Susan was cross. 'What are you suggesting?'

'No, of course you and he were married.' Rosa patted Susan's hand. 'What I'm asking is, when you had sex with Bill, were you married to Dad?'

'Yes. I'm not proud of it.' Susan's head came up. 'But I'm very glad I did.'

'Because you got pregnant with Virginia?'

'Because I got pregnant, yes.'

'Come on, Mum, what happened?' Rosa stroked her mum's arm.

'I was teaching at Little Acorns – it was Westenbury C of E in those days of course. Dad and I had been married over seven years, and I was desperate to be pregnant. To have a baby of my own, but nothing happened. I was at school and there was to be a sort of baby shower – of course we didn't call it a daft name like that, then – it was simply two of the teachers who'd had babies the previous month and had been invited back in, once school was over for the afternoon. You know, come in to show off their babies and be given presents. So, I was there, in the staffroom, cooing and smiling over the most beautiful babies you've ever seen and drinking tea and having a party, and I just wanted a baby of my own. Wanted to cry at the unfairness of not being able to get pregnant. And I knew I had to get out of there before I actually started crying. I slipped out, back up to my classroom to find Bill waiting there.'

'Bill? Waiting there? In your classroom? What on earth for? Had you ever met him before?'

'No, not until that afternoon. I'd totally forgotten I'd written to him asking him if he'd be willing to come in to give a talk about knights and castles, as well as a potted history of Heatherly Hall. He was in the area, he said, and the secretary on reception had shown him up to my classroom and then she'd come to find me, but I was already on my way up the other corridor.'

'And?'

'And I went straight into my stockroom on the pretext of trying to find something – I can't remember what – in order to try and stop crying. But I couldn't stop. I just couldn't stop. And after ten minutes, Bill popped his head round the stockroom door and asked me if I was alright. And he came in and put his arms round me and asked me what on earth was the matter. And basically…'

'Basically what? What, Mum?'

'Well, you know…'

'You had sex in your stockroom with the Marquess of Heatherly? While a baby shower was going on at the other end of the school?'

'In a nutshell – yes. I'm not proud of betraying your father.'

'But why? I can't believe *you*, Mum, had sex in your stockroom with a man you didn't know. In broad daylight?'

'It was dark. It was January.' Susan's eyes, raised to Rosa's own, were challenging and Rosa realised she was seeing a totally different side to her mother. 'I just got carried away. I tell you now, Rosa, that was the most... the most *erotic* moment of my entire life.'

'Mum!' Rosa almost put her hands to her ears. 'You're my mum – I don't want to hear about, you know...'

'I thought you'd understand and be able to forgive when people make mistakes. You know, being a vicar? Have I disgusted you?'

'Disgusted me? No, no, of course not. I'm just utterly taken back, that's all. So, you told Bill why you were crying? Why you couldn't stop?'

Susan shook her head. 'No. To be honest, I couldn't get any words out. He'd no idea why I was crying. He was so lovely; he just put his arms round me and let me cry.'

'Mum, you don't get pregnant by a man just putting his arms round you!' Rosa found she was unable to take any of this in.

'Rosa, I've spent the last forty years trying to work out why I did it. All I can think is that maybe I saw it as the only chance to have a baby. You know, if I had sex with another man? I think I knew, deep down, after seven years of trying, your dad and I weren't going to have a baby together.'

'But, surely Bill, for all his womanising, wouldn't do such a thing? In a school? With someone he didn't know?'

'It happened. It just happened... and I, you know, it was me who... you know... instigated it.' There was, Rosa could hear, a tiny hint of pride in Susan's words.

'And did you tell Bill? Tell him he was Virginia's father?'

'Tell him? Why on earth would I do that? And I didn't know that he *was*. It just seemed a bit of a coincidence that I have... you know... I *do it* with another man, and hey presto I'm pregnant. As far as I was concerned, I was Richard's wife and I was pregnant. The baby I was carrying *could* have been Richard's for all I knew – I told myself it *was* Richard's. To be honest, Rosa, I was so over the moon to be pregnant, I didn't really care how it had happened. I just thanked God that he'd shown me the way.'

'God had? I thought it was Bill Astley who'd shown you the way? The dirty dog.' Rosa stood up and then sat down on the sofa, unable to take it all in. 'So, what happened when you next saw Bill? You know, at school, to give this talk?'

'I didn't. See him again, that is; I was far too embarrassed and guilt-ridden to ever see him again. On the day he was coming in, I rang in to say I had a migraine.'

'A migraine? You've never had a migraine in your life. Have you?' Rosa peered across at Susan.

'Oh, I don't know what I said was wrong with me.' Susan waved an impatient hand in Rosa's direction. 'It wasn't important. The head took the lesson as far as I remember. And then, soon after that, I knew I was pregnant and I just gave thanks for what I'd done. That Bill had been sent to me for a reason. It was all part of God's plan.'

'*God's* plan?' Rosa shook her head, unable to say any more.

Ignoring this, Susan went on, 'And I didn't see Bill Astley again until Virginia was four years old and we left her at home while we had a few days in Paris, surprising Alice at her exhibition. Bill was there, Alice was pregnant with you three and the rest is history.'

'What did Bill say when he saw you?'

'Didn't recognise me. The stockroom, if you remember, was dark and my hair, five years later, had, if I recall correctly, gone from very long and red back to my natural blonde and cut in the short bob I've had ever since. And I think it was probably a time when he was messing around with lots of women, drinking a lot too, after his second wife had left him – I was just one more.'

'Mum, you've shocked me beyond...' Rosa found she couldn't continue.

'Yes,' Susan sniffed, 'I was always the good elder daughter, wasn't I? Always in Alice's shadow. Part of me, over the years, has been desperate to tell Alice. Tell her, yes, *I* had a thing with Bill Astley too. You're not the *only* one, Alice.'

'Right.' Rosa stared at this new, almost challenging, Susan. 'But what about when you took the three of us up to see Bill? When we were little?'

'How often did *I* take you up? Hardly ever. It was always your father who drove or walked you up there. Or, quite often, if you remember, Granny Glenys. It was always Dad who felt you should have some sort of relationship with Bill. It was only when you started working up there, in your teens, that you began to really build a relationship with him. Nothing to do with me by then.'

'So presumably Virginia knows nothing of this?'

'No, of course not. I'm the only one who knows. And now *you*.'

'So, hang on, Mum, the original three tests all came back saying Hannah, Eva and myself were definitely Bill's daughters?'

'Hmm.'

'So, presumably it was Eva given the dud test – the cotton bud? Amazingly good luck on your part, Mum, you don't think? And I can't believe Eva didn't notice the difference? And then how on earth did you get a sample of DNA from Virginia without her being suspicious? Wasn't she away at university at that point?'

'It was the morning of your first day at sixth-form college; you were all excited, more concerned about what you were wearing, and desperate to get off. Why would you notice one swab was slightly different? And Virginia was at home too. She had another couple of weeks before she went back to her teacher training – she'd been working at Piccione's Pickles factory all summer and was shattered. It was easy to tiptoe into her room the next night while she was fast asleep, and take a quick swab from her open mouth.'

'*What?*' If Rosa had been utterly shocked by what her mother had been up to in her stockroom over forty years ago, this new revelation was even more disquieting. 'Isn't there a law against taking things from people's bodies without their permission?'

'Oh, don't be so ridiculous, Rosa. I always used to cut your hair and your fingernails when you girls refused to let me.'

'Yes, I remember, Mum. You once cut my fringe so short and so badly they laughed at me at school.' Rosa had never forgotten it. In fact, she thought, it had probably scarred her for life. 'And you're telling me, Virginia, at twenty-one, didn't wake up while you were firtling around in her mouth?'

'I wasn't *firtling*,' Susan said crossly. 'I was carrying out an essential scientific experiment. I needed to know for sure. And yes, she did wake up; sat up in a total fright.'

'And?'

'And I told her she'd been having a nightmare, shouting out about the pickles on the conveyer belt, and that I was stroking her cheek in order to calm her and get her back to sleep.'

'I don't believe any of this, Mum – you're making it up. What if Virginia *hadn't* been Bill's?'

'Oh, I was 99.9 per cent certain she was. I was never able to get pregnant with your father before or after I was pregnant with Virginia. You only have to look at Virginia to see she has Bill's nose, Rosa. I just wanted to prove it for myself.'

'But weren't you concerned that if Virginia *hadn't* been Bill's daughter, that test – the one you'd labelled with the name of one of us triplets when it was actually the sample you'd filched from Virginia – would have come back negative saying that one of *us* wasn't Bill's daughter? As it obviously has now?'

'Will you stop using language like *firtling* and *filching*, Rosa? You're making me out to be some sort of common criminal. And, a jolly good job I did what I did, don't you think? Knowing what's been revealed today?' Susan was still defiant. 'Because, otherwise, we'd have known there and then Eva wasn't Bill's. And the cat would have been right amongst the pigeons: Eva, at sixteen, would have gone totally off the rails and probably ended up on the streets of Paris and New York looking for her biological father instead of doing A-levels and going off to university to become a dentist. A jolly good job all round I did what I did.'

'And, just to get this straight, Mum, the dud swab *was* obviously administered to Eva.'

'Yes, *obviously*, Rosa,' Susan interrupted crossly. 'The same one of you three girls who it's now been proved has absolutely nothing, whatsoever, to do with Bill Astley.'

'And, big question, here, Mum.' Rosa took Susan's hand once more. 'Will you tell Virginia?'

'Well, I didn't tell her twenty years ago, so I certainly don't intend telling her now.'

'Really?'

'Really. As far as I'm concerned, I borrowed something from Bill.'

'You *borrowed* something? What are you trying to say, Mum?' Rosa shook her head at Susan's set face.

'You know exactly what I mean, so don't go all technical on me, Rosa. Richard was, and is, Virginia's father, just as he was, and is, you three girls' father. It would kill Richard to know the truth about Virginia.'

'But what about Virginia? You don't think she has a right to know? I mean, if Bill had known this, it's quite possible he'd have left Eva's third of his shares in Heatherly Hall, as well as his personal wealth, to Virginia rather than Eva. Oh blimey, what a mess, Mum.'

'It is *not* a mess. I've told you this, but you forget all about it now, Rosa. I will *never* bring it up again. You are a woman of God; I've confessed my sins to God through you and you must now keep it to yourself.'

'Mum, I'm not a Catholic priest.'

'No, but you are my daughter and a vicar and the one I trust implicitly to keep my secret and never divulge it to *anyone* or *ever* speak of it again.'

'Right. OK.'

'So, I'm going home now for a cup of tea. I've done what I set out to do and feel much better for it. And there's an end to it.'

Susan stood, nodded in Rosa's direction, and swiftly and pointedly headed for the vicarage front door.

37

'D on't drink too much of that stuff, Rosa,' Hannah warned. 'You've got Midnight Mass to get through.'

'*Get through?*' Rosa drained her glass of mulled wine. 'You make it sound like some sort of awful task I have to perform before Santa comes down the chimney. I absolutely adore Midnight Mass; it's just such a wonderful atmosphere in any church on this special evening, a real honour and privilege to be in charge of the whole celebration. You have all the regulars in their Christmas dangly earrings and Rudolph antlers as well as the local farmers – who won't have been in church since harvest time – totally singing out of tune. And then there'll be those who've been in the Jolly Sailor all evening and are trying their best to pretend they're not half cut, and the kids who are with their parents and feeling really grown up that they're allowed out at midnight. I've put together a load of Christingle Oranges, as well as enough mince pies and mulled wine to sink a ship.'

'Or Santa.'

'Or Santa,' Rosa grinned. 'There's no way I'm having my flock say I don't celebrate Christmas in style and telling me they'll be off up to St Luke's at Heath Green next year. Gosh, this table looks wonderful. What a great idea of Eva's to have a Christmas Eve supper before we go across for the service.'

They surveyed their efforts in the dining room which, despite being mothballed for years, the two of them had cleaned and polished and strewn with the holly Rosa and Sam had collected up at Norman's Meadow earlier that day. Christmas-scented candles were already alight and combining their heady scent with that of the seasoned logs Sam had discovered in one of the outhouses at the bottom of the vicarage garden.

'Do you think she's OK?' Hannah tweaked a scarlet napkin into submission.

'Is who OK? Eva?'

Hannah nodded.

'With Rayan? I honestly don't know. She seems confused with everything that's going on in her life at the moment, although, I think, a lot less angry with Alice now that Alice has finally told her who her father must be.'

'Oh, I don't know, Rosa. She loved Bill, as we all did, and to find out that he wasn't her birth father after all must be very strange. It was a total shock for her. You don't get over something like that in a couple of weeks.'

'I know, I know, but at least she has the compensation of now knowing that her birth father is the most lauded French artist alive today. I mean, you couldn't make it up, could you? Alice Parkes for your mother and Yves Dufort your father?'

'Dufort is the most recognisable French artist on the international stage. I looked him up as soon as I got home the other day.'

Rosa laughed. 'We all did. Course we did.'

'Apparently he is one of the originators of the concept of the on-the-spot exposition,' Hannah added, almost proudly.

'Right. So, what's that then?' Rosa pulled a face.

'No idea. It's a long time since I did GCSE Art. You do know Eva is planning a trip to Paris? To find him?'

'No, I didn't, but I don't blame her. I'd want to do the same.'

'And Dad says he'll go with her.'

'Dad? Really? Actually, I reckon you and I should go to Paris as well,' Rosa said excitedly. 'Otherwise, Mum will send Dad down with a whole load of corned-beef sandwiches. 'If we go as well, we could eat our way through Paris once we've found Eva's birth father.' Rosa's eyes lit up at the thought.

'Do you not think we're going to have enough on our plates

without you piling them high with *escargots* and *cuisses de grenouilles* on a trip to Paris – you know, with sorting out what's happening up at Heatherly Hall?' Hannah frowned and they both mulled this over in silence, suddenly daunted at the task ahead of them.

'You know, the three of us couldn't have had a better dad than Richard,' Rosa ventured. 'We were thrust upon him by Alice and Mum, and yet he took us in, adopted us, brought us up and loved us. When we're over there tomorrow, for lunch, I think we should raise a glass to him. Let him know just how much we love and appreciate him for being our dad. Our real, proper dad.'

'Absolutely. Let's. In fact, I've a bottle of champagne – the real stuff, not your Co-op Cava – I was saving…'

'For what?' Rosa patted Hannah's arm but said nothing further.

'Oh, you know…' Hannah broke off and sniffed. She tried to smile. 'I'm fine, I'm fine… Honest.'

'You will be,' Rosa soothed. 'You and Ben? Is it honestly really over?'

Hannah sighed. 'I know what I'm doing… *was* doing with Ben was wrong. I reckon I'm just addicted.'

'Addicted?'

'To the adrenaline of it all. You know, waiting for Ben to arrive. Then being let down, then him arriving after all. It gets your heart pounding and you become addicted.' Hannah was embarrassed.

'Just think what we have to look forward to in the new year,' Rosa smiled. 'In charge of Heatherly Hall, for heaven's sake. Your dream of some sort of scheme for Looked After Kids might become a reality. And maybe Paris, as well!'

'I know, I know. Long way to go and I reckon there'll be opposition to it, but I'm already making plans.' Hannah's eyes lit up at the thought. 'And you?'

'Me?' Rosa smiled.

'Are you happy, Rosa? With this rather gorgeous new man of yours?'

Rosa laughed. 'I'm taking it slowly, Hannah... you know? He's a lovely man. Really lovely.'

'But not quite the same as when you met Joe?' Hannah raised an eyebrow, but patted Rosa's arm affectionately.

'I didn't say that,' Rosa tutted, looking cross. 'This is different: we're grown-ups, not kids.' She looked directly across at Hannah. 'So, this addiction thing. Do you think *I* was addicted to *Joe*?'

'No!' Hannah shook her head. 'Absolutely not. Totally different. Joe loved you from the minute he saw you in the alpaca pen up at the hall. And you loved him. Unfortunately, something – or someone – got in the way. You know, I think, if you hadn't met Sam, if Sam hadn't turned up at such an opportune moment, you might have ended up back with Joe.'

Before Rosa could reply, the front door banged and two sets of feet could be heard running down the corridor.

'Aunty Rosa, do you know who's coming tonight?' Laila flung open the dining-room door, but stopped short once she took in the table, the candles and Rosa and Hannah's reindeer antlers on top of their dark heads. 'Ooh, this is lovely.' For once, Laila appeared lost for words.

''ty Wosa, *I* know who's coming to our 'ouse tonight too.' Nora, obviously desperate to spread the news about the expected visitor, attempted to push Laila out of the way. She was followed by both Eva and Rayan, who were, Rosa noted with delight, holding hands.

'So, who *is* coming tonight then?' Rosa laughed, picking up Nora and kissing her. 'Let me guess? Could it be Donald Duck? Dora the Explorer? The Little Mermaid...?'

'No, silly.' Nora gave Rosa such a look of derision, the others fell about laughing. 'It's Father Chwismas.'

'Aunty Rosa, do you really think that Rudolph red nose you have on your face is *suitable* for a vicar to be wearing?' Laila asked with a raised eyebrow.

'I think, Laila –' Sam laughed, coming into the sitting room with the tray of hors d'oeuvres Rosa had made earlier '– I think that *whatever* your Aunty Rosa wears: a red nose, green ears, a fabulously sexy pink dress…'

'Thexy,' Nora lisped.

'…she *would* be dressed suitably. Because, Laila, she is the loveliest, most gorgeous, kindest village vicar in the whole of Westenbury.'

'In the whole wide world actually,' Eva laughed, thrusting a bouquet of Christmas lilies in Rosa's direction. 'Definitely the whole wide world.'

Acknowledgments

The idea for *The Village Vicar* came one morning when, chatting to D who comes every Wednesday for a couple of hours to help clean, she mentioned 'The Trips.' I assumed she meant holidays she had taken, and we chatted further. 'The Trips' were actually newborn triplet girls, now in their thirties, and who D had taken on from birth when her sister was unable to care for them. I was fascinated by this, and my story of the Quinn triplets – Eva, Hannah and Rosa – began to take shape. Thank you, D, for setting the ball rolling.

I knew I wanted one of my triplets to be a vicar and I was very lucky to realise we had a brand-new vicar in my own village. Young, attractive, newly married and happy to talk to me about "vicaring," I need to say a big thank you to the Rev Felicity (Flic) Cowling-Green who gave up her busy schedule one Saturday afternoon to tell me what is involved in the job and the training a vicar needs to go through. It's only now, as I'm writing these acknowledgments, that I see her husband is called Sam, and I can only say that it's a total coincidence that Rosa, my vicar, begins to fall in love with a Sam in the story!

A huge thank you to the very lovely Olivia Woodford (nee Anderson) and her husband Ben, who sat with me one Sunday lunchtime at her mother's house and took me through the experience of being diagnosed with, and treatment for, Stage two Hodgkinson's Lymphoma at the age of just thirty. Olivia also explained the long – and often arduous – process of freezing her eggs prior to chemotherapy. I'm absolutely delighted – and I want to cry when I write this – that Olivia is now totally well and is expecting her first baby, conceived naturally and without the need for her frozen eggs.

As a Youth Magistrate, sitting in the youth court, I was able to ask for advice re Hannah's role as a youth worker from a number of Legal advisors and youth workers. Many thanks to those who gave their professional opinion so freely and helpfully.

Thanks, as always, to my lovely agent, Anne Williams at KHLA Literary Agency, for her unstinting help, advice and loyalty as well as to Rachel Faulkner-Willcocks, my editor at Aria, Head of Zeus who, with the rest of the team, has helped to make *The Village Vicar* the best it can possibly be.

And finally, to all you wonderful readers who read my books and write such lovely things about them, a huge, heartfelt Thank you.

About the Author

JULIE HOUSTON lives in Huddersfield, West Yorkshire where her novels are set, and her only claims to fame are that she teaches part-time at *Bridget Jones* author Helen Fielding's old junior school and her neighbour is *Chocolat* author, Joanne Harris. Julie is married, with two adult children and a ridiculous Cockapoo called Lincoln. She runs and swims because she's been told it's good for her, but would really prefer a glass of wine, a sun lounger and a jolly good book – preferably with Dev Patel in attendance. You can contact Julie via the contact page, on Twitter or on Facebook. Twitter: @juliehouston2; facebook.com/JulieHoustonauthor.